"He closed his eyes and saw the delicate slope of Miss Fairleigh's shoulders . . ."

How vulnerable were the planes of a woman's back; any woman's, but especially hers, in her mended chemise with the fragile bits of lace around the sleeves.

Warmth crept up his thighs as his blood rushed to his center. He was hardening again at the simple memory of her spine. He thought of her buttocks and ached to cup them in his hands. Shaking himself, he turned his gaze to the fog-shrouded window. Should the strength of his reaction worry him? Perhaps he ought to put himself on guard.

But, no. She was a pretty woman; that was all. Any man would have responded. He was glad her powers of attraction were strong. He wanted Freddie happy. He needed Freddie safe.

BEYOND INNOCENCE

Emma Holly

JOVE BOOKS, NEW YORK

This is a work of fiction. Names, characters, places, and incidents are either the product of the author's imagination or are used fictitiously, and any resemblance to actual persons, living or dead, business establishments, events, or locales is entirely coincidental.

BEYOND INNOCENCE

A Jove Book / published by arrangement with
the author

PRINTING HISTORY
Jove edition / July 2001

The Penguin Putnam Inc. World Wide Web site address is
www.penguinputnam.com

ISBN: 0-515-13099-0

A Jove Book®
Jove Books are published by The Berkley Publishing Group,
a division of Penguin Putnam Inc.,
375 Hudson Street, New York, New York 10014.
JOVE and the "J" design
are trademarks belonging to Penguin Putnam Inc.

PRINTED IN THE UNITED STATES OF AMERICA

10   9   8

*To Laurie, who taught me a
thing or two about older siblings.
You're the best, Sis!*

PROLOGUE

❧

London, 1873

"*A footman!*" *Edward* raged. "You were caught in your bedroom with a *footman*?"

Anger had pulled him to his feet behind the study desk. Now he gripped the edge of the carved bog oak as if pressure alone could will his brother's confession away.

Freddie was slumped in the red morocco chair, one foot propped on his knee while he examined his well-buffed nails. The nonchalant pose suited his lanky frame. In blazing white shirt and tastefully embroidered waistcoat, he was the golden boy at rest: his graceful limbs asprawl, his beauty a stylish disarray.

His face, however, was patently miserable.

"It's the calves," he said in a weak attempt at humor. "Never could resist a man with a good pair of legs."

Something strained in Edward's chest. He sat, abruptly weak in the knees. "Freddie, if I believed for an instant you meant that, I'd slit my bloody wrists."

Freddie's head came up, clearly startled by his brother's tone. He opened his mouth, then shut it. Alert now, he dropped his boot to the floor and dried his palms on the front of his trousers.

" 'Course I don't mean it," he said. "You know me.

Can't pass up a quip. We'll call it temporary insanity. Trying to recapture my schooldays or some such tripe."

Edward covered his face. Freddie's light response could not disguise his inner turmoil. Edward never should have sent him to Eton. Never mind the generations of Burbrooke males who had gone before them. He should have known a sensitive boy like Freddie wouldn't survive that pit of adolescent anarchy. Edward had been seventeen when he made the decision, his parents newly dead, his twelve-year-old brother left solely in his care. He'd thought Freddie needed Eton. He'd thought he couldn't take his rightful place in society without it.

A warm hand settled on the back of his neck. Freddie had perched on the corner of his desk. "Here now," he said, gently squeezing Edward's nape. "It isn't your fault. You weren't even there."

Edward let out his breath and looked up. His face hardened. "Who found you?"

Freddie winced. His finger drew a circle on the shiny black desk. "There's the rub, I'm afraid. It was the local squire, invited to the house party because Farringdon's in debt to him up to his eyeballs."

"What's his name?" Edward persisted, determined to turn to the business of cleaning this up.

"Samuel Stokes."

"The brewing magnate?"

Freddie pulled a face. "The very same. Bought his way into the neighborhood after he got knighted. Bit of a mushroom, according to Farringdon."

"But that just makes it worse! If one of our own set had found you, they might make you the latest *on-dit,* but they wouldn't threaten to inform on you. Do you have any idea what would happen if this went to court? You'd be ruined!"

"Actually"—Freddie cleared his throat—"Stokes did threaten to take me before the magistrate. Said I was setting a bad example for the lower orders."

"Oh, Lord."

"But he backed off when he found out whose brother I was." Freddie wagged his brows. "Seems you're well respected among the manufacturing set, despite being a use-less toff."

"Wonderful," Edward groaned. He pushed out of his chair and closed his eyes. His temples throbbed under the weight of Freddie's hopes.

"Maybe you could throw him a sop," Freddie suggested. "Sponsor him to join your club."

"I'll meet him," Edward said, pinning Freddie with his sternest gaze, "and if he's suitable, I'll *consider* putting his name forward at White's."

"But Edward—"

Edward silenced him by laying a hand on his broad young shoulder. Freddie had been a champion rower at school, captain of the team, admired by everyone who met him. He still was admired. Edward knew he'd give his right arm to keep that from changing. His little brother would never be society's laughingstock.

"Freddie," he said, "I'm going to give Stokes my word this won't happen again, and I'm going to rely on you to make it true."

Freddie didn't drop his gaze, didn't in fact say a word. But his lips were pressed so tightly together they'd gone white.

"You can do this," Edward said, letting the love he felt for his brother soften his voice. "You've only to set your mind to it. Remember when you took that first in Maths? Remember when you learned to swim?"

Freddie choked out a laugh. "I learned to swim out of terror."

"Then be afraid," Edward said, softer yet. "People won't overlook this sort of lark, not if you rub their noses in it."

Freddie's sunny blue eyes welled with unshed tears. He bowed his head. "I didn't mean to rub anyone's nose in it, least of all yours."

Edward pulled him into a hug. "I know you didn't. But it's time to put these games behind you." He pushed back and braced Freddie's shoulder. "Why not settle on one of those debutantes who's always mooning in your wake?"

"Don't know who'll have me once this gets around."

Freddie ventured a crooked grin. "The husband-hunting mamas steer clear of me already, me being a younger son and all."

"Idiots," Edward said, echoing Freddie's smile. "They ought to know I'd never see you short of blunt."

Freddie sighed, his expression wistful. Edward had tried to prevent his brother's financial dependence from chafing. Other than a small property their mother had set aside for her younger son, control of the Burbrooke estate was entirely in Edward's hands. He made sure Freddie never had to beg for money and Freddie, while not a pinchpenny, was careful to live within his allowance. That very care told Edward his pride must occasionally sting. But the restrictions of primogeniture were not, apparently, the cause of Freddie's sigh.

"Choosing a wife who's good enough to be your sister-in-law won't be easy," he said.

Edward laughed and slapped his back, but inside, where his love for Freddie lived, he knew the danger had not passed.

CHAPTER 1

With stern face and trembling hands, Miss Florence Fairleigh stepped from the stuffy railway carriage and into a scene from Bedlam. A dizzying population of males—workmen, clerks, and here and there a gentleman in top hat—jostled each other in haste to reach the train she had lately vacated. Above her the roof of Euston Station yawned in two barnlike peaks, its smutted glass filtering a watery species of sunshine more appropriate to dusk than noon. Beneath her . . . well, beneath her the ground did not yet seem quite solid.

Frowning, she smoothed her crumpled black bombazine skirts. None of these observations were to the purpose. Her purpose was her future and her future would not wait on missish fears. She turned to her companion. Lizzie, the Fairleighs' maid-of-all-work, still clung to the carriage door, its grime putting her mistress's best white gloves at risk. Florence's old pink day dress, another loan, hung on Lizzie's slender frame. Though sixteen, and nearly grown, the maid looked all of twelve.

Truly, Florence thought, the only advantage to traveling with a person more timid than oneself was that it served to stiffen up one's spine. She stiffened it now and gestured for Lizzie to come down.

"It is safe," she said with all the firmness she could muster.

Face filled with trepidation, Lizzie tottered down the steps as if the train were a dragon that had momentarily, and perhaps not reliably, agreed to cough her out.

"Oh, miss," she breathed in awestruck tones, "isn't London grand?"

"You must call me Miss Fairleigh," Florence corrected, taking Lizzie's arm to guide her through the crowded train shed. "As is proper for a young lady towards her governess."

This was the fiction they had agreed upon, since Florence could not travel without a chaperone, and a less imposing chaperone than Lizzie Thomas could hardly be imagined. In her dull black gown, Florence thought she looked very much a governess, though not—due to the width of her sleeves and the lumpishness of her bustle—a particularly fashionable one. The ruse had worked well in the dimness of the carriage. When they disembarked at the various watering stations between Lancashire and London, however, Florence had been the subject of interested stares.

Even a governess, it seemed, was not immune to male attention.

"Oh, miss," said Lizzie, calling Florence to the present, "I mean, Miss Fairleigh. However shall we find our way?"

"We shall follow these others," said Florence. "They must be heading towards the street."

A brief argument was required to convince Lizzie she was not to carry Florence's portmanteau. That settled, they soon found themselves under the station's monumental Doric entry arch. To Florence's dismay, the bedlam inside the station merely increased in the out-of-doors. Here the confusion was multiplied by carriages and drays, by costermongers shouting their wares, and by a pungent smell which was half stableyard, half day-old fire. Florence did not have the least idea how to fight through the snarl.

She was swallowing back tears by the time a ragged urchin tugged on the hem of her mantelet. His eyes were huge in his dirty face, but so canny Florence felt a moment's fear. She put her hand on her reticule.

"Need a cab?" he offered. "I'll call one for a penny."

"A penny!" Lizzie exclaimed, her temper restored by this proposed raid on their resources. "You'll do it for a farthing, you scamp."

Florence smiled at her outrage. "A penny is fine," she said, "but we'll pay you after we get in."

This was agreeable to the young man, who proved capable at his task. Within minutes she and Lizzie were climbing into a smart black hansom cab. Florence gave their direction to the driver, which fortunately he knew. After another delay to ease into traffic, they joined the stream of broughams and carts and rumbling double-decked omnibuses. Since the cabbie sat on a high seat at the back of the two-wheeled carriage, his passengers had a clear view of all they passed.

Florence tried to maintain her dignity, but Lizzie was openly agog.

"Look, miss!" she exclaimed, pointing at the distinguished terraces of Bedford Square. "Look at that nursemaid in her apron! Isn't she the grandest thing you've ever seen!"

For her part, Florence took careful note of the classical, columned bulk of the British Museum. If she accomplished nothing else on this terrible trip, she vowed she'd see the Elgin marbles.

The cab continued to the Strand. Florence found the business district crowded and dirty, but strangely exciting nonetheless. Tiny shivers prickled over her scalp as she looked around. Everyone here had an air of purpose. They seemed not to see St. Paul's golden dome, rising behind the sooty haze like a fairy apparition. They were intent on their business, she supposed, and accustomed to the city's marvels. Perhaps someday she would be, too.

At that singular thought, they clopped onto a cobbled side street and stopped before a narrow building with a soot-stained brick face.

"Here you be, miss," said the cabbie.

Florence's heart, which had settled during the ride, resumed its former gallop. She pressed one dampened glove to her stays. This was the moment that would decide her future, the place at which her dreams would be met or dashed. Blowing out a careful breath, she counted a shocking number of coins from her reticule, and helped her supposed mistress to alight.

A small plaque declared the building that of "Mr. Mowbry, Solicitor," so Florence squared her shoulders and tugged the bell. The door was opened by a solid-looking man of middle years who stroked his beard and squinted. His brown tweed frock coat hung open around his belly. From the thick gold fob that gleamed on his matching waistcoat, Florence judged he must be Mr. Mowbry.

"Miss Fairleigh?" he said, peering dubiously from one woman to the other.

Florence flushed, knowing by his expression that they must look quite disreputable.

"I am Miss Fairleigh," she said and offered her hand. The solicitor took it with an air of bemusement. "Please forgive our appearance. We come to you straight from the train. I know such haste is irregular, but we wish to conclude our business quickly."

Her consciousness of the need to obtain a favorable outcome was so great her voice cracked on the final word. At the telltale sound, Mr. Mowbry flashed a kindly smile.

"Of course," he said, ushering her gently before him. "I'm sure I would be pleased to do anything I may for the daughter of my old friend."

Once inside, Florence looked about with interest. Mr. Mowbry's office was small but well kept. The paneling shone with a recent polish, the shelves were filled with heavy vellum tomes, and the dark Turkish carpet showed not the slightest sign of wear—all of which boded well for Florence's hopes. The tightness in her shoulders eased as tea was brought and condolences offered. Lizzie being settled with the charwoman in a little room off the hall, and knowing she should delay no longer, Florence came to the point of her visit.

"As my father's solicitor," she began, "you know he left me a small independence."

Mr. Mowbry nodded. "Indeed. I have been impressed by the conservative manner in which you have drawn upon it. Many young ladies would not have been so sensible."

"Yes," said Florence, and twisted her gloves in her lap. She feared when he heard her plan he would not think her sensible at all. With difficulty, she continued. "I have been careful in the six months since my father's death, but have come to realize the money will not keep me very long. I do not blame my father. He was a genial man and his position as vicar obliged him to entertain. Indeed, not realizing the expense of this little luxury or that, he believed I was able to set something aside from my housekeeping monies. I allowed him to continue in this belief because he was kind and loving and I did not wish him to worry. But now I have forgone everything I can forgo, except for Lizzie, who I dare not discharge even if I would because she is an orphan like myself and I don't know what would become of her!"

"I see," said Mr. Mowbry. The smile that hovered on his lips belied his serious tone. Spreading his arms, he tapped the corners of his desk. "Forgive me for being so bold, Miss Fairleigh, but you are a handsome young woman. Don't you think you might marry before the money runs out?"

"That is my intent," she said, struggling to steady her voice. "Only I should like . . . Perhaps it is selfish of me, but I should like to marry decently. There is only one gentleman at home who could be considered an appropriate suitor, and he wishes me to give Papa's money to a Society and join him on a ministry to Africa. I'm sure this is a worthy occupation and if it were any other man I might consider it, but he is—he is—"

"A sanctimonious prig?" suggested Mr. Mowbry.

"Quite," she agreed, blushing furiously at his frankness but unwilling to contradict him.

"So you have come to London where the gentlemen are many and various."

"Yes," she said and leaned earnestly forward in her chair. "I have heard there are ladies here who, for a fee, will sponsor an unconnected young woman for a Season, who will see she is chaperoned and introduced to respectable men. I would be willing, if you could recommend such an individual, to venture fully half my inheritance upon the enterprise."

Mr. Mowbry opened his mouth to speak, but for the first time in her adult life, Florence cut a gentleman off. This was the crux of the matter and Mr. Mowbry must understand what she wished, before he entered into the scheme.

"I am not aiming high," she assured him. "A younger son will do. Even a tradesman. I know I am not particularly accomplished. A little music and a bit of French is all I claim. But I am, as you say, attractive, and no one has ever complained about my manners. I do not hope for love but only to be treated kindly. Most of all, I wish not to be afraid, to know I shall always have a roof over my head and that it shall be my roof, not that of an indifferent employer or a pitying friend.

"I wish," she concluded, hiding her shaking hands among her skirts, "for a bit of security."

To all this, Mr. Mowbry had listened with an expression of intense concentration. Indeed, it had been so intense Florence had been hard-pressed to hold his gaze.

"Hm," he said now, tapping his lips with folded hands. "I think, Miss Fairleigh, that you underestimate your charms. Of course, your modesty does you credit, as much credit as your looks." Standing, he began to pace back and forth before the glass-fronted bookcase.

His vigor impressed her, as did his obvious seriousness of thought. He was muttering under his breath, saying things like "yes," and "she'd do," and "most delicate, but if it were brought forward in the proper way . . ." Watching him, Florence knew her father had been right to call him Clever Mr. Mowbry. If any man could launch Florence's future, it was this one.

Finally, he stopped in the center of his path and turned to face her.

"I believe I have hit upon a solution." He lifted his hands to forestall a question she had not the nerve to pose. "I make no promises, Miss Fairleigh, but if I am able to pull this off—ah, if!—it could make both our fortunes."

"Oh, no, Mr. Mowbry." Florence shook her head emphatically. "I've no need of fortunes, only a small—"

"Hush," ordered the solicitor. "If I am correct in my surmise, you shall have precisely what you wish: an impeccable sponsor, an amiable husband, and the best possible roof above your head. First, however, we must see to your wardrobe. You cannot call upon anyone in that gown."

Though Florence had known this would be necessary, she could not forbear an inward groan. Ladies' dresses were very deàr, and her little account could scarcely bear the drain. But she knew she must be brave. She must risk all in order to gain any. If the worst came to pass and her money was wasted, she would find a new position for Lizzie, and herself become a governess. Other women had done it, women gentler bred than she. Surely some had faced fears as great as hers. Florence could do no less. She might be shy but she was not, in the end, a coward.

Thus resolved, her hands were almost steady by the time she accepted a hastily scribbled letter from Mr. Mowbry. The red wax seal was warm beneath her thumb. These days most people used envelopes, but perhaps the old gentlemanly habit was one that appealed to a lawyer. Like vicars' daughters, most were neither here nor there in the eyes of society.

"This is an introduction to a friend of mine," he said. "A talented dressmaker, newly arrived from Paris, who is building her clientele. I have instructed her to put what you need on my account. No." He pressed a quieting finger to his lips. "Do not protest. Your father was good to me at Oxford and stood me many dinners when I had not two shillings to rub together. You must consider this repayment of the debt."

"With interest," Florence said, tears springing to her eyes at his kindness.

"With interest," Mr. Mowbry agreed, and called his clerk to hail a cab.

• • •

Mr. Mowbry's friend, Madame Victoire, worked out of a pretty little house near the fancy shops of Bond Street. Bright red geraniums spilled from the ledges of the windows, all of which were open and one of which revealed the slumbering form of an orange cat.

Florence, who had been known to have difficulties with cats, hoped its nap would be a long one.

A parlormaid in black dress and white apron ushered them into the parlor. Though small, the room was lofty, its ceilings molded in the graceful Georgian style. Such light as there was poured through the casement windows. The furniture was old-fashioned and delicate, a medley of gold and cream—a more pleasant room by far than any Florence had lived in, despite her father's love of comfort. The only sign that the parlor figured in its owner's business was the bare dressmaker's form that stood in a pool of pallid sun, and the ell of purple velvet that lay folded in a chair.

On joining them, Madame Victoire bubbled with excitement. Like many of her countrywomen, she was slender and dark, with twinkling gestures and a wide red mouth.

"Oh, la la," she exclaimed, taking Florence's hands to pull her into the silvery light. "Who have we here come to visit my humble shop?"

Florence had no chance to reply for Madame Victoire immediately turned her around and began clucking over her dress. *"Quelle horreur,"* she said, touching the lumpish bustle. "And black! Mademoiselle, you must never wear black. She is not for you, this color."

"B-but I'm in mourning," Florence stammered.

"I take you out of it," Madame Victoire pronounced. *"Immédiatement.* It is a crime to put such a beautiful woman in such an ugly dress." She gestured to the watching parlormaid. *"Regardez* her bosoms, Marie. Look at her glowing cheeks!" With a gasp of excitement, she removed Florence's worn kid gloves. "Her hands are as small as a child's. They are white and—"

Abruptly, Madame Victoire fixed Florence with a deadly glare. Her fingertips had found the calluses on her palms.

"Mademoiselle," she said in a tone of deep affront, "this must be remedied. No more floor-scrubbing for you. You are too perfect to suffer a single flaw."

"I—" said Florence, but the Frenchwoman did not allow her to explain.

"Such beauty is a grave *responsabilité*. Not only to yourself, but to me. You, mademoiselle, are going to be a walking advertisement for the skills of Madame Victoire. Better than the sandwich board man. Mr. Worth will eat the crow when he hears of my triumph."

"Mr. Worth?" Florence said weakly. If the dressmaker meant who she thought, Florence could not, in good conscience, impose on Mr. Mowbry's generosity.

"Yes, yes," said Madame Victoire. "Mr. Charles Worth, with whom I worked in Paris. That is why you are here, is it not?"

Florence dried her hands on her much-abused dress. "Actually, I am here on the recommendation of Mr. Alastair Mowbry. But I'm afraid I cannot afford the services of an associate of Mr. Worth."

"Pah," said Madame Victoire. "Mr. Worth is no associate of me. And you are a friend of Monsieur Mowbry. We will come to the *arrangement.*"

Florence's cheeks burned with the heat of the blood that rushed beneath them. She feared Madame Victoire had jumped to the wrong conclusion.

"Forgive me, madame," she said, "but I am not that sort of friend to Mr. Mowbry."

To Florence's amazement, Madame Victoire burst into peals of laughter. "But of course you are not, little *chou*. I know this because *I* am 'that sort of friend' to him. Granted, he is a gentleman of great strength, but no man is strong enough to require more woman than Amalie Victoire."

This declaration so astonished Florence she could not frame a response, appropriate or otherwise. The best she could manage was to close her gaping mouth. Happily, the silence was broken by the entrance of a noisy little boy. No more than three and dressed in a navy sailor suit, he thundered across the carpet with what looked like a headless bear.

"Look, *maman,*" he cried, seeming more excited than bereaved by the decapitation. "Kitty got him."

He stopped in his tracks when he spotted his mother's guest.

Florence's chest tightened, but once he had seen her, she knew what came next was inevitable. The boy hesitated, staring up at her with round, bedazzled eyes, shyness and interest at war in his face. Then, like a child unable to resist a stranger's toy, his shyness broke and he pounded across the room. For a moment, Florence feared he would actually fling his arms around her legs. Fortunately, he settled for grabbing her hand and tugging it.

"Pretty!" he declared with three-year-old directness. "You come play!"

Florence needed a surprising amount of strength to resist his pull.

"Goodness," said Madame Victoire. "He does not usually behave this way with strangers."

If it had been possible, Florence would have sunk through the floor. She patted the boy's hand in the hope he would loosen his grip.

"Children . . . like me," she explained.

"Children and cats," Lizzie qualified, as if this were cause for pride.

"Well," said Madame Victoire, her lips twitching with amusement, "perhaps Marie should lock Kitty in the bedroom before you suffer more attacks."

"Yes," Florence said faintly. "That would probably be wise."

Once Marie had left to secure the cat, Florence gathered herself sufficiently to remember Mr. Mowbry's note. Madame Victoire took longer to read it than she expected, the message being two pages instead of one. Whatever the solicitor had written inspired much raising of the Frenchwoman's brows. When Madame Victoire had finished, she tapped the missive against her chin. She seemed not to hear the distant rumble of thunder outside her home.

"Hm," she said in precisely the tone Mr. Mowbry had used.

Her "hm" troubled Florence even more than the solicitor's.

He had put something in that letter which he meant to keep from Florence, and for a deeper reason than not wanting to raise her hopes. Oh, how she hated trusting her fate to anyone else's hands! Life with her father, dear as he was, had taught her to rely on no one but herself. How could it be otherwise when one's sole guardian was likelier to forget one's name than remember to pay a bill? Short of giving up her dream, however, she did not see what choice she had. She had to trust the lawyer and his friend. She could only pray his hidden agenda was not a danger to her own.

Edward Burbrooke, earl of Greystowe, was spattered all over with mud. Too tired to ring the bell, he pushed into his Belgravia town house and collapsed on the marble bench inside the door. For a moment, all he could do was stare at his ruined boots.

He straightened when he heard footsteps: Grimby, no doubt, coming to see who'd entered the hall.

"My lord!" he said, obviously shocked by his master's appearance. "You're wet."

Edward snorted at this statement of the obvious and handed the butler his soggy top hat. He should have turned back when it started raining, but the horse had been eager and the park for once uncrowded and Edward's temper too black to miss his daily ride.

This morning there'd been a limerick in the *Illustrated Times*:

> *There was a young viscount of G———*
> *Who couldn't keep off of his knees.*
> *The footman was there, with his hands in his hair,*
> *And his a———hanging out in the breeze.*

Anyone who knew Freddie would recognize the scandal to which it referred. Edward wished he could strangle the supposed wit who'd sent it in, not to mention the editor who'd printed it. That being impractical, he'd vented his frustration on the turf in Hyde Park.

The plop of water from his hat told Edward the butler was still there.

"Sir?" said Grimby. "Shall I call Mr. Lewis to pull your boots?"

"Yes," said Edward, "and have him draw a hot bath."

The knocker sounded just as Grimby disappeared into the servants' hall. Edward heaved to his feet with a weary laugh. Hell, he thought, I can open a blasted door.

The individual behind it, caught digging in his pocket for a card, was so surprised he could only gawk.

"Mr. Mowbry?" Edward said, recognizing the broad, bearded figure of his London solicitor. The man had been his father's lawyer: then a member of a larger firm, now striking out on his own. He was, so far as Edward knew, utterly reliable. But Edward could not imagine why he was calling on him at home.

"My lord," said Mowbry, recovering his composure. "Forgive me for arriving unannounced, but an opportunity has arisen of which I thought you'd want to be apprised."

"An investment opportunity?"

If a man could squirm without moving, Mowbry did so. "No, your lordship. The opportunity regards Viscount Burbrooke."

A chill joined the water that had run down Edward's neck. After this morning's nastiness in the *Times*, he did not want to think what Mowbry's business might entail. He pushed the door ajar. "Come inside. We'll talk in the library." He was halfway there when he noticed he was tracking mud across the cabbage roses of the Brussels carpet. "Blast," he muttered, and stood where he was while Lewis, his valet, rushed towards him in consternation.

This was not how he'd intended to spend his day.

"A vicar's daughter?" Edward said.

"Yes," Mowbry confirmed, sipping his tea with quiet

relish. He and Edward sat by the fire Lewis had insisted on building, any differences in rank leveled by their mutual enjoyment of the warmth.

Edward propped his slippers on the fender. "Fresh from the country?"

"As fresh as can be, but gently bred and exceedingly good-natured. What novel writers like to call a womanly little soul."

Edward balanced his saucer on his thigh. "How womanly?"

Mowbry's white-flecked whiskers lifted in a smile. "Imagine, my lord, if a dewy English rose were to wear Delilah's form. Miss Fairleigh is poor, it is true, but more than enough of a beauty to be considered a catch. Were young Lord Burbrooke to display a partiality to her, no one would think it amiss. And, sir, if you'll forgive me for speaking frankly, I doubt she'd understand the gossip surrounding your brother even if she heard it."

Edward's brows rose. Such innocence was hard to conceive. More to the point, if she were that innocent, would she be able to bring a skittish stallion like Freddie to stud? Still— he rubbed one finger across his lips—the matter was worth investigating. A girl in Miss Fairleigh's position would have few options beyond marriage. Seamstressing or working as a governess could not match the security of wedded life. Certainly, she could do worse than a kind young man like Freddie, who neither drank nor gambled nor cursed in the presence of ladies. As clever Mr. Mowbry had divined, Edward was determined that Freddie marry. In fairness, however, he could not wish Freddie to be the sole beneficiary of the match.

Of course, if Mowbry had exaggerated Florence Fairleigh's charms, the entire matter might be moot. He came to a decision.

"I shall wish to look her over," he said. "Without her knowledge."

The solicitor set his cup and saucer on the tea table. "If you would be amenable to a short ride, my lord, I believe I could arrange for you to see her today."

Edward narrowed his eyes. The lawyer seemed to have been expecting the request. His expression was mild, and suspiciously complacent. Edward could not be certain, but he thought he'd just been managed.

If Edward had known what he was going to see, he never would have called for his carriage. The oddities began when Mowbry directed him to the servants' entrance of the house. A tiny housemaid, quiet as a nun, glided before him through the basement and up the back stairs, which were so narrow his elbows brushed the walls at every turn. On the second floor, they passed a large, well-lighted room where four women bent over sewing machines. Their feet worked busily on the treadles while their hands fed lengths of cloth beneath the needles. Three more machines stood empty. All were black and painted with yellow roses.

This house, he concluded, must be a dressmaker's establishment.

"Almost there," whispered his diminutive guide.

Her accent was French and very pretty, but Edward had no time to consider why she was whispering because she soon led him into a small room. The presence of a secretaire and settee suggested it was sometimes used as a sitting room, but for now the space was cramped with bolts of cloth.

A spindly chair had been pulled between two towers of jewel-bright satin. By gesture, the maid directed him to sit, then hushed his questions with a finger to her mouth.

Feeling somewhat ridiculous, Edward sat, then stiffened when her arm brushed his shoulder. People simply did not touch the earl of Greystowe without permission.

"Pardon," she murmured and pressed a latch that had been hidden among the birds and foliage of the wallpaper. A small aperture opened in the wall.

"Watch," she said. "You will see all you wish to know."

Edward blinked at the peephole, then at his guide, but the little maid was already slipping out the door. His heart beat hard with shock. Were Mowbry's other clients so jaded they could accept this sort of offer without offense? Just how dissipated did the solicitor think he was, expecting him to spy on a half-dressed woman who might conceivably become his brother's bride?

His face warmed with anger, but then he calmed. He'd said he wanted to look the girl over without her knowledge. What better means than this? Besides, for all he knew, she and the dressmaker were merely talking in the other room, fully clothed, with none of their womanly attributes hanging out.

Despite this assurance, his mouth was dry as he pressed his eye against the wall.

The room into which he gazed was small and bright, the gloom outside cast away by the light of a dozen bull's-eye lamps. A tall cheval glass reflected the figures of two dark-haired women.

Heat flashed over his body. The dressmaker was clothed in a smart gold gown, but Miss Fairleigh wore only her chemise and drawers. She was everything Mowbry claimed: lush and rosy with a mass of shining chestnut hair rolled and braided on the crown of her head. The dressmaker had just peeled away her corset. Even without the restraint, her waist dipped in like an hourglass.

Edward swallowed, but did not pull away. No more than medium height, the woman's legs seemed disproportionately long. He could see the shadow of her bottom through the fine linen drawers. A mended patch rested atop one shapely buttock, an endearing imperfection which could not detract from the charm of her derriere. Her flesh was full and well lifted. A man would find a pleasurable handhold should he coax this paragon beneath him. Indeed, he'd find many pleasurable grips. Her breasts were a bounty, her arms both soft and graceful. Her feet— He tugged a sudden tightness at his collar. Her feet were small and white, feet he'd thought only a painter could create, with tiny curled toes and ankles a man could circle with his hand.

A lucky man.

Edward shifted on the stingy padding of his chair. Mere seconds had passed since he'd first looked in the room, but his cock stretched full within its skin. The tip pulsed tight against the placket of his trousers, heavy and urgent, a creature with a mind of its own. The knowledge that what he was doing was beyond the bounds of all propriety simply made the swollen tissues pulse harder.

When he released his bated breath, he realized he could hear as well as see. What struck his ears first was the rumbling purr of an orange cat that had curled adoringly at Miss Fairleigh's feet. Clever cat, he thought, in total sympathy with its instincts.

"We must order three French corsets," the dressmaker was saying as she stretched a measuring tape around Miss Fairleigh's admirable waist. "Two for ordinary wear and one cut low for evening. With one of the new spoon busks, I think. They are *très élégante*. You will like them very much."

Miss Fairleigh opened her mouth, then blushed as the tape moved to circle her bosom. The dressmaker's fingers met at the center of her cleavage, pressing it slightly together. In the glow of the lamps, Edward watched as hectic color spread enchantingly over her chest.

Miss Fairleigh cleared her throat. "I really think one new corset would be enough—if, as you say, I must have a French one."

"As I say?" tutted the dressmaker, kneeling down to measure the length of Miss Fairleigh's legs. The cat mewed with displeasure as she elbowed it aside. "As I *know*, mademoiselle. You must marshal your weapons. A good set of corsets is a powerful weapon indeed."

"But my finances . . ." said Miss Fairleigh, her voice faint. The dressmaker ignored her.

"Stop wiggling," she ordered. "You would think no one but me had ever seen your ankles." With a sigh of satisfaction, she stood and wiped a single curl from her narrow forehead. "It is good. Your measurements are very close to a dress I have on hand today. A snip here, a tuck there, and you shall at once be decent."

Miss Fairleigh's dovelike hands fluttered to her trembling breast. "Oh, no, Madame Victoire. I can't take someone else's dress."

"Nonsense," said Madame. "This customer is late settling her account. Therefore, I will be late with her delivery." And, without giving further heed to Miss Fairleigh's protests, she called for someone named Marie to bring the claret-colored visiting dress.

"Claret?" Miss Fairleigh's tone was rife with dread.

"Non, non," scolded the dressmaker, briskly lacing her into her reputedly inferior English corset. "Do not worry yourself. Your father would want you to go on with your life, would he not?"

"Yes, but—"

"There are no buts. You do what you must. A man will not marry a crow!"

The exchange had Edward smiling, despite the pounding weight between his legs. This woman was so shy and self-effacing that Madame Victoire's attempts to exhort her to femme-fatale-dom could only be amusing. Miss Fairleigh was a peach, he decided, a juicy country peach whose sweetness tempted one to bite.

Of course, he reminded himself, his teeth would not be doing the biting.

Unfortunately, this caution did not quell his fascination as the dressmaker arrayed Miss Fairleigh in the frock. Had he ever watched his mistresses being dressed? If he had, he could not recall it. Surely, few sights could be more seductive than that of a woman tying another woman's petticoats, or steadying a bustle, or dropping a rustling silk skirt over two submissively raised white arms.

Miss Fairleigh herself seemed conscious of the erotic charge. Edward doubted she'd ever had a lady's maid; doubted she'd ever been intimately touched by another human being. Her creamy, broad-boned cheeks were once again pink as Madame Victoire hooked the separate bodice. The fit over her breasts was snug, but the dressmaker seemed more satisfied than otherwise when she returned to consider her front.

"With a French corset," she said, "this would lie perfectly." As if in demonstration, she ran her hands from Miss Fairleigh's shoulders to her waist. Her palms swept the tips of her client's breasts. Edward did not think Miss Fairleigh could feel much pressure through the layers of cloth, but what she did feel had her ears turning scarlet.

He experienced a nearly uncontrollable urge to rush into the room and cuddle her against his chest. Madame Victoire should not tease the girl this way. She was an innocent. She deserved protection!

Which did not change the fact that watching the French-woman touch her had aroused him. His hands were fisted on his thighs, sweat prickled his linen, and the wall beneath his cheek was growing damp. He could not recall a desire this urgent. His body shook with the force of it. His breath came in long, hard pulls. If he hadn't known the house was full of people, he'd have opened his trousers and eased himself. He wasn't prone to self-indulgence, but it would have been a business of moments. As it was, he was heartbeats from exploding.

But Madame Victoire had finished arranging the pleated muslin fraise that framed the dress's neckline. She turned her client to face the mirror. Edward's jaw dropped at the same time Miss Fairleigh's did.

In her chemise and drawers, Miss Fairleigh had been a schoolboy's naughty dream. In the elegant claret dress, she stopped the heart.

She looked a grand London lady, every inch, from her stiff stand-up collar to the train of her polonaise. The complicated draping of her bustle seemed to echo the piquant flesh he knew it hid. Only her expression, wondering and unsure, betrayed her country roots.

"There," said Madame Victoire, her hands on Miss Fairleigh's shoulders. "How does that make you feel?"

Miss Fairleigh touched the waist of the figure-hugging gown as if the silk might burn. "I think it frightens me."

Madame smiled and smoothed a fallen lock into her customer's coiffure. Miss Fairleigh's hair was ruler straight and, if the dressmaker's expression was a guide, quite pleasant to touch. Again he felt that dark frisson of the forbidden. The girl did not know what Madame was doing. The girl could not guess what such gestures conveyed.

"You are seeing your feminine power," said the dressmaker, "without that ugly black dress to dim its light."

Miss Fairleigh lifted her chin in the first hint of stubbornness Edward had seen her display. "A woman shouldn't be powerful just because she's pretty."

"Shouldn't she?" The dressmaker clucked in her droll French way. "Why do you worry about 'shouldn't'? This is the way things are, *chérie*. Women walk a hard road in this world. We must use our weapons where we find them. Just as you must use yours, *non?* You must hunt the nice husband. If your beauty brings him close enough to see how nice he is, what is wrong with that?"

"I've never liked being stared at," Miss Fairleigh confessed.

"Oh, la!" Madame trilled out a laugh. "I would tell you to get used to it, but I know your shyness is part of your charm. Like honey to the bee. When you quiver and blush, you make the men feel big and strong."

Without warning, Miss Fairleigh laughed, as if the absurdity of her complaint had just then struck her. The sound was an infectious warble that seemed to come from deep within her chest. "I shall stop!" she declared between the merry bursts. "I shall never blush again."

And the dressmaker laughed, because her client's face was rosy even then.

Edward stalked to the carriage without waiting for an escort. He was angry with himself for staying so long, angry for being attracted to the hapless country miss, angry at Alastair Mowbry for putting an innocent in that position. That the man had been right about Miss Fairleigh did not calm him in the least, nor did the thought that, most likely, a wish for her well-being had played some part in the solicitor's scheme.

Worst of all was his sense of violation. Edward was sweating with arousal, still half hard beneath his clothes. The minute Mowbry saw him he would guess what he was feeling—as Madame Victoire must have guessed, and the little maid, and perhaps even the seamstresses down the hall. This, to Edward, was intolerable. As wrong as it had been, his experience in that chamber should have been completely private.

His mood was as thunderous as the sky by the time he ducked into the waiting Greystowe brougham. The coachman did not tarry for instructions, but snapped the horses sharply into motion.

Mowbry sat in the shadows of the opposite seat. Silent. Knowing.

"You will fill that peephole at once," Edward said in his coldest, darkest voice.

If the solicitor's expression changed, Edward did not see it.

"It is only for private use," he said. "A game between myself and Madame Victoire. You are the first outsider to have seen it."

His tone was entirely neutral, free of insinuation or censure. Edward forced his hands to unclench. Obviously, he was in no position to judge this man.

"She is all you said," he admitted gruffly.

Wisely, Mowbry didn't take this as an invitation to repeat his estimation of Miss Fairleigh's charms. Edward didn't think he could have borne that. Instead, the solicitor brushed a bit of lint from the bowler he held in his lap. "Have you a sponsor in mind, my lord?"

"My aunt Hypatia," he said, "the dowager duchess of Carlisle. She can bring her forward as some sort of country cousin."

Mowbry simply nodded. He must have known his approval was neither necessary nor welcome. Despite his fury, Edward's estimation of the lawyer rose. Without question, he had behaved abominably, but he had carried it off with rare aplomb.

"You are a man of hidden depths," Edward said.

A small, dry smile acknowledged the warning in his words. "You may call upon my depths whenever you wish, Lord Greystowe. They are entirely at your disposal."

This man is ambitious, Edward thought, but he could not tell whether that boded ill or well.

CHAPTER 2

Edward dropped Mowbry at his office, then ordered the coachman to drive to Lady Hargreave's. The rain continued to fall steadily but not hard, and the wheels made a soft, sticky sound as they rolled through the muddy streets. A mist wreathed the city, muffling the edges of the buildings, slowing traffic and sound until he seemed to ride through a dream. The softness of the air was that of spring, but the color could well have been winter.

He closed his eyes and saw again the delicate slope of Miss Fairleigh's shoulders. How vulnerable were the planes of a woman's back: any woman's, but especially hers, in her mended chemise with the fragile bits of lace around the sleeves.

Warmth crept up his thighs as his blood rushed to his center. He was hardening at the simple memory of her spine. He thought of her buttocks and ached to cup them in his hands. Shaking himself, he turned his gaze to the fog-shrouded window. Should the strength of his reaction worry him? Perhaps he ought to put himself on guard.

But, no. She was a pretty woman; that was all. Any man would have responded. He was glad her powers of attraction were strong. He wanted Freddie happy. He needed Freddie safe.

They reached Regent's Park and the columned marble stretch of Cumberland Terrace, its houses strung end to end so that they looked like a Grecian temple. Edward flipped his watch open. Late teatime. But Lady Hargreave would have no visitors. She'd sent a note that morning, delicately scented, informing him she wouldn't be "at home" to anyone else. Her husband, never the possessive type, was visiting his property in Scotland. Despite the clearness of the field, Edward directed the coachman to a public stable down the street. He preferred not to park his carriage near her house. It was one thing to cuckold a man and quite another to rub his nose in it.

He paused in the act of unfurling his umbrella, caught by a half-conscious thread of memory. Whatever it was, it didn't matter. Nothing mattered but easing the terrible knot of hunger in his groin.

Lady Hargreave awaited in her boudoir. Well aware of how best to display her assets, she was sprawled artistically across an ice-blue chaise longue, with a novel she probably wasn't reading. Her hair, a smooth champagne blonde, spilled like silk down her slender arms. The filmy pink wrap she wore left little to the imagination. He could see the small cones of her breasts beneath it, and the fair thatch of curls that covered her mound.

"Darling!" she cried and, in her usual languid manner, floated to the door to greet him.

His kiss was deeper than was his custom. Rather than let her break it, he gripped her hair to hold her in place. He discovered he wanted to make her melt today; wanted to hear her cry with helpless need.

"My," she said when he finally released her. Her hands slid down his waistcoat to fondle his growing bulge. "Someone's been thinking naughty thoughts."

He did not answer, nor did he want her to speak. He wanted a good hard screw that didn't end for hours. He wanted oblivion and release, and Imogene was damn well going to provide it.

Her hands were clever even through his clothes. She found the tip of his penis and gently pinched it, forcing his linen against the seep of moisture. He gasped as her nails increased the pressure.

"Nice Eddie," she said, and returned to the petting with which she'd begun.

But he wasn't a dog she could cosset to submission. He tore her wrapper down the front and kissed her when she dared to laugh. With inexorable force, he stepped her back to the satin chaise. To hell with adjourning to her bedchamber. He would take her here and now.

"The maid—" she gasped, but her little bosom was heaving up and down. Edward watched it, telling himself he did not wish she were lush instead of lithe, or dark instead of blonde, and that he would not rather she tremble instead of pant.

"Damn the maid." Cupping her breast, he nipped its reddened peak. "Let her get an eyeful."

Imogene laughed and wound her arms behind his neck. "Oh, yes," she purred, crushing her groin to the clothbound arch of his sex. "I like you in this mood."

Their embrace became a skirmish, with Imogene fighting to get on top. Edward used his strength against her, something he had not done in all their times together. She did not seem to mind. In truth, she seemed to like it. Her languor abandoned her. She clutched him as if she could not get enough of his muscle and skin, her hands tearing at his clothes, her throat vibrating with desperate cries.

"Oh, please," she begged when he refused to let her open his trousers. "Please, Edward."

Perversely, he knelt above her, straddling her narrow hips, holding her down with one hand spread between her trembling breasts. With the other, he opened his trouser buttons. As the strain gave way, new blood rushed into tissues already full. He had never been this hard, this needy, and yet he found himself not in the moment but seeing it from a distance. She was lovely, Lady Hargreave, all blonde and pink and eager, her youth wasted on a man twelve years her senior. Edward was what she needed. She had said so many times. Only he could scratch the itch that left her tossing in her bed.

He pushed his trousers to his hips, even that light friction a goad. The air was cool on his fiery skin. Look, he thought. Here's what you want.

Imogene looked, her eyes seeming to glaze as she took in the thick red thrust of his erection. Edward studied it himself: the heavy veins, the nervously jumping sack, the sheen of hunger on the bulbous tip. Why did women want this ugly beast? And why did the sight of it, the feel of it hard and ready, imbue him with a sense of power?

She sighed as she watched it pulse in defiance of gravity's pull. Despite his hold, her hands found him, stroked him, teased him until he ached to drive inside her. He ground his teeth rather than give in. He did not know why, only that something compelled him to delay.

"Fuck me," she whispered, her body writhing between his knees. "I want you inside me."

But he touched her first, because he did not wish to be agreeable. He touched her with his hard male fingers, parting her tangled golden hair. Arousal soaked her delicate folds and plumped her tiny pearl. His fingers slid around the swollen bud. She groaned as he teased it, melting as she never had before, her fair locks clinging to her temples, the pillow rustling as she lashed her head against the chaise. This was what he wanted, to make her helpless, and yet it did not satisfy the formless need inside his soul. With a growl of frustration, he wrenched her legs wide. Enough preliminaries. He would take her and be damned.

He notched her gate and plunged, but found no resistance beyond the stricture of her size.

"Oh, yes," she said, encouraging him to work his engine in. "Oh, yes."

Her knees rose, squeezed the ribs beneath his arms. Back and forth they rocked until her body eased and took him, until his thighs tightened to penetrate the final inch. He stopped and held inside her, his body shaking with desire.

"You're a monster," she breathed, her face white, her pupils huge. "You're the biggest fucking cock I've ever had."

For once he did not doubt this silly claim. He felt like the biggest. He felt as if he could screw the entire world. Her fingers trailed down his spine to grip his straining buttocks.

"Now," she urged. "Do it."

At last, he was willing to comply. With a mutual groan, they thrust in tandem, strongly, smoothly, both selfishly eager to reach their ends. Beyond control, Imogene's nails broke the surface of his skin. Edward grunted and gripped the bottom of the couch to lever deeper, to thrust with greater force. Imogene's neck arched off the cushion, her outward breath a wail.

"Keep going," she gasped, her hips frantically beating his. "Don't stop. Don't stop."

He pounded into her, her flesh tightening around him, his pleasure rising. His cock was steel within her heat, so burstingly hard he could scarcely stand it. He closed his eyes and pressed his brow to the small embroidered pillow beside her head. Images flashed behind his lids: a scrap of lace, a tiny foot, a breast swelling above a corset. The muscles of his belly tensed. He yearned. He ached. And then his partner broke, great shudders of orgasm that milked him to the tooth-grinding edge of release. He pulled out at the very last, coming in heavy, draining spurts against her thigh.

He hung above her on his elbows, shaken by a fear he could not explain.

"Oh, my," she murmured, languidly stroking the scratches on his back. "If people knew how passionate you can be, they'd never call you Edward Coldheart."

He was tempted to inquire who called him that, as this was an insult he'd never heard. In the end, though, he didn't care enough to ask. He looked down at Imogene. Her skin was flushed with satiation, her gray eyes starred. She didn't have the strength to stop him when he pulled away, merely mewled like a disappointed kitten. Too polite to leave outright, he sat by her hip and stroked her arm. Their sexual connection had always been strong, but they'd never shared an encounter this intense. He hadn't spent so fiercely since he'd been a lad of seventeen, nor taken a woman with so little finesse.

Not that Imogene seemed to mind.

"Edward," she sighed, her golden lashes drifting down, "you're enough to make a woman petition for divorce."

He didn't think she meant it, but the declaration rattled him. He didn't feel closer to Imogene. He felt empty. And restless. And weary of the pleasures of life.

He raked his hair back with a sigh. Come to think of it, he felt alone.

His mood was no brighter by the time he called on his aunt Hypatia. Wednesday was her at-home day and he was forced to sit, hat in hand, while some idiot countess and her two marriageable daughters tried to engage him in predictably pointless conversation. They left much beyond the recommended quarter hour, and reluctantly at that. Edward nodded stiffly at the departing girls, but could not bring himself to rise.

"Edward," said Aunt Hypatia, "if you hadn't obviously come on important business, I would scold you for being rude. You're getting too old to dismiss every girl who bats her eyes at you." She patted the spot beside her on the gold and white settee. "Come closer, dear. You're looking unusually dour, even for you. I trust nothing untoward has befallen my investments."

"No," he said, jerkily taking the seat, still warm from its occupation by the countess. For the last few years, he'd been handling the duchess's money. "Your investments are safe. It's this business with Freddie."

"Ah," said his aunt, her unruffled response easing some of the tightness in his chest. Hypatia was a handsome woman, slim and straight despite her years, with a crown of silver-white hair that was all her own. She had not in her youth been a beauty, but her elegance and pride had made it seem as if she were. Now she folded her hands in the pale lavender satin of her skirts. "I wondered when you'd get around to asking my advice."

"It is more than advice I need." He bent forward over his knees and tapped his hat against his shin. "I'm afraid I require your services as a social fairy."

"Indeed," she said, then grabbed his hat and gloves and rang for her rail-thin footman, John.

"Yes, your Grace?" he said in his distinctive sepulchral tones.

"Take Lord Greystowe's coat," she ordered. "Bring the port and bar the door. I am presently indisposed."

"Very good," he said and glided off with what might have been the ghost of a smile.

She would not let Edward speak until the port arrived and he'd downed one brimming glass. "Now," she said, "I suppose your need of my social clout means you've found some chit foolish enough, or desperate enough, to consider a match with the footman's scourge."

"Is that what they're calling Freddie: the footman's scourge?"

"Well, I can think of one footman who isn't. From what I hear, they were having a lovely time before that wretched beermaker burst in. Oh, don't pull that face with me, Edward. I'm older than you and I've seen things a good deal more shocking than young Freddie's peccadillo. Done them, for that matter."

She patted his shoulder and filled his glass again with wine. Edward frowned into its ruby depths. Then a happier thought struck him. If the duchess could view this scandal with levity, Freddie's position must not be as irretrievable as he'd feared.

"Tell me about this girl," she said. "Just how impossible is she?"

"Not too, I don't think, but green. She's a vicar's daughter. Grew up in Lancashire somewhere. Poor as a churchmouse, of course, but *very* pretty."

"Oh, 'very'?" said Aunt Hypatia, with a humorous twist to her mouth.

Edward ignored what his unwitting emphasis might have meant. "She needs polish," he went on, "and someone to sponsor her for the Season."

"What does the Season matter if she's going to marry Freddie?"

"She doesn't know she's going to marry Freddie. I want

him to woo her. I want people to believe this is a love match."

"Does Freddie know what you intend?"

"He will," Edward said, "and he will do what I say."

"I've no doubt he'll try, but—"Aunt Hypatia stopped herself midsentence. Lost in thought, she stacked her hands over the cut-glass stopper of the wine decanter. "No," she said slowly. "You're right. Freddie needs to settle. Better he should do it now, before it becomes impossible."

"So you'll help?"

She turned to him with her still brilliant smile. "You know me, darling: my family right or wrong. Besides, how could I not help my favorite nephew out of a bind?"

The sting of hurt pricked him too suddenly to hide it. True, Freddie had the charm of the family; Edward was accustomed to his little brother being everyone's favorite. The only person who'd ever preferred Edward was their father, a compliment he could not prize since the former earl had been a bastard. But of the people Edward himself respected, he'd always thought— He swallowed and clenched his hands. He'd always thought Aunt Hypatia was partial to him.

Reading the involuntary flash of pain, she clasped his face in her cool, papery hands. "Oh, Edward, Freddie is only my favorite because he needs people's approval more than you do. Why, sometimes I think you'd survive the very Flood all by yourself." She lowered her hands to squeeze the conjoined fist he'd made of his own. "Dearest, I love you every bit as much. What's more, you're the one I would turn to were I in need."

The concern in her eyes made Edward aware of how ridiculous he was being. Of course, Freddie ought to come first. Edward put Freddie first himself. Gently, he pulled his hands loose and cleared his throat.

"No need to talk nonsense," he said. "I'm a grown man, not a child."

"We're all children when it comes to love," said his aunt. "When you're my age, I hope you know that as well as I do."

Edward hoped he would not, but only time would tell.

• • •

The dowager duchess of Carlisle was the most imposing woman Florence had ever met. She was as tall as a man, nearly six foot, and not yet bowed by age. Her clear blue eyes were as sharp as diamonds, and far more penetrating. Her dress was exquisite, a tailored masterpiece of navy and silver stripes with a long basque waist and a bustle so restrained it made one long to burn one's ruffles.

At least, it made Florence long to.

Her knees had begun to knock the moment the ghoulish footman led her up to the drawing room. The ceilings were twice the height of a normal room, with gilded moldings and a teardrop chandelier that no doubt took the servants days to clean. The only thing that saved her from utter terror was an amusing coincidence: the duchess had the same gold and white Louis XV furniture as Madame Victoire. The duchess's, of course, was no papier-mâché imitation.

"Stand up straight," she snapped when a smile threatened to touch Florence's lips. "How can I tell how you look if you slump?"

Florence's eyes widened because she knew she was standing straight. Her cheeks warmed as the duchess stumped around her with an elegant ivory cane. Florence suspected she liked it more for the sound it made than for any support it might provide.

"Hmpf," said the duchess, the awful thumping coming to a halt. She had stopped just behind Florence's shoulder, but Florence didn't dare look around. She felt like an errant soldier on review.

"Who made your dress?" the duchess demanded.

"Madame Victoire of Brook Street, your Grace, a former associate of Mr. Worth."

"Never heard of her." The duchess stumped to Florence's front. She touched her collar, her hands surprisingly gentle on the pleated cloth. "This red is good for you but far too dark for a chit barely out of the schoolroom."

"It was made on short notice," Florence said without a quaver. She'd always found it easier to stand up for others than for herself, and she didn't want the dressmaker's judgment called into question. "It was all she had on hand."

"Hmpf," said the duchess. Her diamond eyes seemed to measure every seam. She began to stump again. "Play the piano?"

"Tolerably well, your Grace."

"Sing?"

"Not for all the tea in China."

The stumping stopped. Florence gasped and held her breath. The duchess's stare seemed to bore holes into her forehead. "Are you trying to be smart with me, girl?"

"No, your Grace, it just popped out."

A noise issued from the duchess's nose which sounded uncommonly like a snort of laughter. "Oh, very well," she said in the tone of someone who had grudgingly conceded an argument. "You'll do. Sit and have some tea. I'm parched even if you aren't. And stop calling me 'your Grace.' To you, I'm Aunt Hypatia."

"Aunt Hypatia?" Florence's knees gave way as she sank into a chair.

"Yes," said the duchess. "After all, I can hardly present a mere vicar's daughter to the queen."

"Oh, your Grace . . . Aunt Hypatia, I wouldn't presume—"

"You had better learn to presume. No protégée of mine is going to scuffle through life like a frightened mouse."

"I am not a mouse," Florence said, even as she pressed her knees together to still their trembling.

Aunt Hypatia glared. Florence lifted her chin. She wasn't a mouse. Shy, maybe. Timid, certainly. But not a mouse. Mice didn't run their father's home. Mice didn't get themselves to London. Mice didn't risk everything to build a solid future.

After what seemed like an eternity, the duchess's face softened with satisfaction.

"Well," she said, "at least you've got spine. Not much, but some. Which is just as well. Most people exercise their temper far too often. Then, when they really need to stand firm, they crumble."

Florence bowed her head. "I'll try to remember that, your Grace."

"Aunt," the duchess corrected, and lifted the pot to pour her tea. "In fact . . ." Her expression grew distant. "I think you'll be my goddaughter."

At that moment, the duchess could have knocked Florence over with a feather. She laughed when she saw Florence's face, her eyes twinkling with the mischief of a child.

"I can hardly wait to take you out," she said, actually rubbing her hands with glee. "You're going to cause a sensation, an ab-so-lute sensation. There'll be so many noses out of joint, we'll have to count them by the bushel."

This was not a prediction Florence could welcome. "I really don't care to cause a sensation," she murmured. "Just to meet a nice, eligible man."

"You will, my dear," the duchess assured her. "Cartloads. But first"—she chucked Florence under the chin—"first we're going to have fun!"

Aunt Hypatia's generosity had just begun. She assigned Florence a spacious room on the second floor, with windows overlooking the fenced-in park at the center of Grosvenor Square. Lizzie had a cozy closet right beside. The girl was atwitter, for she was to be trained by the duchess's own abigail to be a lady's maid.

"It's a dream," she breathed on hearing the news. "Oh, miss, don't pinch me or I'll wake up!"

Florence wished her own enjoyment were as pure. What sort of paragon, she wondered, accepted a perfect stranger into her home and treated her not like a cousin but like a long-lost daughter? The duchess claimed Mr. Mowbry had done her a favor, but Mr. Mowbry must be quite the solicitor to have a duchess in his debt! Nor did Hypatia seem the type to dedicate her life to charitable causes. Openhanded she was, but hardly self-sacrificing. Florence could only conclude some benefit for her lay in the arrangement. Perhaps she had a social rival whose daughter she hoped to put

in the shade. That Florence could believe, though she knew
the suspicion did her no credit. Her father had raised her to
think the best of people: to say "thank you" rather than
"why." He would tell her to count her good fortune, not
question her rescuer's motives.

When Aunt Hypatia wanted Florence to patronize her
dressmaker, however, a woman who lived *on* Bond Street,
not just near it, Florence had to draw the line.

"I'm paying," the duchess huffed. "The least you can do
is let me have my way."

But even if Madame Victoire was a trifle odd, Florence
could not betray her trust.

"If I marry," she said, "I shall be able to pay you back.
Perhaps not at once," she added, thinking of the possible
tradesman, "but eventually."

She held her ground even in the face of the duchess's
glare. Finally, her benefactress gave in with a snort of annoyance. "Next you'll be wanting to pay room and board."

"If your Grace wishes," Florence agreed.

"Cheek," muttered the duchess. "Don't know what girls
are coming to these days."

Happily, when Madame Victoire arrived, the duchess's
feathers were quickly smoothed. Florence had feared the
dressmaker's manner would be too familiar, but her treatment of the duchess was impeccable, almost obsequious—
though the duchess didn't seem to mind.

Their taste was in perfect accord. As a result, Florence
had no say whatsoever. She was to have three new corsets,
all French, four carriage dresses, six dinner dresses, another
six suitable for dancing, and the Lord only knew how many
petticoats, chemises, and shoes. A single pair of satin slippers would have strained Florence's purse, but Aunt Hypatia did not intend for the madness to stop there.

"If you take, we'll buy more," she said. "Since people
will remember what you've worn."

"I feel as if I'm taking enough already," Florence
mourned. "I begin to pity my poor husband. His wife will
be shockingly in debt."

Aunt Hypatia laughed and kissed her brow, but Florence had not spoken in jest.

On Saturday, her cards went out; or, rather, Duchess Carlisle's cards went out with Florence's name written underneath. Florence and the duchess did not accompany the cards. One of her more ordinary footmen drove them around on his own.

"I have only sent out thirty," said Aunt Hypatia. "We are being select."

Thirty sounded like a great number to Florence, but she nodded as if she thought it small. It was the peaceful hour before bedtime. She sat at the duchess's feet in her boudoir, with her new muslin skirts spread around her, idly helping to roll a skein of cashmere yarn. It seemed odd to have no chores. The Fairleighs, even at their most flush, had never possessed sufficient servants to excuse Florence from the nightly round of dishes and water-carrying and stoking or banking of fires. Now she had only to listen to Aunt Hypatia's voice, to admire the Oriental carpets and the lovely watercolors and the flicker of a fire someone else had built to keep the cool May night at bay. She was growing comfortable here; too comfortable, truth be told.

"What," she said, picking up the thread of conversation, "are we selecting for?"

"For those who are powerful," said the duchess, "and those who are so interesting we cannot resist. Alas, those circles very seldom overlap."

"Except in your case, Aunt Hypatia."

The duchess rewarded her teasing with a sharp rap from her fan. "I have not taught you to be so flattering."

"No, your Grace," she dared to say. "You have not had the time."

Aunt Hypatia chuckled. "Ah, child, it's good to see you smile. When you are frightened you tend to look very prim."

"That is preferable to showing terror, I believe."

"Yes," said the duchess with a quiet sigh. "It is."

She stroked Florence's cheek where the fire had not warmed it. It was a brief caress and when it ended, the duchess subsided into thought. Florence watched her regal, time-worn face: the nose haughty and sharp, the eyes wise and heavy. She did not know this woman and yet she felt as if she did. Despite her suspicions, she could not hold out against the tugging on her heart. Florence did not remember her mother. Sarah Fairleigh had died too young. She thought, however, that the tender spot beneath her breast must be the shadow of a daughter's love.

In that moment, her resistance wavered. The most hardened cynic—and Florence was hardly that—could not doubt Hypatia's affection. It was offered too wistfully to be shammed. If the duchess wished to use Florence in some fashion, well, so be it. Florence judged her patroness had more than earned it.

On Sunday morning, the duchess thumped into Florence's room while Lizzie was struggling with the laces of her corset. The new ones would not arrive for weeks, but Lizzie was determined her mistress's waist would come up to London's mark.

"Reach up and grab the bedpost," the duchess instructed, "and let Lizzie give a heave."

Florence squeaked at how well this succeeded, but the duchess showed no pity.

"You'll get used to it," she said, "and if you faint, we'll let the laces out."

Certain she did not welcome the prospect of fainting, Florence vowed she'd somehow learn to breathe. "Do you require my assistance?" she gasped through the constriction around her ribs. "You know I'd be happy to help in any way."

"No, I don't require your assistance," the duchess huffed. "I require your presence at breakfast. In the cream tarlatan with the green velvet bows. The boys will be joining us. You can have your first dry run."

Florence stepped into the first of many petticoats. " 'The boys'?"

The duchess thumped her cane. "My nephews, and your cousins. So no 'my lord' this and 'viscount' that. It's Freddie and Edward to you and don't forget it."

"Oh," said Florence, her heart beating very fast. She was going to take breakfast with men, titled men, the dowager duchess's relatives. Her nerves being what they were, she sincerely hoped the meal wouldn't end up on her dress.

She worried for nothing, though, because the duchess's nephew Freddie immediately made her comfortable.

"Hullo, cuz," he said, rising as she entered the breakfast parlor. He was the handsomest man she'd ever seen, like a hero out of a novel, with wavy, golden brown hair, bright blue eyes, and a smile as sunny as the day outside.

"How do you do?" Florence responded shyly, unable to resist smiling back.

His brother was a tall broad shadow beside the window. Florence wouldn't have taken much note of him if her fingers hadn't tingled strangely in his grip.

"How do you do?" he said, bowing over her hand. His eyes were the same bright blue as his brother's, but his lashes were black as coal. Within that brooding frame, his stare was remarkably penetrating. A peculiar heat curled through Florence's chest. Embarrassment, she thought, but it wasn't precisely that.

"Oh, kiss her knuckles." Impatience incarnate, the duchess waved him on. "The girl needs to get used to gallantry."

With great solemnity, her nephew obeyed. He was graceful but stiff, and when his lips pressed briefly to her skin, she could not suppress a shiver. His mouth had been warm, almost hot. When he straightened, two spots of color flew on his cheeks.

"Enough of that," chuckled his brother. "Edward don't do the pretty like I do."

He took Florence's arm to lead her to the sideboard, where an astonishing array of food was laid out in silver dishes. Florence goggled at the deviled kidneys and eggs, at the kedgeree and kippers, at the porridge and toast and rolls and the pots of jelly that gleamed like jewels. She doubted four people could eat this much in a week, even if two of them were men.

"Shall I serve you, Florence?" Freddie suggested, grinning to soften his use of her Christian name.

"Yes . . . Freddie," she responded and was rewarded with a boyish laugh.

"We'll get on," he said with a friendly wink. "I can see you're a sensible girl."

He could not have picked a better compliment and the meal proceeded with amazing ease. Freddie was a witty raconteur, a bit naughty perhaps, but never over the line.

"My brother," he confided, as that stern fellow cut his kidneys with methodical care, "is the despair of all the mamas in London."

"Is he?" she said, though she wasn't sure she ought to encourage Freddie at his brother's expense. Edward, as she forced herself to think of him, did not seem the type to relish teasing.

"Yes," said Freddie and bumped her shoulder companionably with his own. "They try to snare him for their daughters, but he won't go. Can't even get him to flirt."

Edward frowned at his plate, but did not scold.

"Not all men were born to flirt," Florence said, feeling oddly as if she should defend him. "Perhaps he—I mean you—oh, dear. Forgive me, Lord Greystowe. I ought not speak for you."

"Edward," he said with a chill authority that proved he was Hypatia's nephew.

"Edward," she said, her cheeks aflame beneath his strange, measuring gaze. "I'm sure your reasons for not flirting with the mamas' daughters are very wise."

"Hah!" said Freddie, apparently in no fear of his brother's ire. "He's married to his responsibilities. To his corn and his sheep and his cotton mill in Manchester."

Edward set down his knife and fork. "Now, Freddie," he said with a perfectly sober face, "it isn't nice to say a man is married to his sheep."

Florence almost choked on a piece of toast. One of the footmen had to thump her on the back until she stopped.

"Come, come," Edward chided. "Surely a country girl like yourself is familiar with the animal side of life."

Florence was almost certain he was teasing. Some emotion curled the corner of his surprisingly sensual mouth. His tone, however, was completely serious.

Her nerves in hopeless confusion, she crumpled her napkin in her lap. Whatever this family's reasons for taking her in, she did not want them to think her common, or that her father had not sheltered her as he should. If she'd heard the village lads joking about such things, it was purely by accident! "I know n-nothing of it at all," she stammered. "Why, when Father carved the turkey, he always asked if I'd take a slice of bosom."

She'd meant this to prove the vicar's propriety, but the declaration caused Freddie to cough loudly into his fist. As for Edward, though he did not succumb to humor, a definite glint shone in his eye.

"Very proper," he said. "The white meat is the tenderest."

His head was lowered over his plate, but when he peered up through his lashes, his gaze seemed to rove laughingly across her bodice. She'd never seen a man laugh that way, with nothing but his eyes. It was at once disconcerting and appealing. And it made it utterly impossible not to press her hand to the swell of her breast.

"Edward," Hypatia scolded, "you're making the girl uncomfortable."

The polite thing would have been to deny it, but Florence's mouth wasn't working well enough for that.

"No worries," Freddie said, recovered from his cough. "Old Edward's made his joke for the quarter. You needn't fear he'll try another until August."

"Freddie!" said Hypatia, no happier with his jest.

Despite the duchess's disapproval, Florence felt the heat recede from her cheeks. The brothers' effect on her could not have been more different. Thank goodness for Freddie. His words made her comfortable again: a part of the fun rather than the object of it. When Edward tendered a stiff apology, she was able to accept it with a modicum of dignity.

"See, Edward," Freddie teased, "not just pretty but forgiving."

Florence returned his friendly grin. What an agreeable young man, she thought. If he was a sample of what London had on offer, her quest to find a husband would not be hard at all.

CHAPTER 3

The following week was spent in giving and returning calls. Florence doubted she was "taking," as Aunt Hypatia put it. The blur of faces and names confused her, and she rarely thought of anything to say. How could she? She did not know the people being discussed, nor any more of fashion than Madame Victoire had laid on her back.

Aunt Hypatia, however, gave every appearance of being pleased.

"Modest and unassuming," she pronounced as the footman handed them into the carriage after a visit in posh Park Lane. With an air of satisfaction, she spread her skirts more comfortably around her, then laughed at Florence's grimace. "You mustn't fear being dull, my dear. You would only seem awkward if you tried to be gay. The important thing is for people to meet you and see how pretty you are, which they could not fail to do if they were blind."

Such claims made Florence uncomfortable but, considering how generous the duchess had been and how little else Florence had to offer, she felt she really ought not to complain.

When she was not engaged with calls, Freddie claimed cousin's privilege to squire her around, taking her riding in the parks or on a boat ride down the Thames. She enjoyed herself immensely, for Freddie was a charming companion, full of witty stories but also drawing her to talk about herself. By the end of the week, he knew more about her than almost anyone alive.

She had to remind herself the duchess could not mean for her to fix her affections on him. Her nephew would marry an heiress, she decided, one of those laughing Americans, perhaps, who would not make him stand on ceremony.

"Do you think so?" he said when she shared her theory. He fixed her with an odd, speaking look which, provokingly, did not speak clearly to her.

They were leaning over the rail of a pleasure boat, chugging westwards from the pool of London. The Victoria Embankment lay ahead, and the bristling brown towers of Parliament. They stood so close they bumped elbows but, as ever, she was comfortable with his touch.

"You don't like Americans?" she probed, expecting some quip in response.

Instead, he turned his gaze to a nearby collier. The heavy ship wallowed under its load of coal and Freddie's expression wasn't much lighter. He looked so sad of a sudden Florence's ribs squeezed tight with pity.

"I'm fond of English lasses" was all he said. "Pretty ones, with straight dark hair and eyes as green as glass."

She did not take the implication seriously, not from a flirt like him. No doubt some foolish American had broken his heart, and that was the source of his pain. But if one had, he did not reveal it. The moment passed and he was soon as bright as ever.

His brother joined a few of their outings, which was not an unmitigated joy. Florence did not know why, but he seemed to have taken her in dislike. Freddie's claim that his sibling would not venture more than one witticism per quarter seemed to be correct. Not that she wanted to hear more foolish sheep jokes. One had been enough. Still, she hardly thought it necessary that he frown every time he looked at her. She would have been tempted to evade him but for Freddie's obvious delight. He adored his older brother and, despite Edward's wooden manner, she could see the sentiment was returned. Nor could she fault Edward's politeness. Everywhere they went, he introduced her as their cousin. Shy as she was, she couldn't help being gratified at being seen with these impressive men.

If only the elder of the two could have been a little warmer!

He was not ugly, she decided. To be sure, his build wasn't as lithe as Freddie's, but he was every bit as tall. His shoulders were broader, his limbs heavier and more powerful. His face was interesting if one looked past his glower. His expression had an intensity and an intelligence which was impossible to ignore. True, his brows overhung his eyes, and his nose was as sharp as Aunt Hypatia's. His forehead, however, was truly noble, his jaw strong, and the most exacting critic of human beauty could not have found fault with the sensual perfection of his mouth.

His hands, she thought with a peculiar inward shiver, were also nice. They were large and careful and capable. She found it hard to imagine the task they could not do.

When they all went riding in Rotten Row, her pride in the brothers' company was so great she felt the glow of it in her cheeks. Freddie's style turned every eye and Edward, who rode a magnificent, deep-chested black stallion, was so imposing the other horses sidled away at his approach. His hands seemed barely to move upon the reins. Freddie's gelding frisked with high spirits, but Edward's horse behaved as if he were too proud to do anything except precisely what Edward asked. Florence found this astonishing. In her experience, stallions were rarely fit for anyone but madmen and braggarts to ride—and Edward was clearly neither. He called the beast Samson, for his long caramel-colored mane.

Florence's bay mare, leased from a local stable, seemed inordinately fond of the big black horse. She was a pretty creature, with a gait as light as a cat's, but if Florence's attention strayed for even a moment, she would shoulder over to Samson and rub her muzzle against his neck.

"She's in love," Freddie teased the dozenth time Florence tried to wrestle the mare away. "Edward, you'll have to bring Buttercup back to Greystowe for Samson's harem."

Florence had heard such talk before, of course. Back home, horses and their breeding were as great a topic of conversation as the weather. Nothing Freddie said should have embarrassed her. For some reason, though, maybe because Edward's eyes were on her, or because the mare chose that moment to press even more amorously into Samson's side, a great wash of heat poured through her limbs. From head to toe, her body pulsed with the fiery tide. Florence had never experienced the like. Sweat prickled between her breasts and where her thigh was jammed against Edward's burned as if his leg were made of coal.

With a soft cry, she thrust out her hand to keep from being crushed between their mounts. Her palm caught Edward's hip, right where his buff-colored breeches stretched across his groin. His leg was harder than she expected. Her fingers curled in reaction and, as a muscle shifted abruptly beneath her touch, the strange throbbing heat intensified inside her.

Edward wrenched away with a curse. "For God's sake," he exclaimed, his color high, "watch where you lay your hand."

"I—I—"said Florence, but before she could get the apology out, he was tearing through the trees towards the Serpentine's banks, clods of turf kicking up beneath Samson's hooves.

Mortified, Florence tried to contain her tears. In all her life no one had spoken to her so coldly. Of course, she could not deny she deserved it. He must think her twice the fool: first for not controlling her horse and second for having the temerity to touch him where no lady should. That she hadn't meant to hardly mattered. Worst of all, there were witnesses to her shame. Two young women in jaunty feathered hats had stopped beside the sandy path, and now were tittering behind their gloves. Florence had the awful feeling she'd met them on one of her calls. The Misses Wainwright, she believed, whose mama had asked so many pointed questions about Freddie and his brother. The woman had been

most encroaching and Florence had thought perhaps it was
her nose Aunt Hypatia meant to put out of joint by launch-
ing her.

Florence certainly hadn't helped that ambition today.
They, too, cantered off before she could decide whether she
ought to nod.

The only saving grace was that Freddie hadn't seen them
cut her.

"Don't mind Edward," he said, giving her horse's with-
ers a soothing pat. "God love him, but he's moody."

"He's right," she said, every part of her aquiver. "My
failings as a horsewoman are undeniable."

"Pooh." Freddie waved the suggestion away. "Got as
fine a seat as anyone. Not your fault Edward chose a horse
with a fancy for his."

Her heart picked up strangely at his words. "Edward
chose my horse?"

"Didn't he just! Wouldn't trust the job to anyone else.
Drove the man at Tattersall's batty. Nothing too slow, he
says, but nothing too fast and, no, that one ain't near pretty
enough. And what does he get for his pains but this lovelorn
creature?"

The mare whickered as if she took offense. Most of Florence's hurt was lost in the laugh she and Freddie shared.
Not all of it, though.

Lord Greystowe's disapproval had a powerful sting.

Edward rode full out until he hit the quiet of Kensington
Gardens. Up till then, the necessity of dodging phaetons
and buggies had kept his mind from the brand Miss Fairleigh's palm had seared onto his thigh. The girl was too
innocent for her own good. Too innocent for *his* good.

With a muttered curse, he dismounted beneath the wil-
lows that lined the Long Water's banks. His lingering erection made him awkward but he ignored it. He was used to
it by now, or should have been. He had only to think of the
girl and his sex began to fill. Worse, he was beginning to
like her. Most girls in her position would have been grasp-

ing or sly, but she was an amiable little thing, and so tempting to tease. A hundred times a day he thought of some quip to make her blush, then had to remind himself that charming her was Freddie's business. Sighing, he removed his hat and raked his sweaty hair back from his brow. A heron stalked the placid lake before him, its stately progress calming his disordered nerves. As if to remind him how hard he'd been working, Samson blew impatiently in his ear.

"Yes," said Edward, stroking the horse's lathered nose. "You're a good fellow."

A better fellow than his master. Samson hadn't lost control when that mare rubbed up against him. Nor was Samson contemplating another visit to Cumberland Terrace. Three times this week that made, with each encounter more frenzied than the last. Imogene was cooing.

He shook his head in disgust and opened his collar to the breeze. He couldn't keep exorcizing his lust for his brother's intended with his mistress. Even if Imogene didn't know, it wasn't right. No, he had to wrestle this demon to ground himself. Florence wasn't for him. Florence was for Freddie. And they were getting on famously. Per instructions, Freddie was giving a fair imitation of an increasingly besotted man. Nor did his interest seem feigned. He was fond of the girl, genuinely fond. He repeated things she'd said, planned excursions for her pleasure, and, as far as Edward could see, enjoyed their time together.

Just the other day, he told Edward how she'd charmed the duke of Devonshire's horse. "Silly beast tried to eat the girl's hat," he'd laughed. "You know what she said? 'Why, your Grace. I'd no idea that hat had such good straw.' That shows pluck, Edward. Pluck. Especially for a girl who'd jump at her own shadow." Freddie was proud of her, as a man should be proud of his future wife. All in all, Edward's plan could not have been progressing better.

If he hadn't been so attracted to her himself, he was certain he would have been glad.

•   •   •

Freddie, Florence, and the duchess stood in a courtyard behind a big Palladian building on Piccadilly, waiting for Edward to arrive. For the last four years, this brown and white mansion had housed the Royal Academy of the Arts. According to Aunt Hypatia, the private viewing of the spring show, for which they had come, was the first great event of the Season. The look of the crowd upheld her claim. All around them, the cream of London society filed slowly towards the entrance, their clothes exquisite, their demeanor impossibly proud. Always an object of attention, the duchess nodded at many who passed, all of whom seemed pleased to be acknowledged. Surprisingly, many nodded at Florence as well. Florence did her best to smile and bow, but was far too agitated to attempt more greeting than that. To her relief, she did not see the Misses Wainwright.

"Don't fidget," said Aunt Hypatia, softening the order with a pat.

Florence barely heard her. She did not know if she was glad or sorry Edward had chosen to see the show. The duchess could use his arm, of course, and Freddie was always happy to have him, but Florence was finding Edward's company increasingly oppressive to her nerves. She could not seem to catch her breath when he was near. If he should chance to touch her, her hands would begin to shake. The mere sight of his shoulders in one of his conservative black coats caused a peculiar palpitation of her heart.

Today, his top hat did her in. It was perched with perfect straightness on his head, its gleam no richer than that of his wavy hair, which was clipped so close to his neck the locks didn't dare curl over his collar. What drove a man to treat his hair as if it were in danger of running wild? And what, she wondered, would happen if he let it?

The question was nonsensical, of course, and the answer not her concern. Determined not to pursue it, she folded her hands at her waist and composed herself to greet him.

He met them with his usual stiff bow and frown, a frown that deepened as he took in her long-waisted apricot gown. She wore one of her new French corsets beneath it, laced only a little tighter than she was used to. The color was flattering, as was the ecru lace that spilled from its neck and sleeves. The bustle was modest, the sweep of the polonaise no more extravagant than any woman her age might wear. Her hat was a marvel of simplicity: a tilted satin chip with a single white feather in its brim, so small it perched atop her upswept hair like a saucer to a teacup. Freddie had gone into raptures when he saw her; said she'd outshine anything the painters could devise. And Freddie knew fashion. Because of this, Florence refused to believe Edward was frowning at her outfit.

Which meant he had to be frowning at her.

"Florence," he said, no more than that, and turned to escort his aunt.

The deflation she felt once his eyes had left her was completely inexplicable.

"Are you sure he wanted to come?" she whispered to Freddie as they, and the rest of the crowd, crept up the double staircase in the hall. "You didn't bully him into it, did you?"

"Me?" Freddie's eyes widened in surprise. "Lord, no. Couldn't keep him away. Edward's a true patron of the arts. You watch. Everyone else will be gossiping about who's wearing what and who's wooing whom and old Edward will be looking at the pictures."

Freddie, apparently, belonged to the gossiping set. She lost him to a group of laughing men as soon as they entered the hall. He waved at her to join him but she didn't want to go, not only because his companions looked a trifle fast, but because she wanted to see the show. This, to her, was the lure of London. Not parties, not *cartes de visites,* but plunging into the heart of art and culture. When she couldn't spot Edward or the duchess, she resigned herself to touring alone.

Happily, no one paid the least attention as she wandered from room to room. Each wall took a good deal of study, for the paintings were crammed together, one atop the other, all the way to the ceiling. Florence didn't mind the confusion. She loved seeing these works in person, rather than as engravings in a magazine. Even the bad paintings pleased her, for she could see the brush strokes and the colors and imagine the real live painter at his work. How wonderful it must be, she thought, to have the ability to create.

Some of the pictures were very fine. For long minutes, she stood entranced by Mr. Millais's portrait of the grand Mrs. Bischoffshein, her character captured so thoroughly Florence felt as if she knew her. A termagant, she thought, but one with a sense of humor. She stopped as well when she reached Tissot's *Too Early,* which, by luck or design, hung by itself above a lovely marble fireplace. The picture depicted four lovely, but obviously embarrassed, girls, waiting with their escorts in an empty ballroom.

"Do you like it?" said a deep familiar voice.

Florence's heart began to pound. She couldn't recall Edward soliciting her opinion before. She snuck a look at him but, thankfully, his stern blue gaze rested on the painting. She answered as steadily as she could.

"I like it very much," she said. "The artist has so perfectly captured the awkwardness of arriving first one can hardly help but smile."

Edward tugged his lapels. "You like a picture that tells a story?"

"As long as the story is interesting."

"What about that French fellow, Monet, or Mr. Sisley?" For the first time, he looked directly at her, both his gaze and his tone challenging. Florence felt an odd swooping in her stomach. No man should have lashes that thick. For a moment, her face was so hot she thought she'd faint. She had to swallow before she could speak.

"I'm afraid I'm not familiar with their work."

Edward nodded as if her answer was no more than he'd expected. "Come with me," he said. "I have something to show you."

To her amazement, he took her not by the arm but by the hand. Even through her gloves she could feel the warmth of his hold. Her fingers were utterly swallowed in his grip. She could only pray he did not sense the sudden dampness of her palm.

He led her through a maze of arched doorways to the very smallest of the galleries. There he handed her a pair of silver opera glasses and pointed to a painting which hung, as if the Academy were ashamed to have accepted it, in a high, dingy corner near the ceiling.

Florence put the glasses to her eyes. "Am I looking at Mr. Monet or Mr. Sisley?"

"Neither," he said, with the perversity she had come to expect. "This work is Mr. Whistler's."

She could feel him breathing, slowly, steadily. He stood directly behind her, his long legs brushing her skirts, his big hands tilting the binoculars to guide her gaze. Her arms began to tremble. They only stopped when she focused on the painting.

"Oh," she sighed, unable to keep her wonderment inside. The picture showed a bridge just after sunset on a misty night, with the shadow of a solitary boatman punting the current underneath. She'd never seen anything like it. It was a completely new thing, a blur of subtle colors which somehow created a world. She felt her mind open in the strangest way. This, she thought, is a painting of the future.

Edward seemed to share her excitement.

"Isn't it something?" he said, the words a gentle stir beneath her hat.

"It's extraordinary! Why, it's nothing but smears of dark and light blue, but you know exactly what it is. He has it precisely: how the water looks at night, even how it feels, as if the whole world had gone to sleep but you. It makes me want to cry just looking at it and yet it's quite, quite beautiful."

Lost in admiration, she didn't even jump when Edward's hands settled briefly on her shoulders, just a quick, warm squeeze and they were gone.

"I was thinking I would buy it," he said.

Florence couldn't help herself. She lowered the glasses and turned to him. His expression was musing, his exquisite mouth relaxed. For once, he looked as young as Freddie. Oh, I could like him, she thought. If only he behaved this way more often, I'm certain we could be friends.

"Do you know," she said, "I've never known anyone who bought a painting."

He laughed at her admission, a soft, open sound that brushed her ears like a puppy's growl. "Careful, Miss Fairleigh. You betray your origins by such a statement."

His eyes were twinkling so kindly she knew he was teasing. All the same, she found it impossible to hold his gaze. It was too blue, too warm. She looked at her hands instead, still clasped around his opera glasses. "My origins are difficult to hide," she said, smiling a little herself. "Aunt Hypatia says I mustn't even try."

"Well, if Aunt Hypatia says . . ." he agreed, and smoothed back the little white feather which had fallen forward from her hat. It was a gesture his brother might have made, thoughtful and protective. Florence shivered under it as she never had with Freddie.

"Are you cold, Miss Fairleigh?" Edward asked, his voice low and oddly husky. He had bent forward to view her face, an action necessitated by his greater height. She could see the shadow of his whiskers beneath his skin; could smell the woodsy aroma of his cologne. She wouldn't have thought he'd wear scent, a sober man like him. The fact that he did pricked her deep inside. He has secrets, she thought. He is not at all the man he seems.

"Miss Fairleigh?" he said. So lightly she might have dreamt it, his finger brushed the curve of her cheek. Its tip was bare and slightly rough. He must have removed his gloves. Her stomach tightened at the unexpected intimacy.

"I am well," she said, just a shade too loudly. "Quite."

Edward stiffened at her tone and took half a step back. He buttoned his elegant coat and smoothed it down. "Perhaps we ought to rescue Aunt Hypatia from the tea room."

"Yes," she said, both relieved and disappointed.

He offered his arm this time, the elbow held well out from his side. When Florence put her hand through it, his yielding had disappeared. The limb might as well have been a block of wood. A sigh escaped her corseted lungs. She'd thought Freddie's brother was warming to her, and had been foolish enough to welcome the change. She should have known better. Clearly, it would take more than a moment's amity to melt this man of stone.

Lewis tapped on the door to the dressing room just as Edward slid an onyx stud through the front of his stark white shirt. He was planning his strategy for tonight's ball, a strategy that did not include forgetting himself as he had at the Academy. He would be civil to Miss Fairleigh, no more. He would not touch her. He would not smile at her. Most definitely he would not dance with her. Until he found a means to control his disturbingly volatile reactions, he was not going to get close to her again.

He didn't care if her eyes were as green as Irish grass. He didn't care if she did agree that Whistler was a genius, or that her blushes made him want to crush her to his chest and kiss her senseless. From now on, distance would be the lynchpin of their relationship.

"Sir?" said Lewis. Having failed to get a response from his master, the valet stepped just inside the door. "I'm afraid a small problem has arisen."

Edward's mind flew to Freddie, and footmen, but he pushed the thought aside as quickly as he could. Freddie had given his word. That was all Edward needed to know. He fastened the stud beneath his pointed collar. He reached for his white bow tie. "What small problem?"

"It's Miss Fairleigh."

Edward's heart skipped a beat. Damnation. Her name was enough to tighten the muscles of his groin. "Is Miss Fairleigh unwell?"

"Not precisely, my lord." Lewis took the tie from Edward's hands before he mangled it. "Apparently, she's grown so anxious over the prospect of her first formal ball that she is . . . prostrate."

" 'Prostrate'?" Edward lifted his chin for Lewis to tie the bow. An image of Miss Fairleigh fainting drifted disturbingly through his mind. He could almost feel himself catching her.

"A disturbance of the stomach," Lewis elucidated.

In spite of a rush of sympathy, Edward laughed. "You mean she's so frightened she cast up her accounts."

"Yes, sir," said the valet. "Her courage has failed her. She swears she'll return to Keswick tomorrow, rather than make a fool of herself tonight."

"Keswick?" With a frown, Edward submitted to a subtle rearrangement of his hair.

"Her home village," Lewis explained and Edward experienced an illogical prick of annoyance that his servant knew this when he did not. "Duchess Carlisle is at her wit's end. She sent her footman over to see if young Lord Burbrooke can talk some sense into her, but your brother has already left for his dinner engagement at the Brawleighs'."

"Surely my aunt could—"

"She says it's a job for a man: the voice of authority appealing to the rational in a woman." Lewis looked as if he doubted this quality existed in female form. Then again, for the past year, Lewis had been trying without success to coax the senior chambermaid into his bed.

"I'll speak to her," Edward said, though he knew it flew in the face of his resolutions. "Most likely she only needs to be reassured she won't be left standing through the waltzes."

"Yes, my lord." Lewis held up his waistcoat for him to slip his arms into the sleeves. The design was very plain, black with a smooth shawl collar and a satin back. It fit like a second skin.

Edward ignored the tingle of excitement that warmed his spine. This mission of mercy posed no danger. After all, how appealing could a "prostrate" woman be?

"Brush your teeth," said Lizzie, holding out the tin of tooth powder.

Florence buried her face in the pillow. She was never leaving this room. The Vances were expecting five hundred people at their ball. Her stomach lurched at the very thought. She'd been brave up till now; she truly had, but this was too much to expect. Five hundred people! And

Aunt Hypatia wanted her to dazzle them. She'd be lucky if she survived.

"Already brushed them twice," she mumbled.

"Once more before you go," Lizzie insisted. "Duchess's orders."

"But I'm not going. I'm not, I'm not!" She knew how hysterical she sounded, but she could not stop herself. She couldn't go. She simply couldn't. She might be pretty but she was hopelessly inept. With a groan, she piled the pillow over her head.

"Honestly," Lizzie huffed, and Florence knew she'd put her hands on her skinny hips. "You make me ashamed to know you, Miss Florence."

"And you should be ashamed," said a voice that had her bolting up with the pillow clutched to her chest, though her dressing gown was perfectly modest. Her hair was down. And this was her bedroom. And he was a man. All of which was enough to throw her into a panic.

"Lord Greystowe!" she gasped.

He sat very gently on the edge of the bed, as if she were an invalid. She thought he would take her hand but he only stroked the coverlet beside her hip.

"Now, Florence," he said, "tell me what has frightened you."

He made her feel foolish by simple virtue of asking the question. But she wasn't foolish. No one understood how terrible this was for her, least of all this man, who'd probably never been frightened in his life. She plumped the pillow in her lap and sniffed back a tear. "Aunt Hypatia says five hundred people are coming to the Vances' ball."

"And?" he said, as if five hundred people were nothing. Her tears welled again, but now they were tears of resentment.

"They'll stare," she said, her nails curling into her palms. "They'll stare and they'll titter and they'll talk behind their fans as if I were a cow at a county fair."

"Because you're pretty," he said in that same infuriatingly reasonable tone.

"Yes!" she said, almost shouting it.

Edward smiled and her temper abruptly snapped. How

dare he mock her fears? Before she could stop herself, she pounded his chest with both hands. Edward caught them before she could land a second blow.

"Hush," he said, and pressed a gentle kiss to the knuckles of each fist. This procedure so astonished her she didn't think to pull back. His eyes shone with humor and something that in any other man she would have said was fondness. "Allow me to explain the economies of size, Miss Fairleigh. With five hundred attendees, at least half of them women, you can count on, oh, fully twenty being prettier than yourself. A good many will have jewels more dazzling than your own. A fair number will be dressed so inappropriately anyone who sees them will not be able to look away. Add to that those guests who are either the subject or repository of gossip, and you'll find no more than a tenth of those present will stare at you even once."

"And a tenth is only fifty," Lizzie put in, who was proud of her skill at math.

Florence was neither impressed nor reassured.

"All I know are country dances," she said, her voice still quavering. "I don't remember a step Aunt Hypatia's dancing master tried to teach me."

Edward squeezed her hands. "You'll remember. The moment the music starts it will all come back. Come now, Florence. Where's the girl who charmed the duke of Devonshire with her wit? Where's her courage?"

"In the chamberpot," Florence muttered.

"Nonsense," said Edward. "That was only lunch."

"And since it's gone," Lizzie added with country practicality, "you needn't worry about being sick."

Florence's shoulders sagged. She didn't want to be strong. She wanted to be weak and helpless and stay where she was safe. But Lizzie was counting on her and so was Aunt Hypatia, and even Edward, in a way. If his "cousin" proved a coward, it would not reflect well on him.

"I suppose I have no choice."

"No choice at all," Edward agreed. He smiled at her. Florence saw a hint of pride in it and thought perhaps she wouldn't fail after all.

CHAPTER 4

❧

A burning shiver swept the bare expanse of Florence's shoulders. Edward was watching her descend Aunt Hypatia's curving stairs. He wore an expression of utter stupefaction.

"Perhaps," he said, in an unusually faint tone, "I have misled you."

Florence didn't know what to make of his reaction—or her own. Edward had never looked at her like this, as other men did, as if she were a meal they wished to devour. Usually this look discomfited her. She couldn't imagine why she welcomed it from him. Certainly, she didn't *desire* his attention. He was the opposite of everything she valued in a man: not gentle, not affectionate, and certainly not safe! No, indeed. Most likely her response was merely nerves.

"Misled me?" she said, the question dangerously close to a squeak.

"Yes," he murmured and pressed his hand to his pristine shirtfront. His father's ruby signet gleamed on his smallest finger. "I fear you *shall* be the prettiest woman there."

"Enough," said the duchess, thumping her ivory cane. "Move aside so I can see."

At her instruction, Florence turned slowly before her. She knew she looked her best. Her gown was daffodil satin, cut low off the shoulder and draped at capsleeve and train with dotted tulle. Beneath this ephemeral net, the skirt gathered yard upon yard of fabric, an extravagant expanse from whose folds peeped vines of pink silk roses. More roses decorated her elaborately braided chignon. Around her neck a stunning choker was clasped, formed by thousands of seed pearls strung into the shape of flowers. The gown's waist required such stringent lacing Florence felt as if two large hands were wrapped around her ribs. The sensation was unexpectedly pleasant but, as a result, her breasts were forced so dramatically upward she feared she was overly décolleté.

If she was, Aunt Hypatia did not disapprove. Instead, she touched the necklace with one age-stiffened finger. She nodded brusquely.

"Suits you," she said. "Never did believe in girls wearing ribbons around their necks. Not if they've got something better."

"I'm grateful for the loan," Florence said, knowing the duchess had worn these pearls when she was Florence's age. "I shall take good care of them."

"Know you will," said Aunt Hypatia. The light from a wall sconce caught a sudden glitter in her eye. Was she thinking of her dear departed duke or some other youthful conquest? Assuredly she had had them. The duchess was too self-assured for it to be otherwise. But Florence doubted she would share the tale. Indeed, as soon as Hypatia blinked, the glitter disappeared. Once more in command of herself, the duchess rapped her cane against the footman's calf.

"Well, John," she snapped to the senior man, "have them bring around the carriage."

"Yes, your Grace," he said in his eerily drawn-out voice, as if being struck by his mistress were an everyday occurrence.

It made Florence wonder what she'd gotten into when she let the duchess take her under her wing. If she failed to live up to Hypatia's plans, would her calves be stinging, too?

• • •

Her heart had plenty of time to flutter before their coach crawled its way up the line of carriages to the door. Such dresses she saw as they waited! Such silks and jewels and clouds of expensive perfume! For once, she was glad Madame Victoire had spared no expense on her couture. She would at least look as if she belonged.

When they reached the fancy overhang of the porte cochere, Edward lifted her out of the carriage. The clasp of his hands made her even more breathless than the corset. She hadn't supposed a man could be that strong. She seemed to weigh nothing in his arms. As he set her on the pavement, their eyes locked. Edward's shone like hot blue flames, intense but mysterious, and completely focused on her. Warmth spread over her breasts. Wish though she might, she could not quell the reaction. Embarrassed, she touched the tulle that swathed her bodice. Edward looked away.

"Watch your train," he said, as gruff as ever, and helped the duchess down.

When she was settled, they ventured together up the stairs. Grateful for the distraction, Florence could not contain her curiosity. She'd never been in a house this grand. To her it seemed a palace. A pair of torches shaped like nymphs, with gas globes balanced on their shoulders, lit the reception area inside the door. While the liveried footman announced their names, Florence goggled. The nymphs bore no more covering than a gauzy, scarflike cloth which seemed to have blown across their privy parts. Their breasts were bare and topped with swollen nipples—not stiffly swollen, as if the nymphs were cold, but soft, as if the breeze that blew the scarves had gently kissed their skin.

An irrational yearning pulled her closer. She would have liked to touch that polished bronze. Even more puzzling, she would have liked to stand in the nymphs' place, equally bare, to be kissed by the balmy breeze and admired by passersby. A statue could not be shy, after all. A statue could only be adored. She touched the metal plinth, surprised to find it cold.

"Florence," hissed the duchess.

She hurried after her with a gasp. What was she thinking? Without a doubt, her recent fears had disordered her mind!

In its way, the Vances' home was as confusing as Euston Station. The mansion in Knightsbridge had been designed by Robert Adam in an opulent, classical style. Every public room—and there were many—boasted marble columns and gilt and inlay and magnificent stuccowork ceilings. The paintings were as fine as any she had viewed at the Academy. With difficulty, she tore herself past Gainsboroughs and Reynoldses and followed a female servant up the stairs to the women's cloakroom.

In this bustling boudoir, an obliging lady's maid took her wrap and smoothed her hair and, best of all, showed her a quiet corner where she could sit. There, behind a sheltering screen of potted palms, with the sweet night air flowing in through an open window, Florence shut her eyes and tried to catch her breath.

She told herself she could do this. She would take the evening slowly. She would speak when spoken to, dance when asked, and—above all—pay attention to any nice gentlemen she met. The sooner she settled herself, the sooner she could repay Aunt Hypatia's faith, not to mention her purse.

Her face had begun to cool when a trio of women stopped on the other side of the wall of greenery. To her dismay, two were the Misses Wainwright, in matching white tarlatan gowns. They stood so close she could not possibly leave without them seeing her. But perhaps she would stay where she was a little longer. Discretion was, after all, the better part of valor. Her cowardice thus justified, Florence steeled herself to wait as quietly as she could.

"They say he's smitten," the elder Miss Wainwright was saying. Her name was Greta, Florence recalled, and the younger's name was Minna. Both sisters were handsome, built on Amazonian lines with dark gleaming hair and equally dark and gleaming eyes. Their curls, the likes of which Lizzie despaired of ever coaxing from Florence's hair, hung in perfect corkscrews to their shoulders. They sang charmingly, she had heard, and possessed a wealth of airs and graces. Their only flaw, if it even was one and not a figment of her imagination, was a certain petulance to their mouths. Truthfully, whatever Hypatia's ambitions, Florence could not imagine outshining these lovely girls.

"I can't believe his affections are engaged," said a third woman whom Florence didn't know. "Everyone knows he's an incorrigible flirt. I'm sure he's simply being cousinly."

"Perhaps," drawled Miss Minna in a cool, superior tone. "But one of her cousins doesn't welcome the association. I saw him cut her myself. Galloped off without a word when the hopeless ninny bumped his horse. I thought she'd burst into tears right there."

Heavens, Florence thought, starting up in her chair. They were talking about her, about her and Edward. Heart thundering, she shrank back and willed the women not to see her. Fortunately, they were too caught up in their gossip to look around. Even as Florence held her breath, the third whispered furiously in Minna's ear. When she'd finished, Minna's curls trembled with indignation.

"Now that," she pronounced, "is the grossest slander yet. Freddie Burbrooke adores women. Any female who's met him knows that. In any case"—she snapped her painted fan—"I don't see why we should concern ourselves with such a nobody. Why, if it weren't for that tired old dragon who's carting her about, no one would pay her any mind."

"She *is* pretty," Greta said in the tone of one too sure of her own beauty to be threatened.

"Milkmaid pretty," Minna scorned. "And who among us believes those blushes don't come out of a pot?"

If the trio had seen Florence then, they would have known her blushes were real. Her very ears were hot. With relief, she watched the women moving towards the door. The third, alas, had a final parting shot.

"It's animal magnetism," she said as they rustled off. "She's coarse and fleshy and men are the biggest animals of all. Didn't you hear what Devonshire's horse did to her hat?"

Florence clapped her hands to her cheeks. Were people really talking about that?

A low, musical laugh broke through her shock. Florence looked up. A slim young woman with frizzy gold hair and freckles was parting the fronds beside her ear, like an African hunter who'd found his game.

"I see from your horror," she said, "that you are the infamous Miss Fairleigh."

The woman's words were so mischievous Florence couldn't help but laugh. She rose and dropped a small curtsey. "I am," she said. "Milkmaid blushes and all."

"And I," said the girl, "am Meredith Vance, the plainest deb in London." She gave Florence's hand a brisk, unfeminine shake. "Shall we walk down together and show those silly cats that plain girls and milkmaids know how to behave?"

Florence had not met Miss Vance before, but knew her to be the daughter of their hosts and, therefore, the daughter of a duke. Consequently, she was momentarily flustered by her offer.

"It would be my honor, Miss Vance," she said once she had found her voice.

Miss Vance wrinkled her nose. "Call me Merry," she said, as if Florence herself were the daughter of a peer. "All my friends do and I'm certain we're going to be friends."

Miss Vance's kindness stole her breath. Dear as Keswick was, the village had been home to a great many genteel old ladies. Florence couldn't remember when she'd last had a friend her own age. Of course, she thought more soberly, Miss Vance's generosity meant she couldn't hide in the cloakroom all night.

"My brothers are going to swamp you," her rescuer predicted.

Florence endeavored to look as if this news were good.

Edward leaned against the wall with his champagne punch, watching an endless succession of males whirl Florence Fairleigh around the floor. She was, as she'd predicted, an awkward dancer. Not surprisingly, none of her partners seemed to mind. Rather, they gazed at her with puppyish eyes, trying to coax her to lift her shyly lowered lashes by telling amusing tales. Even the older men played this game, as if she in her innocence made them remember theirs.

Only Freddie succeeded. He arrived late with a shower of apologies and immediately swept Florence into a waltz. Within minutes, she was shaking her head with laughter, easy in his arms as she was in no one else's. Her smile dazzled Edward all the way across the room. Freddie was good for her. Freddie brought her into her own. Even when he took her to meet his friends, she did not lose her glow. Edward saw her speaking to them and watched them laugh at whatever she'd said. Somehow, Freddie had found a way to share his charm with her.

Her earlier terror might as well have been a dream. Certainly, she didn't need Edward's assistance now.

He thrust his hands into his pockets, glummer than he could ever remember being. He shouldn't stare at her like this. He was only torturing himself. But how could he look away? Peter Vance was dancing with her now, a sprightly polka which could not have shown her stiffness to worse effect. Why did her awkwardness enthrall him? His heart thumped at the way she craned her slender neck to watch her stumbling feet, at the way her skirts caught Vance's legs, at the way—God help him—she blushed when Vance bent to whisper some tease in her shell-like ear.

Edward ground his teeth. He was an idiot. A complete and utter idiot. The obsession he felt for this girl made no sense whatsoever. It did no one any good: not him, not her, not Freddie.

"People are saying you snubbed her," said a throaty, boyish voice.

Caught by surprise, Edward looked down quite a few inches and found himself gazing into the wide freckled smile of their hosts' youngest daughter. He'd met her at Tattersall's, he recalled, a horse-mad girl, as plain in speech as she was in appearance.

"Miss Vance," he said, and bowed politely over her hand. "Forgive me for not noticing your approach."

She gave him a rap with her fan that put him more in mind of Aunt Hypatia than a seventeen-year-old coquette. "Didn't you hear me? People are saying you don't like Florence Fairleigh."

Edward squinted in confusion. "Are you acquainted with Miss Fairleigh?"

"Oh, yes," she said airily. "Your cousin and I are great friends—ever since I heard those Wainwright witches taking cuts at her in the cloakroom."

Edward's spine snapped straight. Someone had hurt Florence? Someone had dared? "What Wainwright witches?"

His unwitting growl made his companion laugh. "The same Wainwright witches whose mama has been stalking you these past two years."

"Oh," he said, unconsciously pursing his mouth in distaste, "Greta and Minna."

"Yes. Greta and Minna. And if you don't dance with your cousin, they'll convince everyone you disapprove of her." Her eyes narrowed and she poked the center of his chest with the end of her fan. "You don't really dislike her, do you? I'd hate to think so. Because she's obviously a nice girl and just as obviously perfect for your brother. If you meant to be cruel, I would be forced to greatly lower my estimation of your character."

Edward was startled to hear Miss Vance had any estimation of him at all. Taken aback, he had only enough presence of mind to blink when she grabbed both his wrists and pulled him onto the crowded floor. What a hellion she was to behave this outrageously in public!

"We'll dance straight to her," she said, lifting his arms into the appropriate position. "My brother Peter has got her now and he's already stood up with her twice. Once more and Mama will fear he means to make a declaration. He'll know he must relinquish her to you."

Contrary to Edward's expectations, Miss Vance, the freckle-faced, horse-mad girl, proved a neat dancer. Almost before he knew it, she'd spun them through the other couples to Florence's side. He wasn't certain, but he suspected Miss Vance had been leading.

Florence's world shrank down to a single soul. Edward stood before her. Tall Edward. Grave Edward. Edward of the burning eyes and the beautiful mouth. Peter Vance faded into insignificance, though he'd stepped a mere foot away. Freddie's older brother was all that she could see. This was not good, she thought, not good at all.

"Oh," she said stupidly, and put one hand to her stays to keep her heart from bursting through. "Edward."

"Florence," he said, with a low, formal bow. How broad his shoulders were, and how well his black tailcoat showed off the trimness of his waist! With customary dignity, he straightened. "Might I have the honor of this dance?"

Florence blinked. "You wish to dance with me?"

He frowned and at once she felt more clearheaded. A scowling Edward she was used to.

"Yes, I wish to dance with you. Have you some objection, cousin?"

"Oh, no," she said. "I—I'd be happy to."

"Well then," he said.

As if on cue, the orchestra struck up a waltz. Her skin tingled as he took her in his arms. At once, she knew this dance was different. Edward held her with complete assurance, born to rule the ballroom. The hand he'd placed on her waist almost lifted her through the steps.

"Stop looking at your feet," he whispered, his cheek for one moment pressed to hers.

At the touch, her limbs turned to honey, liquid and warm, as if she'd been set in the sun. "Oh," she said, enchanted in spite of every scrap of sense that spoke against it. "Oh, my, you dance divinely."

He laughed, the second time she'd heard him do so. She wanted to hear that happy sound again. She wanted to hear it every day. His arm tightened and suddenly her breasts were pressed lightly to his chest. That, she thought dizzily, was even better. His legs, so long, so sure, brushed the front of her skirts. She had only to follow their motion; had only to let him lead.

"It's like flying," she said, helpless to keep her smile inside.

He grinned back at her, his face creasing upward, his bright blue eyes agleam. "It's dancing, Florence, the way it was meant to be."

She caught her breath with pleasure as he spun her even faster. The other couples seemed to part like the sea before them. The music swooped, giddy, magical. She took a firmer grip on his shoulders and closed her eyes.

"You're as lovely as a rose," he murmured, just loudly enough for her to hear.

With a quiet sigh, he gathered her closer still. She felt the warmth of his body, the hardness of his chest. His breath came quickly from his exertions. In. Out. Stirring her hair. Warming her cheek. The sound put a spell on her. Something throbbed inside her: an ache, a nameless want. She thought she heard him whisper her name. *Yes,* she thought, and her lips moved soundlessly on the word. He must have seen her do it. His hand tightened on hers, his fingers strong, sending a message her body could not help but read. Without warning, a flood of heat washed through her flesh. Her knees wobbled and gave and she stumbled over his foot.

Edward caught her before she fell.

"Goodness," she said, mortified by her near collapse. "I'm afraid all that twirling has made me dizzy."

For once, Edward's frown was more worried than disapproving. He put his arm around her waist to steady her. "Come. Let's get you some air."

He would not listen to her demurs, but led her from the stuffy ballroom and down a corridor to a large conservatory. Florence would have liked to see this marvel by daylight. Arched high above their heads, the white iron framework glowed faintly beneath the moon. Perhaps, like the Crystal Palace, the great Paxton had designed it. The structure was certainly grand enough. Small Japanese lanterns shaped like gold and black pagodas lit the winding paths. Ankle boots crunching on the pebbles, Edward guided her past towering palms and banks of ferns and a large lily pond beneath which orange fishes hung in sleep. He stopped at last under a cool dome of glass where roses of every imaginable hue grew in lushly scented profusion.

"Here." He seated her on a pretty cast-iron bench. "Close your eyes and breathe." To her surprise, he sat beside her and patted her hand. "Lizzie laced you too tightly, didn't she?"

"Oh, no," she said, her eyes flying open to find his gaze. "Aunt Hypatia's maid wouldn't let her. It was the dancing, I think. All that swooping around. It was wonderful, of course, but suddenly I felt so hot."

His brows lowered, shading his eyes to blackness. His expression was most peculiar. "You felt hot."

"Yes." She fanned her face at the memory. "Astonishingly hot. As if someone had dropped me in a pot of steam. You don't suppose I've taken ill, do you?"

She knew the words were hopeful. Though the ball had not been as terrifying as she'd feared, she still would have liked to go home.

"No," he said, but he touched her cheek with the back of his hand.

"There it is again!" she gasped.

"Florence," he said, half laugh, half groan. "You cannot be so ignorant you do not know why you are flushed."

"Well, I—" she began and then her gaze caught on his smiling lips. "I'm sure it's not—I've found men appealing before, you know, and they never affected me like this!"

"Didn't they?" His eyes were heavy, his tone a soft, insinuating growl. "Didn't they make you hot from the inside out? Didn't they make you yearn and ache and feel as if you would die unless you held them?"

His head drew closer, lips brushing her cheek like heated satin.

"Edward," she gasped, a shiver supplanting her flush. She wished he wouldn't speak so; wished he wouldn't draw so close. "You can't be meaning to kiss me!"

"Indeed," he said with that same groaning laugh, his

mouth sliding along her jaw. "I assure you I don't mean to. Common sense forbids it. And decency. And every drop of affection my brother pulls from my heart."

She didn't know what Freddie had to do with it, but she was certain what he was doing qualified as a kiss. His lips had slid over hers, soft but firm and parted for the rush of his breath. She brought her palms to his chest, meaning to push him away but mysteriously unable to do so. She felt like the victim of a mesmerist, caught in the spell of his magnetic power. His chest was so hard, so warm. Helpless to resist, her fingers curled into the starchy linen of his shirt.

"Stop me, Florence," he whispered, shivering beneath her touch. "Stop me before I hurt us both."

"Stop yourself," she said, though she couldn't imagine where she'd found the wickedness to do so.

At least he was not angry. Chuckling, he nipped her chin, then did what no one had ever done before. First he licked her lower lip, then pressed beyond it with the tip of his tongue, actually breaching the outer reaches of her mouth.

"Sweet," he said, and did it again, more deeply than before.

Florence was shocked beyond fear. The smooth wet curve slid past her teeth before she could gather her wits to stop him. She could taste the champagne punch he'd drunk; could feel the texture of his tongue as it stroked her own. The effect was peculiarly seductive. It made her want to lick him back; made her want to close her eyes and sigh. But it was an unconscionable intimacy, a thing even a husband might not do. And now he was sucking her, pulling at her tongue as if he meant to lure it from her mouth. Her shoulders stiffened and her hands clutched his arms. Her heart beat like a fox chased to ground. A kiss was bad enough, but this . . . this blatantly carnal invasion—she could not allow it, simply couldn't.

"Let me," he whispered when she twisted her head away. "Oh, God, Florence. I'll go mad if I can't kiss you."

A sound broke in her throat, a hopeless whimper. His sweet, husky plea made her tingle from head to toe. He was right. She was attracted to him. That honeyed warmth was pouring through her veins, curling low in her belly and thighs, like a tide no force of will could stop.

"Let me," he said, as if he sensed her weakening. He nibbled her neck, then the lobe of her ear. "One kiss, Florence. One kiss to satisfy us both. No one will see. I'd never let anyone see."

She tried to think of Aunt Hypatia, of the five hundred guests who might take it into their heads to wander out. She tried to think of what she'd come here to find. A nice, safe husband. Not a moody, black-hearted wretch who insulted her one moment and begged for kisses the next.

Sadly her efforts were for naught. "Just one?" she asked in a shameful rush of breath.

He covered her mouth with a sighing moan, his tongue searching, caressing, his arms slowly circling her back. This time she kissed him back. She couldn't help it. He was gentle but unstoppable, like treacle rolling down a heated pan.

"Yes," he praised at her tentative foray. "Kiss me, Florence. Kiss me as deeply as you can." One hand slid up her spine to cup her head. He was tilting her neck: guiding her, she thought with an odd, warm start, so that her vulnerability to his possession would be complete.

And then her neck wasn't the only thing that was tilting. He was tipping her backwards, dizzying her as he laid her down along the bench. Satin rustled and hissed. She had to clutch his back to keep from falling and then she *wanted* to clutch his back. Its breadth was a pleasure she could not resist: its warmth, the slow, shifting strain of its muscles. His mouth lifted for breath, then sank again.

Oh, her head was spinning. His hand gripped her waist, then her hip, then wedged beneath the bulk of her bustle to squeeze her bottom as if he loved the give of the generous flesh. Her moan was not the protest it should have been. His weight felt so right between her legs. This was what men and women were meant to be. His hardness was the match for her softness, his pressure for her yielding. She gave in to the urge to hold him tighter, sliding her arms beneath the cover of his coat.

To her surprise, his shirt clung damply to his skin.

"Florence," he groaned. "You don't know what you're doing."

But then he kissed her even harder, as if his life depended on the total plunder of her mouth. His fingers tightened on her neck, sliding under Aunt Hypatia's pearls. When his father's signet pressed her skin, the metal was fever-warm. His scent surrounded her, not merely cologne but a subtle, animal smell. He began to push his hips against hers, slowly but with force, rubbing up and down the very center of her heat. That heat seemed to double as she realized his manly organ was not soft. Rather, it was thick and thrusting and hard, like a creature that needs to mate.

Abruptly panicked, she struggled to get away, but he only held her tighter. He was groaning her name now, grinding her with his hardness. His body seemed beyond his own control.

Florence could not wait for him to control it; could not stop to think. She did what she'd heard the village lads joke about. She reached around his legs and gave his parts a forceful squeeze. Apparently, she'd done it right. Swallowing a yelp, Edward shoved back as if she'd stabbed him. The blackness of his glare was enough to make her quail. Burning fingers pressed to her mouth, she struggled to sit upright.

"I'm sorry," she said, barely able to get it out. "Did I hurt you?"

"Did you—? Good Lord!" He raked his hair with both hands, then dropped his head back and breathed: long, slow breaths that lifted his belly and chest. The place she'd pinched was still humped between his legs, a rise of black cloth that pulsed like a living heart. Seeing it, she went hot again and knew she'd lost her mind. Surely she couldn't regret calling a halt to his affront!

As if he sensed her stare, Edward opened his eyes. Unlike her, he seemed to have regained his calm.

"You did precisely as you should," he said. "It is I who must beg forgiveness. I drank more champagne than I ought tonight, and took advantage of your inexperience. It was utterly despicable and I promise it shall never happen again."

He was saying he'd only kissed her because he was drunk. The confession should have comforted but it didn't. She wound her hands together in her lap. "What you did wasn't completely terrible."

He laughed, the sound harsh. "I'm glad it wasn't terrible, but it was wrong. You mustn't let other men get you alone where they can try it."

"I'm not so green I don't know that," she snapped, with a salutary hint of anger. "It's just you're, well, you're supposed to be my cousin!"

"Quite." He sighed and dragged his hand through his hair again, causing it to stand up rather comically. He was right to worry about his wavy locks. They could turn wild. But he didn't seem to notice. He nodded towards the path. "Perhaps you should go. I wouldn't want anyone to miss you."

She knew he was right. She stood and smoothed her skirts, perversely reluctant to leave. "Are you sure you're well?"

"Yes," he said sternly. "Now go."

She trudged two steps and turned back. "Your hair."

He furrowed his brows at her.

"It's sticking up. You need to smooth it."

"I shall," he assured her. And then she had no more excuses to stay.

As soon as she'd gone, Edward sagged over his knees. How could he have been so irresponsible? Anyone might have walked in on them. Florence would have been ruined, not to mention his plans for saving Freddie. Edward couldn't imagine what had come over him. All his life he'd known the value of discipline. Even before his parents died and left him alone to care for Freddie, he'd been the master of his passions. Edward didn't cry when he was scolded, or skinned his knees, or was shunned by his schoolmates because he refused to bully the boys in the lower forms. Edward was a Greystowe, an English earl. Edward set his course and followed it.

He certainly didn't drive a vicar's daughter to pinch his balls.

"Damnation," he said, and wished he knew just what he cursed.

With a long, low sigh, he pushed to his feet. He tidied his hair as well as he could and marveled at Florence's consideration in giving him the warning. What she must think of him, he couldn't guess—nor could he afford to lament the loss of her good opinion. If she stayed away from him, all the better. Clearly, he could not be trusted to keep his vows.

Imogene Hargreave cornered him halfway down the corridor to the ballroom. He had no chance to avoid her. Apart from the distant hum of merriment, and a marble cherub with a mass of roses in its arms, they were alone.

"There you are," she cooed, tiptoeing her fingers up his chest. "Charles is staying at his club tonight. I thought you might whirl me around the floor."

He caught her hand and held it away. Her hair gleamed like flax in the flickering gaslight, her skin like ivory. She was as seductive as ever, as beautiful and as skilled, but she moved him no more than a statue.

"I'm on my way out."

"Are you?" Imogene chuckled. "I'll admit the Vances' parties are a bit tame, but your aunt and her little charge seem to be enjoying themselves. Quite the sensation, that one. You'd better take care or you'll have more than a cousin on your hands. Your brother is acting smitten."

Edward stiffened at her tone. "Florence Fairleigh is a perfectly respectable young woman. If my brother chooses to pursue her, the duchess and I would hardly disapprove."

Imogene's eyes widened. "Well, of course. I'm sure she's everything that's agreeable."

"She is," Edward insisted.

Imogene cocked her head, then shook off her puzzlement. She stroked his arm. "Come, darling, let's not talk about your relatives. Let me give you a ride home." Her brows rose suggestively. "To my home, if you like."

Edward hesitated. He had no doubt Imogene intended the journey to end in her bed, a place he'd vowed not to visit again. On the other hand, if he took the carriage he came in, he'd have to send it back for Hypatia. Going with Imogene would save the coachman an extra trip. Besides which, he'd put off talking to her longer than he should.

"I'll be going to my home," he said, "but if the offer stands, I'd be happy for it."

"Of course it stands," said Imogene, playfully swatting his shoulder.

As he'd suspected, she was planning to change his mind. The carriage hadn't left the Vances' drive before she'd slid over to his seat and pulled the shades. The lantern that swayed from the hook above the door made a glowing nest of the interior. The coach's upholstery was blue, a sleek, pale satin that echoed Imogene's eyes.

"There," she said, giving him a deep, practiced kiss. "This is more like it."

He did not stop her. He was waiting—hoping, he suspected—to see if her kiss could do to him what Florence's had. But the truth was as he'd feared. The memory of Florence's touch, innocent as it was, was more exciting than the reality of Imogene's. That pleasure had been fresher, sharper—more right, God help him. Kissing Imogene was wrong in ways he hadn't the courage to examine.

After a moment, he eased back. "We need to talk."

"Oh, dear," she said with a high, brittle laugh. "I'm sure I don't like the sound of that."

He covered her hand where it lay soft and supple on her thigh. "You know I admire you, Imogene. You're one of the most beautiful, vibrant women I've ever known. You can't imagine how grateful I am for the time you've given me."

"Edward." She pulled her hand away, a flush staining her cheeks. "I don't want your gratitude. Why are you doing this? We're good together. The passion we share is special."

Edward watched her hand where it clutched her satin skirts. There was no way to say this without hurting her, but perhaps that was best. Perhaps the gentlemanly thing would be to let her hate him. "It doesn't feel special to me," he said as gently as he could.

She shook her head as if she couldn't believe what she was hearing. "My aunt was right about you. You are a cold-hearted bastard. Just like all the Greystowes. Unless there's another woman?" She narrowed her smoky eyes. "Tell me it's not Millicent Parminster. That two-faced bitch. I'll rip her bloody hair out."

"It's no one," he said, wondering when he'd met her aunt. "I just can't do this anymore."

She snorted. "I'll believe you can't do it when someone tells me your stones have fallen off."

"It's over, Imogene," he said. "I'm tired of feeling dirty."

He was sorry he'd said it the instant it left his mouth. Her lips moved to repeat his final word. Then she covered them with her hands. "It's your cousin, isn't it? The blushing miss who's been batting her eyes at your brother. She's a clean one, all right. Clean enough to squeak!"

"It's no one," he repeated, the denial a threatening growl.

Imogene wasn't fooled. "Bloody hell," she laughed, the sound like glass. "The mighty Edward Burbrooke has fallen for his brother's country mouse!"

He caught her arm. "You breathe that to a soul and I'll see you ruined."

In that moment, he meant the threat, unfair as it was. Fortunately, Imogene seemed to believe him. "Oh, I won't repeat it," she sneered. "That timorous twit is going to dish out all the revenge I need. I hope you stew without me, Edward. I hope you spend your whole bloody life dreaming of a woman you can't have."

Then she rapped the roof with her fan, ordering the coachman to set him down by the side of the road. He was miles from home, but Edward didn't protest. He knew the walk would not be as bad as the memory of her curse.

CHAPTER 5

❖

The picnic was Freddie's idea. A reward, he said, for Florence's having braved three balls in one week—not to mention a presentation to the queen. Curtseying to the monarch had been by far the easier ordeal, despite having to practice walking backward in a train. Not the least bit terrifying, Queen Victoria had reminded Florence of the plump, kindly widows back in Keswick. All the same, she was grateful the business was over.

Momentarily free of obligations, they spread their blanket across the grass in Aunt Hypatia's town house garden, a small stretch of ground enclosed by a tall brick wall. A sundial shaded Freddie's shoulder and a picturesque urn spilled ivy down a pedestal of stone. Florence's relaxation had as much to do with Freddie's presence, and the lack of anyone else's, as it did with the glass of currant wine he'd pressed into her hand. At peace for the first time since Edward had taken leave of his senses at the Vances' ball, she sat in the circle of her dark chintz skirts—housecleaning clothes from Keswick—and watched Freddie pick idly at the remains of their cold repast.

He lay sprawled on his belly, his jacket discarded, his sleeves rolled to his elbows. Florence knew she could stare at him for hours. His profile was that of a Greek coin; his physique, a young athlete's. More than either of these things, however, his visible good nature drew her eye. He had, she thought, the most agreeable face she'd ever seen.

He'd been quiet today. More than once, she'd caught him gazing at her in a deeply considering manner. He didn't appear to be smitten. Fond, yes, but not smitten. Spiteful or not, the Wainwrights' friend seemed to have been correct. But that was fine with Florence. She hadn't the least desire to threaten Freddie's heart.

"Penny for your thoughts," he said and batted her sunhat with a tasseled blade of grass.

"I'm happy," she said, "because I'm sitting in the sun without my corset."

He hid his smile by drawing circles on the blanket. "As a gentleman, I'll pretend I didn't hear that."

Florence grinned back and wondered if she'd ever find a suitor she felt as comfortable with as him. She touched his shoulder with the tip of her finger. "May I ask you a question?"

He rolled onto his back. "Ask away, dearest."

"It's a personal question," she cautioned, "one that might inspire sad thoughts."

"I shall not renege my permission because of that."

She set her wine in the grass. "I know you lost your parents when you were young, but I don't know how they died."

"Ah," he said, and closed his eyes. To her relief, he was not offended. "They took a trip to Egypt to see the pyramids. On the journey back, one of the passengers brought the yellow fever onto the ship. It was a bad outbreak. Twenty-two died before they were able to contain it, my parents among them. My mother was one of those who nursed the sick. She saved a few, they say, and died a heroine. I imagine Father was proud of her in the end."

Here, at last, was a hint of sadness. Florence wanted to comfort him, but wasn't sure she should. Had his father been ashamed of his wife? Had he reason? The question seemed too prying. Rather than ask it, she pleated the worn flowered cotton of her dress. "That was when Edward became your guardian."

She could not forestall a blush at speaking his name, but Freddie did not notice.

"Actually, Aunt Hypatia became our guardian. Edward was only seventeen, and I was twelve. But he fathered me from then on, if that's what you mean."

"Was it difficult?"

"To let Edward have charge of me? Not in the least, for he'd been doing it all along. Even as a boy, he took his duty as elder brother seriously." His face softened with memory. "Our father was strict. A hard man, you'd say, to the point where he sometimes seemed cruel. His father had been the same. According to family lore, our great-grandfather was a wastrel. Nearly gambled Greystowe into the poorhouse. Perhaps the generations left to repair the damage were right to run a tight ship. Whatever the reason, many times Edward stood between my father's rod and me."

He rolled onto his elbow and covered the hand that was crumpling her skirt. "Shall I tell you the best Edward story?"

Ignoring the sudden skipping of her heart—for why should she care about Edward's part in the tale?—she smiled into his boyish face. "Of course you should tell me."

He composed himself by propping his jaw on his hand. "You may not know this, but Greystowe is built above a lake with an island in its center and a family of proud black swans who return each year to raise their brood."

"*Black* swans?"

"None other. Nasty, noisy things, if you want to know the truth, but handsome enough to look at. At any rate, when Edward was seven, our father decided he ought to learn to swim. He rowed him to the deepest end of Greystowe Lake and pushed him over the side of the boat. Edward, of course, immediately flailed around and went under. When my father judged he had swallowed enough water, he hauled him out, let him catch his breath, and did it again."

"Heavens!" said Florence, her hand to her breast.

"I told you my father was stern. I imagine his father did the same to him. He liked to say Greystowe men were made of iron."

"But Edward might have drowned!"

"He learned not to soon enough," Freddie assured her, and soothingly patted her hand. "Edward being who he was, when it came my turn to learn, he insisted *he* be allowed to teach me. Told my father the responsibility would prepare him to be a leader. He always was better at getting around the earl than I was."

Florence shook her head against a dawning horror. "You can't mean to tell me Edward dumped you in that lake!"

"Indeed, no." Freddie laughed and her shoulders unwound in relief. "But he did take it into his head that I had to learn in a single day or Father would do it instead. We stayed in that lake till midnight, a shivering pair of prunes."

"And did you learn to swim?"

"Enough to satisfy Father. And better over the course of the summer. Edward was so pleased he gave me lessons every day. Two years later, I won a swimming prize at school. Edward doesn't know I know this but, to this day, he keeps that medal in a cabinet by his bed."

Florence blinked her stinging eyes. "What a wonderful story. It makes me wish I really were your cousin, so I could have been there to cheer you on."

"I should have liked that." He touched her cheek where a single tear had slipped away. "Now you must let me ask you a question."

"Oh, Freddie, you know I can't tell stories like you."

"It's not a question that requires a story. At least, I don't think it is."

"Very well," she said, and smoothed her simple skirt. "Ask me anything you like."

He cocked his head at her answer, eyes twinkling, but all he said was, "What do you think of Peter Vance?"

"The duke of Monmouth's son?" She sat straighter in surprise.

"Yes. Aunt Hypatia tells me he sent you violets this morning and invited you to the opera with his family."

She squirmed at the memory of the card that had accompanied his bouquet. Something about the "violet hiding in the shade" and the "sweet and simple beauty" that its perfume betrayed. The sentiment was flattering, even poetic, but Florence had felt supremely uncomfortable when she'd read it.

"I'm sure he only sent them to please his sister," she said. "And even if he didn't, he's the son of a duke."

"The youngest son," Freddie interposed.

"Yes, but I don't think he is someone I should consider. I am only a vicar's daughter."

"You may consider anyone you please. You're a sweet and pretty girl. The question is, does Peter Vance please you?"

Florence gazed at the sky, at the sheer white clouds and the swallow that soared above them towards the greensward in Grosvenor Square. Did Peter Vance please her? He didn't have half Freddie's sense of humor, but he was handsome and ardent and undeniably better than a simple girl like her deserved. Instinct told her he'd be kind to his wife and take a mistress in half a year. Which did not rule him out as husband material—at least, not the sort of husband she'd told Mr. Mowbry she was seeking.

If her thoughts had been haunted of late by a taller, darker, and infinitely more dangerous figure, that was a foolish romantic notion she would do her best to quash.

"I suppose he pleases me," she said. "But how can I tell? I have danced with him and talked of nothing. He has brought me punch and paid compliments to my hair. All I really know is that he likes horses, is pleasant to look at, and has an agreeable sister."

"Agreeable sisters are important."

He seemed to be teasing, but Florence couldn't smile. "You must think me terribly cold-blooded."

"You, Florence? Never."

"But to hunt for a husband this way, as if he were a bit of beef, rather than a living human being who would be yoked to me for a lifetime."

"What a horror that would be!"

She shoved his muscular shoulder. "Scoundrel. You always make me laugh. I must confess, I halfway wish I could marry you."

This stilled him.

"Do you?" he said, eyes hooded from her gaze. She wondered if she'd alarmed him.

"I'm afraid so," she admitted as lightly as she could. "But please don't tell your aunt. She'd be aghast."

"I don't know about that. From what I've seen, she's very fond of you."

"Not fond enough to invite a silly nobody into her family!"

He peered at her from under his brows, the same measuring look he'd been turning on her all day. "You might be surprised." He smoothed the blanket beside her knee. "Florence, would you really want to marry someone like me?"

"How can you doubt it? You're quite the nicest man I've met. You're funny and you're kind and when I'm with you, I almost feel brave."

He pressed his hand to his heart. "Goodness. I am a paragon."

She clucked her tongue at him in scold. Though his eyes shone with more than laughter, she should have known he couldn't be serious.

But then he cleared his throat. "Florence?"

"Yes, Freddie."

He drew a breath and let the words out in a rush. "Would you marry me? Would you really? I know I'm not as good as I could be, but I'm not as bad as some. I don't drink or gamble or curse. I don't often work hard, but I can, and I'd always do my best to keep you happy."

Her eyes felt as round as saucers. He wanted her to marry him, the man she'd made a model for her ideal. She should have been elated—indeed, part of her was—but behind the elation, a sensation uncommonly like panic was expanding in her chest.

"You can't be serious," she said, half of her wanting him to admit he was teasing.

"Yes, Florence, I am." He sat up and took her hands. "I'd

very much like to marry you. That is, if you think you'd enjoy yoking us together."

Her heart was pounding like a drum. She told herself only the thought of Edward kept her from jumping into Freddie's arms, because he'd kissed her, because he'd made her pulse race and her skin tingle from head to toe.

But Edward wouldn't marry her. Even if he would, he wasn't what she needed. Peter Vance might disappoint her, but Edward would break her heart. She knew that as surely as she knew her name. She'd promised herself she wouldn't end up like her father, half her soul lost to mourning a love she could never find again. Florence was not some hearts-and-flowers ninny. Florence was a sensible girl. Despite which, she couldn't quite make herself accept.

"I don't know what to say," she said.

"Say yes," Freddie urged.

"Oh, Freddie. How can I? Your aunt will think I've betrayed her trust."

"I assure you she won't, but I'd face even that if you feel certain you'd like to have me."

She searched his dear, kind eyes, eyes that for once seemed as shy and unsure as her own. She could make him happy, she thought. They were not in love, but there was fondness between them, and respect. She could make a home he would be pleased to call his own. She could ease the sadness she sometimes saw behind his smile. As for her . . .

She would be safe, as safe as she'd ever dreamed. Freddie was a good man: young in some ways, but decent to the core.

"Yes," she said, squeezing his hands. "I'd be honored to be your wife."

She was not sure whose palms were colder: Freddie's or her own.

"Congratulations," Edward said, his jaw almost too stiff to force out the word. His brother had broken the news in Hypatia's private parlor, amidst the comfortable chairs and

the thick pile rugs and the knitting work she loved to nod over by the fire. "You'll want a quick wedding, of course."

Florence furrowed her brow and looked to Freddie, who pressed a kiss to the back of her hand. The gesture was given and taken so naturally Edward's heart twisted in his chest.

"Yes," Aunt Hypatia agreed. "A small, quiet wedding, so as not to break your mourning too badly. The vicar at St. Peter's is a friend of mine. I'm sure he can fit you in."

"I don't understand." Florence looked from Edward to his aunt. "You aren't upset. You seem pleased. I don't mean to insult you, your Grace, but I honestly thought you'd agreed to sponsor me because you hoped I'd upstage Greta and Minna Wainwright."

"And you think this won't do that?" Hypatia barked out a laugh. "No, no, my dear, while I admit the thought of foiling their mother's ambitions lends this match an extra savor, I assure you I had no such ulterior motive. I'm fond of you, Florence. More so now than ever. You've made my nephew a happy man."

"But I'm only—"

"Only my goddaughter," said Edward's cheerfully mendacious aunt as she leaned forward to kiss her cheek. "We're not snobs. I'm sure you'll be a credit to the Burbrooke name."

Florence began to cry, slow fat tears she tried to hide behind her hands. With a fond smile, Freddie pulled her into his shoulder and stroked her hair. She looked as if she belonged there, as if they were married already.

"There, there," he said. "It's nothing to cry over."

"You've been so kind," she said, with a teary hiccup. "I don't know how I shall repay you."

"You can repay us by being happy," Freddie said. "That's really all we ask."

His gaze met Edward's over her shoulder. His expression held a grief Edward could scarcely bear to face, a grief not so much for himself as for Florence—as if, between them, they were committing some terrible sin against the girl.

But they weren't. Edward tugged his lapels and set his jaw. They were saving her. They were making her happy. Any idiot could see she and Freddie were meant to be. This would not be a marriage like his parents', with one partner cold and the other miserable. This would be as near to a love match as Edward had ever seen. If a deception made that possible, well, so be it.

"We all want you happy," he said, his voice gentler than he'd intended.

She looked around at him, her cheek still pressed to Freddie's chest. Her eyes dazzled him, soft with emotion, green as the buds of spring. With no more weapon than that, she speared him to the floor.

Good Lord, he thought, chill with horror. I love her.

"Thank you," she said, as if his approval meant the world. "I'd be proud to join your family."

She held out her hand to him, her small, soft hand.

He thought the hardest thing he'd ever done was clasp it and let it go.

CHAPTER 6

Edward's idea of a quick wedding was not the same as his aunt's. He saw no reason to wait beyond the obtainment of a special license. She, however, cautioned against the appearance of undue haste.

"It won't do," she said. "Anything less than six months is simply vulgar."

But that was before Imogene Hargreave extended her claws.

Hypatia heard the news before he did. He was sitting down to breakfast when her carriage dropped her at his door. She didn't wait for Grimby to announce her, but strode straight through. Edward looked up from his plate, too stunned by his aunt's appearance to venture a greeting. Her skirts swished loudly with her haste, then released a cloud of lavender as she flung herself into a chair. Her hat was askew, her yellow gloves an offense against her purple dress. Her cane was nowhere in sight.

"We have trouble," she said, yanking off the gloves as if she wished to do them harm. Her hat followed with equal force.

Edward swallowed his final bite of toast. A hank of silver hair was standing up from Hypatia's head. Suspecting she needed bracing more than he did, he slid his steaming cup of tea in front of her. "What trouble?"

Her face twisted with anger. Edward hadn't seen her in such a fury since the one and only time his father had struck him. Freddie had been six, as he recalled, and the earl had decided to take him cub hunting, it being common practice for inexperienced riders to be set after the younger foxes before the season. Freddie hadn't understood what would happen until it came time to "blood" him with the kill. He'd turned hysterical then, refusing to let their father smear his forehead—no surprise, since the boy still slept with a stuffed rabbit. Only Edward's intervention had stopped the earl from shouting his younger son deaf, for which act Edward had earned a black eye.

He'd known at once his father regretted lashing out. The earl had grown very quiet; actually picked Freddie up and carried him back to the house—gently, too, as if he meant to comfort him. When Aunt Hypatia discovered what had happened and slapped her elder brother across the face, the earl accepted her judgment without a word.

She looked as if she wanted to slap someone now, but her fingers merely tightened on the teacup. "It's that bastard Charles Hargreave," she said. "He's telling people he saw someone who looked 'uncommonly like Freddie Burbrooke' coming out of an introducing house on Fitzroy Street."

Edward sagged back in his chair. Despite his fears, the news caught him completely unprepared. An introducing house was a homosexual brothel that specialized in underage boys. If it was true . . .

"I don't believe it," he said, breathless and hot with shock. "Freddie gave me his word. Even if he hadn't, he would never do anything to take advantage of the young."

He wouldn't, he told himself, the possibility unbearable. Not Freddie. Not the brother he loved. His hands clenched so tightly the skin over his knuckles stretched white.

"I'm inclined to agree with you," said his aunt. "Whatever his faults, Freddie has never been a bully." Her mouth pursed with distaste. "To do what one would rather no one did, with those too young to give permission, to even understand what they risk, isn't something I want to think he would consider. But it hardly matters whether the story is true. If people believe it, the damage will be great enough."

Edward smashed his fist into his thigh. "It's Imogene. That bloody bitch put her husband up to it."

Hypatia stared at him, one thin brow raised in judgment. That she'd indulged in similar language did not seem to matter. Edward rubbed the ache in the center of his forehead.

"Sorry," he said. "Shouldn't have lost my temper."

"Of course you should have. Hargreave's behavior is despicable, even if his wife is behind it." Calm now, she turned the blue and white teacup in a circle. She reminded him of merchants he knew, planners, men of business. Her gaze was as cool as theirs. "I won't ask why Lady Hargreave might have a grievance against this family. I simply trust that no one in it will have anything further to do with her."

Edward's laugh was brief and bitter. "You can rest easy on that."

"Good." With a brisk rustle, the duchess rearranged her skirts. "Now all we have to do is decide how to get Florence to Greystowe."

He blinked at this change of tack. "To Greystowe?"

"Well, we can't let her stay in London. She's bound to hear the gossip. And we can't send her anywhere alone. She's half in love with Freddie already. If we throw the two of them together, she'll be committed to him by summer's end."

Without quite realizing he'd done it, Edward pressed a hand over his stomach. *Summer's end.* Was that all it would take? "They'll need a chaperone," he said, his voice strangely distant to his ears. "Are you willing to accompany them?"

"More than. But I think you'd better come, too."

"Me?" The ache in his belly increased.

"I trust Freddie," said the duchess. "But I trust him more when he knows your eyes are on him."

Edward wished he could close those eyes and shake his

head. Florence. In his house. With Freddie. Leaving her scent in the hall. Her laugh. Her twinkling footsteps. His aunt had no idea what she was asking.

Which was good news, really, even if it meant he'd be living out Imogene's curse. She'd kept her word, damn her; she seemed not to have told anyone that Florence had enamored him. She'd found a better way to hurt him: through Freddie, through the brother who was his heart. But at least they'd be taking Florence beyond her reach. He didn't trust his former mistress to hold her tongue should the two meet face-to-face.

Edward's chance to speak to Freddie came that afternoon. He found him in the study, slumped in a chair with the curtains drawn, a bottle and glass close to hand. A single lamp burned on the table by his elbow. The low yellow light turned his wavy brown hair to gold. From the rumpled state of his clothes, it appeared he'd been sitting—and drinking—for some time. His collar was open, his tie a draggle around his neck. He looked a fallen angel, one who mourned his former state of grace. Where had he heard the news? At his club? On the street? At a loss as to how to begin, he walked to Freddie's side and looked down. His brother did not look up.

"Join me?" he said, his voice slurred but steady. "We can drink to the end of Freddie Burbrooke as we know him."

Edward's breath came faster. "I know you didn't do what they're saying."

Freddie finished his drink and poured another. The decanter clinked against the cut-glass rim, but the liquor did not spill. "How do you know?" he said, eerily calm. "I'm a deviate, aren't I? The victim of unnatural urges. Who can say where my depravity ends?"

Edward grabbed his shoulders and shook him. The glass tumbled down Freddie's shirtfront, spraying whiskey over them both on its way to the floor. Freddie's head rolled back and forth like a rag doll's, but Edward could not stop.

"I know you didn't do it," he said, almost shouting. "I know!"

With a sudden burst of energy, Freddie pushed him off. He wasn't as strong as Edward but he was strong enough. He stood and put the chair between them. "You don't know, damn you. I can see how afraid you are. I can hear it in your voice." He raked his hair back with a curse, then pointed in accusation. "You can't know because you don't know anything about that side of me. You don't know how it works. You don't know how it thinks. I don't blame you for doubting me, Edward, but I swear to you, I'd rather die than do a thing like that."

Edward stepped to the front of the chair and laid his hand on Freddie's shoulder. His brother was shaking, his teeth chattering with the force of his distress. His eyes were red but dry. They seemed to burn as they met Edward's gaze.

"Never," Freddie said, tight and low. "Never with anyone but an equal. Never with anyone who didn't want it as much as I did."

The terrible doubt inside him eased. He knew Freddie was telling the truth and yet, as grateful as he was, he didn't want to hear this; didn't want to know there had been others besides the footman, besides the boys at school. He looked down at the empty chair, at the drying liquor stain on its seat. "Aunt Hypatia and I have decided we need to go to Greystowe: you, me, the duchess, and Florence."

"Florence?" Freddie's brow lifted in astonishment. "Edward. You can't mean to go through with this engagement. Florence is bound to hear."

"That's why we're going to Greystowe."

"For the rest of our natural lives?"

Edward stooped to retrieve the fallen glass. "Just for the summer. Memories are short. The next scandal will push this one from people's minds."

"And if it doesn't? Good Lord, Edward, think of Florence. It's hardly fair to—"

"Why not? You're the same man who proposed to her.

The same man she clung to with joy. The same man who'll keep a roof over her head and a meal on her plate."

"There's more to life than roofs and meals."

"You are more than a meal to her, Freddie. You're her friend." Edward knew he spoke the truth, just as he knew this was the way things had to be, for all their sakes. Maybe Florence did deserve to marry more than a friend. Maybe she deserved the world. That didn't mean she wouldn't be perfectly content as Freddie's wife. And Freddie would be content as Florence's husband: content and safe. In this sorry old world, who had the right to ask more than that? Throat tight, Edward opened the decanter and poured. Freddie watched wide-eyed as his brother tossed back the drink. The fine Irish whiskey hit his belly like a punch. He coughed before he spoke. "I'm telling Lewis we leave tomorrow."

"Tomorrow?"

"Tomorrow," he rasped, and prayed the decision would not destroy them all.

Florence was exiting the library with a book when the senior footman informed her that her cousins were in the drawing room.

"My cousins?"

"Lord Greystowe and Viscount Burbrooke."

"Of course," she said, nervously smoothing her skirts. "Thank you, John. I'll go right up."

She wondered what they wanted, as it was past the hour for calls. Business involving the engagement, perhaps? But it seemed unlikely they would discuss that without the duchess, and she was spending the evening with friends.

"Gentlemen," she said, striving to present a calm exterior as she entered the elegant room.

The men rose and bowed. To her consternation, both wore matching sober faces. Indeed, Florence had never seen Freddie so serious. Heavens, she thought, her heart giving the oddest leap. They must be calling off the betrothal.

"Is something wrong?" she said aloud, her hand pressed

to her throat. "Aunt Hypatia hasn't met with misfortune, has she?"

"No, no," said Edward. His smile seemed forced even for him. "Freddie here"—he slung his arm around his brother's shoulder—"has a surprise for you."

Freddie looked a bit green around the gills but he nodded in agreement. "Thought you might fancy a trip to Greystowe. See my boyhood haunts and all."

Florence blinked at him, then broke into a grin. "I'd love to, Freddie. Absolutely love to." She skipped across the room to squeeze his hands. "How did you know I'd been longing for the country?"

"You don't have to go," he said. "Only if you really want to."

There was something in his eyes she didn't understand, some inexplicable discomfort, as if he were making this offer under duress. Edward cleared his throat.

"What's the matter?" she asked, her hands slipping to Freddie's lapels. "Don't *you* want to go?"

" 'Course I want to go. Just thought you might regret missing the rest of the Season."

Florence had to laugh at that. "I'd pay to miss the rest of the Season. But are you well, Freddie? You look pale."

"Drank too much at my club," he confessed, pulling away and giving his coat a tug. "Think I'd better see if Aunt Hypatia's footman has a cure."

With that, he hastened from the drawing room as if he were being chased. Florence stared after him. "How peculiar," she said. "It's not like Freddie to overindulge."

"I imagine his friends wanted to toast his engagement."

The explanation rang false, but she shrugged the mystery off. No doubt Edward was hoping to keep some prank from Florence's ears. She could not worry about it now. Freddie's abrupt departure had left the two of them alone. As always, Edward's presence, and all the unsettling feelings it inspired, was quite enough to occupy her mind.

"Shall I ring for refreshment?" she asked even as she hoped he would refuse.

"No," he said, and turned his black silk hat between his

hands. She thought he'd make his excuses then, but he remained where he was, as if rooted to the Axminster carpet.

"Brandy?" she offered.

Again he shook his head, then seemed to gather his will. "You are happy, aren't you?"

The question was more accusatory than concerned, and more personal than he had any right to ask. Her temper rose. "Of course I'm happy. Why wouldn't I be? Freddie is a wonderful man. A true gentleman."

Edward flushed at her barb, then tightened his jaw. "Glad to hear it," he said in a patently scornful drawl. "I'd always hoped my brother's wife would appreciate the noble virtues."

"More than you can," she said, and matched him glare for glare.

She didn't know when they'd drawn so close but they were nose to nose now, each vibrating with fury. His scent threatened to seep into her skin, musk and salt, heating her blood against her will. Damn him, she thought, for being so blasted masculine.

"If you hurt him . . ." he warned.

"*I?* I hurt him? You're the one who—" But she snapped her mouth shut on the rest. A real lady would pretend their encounter in the Vances' conservatory had never happened.

Not that Edward would let her be a lady. "No, no," he urged. "Finish what you were saying. I'm the one who what?"

She drew herself up and turned her face away. "It could not be of less importance."

"Oh, it couldn't, could it?"

When he gripped her jaw and forced it back, she felt as if she'd been waiting all night for him to do this very thing. Her body thrummed with excitement even as her heart sped up with fear. Her lungs were working like a bellows.

"Florence," he growled, his nostrils flaring as if he, too, could scent her secret flesh. His mouth crashed over hers, all searing male power. He invaded her, drew on her, his hand like iron around her jaw. He kissed her until her knees began to wobble, until her hands fluttered to grab his coat.

He kissed her until she whimpered, until every shred of rational thought escaped her brain. The sinews of his neck were damp beneath her palm, his breathing ragged on her cheek. He pulled her up against him, his hold crushing her dress, his thighs hard and hot through the fragile cloth. With one forearm banded beneath her buttocks, his hips began to rock like that night at the ball. The ridge between them was extravagantly large. He seemed to want to brand her with it, to force her to take its measure against her skin. She could not get away; could barely even squirm, but the long, grinding press did not frighten her as before. Instead, to her dismay, she wished she could explore him with her hands; wished she could see the shape of his desire. Here was a passion a woman could drown in. Willingly. Recklessly. Until she begged her seducer to do with her what he pleased.

Of course, she should have known what Edward pleased had nothing to do with her.

Just as she was ready to add her own hunger to the kiss, he tore his mouth away and held her off from him by the shoulder. "Now *that*," he rasped, "could not be less important."

He strode from the room without another word. *Beast,* she fumed. Horrible, arrogant beast. She couldn't be attracted to a man like that. Simply couldn't. What was he trying to prove? That she liked his kisses? That she wasn't enough of a lady for his brother?

"I am," she swore to the silent room. "I am."

She released a long, tremulous breath, then smoothed her hair into its coiffure. She was not a heroine from a penny weekly, tripping blithely down the road to ruin. She was a vicar's daughter, a gentlewoman born. This . . . anomaly in her feelings would not sway her. So long as Freddie Burbrooke wished to marry her, she was more than happy to marry him.

Whether she was more than happy to be Edward's sister-in-law, however, was a very different matter.

• • • •

Bloody insane, he thought, sagging back against the drawing room's heavy door. He'd kissed her. Again. For no better reason than her implication that his kisses didn't matter. What did he expect her to say? That she was secretly in love with him and that Freddie, "the perfect gentleman," could go hang? As if that would help. He covered his eyes and wagged his head. Better he should pray she hated him.

Of course, after tonight's fiasco, chances were good she did.

The journey to Greystowe was as different as night and day from the one she'd made to London. Edward, it seemed, owned a railway carriage.

"The spoils of dirtying one's hands in industry," Freddie teased as he handed a gaping Florence up the stairs.

Inside, the car was as fancy as the duchess's drawing room. The walls were lined in bird's-eye maple, the couches and chairs upholstered in dark green satin. Quilted black silk covered the arch of the ceiling and a rich Chinese rug, intricately patterned in red and gold, muffled the floor. The effect was one of sumptuous, masculine splendor, so sumptuous Florence blushed to see it. She couldn't help imagining Edward stretching some eager maiden across that couch, kissing her perhaps as he'd kissed Florence. How smooth that silk would feel beneath one's skin; how it would whisper when one moved. With a tiny shudder, she pushed the senseless image aside.

That way lay disaster.

"Heavens," she exclaimed, then lowered her voice because Edward was climbing in. "He doesn't own the whole train, does he?"

Freddie laughed and turned to his brother. "Florence wants to know if you own the train."

"No," he said, with his customary curtness. He reached for the duchess's hands. "That honor belongs to the Midland Railway."

His tone suggested Florence had been foolish to ask. She sighed and turned away. Moody, Freddie had called his brother, but no one seemed to bring out the worst of his moods as well as she. Fortunately, she had one of Mr. Dickens's novels to while away the ride. As luxurious as it was, this carriage was not big enough for her and Edward's moods.

He seemed to feel the same. First he buried himself in the *London Times,* and then in a pile of correspondence. She told herself she did not care, could not possibly care. She'd enjoy the trip, just as she'd enjoy their stay at Greystowe.

She had plenty of time to test her vow, for the journey was not a short one. Greystowe, Freddie informed her, was in the East Midlands, not far from the Peak District. As they clattered and chuffed towards the heart of England, they passed picturesque villages and thriving market towns. To her relief, the stench of London quickly cleared the air. The building stone turned gold and soft, and the landscape took on a pleasing roll. Sheep grazed the slopes, but crops had been planted as well. They shimmered low and green beneath the clear June sky.

The country girl inside her drank it in like a healing balm.

At last, as the sun began to sink behind the hills, they entered a sheltered valley. Its fields were fed by the Derwent River and separated not by hedgerows, but by weather-worn walls of stone. Ox-eye daisies waved at her from the side of the track. The grass was wonderfully green. After her stay in London, the color almost hurt her eyes.

The station bordered the village of Greystowe, a handsome tumble of half-timbered Tudor shops. Edward's car was unhooked from the rest and towed onto a private siding.

"Thank God," Freddie said, stretching until his spine cracked.

Florence echoed his sentiment with a smile, but saved her stretch for later. Aunt Hypatia would not have approved, even if she had been sleeping for hours. With a tenderness that belied his surly mood, Edward touched his aunt's shoulder. His face was achingly beautiful in its kindness.

The duchess awoke with a start. "Goodness," she said. "Must have dropped off for a minute."

No one was rude enough to contradict her, but even Edward joined the exchange of grins.

A big old-fashioned coach awaited them on the road, accompanied by a much plainer wagon into which half a dozen liveried servants were loading their luggage. Their silent efficiency was impressive to behold. Clearly, Edward's arrival had whipped them to their best.

"Not far now," said Freddie, and draped his arm around her back. His warmth was twice as welcome after all those hours of Edward's chill. She had to admit, though, she was surprised to find him eager to resume his rural life. If ever a man had been made for the city, it was Freddie. He loved people and parties and gossiping till dawn.

"Tell me Cook has a big dinner waiting," he called to the coachman, obviously an old retainer.

"Could be, sir," said that large, grizzled fellow. "Did think I smelled a Yorkshire pudding afore I left."

Florence's stomach growled at the mention of food. They'd had a light tea on the train, but that was all. Freddie, of course, could not ignore the unladylike sound.

"Roast beef," he said, rubbing his hands in exaggerated glee. "Horseradish sauce and gravy."

She laughed and pushed his shoulder to make him stop. "You'd think you'd been fasting for days!"

Beside her, Edward rediscovered his frown.

The church was farther into town, with a handsome stone school beside it. The town fathers—here she glanced at Edward—had not stinted on the windows, all of which would be taxed. She smiled when she remembered her father bullying the council to put in his windows. *Children need light,* he'd exhorted. *Light and air and a place for little eyes to wander.* As always, the thought of him brought a touch of sadness. Poor Papa. So much love in that big, warm heart and no one to spend it on but his daughter and his flock. They hadn't been enough. Hard as he tried to hide it, she'd always known a part of him had broken with her mother's death.

Freddie noted what had drawn her attention. "You'll have to visit when school starts up."

"Yes," she said and shyly squeezed his hand. Would they be here then? Did Freddie mean for them to live at Greystowe? Would he allow her to teach? Florence had done so at home. As the vicar's daughter, it was expected. When she married Freddie she'd be a lady but, oh, how little she'd like that honor if it meant she had to sit home all day and stitch!

These questions massed inside her as they rolled through the pretty town, but Edward's presence compelled her to hold them back. She didn't know if Freddie had spoken to his brother about the future. Would they have a small place of their own? Would Freddie want one? She could have burst with all she wished to ask. Even not knowing, the thought that this might be her home added interest to every soul they passed.

People called out to Freddie, she noticed, and tipped their caps to the earl.

All thoughts of the future faded with her first glimpse of the estate. The railway carriage should have warned her, and the mention of the cotton mill. Despite these hints, the sheer size of the place took her aback.

Greystowe sprawled across its grassy rise like a small Gothic town: a fortress town. Though of relatively modern construction, with all the attendant tracery and windows and archwork, the house was topped by battlements of stone. The lake reflected its blocks and towers, not so much in vanity as in emphasis. Swans aside, Florence couldn't help being reminded of a moat. This house made no bones about its intent. It was built to impress, to dominate, to hearken back to a time when lords were lords and everyone else was not.

Her lips twitched as she snuck a look at Edward's stern, feudal visage. She bet he'd have liked clumping about in armor, or galloping off on Samson to terrorize England's foes. What a step down he must feel it, to be reduced to terrorizing country mice!

"Home, sweet home," said Freddie, and Florence's burst

of humor faded. Anything less like a home she could not imagine. The setting sun flamed across a numberless march of windows: rose on the lower stories, lime on the upper.

It would take a miracle, she thought, to make a girl like her feel comfortable here.

Even as she pondered this impossibility, the front door—a great ironbound arch that required two brawny footmen to prop it open—released a long double line of servants. They filed down the wide granite steps, crisp as you please, like a regiment forming ranks. Their livery was black and fawn, with shining brass buttons on the coats. Edward waited for them to assemble, precisely as if he intended to review them. When they'd finished, one man and one woman stepped forward.

The man was tall and elegant, with salted black hair and pale gray eyes. The woman, a bit older, was round and merry. Good humor notwithstanding, she held herself with authority. Florence suspected she was the housekeeper.

"Welcome home, your lordship," said the man. "We received your telegram and everything is in readiness."

"I've prepared the best upstairs apartment for the young lady," the woman added, "and the duchess"—here she dropped a curtsey—"shall have her usual rooms on the ground floor."

"Very good," said Edward. He turned to Florence, his eyes strangely wary. If she hadn't known better, she'd have said he was worried about her reaction. "Florence, this is our steward, Nigel West, and our housekeeper, Mrs. Forster. They've both been with us for years. Should you require anything at all, one or the other of them will be happy to oblige."

"And may we say," Mrs. Forster put in, "that we're very pleased to meet young Lord Burbrooke's intended?"

"I believe you have said it," Freddie cried, and pulled the older woman into a hug.

The woman laughed as he spun her around, her dignity forgotten. Florence smiled at the spectacle. Leave it to Freddie to put everyone at their ease. Edward, naturally, called a halt to the merriment. "We should go in," he said. "I'm sure the ladies would like to freshen up."

Mrs. Forster immediately squirmed down and sobered. "At once, my lord. If the ladies would follow me?"

He's an ogre, Florence thought as the housekeeper led her up the main stair. He's an old sourpuss who can't bear to see anyone happy. The thought steadied her, as if it were a shield against confusion. But when she stepped into the blue and white splendor of her rooms, something awaited that put her to shame. It wasn't the huge tester bed, or the breathtaking view of the lake, or even the gorgeous carving on the fireplace. It was the picture that hung above it: Mr. Whistler's blue bridge, even more beautiful than when it had hung in that poor dingy corner of the Academy.

"Oh, my," she breathed, hands to her mouth. He'd remembered her admiration for this painting, and deigned to share the pleasure of owning it with her. That the same horrid creature who'd used his kisses to insult her could be so thoughtful was beyond her power to fathom.

Mrs. Forster was a step behind her. "Funny sort of mess," she said. "Lord Greystowe claims it's art, but if you don't like it, I'll take it somewhere else."

"Oh, no," said Florence. "There isn't another picture I'd like to look at more."

She hadn't been fair, she thought as the housekeeper withdrew. Perhaps he had some reason for his behavior, perverse as it was, which she did not comprehend. Perhaps, in fact, he meant this as an apology.

And perhaps pigs will fly in Hades, her more practical self put in. But if there was even a chance he wasn't set against her, that he was only concerned she would let his brother down, she had to do her best to win him over. And that's all I want, she promised herself: to be friends, to turn the other cheek as her father would have wished. For the sake of her and Freddie's happiness, she knew she had to try.

Dinner, which had been blissfully quiet apart from Florence's attempt to thank him for hanging that blasted painting in her room, was followed by a stroll through the back garden. Edward didn't see why he had to go along, but when his aunt took his arm he couldn't find a mannerly way to refuse. In spite of his annoyance, Florence's pleasure was a joy to see. He knew the house had shocked her. Greystowe was far too grand to welcome a simple vicar's daughter. She loved his gardens, though. Her eyes shone with it. Her cheeks flushed. When they passed the tangled grape arbor, she actually clapped her hands.

Like his father, Edward favored simple landscaping. Greystowe shunned Frenchified bedding arrangements for a more natural, parklike effect. Nothing was allowed to run wild, of course; the thickets and glades were strictly planned. But in appearance, at least, the grounds might have been dropped from God's hand. Even the rose garden, his mother's special project, bore an admirably spontaneous air.

Florence had just stepped onto its crushed oyster shell walk when a sudden belling from the hounds warned Edward that one segment of the household's population had yet to welcome them home. The pack raced across the lawn in full cry, their tails wagging madly, their keeper in hot pursuit. "Hoy," yelled that hapless fellow. "Hoy there, lads. Hold up!"

Edward braced himself for an embarrassing scene. He was not disappointed. In a matter of heartbeats, the wolfhound's paws struck his shoulders. Nor was he the last of the assault. Between barks and whines of joy, a dozen tongues lashed his hands, and a dozen noses snuffled whatever they pleased.

"Enough," he said, thrusting the worst of them away. To his amazement, he was obeyed.

Then he saw why.

Every one of the smaller dogs was groveling furiously at Florence's feet. True, she had knelt down to pet them, but even so, the division of attention was unprecedented. Even Freddie, whom the dogs knew, didn't warrant such a greeting.

Florence looked up from the tangle of wriggling bodies.

Her eyes, both laughing and sheepish, found his. The moment hung. To save his life, he could not look away. Her gaze flushed him hot and cold. He hardened, abruptly, fiercely, but his body's reaction was a distant thing. Looking at her, he felt a sense of union he could not reason away, as if the affection of the dogs had mysteriously linked them together. *This one is the same,* their favor seemed to say. *This one is the same as the one we love.*

Ridiculous, he thought. Totally ridiculous.

"Well," Aunt Hypatia observed, "people are right to speak of your animal magnetism."

Florence's head came up in alarm, the pink of her cheeks rivaling his mother's roses. "Oh, no," she said. "I never have this effect on dogs. Only cats and . . . and small children. I'm sure I simply smell of dinner."

That, Edward thought, did not explain the effect she had on him. Even now, in front of his family, in front of the gamekeeper and God, he couldn't control his lust for his brother's future bride. His palms itched to hold her, to touch her in any way. Even to stroke the soft curves of her face, to kiss the tip of her nose, would have brought him satisfaction. Never had he yearned like this for a woman. Aunt Hypatia had spoken true. He was an animal. And Florence, apparently, was the magnet he couldn't resist.

Florence had survived the day: the train ride and the silent dinner and Edward's obvious disapproval over that stupid business with the dogs. As if she'd wanted them to make a cake of her! Now she stood by the window in her darkened sitting room, quiet but for the sound of Lizzie's snores from the room next door. The maid was understandably tired. She'd ridden to Greystowe on the public part of the train, along with the duchess's maid, Edward's valet, and a few of the footmen who weren't needed to keep the London house. Lizzie had been sorry to leave the city until she'd discovered they weren't trading it for a drafty, antiquated heap.

"They've got running water," she'd imparted in a breathless tone. "Hot and cold. And baths in the servants' wing.

It's a right palace, Miss Florence. Why, the ground floor has gas!"

This last pleased her most. Lizzie had never relished the messy chore of trimming lamps. Not that she would have been asked to do it here. Thanks to Aunt Hypatia, Lizzie had climbed to the top of the servants' heap. Only the steward and the housekeeper had the right to order her about, a fact that was only beginning to sink in. "I've never been so happy," she said. "Never."

Florence should have been able to say the same. Freddie was a wonderful man. Her future was nearly assured. But instead of enjoying the accomplishment of her dream, she stood sleepless, restless, her forehead pressed to the glass, her mind on a single thorn. Sighing, she gazed out at the grounds. The window overlooked the moonlit lake at the front of the house, the selfsame lake in which Freddie had learned to swim. An arched stone bridge connected its bank to the island in its center. Between the tops of the trees poked a pointed Moorish roof. She wondered what the building beneath it was used for, if it were simply a folly or a place one could shelter from a storm. It seemed large, its architecture unlike anything on the grounds. Florence shivered and rubbed the curtain's gauzy liner against her cheek. The building was exotic, Eastern, a place for self-indulgence and assignations: a man's place.

How easily she could picture Edward there, despite his stuffy manner. He'd furnished his train car, hadn't he? He must harbor a streak of the sybaritic. He'd smoke cigars in that hideaway, she mused, and drink expensive wine. And meet women, of course. The local widows. The saucy laundry maids. They'd know more than his kisses. They wouldn't be too frightened to unwrap the mystery that hung between his legs. They'd touch it bare and feel it harden. They wouldn't fear, not them, not with Edward to guide the way. Edward would know how to protect a woman from the consequences of indiscretion.

With a soft cry of annoyance, Florence banished her foolish thoughts. Indistinct as they were, her imaginings disturbed her. Her heart was beating too fast and a heavy velvet warmth had settled under her belly. The reaction was pointless. What did it matter what Edward did with other women? It was nothing to her. Nothing.

Then, just as she was about to turn away, she saw a figure on a horse, cantering smoothly around the lake. Edward. And Samson. They seemed a creature out of myth, one being. As she watched, Edward slowed the stallion to walk him through a patch of stones.

He cares for that horse, she thought, far more than he'll ever care for me.

Then it came to her: what she could do to win his respect.

Her hand tightened on the drapes and her body tingled with a different sort of thrill. This was the answer. She was sure of it. I must learn to ride, she thought, as well as a lady born.

Heart pounding with resolve, Florence found Freddie in the billiard room after breakfast. Appropriately enough, he was dressed to ride, though, at the moment, he was merely knocking balls around the table. When he looked up from his shot, his eyes glowed with approval.

"Well," he said, "don't you look smart!"

Uncustomarily nervous, at least for an interview with Freddie, she smoothed the front of her teal-colored habit.

With a smile, Freddie set down his stick. "What would you like to do today? We could go into town and meet the shopkeepers, who—believe me—will be delighted to hear there's a lady in residence. Or we could visit the canal. We're not too far from the lock, and the boats hereabouts are the sort of works of art a Philistine like me can appreciate. The owners paint them, stem to stern, like gypsy wagons. They're very pretty. Plus, I'm sure the Quack and Waddle would be happy to have us for lunch."

His enthusiasm was catching, but Florence resisted it. "Sometime I'd like to do that. Especially the Quack and Waddle. For today, though, if you wouldn't mind, I'd simply like to ride. I never got much chance at home. We couldn't afford a lady's horse. I've been thinking I ought learn to do it better."

Freddie cocked his head at her. "You don't ride badly."

"Not riding badly isn't the same as riding well. You and I are . . . are going to be married. I don't want you to be ashamed of me."

"I couldn't be ashamed of you if you rode like a sack of potatoes."

Florence looked down at her hands, folded now across her waist. She was uncomfortably aware that she wasn't being honest with him; that it wasn't Freddie's judgment she hoped to improve. Still, his brother's opinion mattered to him as well. If Florence won Edward over, Freddie would be happier, too.

"I'd like to ride better," she said, and forced herself to meet his eye. "You don't have to teach me yourself. One of the grooms could if you'd rather. Anyone who knows more than me would be a help. Please, Freddie. I'd really like to learn."

"I see that," he said. He seemed perplexed by her persistence. The lift of his golden brows wrinkled the skin of his forehead. "Very well. I'd be happy to teach you what I can."

"Are you sure you don't mind?"

"Not at all." He rolled a green ball into the corner of the table, then grinned. "It will be fun. You have a nice enough seat already. You'll be a nonpareil in no time."

"Oh, Freddie. I don't—"

"I know." He laughed. "You don't want to attract attention. We'll turn you into a quiet nonpareil, a perfectly unobjectionable equestrienne."

Florence was so grateful she rose on tiptoe to kiss his cheek. "That," she said, blushing for her boldness, "would be marvelous."

CHAPTER 7

The day was perfect for a ride: warm with a light, rose-scented breeze and a flood of sparkling sunshine. She and Freddie crossed the back grounds to reach the stable, a longer walk than she'd expected. Greystowe's servant wing took up fully half of the sprawling house, and the stable was no smaller in scale. Like the main structure, it was built of stone. Blue slate protected its barrel roof and tall arching windows opened onto each horse's stall. The horses were cleaner and better fed than many of the people she'd seen in London. Even the cats looked sleek and fat.

They, thank heavens, took a few twists around her ankles and let her be.

With the efficiency that characterized all of Greystowe's workings, Freddie was mounted on a dappled gray and Florence on a nervous brown mare with the unpromising name of Nitwit.

"She'll settle," the groom assured her when the horse shifted from side to side. "It's the stable she don't like. Once you're in the open, she goes as pretty as you please."

Since they were already in the yard, Florence wasn't certain she believed this. Nitwit had her swaying like a tipsy sailor. Happily, the mare did calm as they left the home paddock behind.

"Watch your footing," the groom called after them. "We've had badgers."

Freddie smiled and waved and clicked his horse to a brisker pace.

"We'll take you across the downs," he said, "and get a look at your form."

The downs were an expanse of low, grassy hills, dotted with sheep and crossed by a narrow stream. After a short ride, Freddie pulled up at a flat, clover-strewn stretch of grass. "Here's a likely spot. 'Course, you probably shouldn't gallop a horse you've never ridden. Would you mind if Sooty and I shake the bugs out while you wait? I can tell he wants to run."

The dappled horse blew noisily in agreement. Florence laughed. "By all means, shake out all the bugs you please. Nitwit and I will enjoy the view."

In truth, Nitwit enjoyed the clover more than the view, but Florence was admiring enough for them both. Freddie rode as well as his brother, though his style was different: more full out, as if the horse's spirit drove that rolling gallop, rather than Freddie's driving the horse. He crouched low over Sooty's neck, his seat rising out of the saddle, his golden hair streaking like a second mane. He was tall for a jockey, but Florence had never seen one with more dash.

He was free out there. She'd never thought of him as less than free, not like his brother, but seeing him today she knew that he, too, had constraints he needed to leave behind.

Horse and rider slowed to a canter, quartering back the way they'd come. Sooty's gait was smooth as butter, a joy to watch. As if to share the pleasure, Freddie hooted and waved his arm.

Until Sooty found the hole.

It caught his right foreleg. She heard the horse scream and saw him fall. Freddie went down with him. He let out a yell, and then she heard nothing. Sensing her alarm, Nitwit began to sidle but Florence dug in her heels and forced her across the field.

"Come on," she urged, her skin all over sweat. "Come on!"

Ten feet from the fall, Nitwit refused to budge.

Even that close, Florence couldn't see Freddie, just the
thrashing horse. Lord, she thought, Freddie must be underneath. She jumped from the saddle. The break was bad.
Sooty's right cannon bone stuck out beyond his skin, the
edges showing ragged through the blood. The horse was
rolling his eyes, moaning low in his throat for help. She
wished she could stop but she couldn't until she'd seen to
Freddie.

As she feared, he lay under the horse, legs trapped by its
weight, eyes wide and staring.

"Freddie!" she cried, kneeling beside him. He was pale
as parchment.

And he wasn't breathing.

Her moan echoed the horse's. He couldn't be dead. He
couldn't. What would Edward do? Edward would die himself. She touched Freddie's throat. A pulse. She felt a pulse.
She had to do something. She couldn't move him, but she
had to wake him. She had to make him breathe. God, she
thought, praying this time. Please, please tell me what to
do.

She didn't know if He answered but she drew back her
arm and slapped his face. "Freddie! Freddie, wake up!"

His body shuddered so she slapped the other cheek. This
time he gasped, his chest lurching upward in a pull for air.
His eyes jerked wildly as if he didn't know where he was.
A second later, he tried to sit up. His groan was almost too
low to hear.

"Don't move," she ordered, pushing him back. She
gasped for air herself, so relieved she could barely speak.
"You've had a bad fall. I think you got the wind knocked
out of you, but you might have hurt your spine."

"Fall?" Then he saw what was lying across his legs.
"Bloody hell," he said, the first time she'd heard him curse.
"He told me. He told me about the bloody badgers and I
forgot." He pressed his arm across his eyes. "God damn it,
I've killed my horse."

His fist pounded the grass. Florence caught it before he
could hurt himself any more. "Freddie, it was an accident."

"An accident no one but an idiot would have had, a stupid, worthless— Everything I touch goes wrong. I should be shot. I should be drawn and quartered. Edward's never going to forgive me."

Florence stroked his bone-white, clammy face. More than his language shocked her. "Freddie. Edward might be disappointed, but the only thing he'd never forgive is if you'd killed yourself."

Freddie lowered his arm. Tears streaked his face, but she saw her words had calmed him. "You have to ride to the house and get him. Tell him to bring some footmen. And a rifle." Florence looked at him, then at the panting horse. He covered his eyes again. "Hurry, Florence. I don't want Sooty to suffer."

She hurried as well as she could on a horse who tried to skitter sideways every time she saw the house. She had to lash the mare hard before she'd gallop, and then it was only will that kept her in the saddle. Sliding off at the rose garden, she picked up her skirts and ran.

"Edward!" she shouted with the last of her breath. "Edward!"

He appeared, with Nigel West, on the first floor landing. She thought she'd never been so grateful to see anyone in her life.

Edward paled when he saw her. "Florence, what's wrong?"

"It's Freddie. He fell. The horse." She held her stomach and gasped for air. "You need to bring some servants and a rifle."

Both men had run down the stairs in the time it took her to say this. Now Edward grabbed her arms hard enough to bruise. "Is Freddie all right?"

"Yes, I think so. But he's trapped under the horse and the horse has a bad break. Freddie thinks he needs to be put down."

Edward emptied his lungs. Then, visibly in control again, he addressed his companion. "Nigel, you get the men and the gun. We'll meet at the stables and Florence will lead us to where it happened."

The steward pulled himself straighter. "We should bring Jenkyns, too. He can patch Freddie up if he needs it."

"Good," said Edward. "Do it."

He hustled her into the garden before her brain had finished following what he'd said. Fortunately, she'd remembered to loop Nitwit's reins around a bench, though she didn't remember how she'd gotten onto the horse's back without a mounting block. Now Edward tossed her up so quickly, she nearly slid off the other side.

He shook his head, took the reins from her hands, and led her to the stable as if she were a child. His anger was a cold, palpable force. The mare minced after him like a beaten dog. Florence wasn't beaten, though, not when it came to protecting those she loved.

"Freddie's sorry," she said, her jaw tight from steadying her voice. "He's sorrier than you could make him if you tried. There's nothing I can do to stop you from yelling at him, but I really don't think that's what he needs."

Edward stopped. He stared at her as if she'd grown a second head. When he turned away, he quickened his pace. "I've no intention of yelling at my brother."

"What about glowering at him? What about making him feel as if that horse means more to you than he does?"

A muscle bunched in Edward's cheek. "My brother knows better than that."

"Not right now, he doesn't."

Edward walked faster still. Florence knew she had no right to dictate his behavior, but she refused to withdraw a single word. Freddie thought he was worthless. Freddie thought everything he touched went wrong.

"You have to be nice to him," she insisted, though her heart was pounding in her throat.

Edward snorted. "I'll shower him with the milk of human kindness."

His tone was as dry as she'd ever heard it. She could only hope she'd made her point.

·   ·   ·

She thought he was a monster.

Even as Edward issued orders, Florence's scold played through his mind. Even as he waited for Jenkyns to gather his supplies, even as they rode like thunder across the downs, her estimation of his character made him grind his teeth.

She thought he was a monster.

But when they reached Freddie every worry but his brother left his mind. The horse lay over him from the waist down. This couldn't be good. In a single motion, Edward swung off Samson and tossed his reins to someone else. His knees hit the turf by Freddie's side.

Freddie's eyes fluttered open. His face was the bluish white of too-thin milk. It glistened with perspiration. He was in pain, Edward knew. Bad pain.

"Eddie," he said, a name he hadn't used since they were children. His voice was thready. "Tried to move, but my leg—" He grimaced. "Think I broke it. Only fair, I guess, since I broke the damn horse's."

"Sh," Edward soothed, brushing the hair from Freddie's brow. Freddie's tone alarmed him. Was Florence right? Did his brother think the horse meant more to him than he did?

"Stupid," Freddie said, rolling his head from side to side. "The groom warned me."

By this time, the stablemaster was kneeling by Freddie's other side. He touched Edward's arm. "I'd like to get a look at his eyes, my lord. See how bad a thump he took. Then the men can hoist up the horse and we'll slide him out."

Edward nodded. Jenkyns was the best doctor Greystowe had, a man of sense and experience, with people and horses. Not knowing what else to do, Edward moved to Sooty's head and held his tossing muzzle. "There," he said, over the horse's ragged pants. "You'll be out of this soon."

Sooty's great, liquid eyes held such pleas, and such faith in Edward's ability to grant them, that he felt as if a vise were tightening around his ribs. "You're a good fellow," he said, the words like gravel in his throat. "You've been a good friend to my brother."

"Your lordship?" said Nigel. The steward stood one polite step behind him. "Jenkyns is ready to move him. We need your help to lift the horse."

"Of course." Edward gave Sooty a last pat and got to his feet.

To his surprise, Florence moved in as well. Though he couldn't imagine what help she'd be in lifting a horse, some corner of his mind was pleased she wasn't hysterical.

"She's to steady Lord Burbrooke's legs," Jenkyns explained. "We don't want them jostled when we slide him out." The wiry stablemaster had positioned himself behind Freddie's shoulders, ready to pull the moment Edward gave the signal.

"All right," Edward said to the other men. "On three."

They got him out on the second try. Both Freddie and the horse cried out at being moved.

"Stand back, Florence," Edward said once his brother was free. He could tell from Freddie's pallor that he was about to be sick. Florence seemed to reach the same conclusion. Despite the warning, she rubbed his back while Jenkyns rolled him gently to his side. She didn't cluck or fuss, just stroked him the way a mother would a weary child.

When his sickness passed, they immobilized Freddie's leg and laid him on a canvas stretcher. Nigel took one end and Jenkyns the other. Woozy with pain, Freddie still reached for Edward before they could carry him off.

"You take care of Sooty," he said, his grip surprisingly strong on Edward's wrist. "He knows you. I don't want him to go without a friend."

"I will" was all he managed to get out.

To Edward's surprise, Florence did not leave with her fiancé.

"I'm staying with you," she said, her face tear-stained but determined.

"With me?"

She glanced at the footman who'd carried the gun, then lowered her voice. "I wronged you, Edward. I should have known you wouldn't treat Freddie harshly. And I want to make sure you're all right."

His mouth fished open and shut. Protests streaked like quicksilver through his head: that he might have yelled at Freddie if she hadn't been there, that a man like himself did not require coddling, that Freddie needed her more and that her continued presence was hardly proper. She was the gentler sex. She was the one who shouldn't see this. Instead, he gazed into her sweet, stubborn eyes and knew he could not refuse her gesture.

"As you wish," he said. Though he'd meant the words to come out cool, they were as low and caressing as a lover's midnight sigh. Embarrassed, he shouldered the rifle and cleared his throat. He pressed the muzzle to the gelding's skull. As if he knew what was coming, Sooty calmed.

"Stand back," he said. "I don't want you spattered."

Florence made a half-swallowed sound, more concern than horror. Edward didn't mean to look at her again, but their eyes locked just as they had over the hounds. A strange, drawing sensation pulled at his breastbone, a thin, painful tug, as if his soul were trying to reach her.

You ought to be mine, he thought. Only I can make you happy. But that was pointless. She belonged to Freddie. She was Freddie's saving grace.

He squinted down the barrel of the gun and blinked to clear his vision. The horse gave one last sigh. Edward gritted his teeth and pulled the trigger.

The recoil knocked him back a step, but the kill was clean: just a pool of blood that soaked quickly into the ground. When he lowered the gun, his arms were shaking as if he had the ague. He didn't resist when Florence tugged him away.

Edward did not make it from the stable to the house. Even though he must have been anxious to check on his brother, his legs refused to carry him. Florence watched him go paler and paler until finally, in front of a big oak with a rustic bench beneath, he tightened his hold on her arm and forced her to a stop.

"I have to sit," he said, his voice a ghost. "I can't let Freddie see me like this."

He dropped to the bench and propped his head on shaking hands. Florence sat beside him, her knees turned towards him in worry. He was sweating, and not from exertion. She pulled off her gloves and reached between his arms to unfasten his collar. As she did, he looked at her, his expression naked, his eyes pleading for something deeper than understanding.

"It's all right," she said, laying her hand behind his shoulder. "Breathe slowly. I'm sure you'll feel better soon."

She kept to herself the certainty that his brother would not think ill of his reaction. This was not about Freddie's opinion of Edward, but about Edward's opinion of himself. Gradually, as he breathed in a measure of control, the color returned to his face.

"Father wouldn't have turned a hair at this," he said, his head still lowered. "He'd have put down that horse and called for lunch."

Though Florence knew he was jesting, she did not laugh. "Forgive me for saying so, Edward, but—your father's strength of character aside—I think you're entitled to turn more than a hair. And not over the horse."

"No," he agreed with a grimacing shake of his head. "Not over the horse." He pushed himself upright and let the tree's breeze-blown leaves dapple his face with sun. Florence had never seen him so weary. She longed to hold him, to cradle his head against her breast. Her hands curled with the intensity of the urge and she blushed for fear he might look at her and read the forbidden desire. She sat in agonized silence, not knowing what to say but unable to leave. At last, he sighed and twisted his father's signet around his smallest finger. The cabochon ruby flashed in the dancing light.

"I always got on better with the earl than Freddie did," he said. "Father . . . respected me."

She lifted her gaze to his face, an intimacy that was possible only because he was staring out across the grounds. "Is that a bad thing?"

His lips twisted in a smile. "My father gave me my first horse when I was nine, to ride when I wished without the company of a groom. Freddie never earned that privilege, though he was twelve when Father died. Whatever he did, he came up short. According to Father, he was always too soft or too flighty or too much a mama's boy. My mother—" Edward pinched the bridge of his nose. "My mother was delicate, easily upset, but very sweet-natured. She needed the kind of love Freddie gave her. Unqualified. Unquestioning. But Father couldn't see that. If Freddie wanted to ride alone, he had to sneak a horse out of the stables. He had to break my father's rules and risk getting whipped."

"Are you saying that if your father had let him have his own horse, this accident wouldn't have happened?"

"No. Freddie was born to ride. More than I was, to tell the truth." His hand moved towards her face. With the pad of his thumb, he swept a windblown lock from the corner of her mouth. "I suppose I'm trying to confess I liked it."

His touch befuddled her. Enchanted and confused, she sat frozen while he traced the curve of her lower lip. His expression was musing, almost absentminded. Did he know what he was doing? Could he possibly? Only when his hand fell could she speak. "You liked what?"

"Being first," he said. "Being Father's favorite."

"Surely that's natural. You were just a boy."

"I don't know. Sometimes I think I shouldn't have— well, I admired him, you know. I knew he was a bastard but I wanted his approval."

"He was your father."

"Freddie was my brother, and a far truer soul." Edward turned his body towards her, his forearm on his knee. "You were right to scold me today. Sometimes I'm too much like him. He hurt Freddie. Made him feel the lesser son. But he wasn't less. He simply couldn't be molded into the shape my father thought appropriate for a Greystowe male. In that, Freddie was stronger than I was."

"If Freddie was stronger than you, why did you have to protect him?"

Edward brushed her knee, restlessly smoothing the folds

of her riding habit. Her body tensed deep inside and she
willed her reaction not to show. Fortunately, he watched his
hand rather than her, his extravagant lashes shielding his
eyes. His mouth held a soft, ironic curve. "I liked protecting
Freddie. I liked that better than if my father had treated us as
equals."

This, Florence saw, was the true confession. This was
what had tightened his jaw and set that subtle tremor in his
hands. But what a thing to feel guilty for, and for so many
years! Aching for him, she gave in to the urge to stroke his
rich dark hair. Even as she tried to soothe him, she reveled
in the feel of that silk sliding through her fingers. She was
shamefully glad she'd removed her gloves.

"A thought has consequences," she said carefully, gently. "My father taught me that. But a thought is not a deed.
Your enjoyment of protecting Freddie did not cause your
father to be cruel. Nor do I think you should worry over-
much about the possible disloyalty of your emotions. Children need to be loved by their parents. Freddie was your
mother's favorite, wasn't he? You may as well blame her
for what happened—though I know you will not."

Edward was silent for a moment. When he spoke, his response was low and heartfelt. "You are a wise young
woman. And a kind one."

"You are easy to be kind to." Moved by his tone, she
dared to pet his cheek. He turned his head, pressing his
cheekbone to her fingers, brushing his mouth across her
palm.

Then, as if he'd done something he devoutly wished he
hadn't, he jerked away and stood. Briskly, he tugged the bottom of his waistcoat. "I must consult with Jenkyns," he said.
"Please stay until you are ready to go in."

He did not wait for her to follow. Indeed, his words
made following impossible. Instead, she watched him stride
stiffly towards the house, once again himself, while she—

She no longer knew who she was.

• • •

Florence paced the hall outside Freddie's room. She was waiting for Edward's steward to finish settling him. The stablemaster had given Freddie a dose of morphine, but he wasn't yet asleep. Though Florence knew she ought to wait till morning to see him, she felt too restless, so restless she was wringing her hands like a heroine in a play.

She couldn't push Edward's expression from her mind. When he'd looked at her as they sat on that little bench, she'd thought—she'd wished—

She wrung her hands and paced the other way. For once, his heart had been in his gaze. When she met it, she seemed to know his every thought: his regret for the horse, his fear for Freddie. Most of all, she'd sensed his hope that no one would guess how weak he was. But Florence didn't think him weak. Instead, she thought him the strongest man she'd ever known.

Was that the real Edward: the man whose heart could break for a wounded horse? Who could torture himself over the tangled motivations of his childhood? Who could worry that his love had not been perfect? And if this was the real Edward, what did that mean for her? Attraction was one thing. Even infatuation could be dismissed. But the pull he exerted when he bared his soul would not be easy to evade. She wasn't even sure she wanted to.

The dilemma seemed destined to remain unsolved. Nigel West stepped out of Freddie's room and carefully shut the door. As befitted his position—the steward ran Greystowe when Edward could not—he was a dignified man of middle years, slender, his temples lightly shot with white. He would have appeared as serious as his master but for his extraordinary gray eyes. They were kind and quiet and crinkled pleasantly at the corners when he smiled. He smiled now at Florence.

"I'm afraid he's dropped off, Miss Fairleigh. Didn't even wait for me to finish plumping the pillows. You can go in, of course, but I doubt he'll wake."

"Oh," she said, feeling as if an escape route had been blocked. "I wouldn't want to disturb him." She started to go, then turned back. "Will you be looking after him, Mr.

West? I know the housekeeper or one of the maids could do it, but he'd probably be more comfortable with a man."

Nigel's brow puckered as if her words held some significance she didn't understand. She wondered if she'd overstepped her place. She had no authority here, nor would she have much more as Freddie's wife. Greystowe was Edward's to arrange. Just as she was about to withdraw the request, Nigel shook himself.

"I imagine I shall be looking after him. With Edward home, I'm rather at loose ends."

Relieved she hadn't put her foot wrong, Florence smiled. "You've been at Greystowe a long time, haven't you?"

"Since his lordship's father paid for my schooling." Nigel grinned at her shocked expression. "You've heard the stories then. All true. The old earl was a devil. But he did believe in fostering potential. I owe this family more than I can say."

Eyes abruptly pricking, Florence gazed past him down the hall. She owed this family a good deal herself, too much to think of betraying their trust. They'd welcomed her, a simple country girl, as Freddie's bride. And Freddie . . . Freddie was the dearest man she'd ever known. "They're complicated, aren't they?" she said. "Even Freddie."

"Yes," Nigel agreed, the gentleness of his tone forcing her to blink back tears. "But steadfast every one. You couldn't want for truer friends."

Friends, she thought. If only her wishes were that simple.

Shortly after midnight, Edward crossed the hall to his brother's room. He had no intention of waking Freddie. He simply wanted to stand in the dark and listen to him breathe. The leg with the splint made a funny shape under the sheets, as if a mummy were sharing his bed. Edward was still too shaken to be amused. He didn't know what he'd do if he lost his brother; didn't know who he'd be. He'd built his life around protecting him. Without Freddie alive and well and happy, none of his accomplishments meant a damn.

He turned to the window, hands clenched, muscles tight. Florence, he thought. Oh, Florence. Why do I have to care about you, too? The night could not answer. With dreamlike slowness, the draperies belled in the breeze that cooled the room. Their sheer white hems whispered across the carpet. Edward looked back at the bed. The night was mild, but Freddie could not afford a chill. One good leg had been enough to kick off half the covers. Smiling wryly, Edward pulled them up his chest.

Disturbed by the movement, Freddie snuffled in his sleep and rolled partway onto his side. His arm flopped out, hitting Edward's leg. His eyes opened. "Nigel?"

Edward hunkered beside the bed. "It's Edward. I just came to check on you."

Freddie smiled, his eyes sliding shut again. "You haven't checked on me since Mummy and Daddy died."

"I didn't know you saw me do that."

Covers rustled as Freddie shrugged. "I figured you wanted reassurance that you weren't alone. I didn't mind. It made me feel safe."

"You are safe. I'll always keep you safe."

Freddie laughed under his breath. "Can't promise that, old man. You ain't God yet, though I know you'll try."

His singsong tone told Edward he still felt the morphine. He'd have to warn Jenkyns to watch the dose. He didn't want Freddie getting used to it.

"She did it for you," Freddie said, his fingers plucking idly at the sheet.

"Who did what for me?"

"Florence," he said. "Asked me for riding lessons. She didn't say so, but I know it was you she wanted to impress."

Edward's breath caught. Was it true? Did Florence value his opinion? He'd thought today, when she stroked his face, that she must hold him in some esteem. But how could he know? She was a sympathetic soul. Perhaps she'd have touched anyone as tenderly. Surely after all he'd done she couldn't still care what he thought.

Freddie laughed again. "Thinks you don't like her. Big old grouch."

"Florence called me a big old grouch?"

But Freddie's drug-fogged mind had already wandered on. "You'll have to take over for me. Teach her yourself." He smacked his lips and burrowed deeper in the pillows. "Be like when you taught me how to swim."

Alarmed by the suggestion, Edward stood. Be alone with Florence? Teach Florence? Not on his life. Not unless he wanted his brother to marry a ravaged bride.

CHAPTER 8

According to Jenkyns, Freddie couldn't be moved until his bones had a chance to set. Nigel was seeing to his meal when Florence knocked.

"I don't want your blasted broth," she heard Freddie snap. "My leg is broken, not my stomach." Clearly, his pain had made him peevish. Despite his discomfort, he brightened when he saw her. "At last. A kindly nursemaid. Tell this loathsome bully to take his nursery food away."

Florence kissed his brow without a blush. "I'm sure Mr. West is only following doctor's orders."

"Bloody horse doctor," Freddie muttered, then squeezed her hand in apology. "You should go, sweetheart. Have your own breakfast. I'm a bad invalid. Always have been. I'm afraid if you stay, you'll throw me over for a banker."

Florence clucked her tongue and roundly denied the charge. She did as Freddie asked, though, for he was obviously not in a humor to see her. He and Nigel were squabbling again as soon as she shut the door.

Poor Nigel, she thought. She was glad the steward had taken him in hand. Freddie would have talked his way around any of the maids. She proceeded to the breakfast parlor, a pretty yellow room with a view of the breeze-ruffled lake. To her dismay, only Edward sat inside.

"Is Aunt Hypatia—?"

"Sleeping," he said, as short-tempered as ever.

So, she thought, the grumpy earl returns. She filled her plate at the sideboard: eggs, sausage, a freshly baked roll, and strawberries. Refusing to give in to fear, she took the seat around the corner from his. For long minutes, the only sound was the clink of china and the rasp of a snore issuing from the ground floor bedroom next door. Never an early riser, Edward's aunt must have been exhausted by the previous day's excitement.

Florence wanted to smile, but she doubted Edward would appreciate the jest. His mood was blacker than Freddie's—and both his legs were sound. She was beginning to think she'd dreamed the man she'd seen the day before.

"Do you think we ought to call a real doctor?" she asked, perversely wanting him to look at her. Even his scowl was preferable to being ignored.

Edward set down his knife and fork. When the morning sun struck his eyes, they glowed like clear blue gems. His riding coat was for once not black, but a soft brown tweed. His shirt was white and collarless. He looked wonderful: big and broad-shouldered and country-squirish. Not relaxed though. She couldn't imagine Edward ever being relaxed. A short, deep line appeared between his heavy brows. For him, the expression was friendly.

"I'm afraid the doctor in town is a bit decrepit. Jenkyns knows more about broken bones than he does. If we encounter complications, I'll send to London for my physician."

His gaze remained on Florence even after he finished speaking. She'd wanted him to look at her but now that he was, she could barely sit still. His regard, steady and inscrutable, inspired a powerful urge to squirm. When he tipped his coffee to his mouth, his lips drew her eyes like a magnet. Those sensual lips, so at odds with his forbidding face, stirred memories better left alone. He licked them as he set down the cup.

Those lips had kissed her, and those hands, those big, sun-darkened hands had held her head, had run down her spine and cupped her bottom. The last time they'd done it he hadn't had drink to excuse him. He did desire her, even if he didn't like her. Perhaps, she thought, he remembered their kisses as vividly as she did. Perhaps he wanted to kiss her now. The possibility made her shiver. She did squirm then, just a little.

"Florence," he said, his voice deeper than usual.

Startled, she glanced guiltily back at his face. "Yes, Edward?"

"I'm arranging for Merry Vance to visit Greystowe, so you won't be bored while Freddie's laid up."

"Oh," she said, surprised he would concern himself with her comfort. "That's very kind, but won't she mind leaving London during the Season?"

His laugh was dry. "She's only seventeen. I suspect she wouldn't be out at all if she hadn't wrapped her father around her finger. I thought she could take over training you from Freddie. By all accounts, she's quite the horse-woman."

"Oh," said Florence, the only word she could think of. Her tea and sausages sat like stones in her belly. Suddenly, the reason for Edward's consideration was clear.

He didn't want to teach her himself.

She looked at her lap, where her traitorous hands were twisting her napkin into a ball. She swallowed. She was being ridiculous. She shouldn't let him hurt her. It wasn't as if having him teach her would be fun. More often than not, he wasn't nice to her at all. Against her will, she thought of Freddie's swimming trophy, the one Edward kept in the cabinet by his bed. She knew then; couldn't deny it any longer. She wanted more than Edward's respect. She wanted him to like her, to care as deeply for her as he did for his brother.

"I'm sure you'll do well," he said, the assurance uncustomarily soft. She had the impression he was leaning towards her, though she didn't dare lift her head. "I'm sure Freddie will be proud."

"Thank you," she managed to say. "I liked Merry Vance very much. It was kind of you to think of her."

"You are easy to be kind to."

Florence couldn't help widening her eyes. Did he mean to remind her of her words to him in the garden? He'd behaved as if he wanted to forget his confidences, and expected her to do the same. But perhaps the reminder was unintentional, or some obscure setdown she was simply too thick to fathom. Oh, she would never understand him, never!

Unfortunately, knowing that did not keep her from wanting to try.

The rose garden buzzed with dragonflies and bees. Two days had passed since Freddie's accident and Florence was taking tea with Aunt Hypatia. According to the duchess, Florence's simple flowered cotton gown—one of her own—was woefully inadequate.

"You look like a farmgirl," she complained.

Florence did not take offense. The duchess liked complaining as much as cats liked cream. She hid her smile behind the gold-plated rim of her cup. "I thought tea dress was meant to be more comfortable."

"It is, but in a picturesque and romantic manner. Here." With the agility she displayed when she chose, she pushed from her chair and snipped two budded yellow roses. The small silver scissors that hung from a cord at her waist made quick work of the thorns. That done, she removed one of her hat pins and fastened the flowers, leaves and all, to Florence's bodice. "There. Marginally better. We won't always be taking tea alone, you know. I do have acquaintances here."

"I'd forgotten that," Florence admitted. "You were born in this house, weren't you? With Freddie's father."

"Wonder is, I survived it," the duchess grumped, though the sparkle in her eye led Florence to believe her memories weren't all unpleasant. "My brother, the thirteenth earl, was the worst scamp you could imagine. The trouble that boy got me into!"

"I thought he was very stern."

"Not until he got the title. Then he had to be a 'Greystowe man.' " She pulled a face Florence suspected was an imitation of the haughty earl. "The peerage ruined him. Destroyed every shred of humor and humanity he had. After that, nothing mattered but the family honor. He threw over a girl he'd been seeing for well on seven years. Everyone assumed they'd marry. But a baron's daughter wasn't good enough for him. He had to take up with the boys' mother and make her miserable, too." She shook her head. "Suzanne was as sweet as spun sugar and about as tough. I doubt anyone had raised their voice to her before her marriage. As for me, when Stephen gained an earldom, I lost a friend. Didn't so much as pat my back until the day I married my duke. That earned me a brother's embrace. That made him love me again."

Florence reached past the tea things to clasp her hand. With a fond smile, the duchess returned the pressure. "No, dear. You mustn't pity a rich old lady. All that happened long ago."

But it wasn't the duchess who worried Florence most.

"Aunt Hypatia," she said, "you don't think Edward is in danger of . . ."

"Becoming like his father?" Aunt Hypatia laughed. "It's good of you to concern yourself, but there's not much chance of that. Sometimes—I fear this will sound callous, but sometimes I think it's better my brother died young. Certainly better for Freddie." Her face softened as people's tended to at his name. "Freddie was raised with love. He'll be a good father someday because Edward was everything my brother should have been. Edward still has his heart."

Did he? Sometimes Florence thought so. Other times, she doubted it very much. She would have liked to sit quietly then, to mull over what she'd heard. Her wish was not to be, however, because Mrs. Forster, the housekeeper, chose that moment to announce the arrival of Merry Vance.

When she stepped onto the terrace she looked a different creature from the impeccably dressed young lady Florence had known in London. Her hair was disheveled, her color high, her smart yellow gown wrinkled and dulled by the dust of travel. Her grin, however, was as wide and engaging as ever.

"Yes, yes, I'm early," she said in her happy, breathless way. Holding both gloves in one hand she leaned down to kiss Florence's cheek. "London has been as dull as dishwater without you. I simply couldn't wait to say hello." Her eyes twinkled as she bobbed a curtsey to the duchess. "Please forgive my informality, your Grace. I assure you it isn't personal. Anyone you ask will tell you I'm a hellion."

"Will they indeed?" intoned the duchess.

"Miss Vance," Edward said, appearing at the edge of the grass. His nod was grave but his face creased upward as if he were about to laugh. No doubt he'd caught the duchess's frosty response. "I trust you and Buttercup survived the train from London."

Buttercup? Florence thought. Her cat-light mare from London? Was it possible Edward had bought the horse for her? It would have been an extravagant gesture, and one she really shouldn't accept, but, oh, if he had! But Merry Vance dashed her irrational hope almost before it had time to form.

"I can't thank you enough," she said, "for arranging her as my ride. Teaching is so much easier when you have a good mount."

Edward looked down. This, of all things, seemed to embarrass him. He glanced uncomfortably at Florence, his gaze catching for an instant on the roses the duchess had pinned to her bosom. With an air of distraction, he shook his head and returned his attention to Merry. "Ah, well, pleased I could oblige. I had to buy her in any case. My stallion was moping."

Merry laughed, a surprisingly feminine sound. "How grand! A romance among the stalls. I shall have to keep on top of developments while I'm here."

She smiled at Edward as she said it, as if her words held

a meaning known only to the two of them. She wasn't plain then, not with that gleam in her eyes and the sunshine blazing in her cloud of golden hair. She was a little Valkyrie, lithe and strong, if not quite up to a large breast-plate. The realization that Edward might find her attractive made Florence distinctly ill at ease.

He doesn't want her, she assured herself. His manner was too casual, too matter of fact.

Even if he had given Merry her horse.

"You'll want to freshen up," Edward said, though not as disapprovingly as the duchess would have.

Merry trilled at the gentle suggestion. "Indeed," she cooed, tapping Edward's chest with the tip of her finger. "Fresh is my middle name."

Florence experienced a nearly uncontrollable urge to pinch her, but Edward was not put off. "Shall we hold tea for you?" he asked.

"Oh, no." Merry tossed her golden hair and turned towards the house. "I'm sure I can cozen something out of the kitchen when I get back. You three enjoy. I'll find my poor old maid and the next time you see me, I'll be free of dust and decent."

"Not too decent," Edward said, perfectly straight-faced.

"My, no." Merry threw a wink over her shoulder. "What fun would that be?"

Florence could barely lift her jaw. As Merry sauntered across the terrace, her little bottom twitched beneath her dusty bustle. She'd been flirting with Edward. And Edward had flirted back.

"Hm," said Aunt Hypatia once Merry was out of earshot. "That girl bears watching."

Florence didn't know if she meant this as an insult or a compliment, nor was her nephew's demeanor any clue. Still facing the direction Merry had taken, Edward clasped his hands behind his back. Florence sincerely hoped he wasn't watching Merry twitch.

"She's Monmouth's daughter," he said.

"Yes." The duchess stirred her tea. "In a year or two, she'll make some man a fine wife."

"You mean she'll make some man a fine handful."

"That, too," said Aunt Hypatia.

Florence pushed her cucumber sandwich to the farthest edge of her plate. Her appetite had fled, along with her enjoyment of the afternoon. A fine handful indeed! She might not have the right to mind it, but she knew she didn't like the sound of that.

CHAPTER 9

To Florence's dismay, Nitwit had become "her" horse.

"Today you'll groom her," Merry announced as they entered the busy stable. To Florence's amazement, Merry wore breeches. For once, another woman drew more stares than she did. She didn't know whether to blush for her friend or admire her brazen style. Merry behaved as if she were dressed to meet the queen and, while no one so much as whistled, Florence suspected Greystowe's grooms would be talking of this for years. Everywhere they passed, jaws dropped. Apparently, the only males immune to the shock of visible female legs were a trio of school-age boys who were forking soiled hay into barrows.

Grateful for their efforts, Florence picked her way across the hard-packed floor. She sighed when they reached Nitwit's box. The top of the stall door was covered in equine tooth marks, mute testimony to the mare's restless habits. Equally unimpressed with Florence, Nitwit curled her lip and made a rude noise.

They eyed each other while Merry went to Jenkyns for supplies.

"It wasn't my choice," Florence said as the mare deigned to swivel her ears. "We'll simply have to make the best of it."

Merry caught the tail end of the exchange. "Good. You're getting acquainted. You can't ride well if you and the horse aren't comfortable with each other."

As if to prove the unlikelihood of this happening, Nitwit kicked the back of her box.

"We'll have to lead her into the yard," Florence said. "Being inside makes her snappish."

"Nonsense," said Merry. "She only needs settling."

With a sense of resignation, Florence followed her into the stall. Ten minutes later, after Nitwit had clipped Merry twice on the boot, they trooped out.

"Maybe we should ask Jenkyns for another mount," Merry said.

"No, no. She'll be fine once we get her into the paddock." Florence was reluctant to admit it, even to herself, but she was feeling more kindly towards the mare since she'd tried to kick her teacher. Merry's good-humored air of competence was wearing on her nerves. It didn't seem right that someone younger than herself should be so skilled, or so fearless.

Or that someone who obviously didn't need a nice horse should be given one like Buttercup.

She bit her lip at her unkind thoughts. Her father used to say envy was a bitter pill. Now she knew how true those words were. She could barely choke her resentment down. It wasn't justified, of course. Merry was a nice girl, a generous girl to come and teach her this way. And still Florence exulted when Nitwit proved her right. The mare did like being brushed in the open air. She barely twitched when Florence curried her sensitive underbelly.

"Now lift her feet," Merry said. "Let's see if she'll let you check her shoes."

Florence did as she asked, too annoyed to feel a moment's fear.

"Good," Merry exclaimed when Nitwit did not protest. "Horses are flight animals. When they let you hold their feet, that means they trust you."

Florence was tempted to tell her most animals trusted her, but managed to hold her tongue. Merry didn't know about the cats. Merry was only trying to be encouraging. The least Florence could do was pretend to be grateful.

I am grateful, she thought. I am.

But she had to struggle not to grind her teeth.

After they checked Nitwit's shoes for stones, Merry had Florence saddle her and mount. Then, instead of watching Florence ride, she took the halter and told Florence to release the reins.

"Hold your arms out from your sides," she instructed. "And don't put your foot in the stirrup or hook your knee around the head. Sit face front and tuck your leg behind the horn. I'll hold Nitwit steady. You concentrate on centering your weight over the horse's back. That's how you develop a sense of balance."

As far as Florence could tell, she wasn't developing anything but a sense of embarrassment. Her arms shook from lifting the heavy saddle over Nitwit's back. The smallest movement felt as if it would send her sliding. Even worse, the three stableboys had perched on the paddock wall to watch the show.

Either that, or they weren't too young after all to notice the fit of Merry's breeches.

"Doing fine, miss," the tallest one called. The shortest, a round, straw-headed elf, decided to play tightrope on the stones.

Oh, Lord, thought Florence, his antics making her dizzy. She hardly dared breathe for fear of falling off. Nitwit was taller than Buttercup and the ground seemed a long way down.

"Are you ready for me to lead you around?" Merry asked."

Florence's "no" was almost a shout. Merry laughed and patted Nitwit's neck.

"Never mind," she said. "You just sit today. We'll save walking for tomorrow."

Tomorrow, Florence thought, and wished she were enough of a coward to give up.

• • •

To Florence's immense relief, the next day was better, and the next better still. On the fourth day of lessons, Merry put Nitwit on a long leather lead called a lunge line and had her circle the paddock with Florence on her back. First they walked slowly, then swiftly, and then they tried a gentle trot. Merry let her hook her leg around the head for this, but Florence fell off all the same. She was determined, though, especially with her trio of fans. She didn't know if Jenkyns had given them permission or if they'd simply sneaked away, but the three muddy boys managed to watch her every day.

"No worries," they'd call each time she hit the dirt. "You'll get it next time."

Despite her embarrassment, and the fact that her bottom was all over bruises, Florence was glad they were rooting for her. These boys were too old to be the victims of her peculiar charms, and too young to be interested in her ordinary ones. They had to be there by choice. They had to be there because they liked her.

"Forget posting," Merry said when she tried to raise up and down. "Posting is for ninnies. You want to rock back and forth from the hips. With the horse's movements. Easy. Feel how your weight shifts with the horse's steps."

"Woo-hoo," hooted the boys at Merry's suggestive demonstration. Merry merely laughed.

"With the horse," she coaxed. "*With* the horse."

Finally, on the seventh day, Florence got it. Nitwit snorted and pranced as if Florence had performed a miracle. Truth be told, she felt as if she had. How easy this was! How right! It was just the way her body had been wanting to go all along.

Then Merry let her put her foot into the stirrup.

The security Florence felt astounded her—and she had yet to use her hands. Merry was a genius. Even a canter didn't shake her. Oh, her heart was pounding, but her seat was as steady as a rock. When they tried a gallop, Florence thought her soul had taken wing. The rhythm of the gait made the most of Merry's lessons and Nitwit, bless her, flew over the ground as if her legs were pistons and her hooves set on tracks. For the first time in her life, Florence knew what people meant by horse and rider being one. Nitwit might not be as light on her feet as Buttercup, or as even-tempered, but she was strong and fast and as sure as a mountain goat.

"What a goer!" Merry exclaimed and Florence was proud for her mount's sake, too.

As luck would have it, Edward was the first person to meet them coming out of the stable. Florence was too elated to mind her manners. "I did it!" she said, grabbing his hands and bouncing up and down. "I galloped on Nitwit without the reins."

Edward smiled at her. His grip was firm. It even swung a little. "I saw," he said. "That was very brave. I suppose next you'll be wanting to join the circus."

The warmth in his eyes made her shy. "Not the circus. Not me."

"She's a trooper," Merry put in. "A mouse with the heart of a lion."

Her words seemed to remind Edward that he was holding Florence's hands. He dropped them as if they burned and turned to Merry. "You've done a good job, Miss Vance. My stablemaster has been singing your praises."

"She's a wonderful teacher," Florence agreed, too exhilarated to be jealous. "I never believed I could ride a horse like that."

"A girl can ride anything she puts her mind to," Merry said, her eyes laughing suggestively at Edward's. "That's what we're built for."

Even Florence could not fail to catch that double meaning. Edward's lips thinned wryly as he shook his finger. "Your father would wash your mouth, Miss Vance."

"It's Merry," she said, but he was already walking off. Her sigh as she watched him go spoke volumes. "Lord above. Did you ever see such a pair of shoulders?"

Florence looked at them, then at Merry. Merry's hand was pressed to her bosom and her gaze was soft with yearning. Knowledge dawned with a sinking of her stomach. Merry hadn't come to Greystowe because she liked Florence, or because she liked teaching, or even because she was still too young to take the Season seriously. All those things might be true, but Merry had come to Greystowe because its earl made her swoon.

When Merry looked back at her, her awareness must have shown. Her teacher smiled, crookedly, ruefully. Florence's heart squeezed with sympathy. Merry might not know it but, in this, they were two of a kind.

"The first time I saw him at Tattersall's," Merry confessed, "my toes curled in my boots. If only I were bold enough, I think I could have him. I'm not too terribly ugly. And he does think I'm funny. Men have been known to fall for less."

Florence supposed they had. She drew breath to assure the girl she wasn't ugly, then thought better of it. "Maybe you should be careful. You are young, and he is a grown man."

Merry made a sound halfway between a gurgle and a moan. To Florence's dismay, she knew precisely what it meant. Edward was more than a grown man. Edward was the epitome of all that was male and, as such, he called to the most primitive urges a woman had. A man like Edward made a woman want to forget everything: promises, propriety, even common sense. But perhaps she ought to be glad he had the same effect on Merry. Perhaps Florence's feelings were nothing to be concerned over. A natural human temptation. Vicar's daughter or no, Florence had always known she was human.

"I hope you don't think I'm awful," Merry said, her hand on Florence's arm. "My friends in London say silly things or scoff. You, at least, know how I feel. After all, you and Freddie must have stolen a few kisses. Freddie's a handsome young man in his prime." Confidence recovering, she wagged her strawberry brows. "A man with needs, Florence. A man who's practically chained to his bed. Believe me, were I in your place and Edward in Freddie's, I know what sort of nursemaid I'd be."

Her words painted a picture Florence could not thrust away. She saw Edward wrapped in chains, his chest as bare as a marble statue. And her hand. She saw her own hand reaching for the secrets she'd been too timid to explore. That thickness, that shifting, swelling shape . . . Her body clenched, low and tight. She was liquid inside, and hot. But she couldn't let Merry guess how she felt. She couldn't let Merry think what she was planning was appropriate. She eased her arm from Merry's hold.

"Freddie is a perfect gentleman," she said in her most repressive schoolteacher tone. "Freddie would never do anything to compromise a lady's honor."

"Of course not," Merry said, obviously unconvinced.

And Florence knew nothing she'd said had sunk in.

She watched them together after that; watched how easy Edward was with Merry, how he laughed at her jokes, how his eyes sparked when they debated the merits of various equine traits. Merry would not back down when she thought she was right. Merry would rise out of her seat and pound the table.

And Edward didn't seem to mind.

Was Merry right? Did Edward merely need a push? He didn't act like a besotted man. At least, not the besotted men she knew. But Edward was a creature apart, so perhaps he felt more than he showed.

She watched to see if he touched her, measured his smiles, compared his stares to those he'd shared with her. They weren't the same. They weren't hot and riveting and as sharp as a whetted blade. She could see the difference and she was dreadfully wrong to care. She even watched his hidden flesh to see if it grew large when he and Merry were together. He caught her at it once and gave her the strangest look. Her face had burned like flame. Other things, too. Other things she didn't have names for caught fire between her legs.

She told herself Edward's amours were not her concern.

She told herself if only she knew the truth about his feelings for Merry, she could face them.

But the truth was the last thing she could face. The truth

was pressing up inside her, dark and restless, as if Pandora's box were striving to open itself. At her wit's end, she sat on the lid and shut her eyes. She did not know how close the secret was to breaking free.

Florence convinced the housekeeper to let her take Freddie's lunch tray. She'd allowed Nigel to shoulder too much of her intended's care. That was going to change. She couldn't do everything, but she could fluff pillows. She could smooth brows and banish boredom. She could let Freddie know she would never, ever neglect him.

With that resolve, Florence shifted the tray to her hip and rapped lightly on his door.

"You do *not* want to do this," she heard Nigel saying sharply through the wood. When he opened the door a moment later, his face was flushed. He and Freddie must have been fighting again. She'd come just in time, she decided. The poor man must be desperate for a break.

"Sweetheart!" Freddie exclaimed. He had a pillow on his lap and his hair was mussed as if he'd been running his fingers through it. As always, he put on his best face for her. His smile was brilliant. "Your timing is perfect. My warden here was about to thrash me."

"I'll leave you two alone," Nigel said, sounding as stiff as the earl.

Florence clucked at Freddie as soon as the steward was gone. "You shouldn't bait him."

Freddie helped her slide the tray over his lap. "Bait him?"

"I know it's hard on you being shut up like this, but it's hard on him, too. Mr. West wasn't trained to be a nursemaid. Now and then you could squabble with me instead— if only to give the poor man a rest."

Freddie blinked as if he hadn't understood a word. Florence uncovered the beef and barley stew Cook had made to keep his strength up. She knew better than to believe his innocent air. "I know you two were arguing. Mr. West's face was as red as a beet when he opened the door."

For some reason, this made Freddie red, too. He toyed with his fork. "Ah, um, that. We were, um, arguing the merits of a Bath chair. I say I'm ready to go out in one. He says I'm not. Hence our contretemps."

Florence offered him a napkin to tuck into his shirt. His embarrassment spoke well for his conscience, but she couldn't drop the matter yet. It wouldn't be fair to Mr. West. "I'm sure Mr. Jenkyns can decide if you're ready to be wheeled around."

"Of course," he said. "Of course."

He lifted a bite of stew, then set it down. His gaze met hers. His arm rose and, with almost alarming tenderness, he cupped her cheek. He murmured her name, his fingertips stroking the edge of her hair. All her affection for him came rushing back. With relief, she knew she did love him. She might not yearn for him as she yearned for Edward, but she loved him in a good, steady way. A way that would last. She smiled at him and covered his hand with her own.

"You're the dearest woman I know," he said. "Even when you're scolding me."

His tone was oddly wistful.

"I've made you sad," she said, "and I don't even know how."

He shook his head. His hand dropped, its warmth fading quickly from her skin. "I'm only sad for you, Florence, for agreeing to marry a ridiculous creature like me."

"You're not ridiculous. Merely a bad invalid. My father was the same. But I shall pay more attention to you now, and make sure your spirits do not sink."

"If only everything were sinking," he said, with a laugh she did not understand.

"I'm sure Mr. West would help cheer you up if you would let him."

He laughed again, a brief, sharp sound. "Mr. West disapproves of too much 'help.' Considers it a betrayal of the family trust. In which belief he is perfectly correct."

Florence expected such acerbity from his brother, but not from him. Before she could ask what he meant, he shook off whatever had troubled him. He took her hand and

Emma Holly

pressed a soft kiss to its palm. Her toes did not curl in her boots, but that was because she was a sensible vicar's daughter, not a headstrong girl of seventeen. She and Freddie would be happy. That was all she needed to know.

Or so she told herself as the darkness inside her grew.

Nigel wasn't in his office. Edward wanted to ask him about the history of some correspondence with the mill, but Freddie must have needed his assistance. He frowned, annoyed that he'd have to put the matter off. Though it probably wasn't urgent, he'd wanted, needed actually, to bury himself in work.

He couldn't stop thinking of Florence. His feelings had escalated beyond control since their talk in the garden. He didn't know why he'd confessed those things about his father. Shock, he supposed, or simply the presence of a sympathetic ear.

Her sympathetic ear.

He'd known she was sweet, but hearing her words—so simple and wise and kind—made his yearning that much worse. He could still feel her small, warm hand against his cheek, the memory of that gentle touch as inflaming as a kiss. She was an ache in his bones, a fierce, impossible desire.

The devil whispered to his conscience. *She cares for you, Edward. You could make her happy; could love her like no other man. Let Freddie fend for himself. Don't you deserve to be selfish just this once?*

Disgusted by his own weakness, he stalked down the hall with a growl. A scullery maid jumped at the sound, nearly dropping the tray she was carrying to the servants' midday meal. He helped her steady it, which made her tremble all the more.

"I am not an ogre," he snapped.

"Of course not, my lord," she said, eyes showing white as she backed away. "Not at all."

Blast, he thought, his fist thumping a doorframe. Nothing brought him ease. He could have taken every woman between Lancashire and London. He could have humped a stone. He could have spilled a river of seed and still come up for more.

The only woman he wanted was her.

He wanted to lock her in his rooms for a fortnight. Wanted to chain her to his bed and slide inside her from dusk till dawn. He wanted her heat, her touch, her gasp when she saw the rigid evidence of his lust. He wanted her silky hair across his chest. He wanted her tender rose-red mouth. He wanted her hips, her breasts. He wanted to wrap his hands around her knees and spread them wide.

He wanted to make her his.

He leaned straight-armed on the wall and hung his head, breathing hard, trying to pull himself together. A line of boots sat inside the room where he'd stopped, clearly awaiting a polish. One of the pairs was smaller than the rest: soft gray kid with matching laces. Before he could stop himself he picked them up. The ankles were soft and supple against his palm. The leather was new yet, the stitching on the toe a series of fancy, twining curls. He ran the tip of his finger over the pattern, knowing the boot belonged to Florence. There wasn't a woman in the house who had a foot as neat. An image formed in his mind, as unstoppable as the tide, of Florence at the dressmaker's, standing barefoot in her chemise and drawers. She'd had such tiny white feet, such adorable toes. Kissable toes. Suckable toes.

The sound of his rumbling groan restored him to his senses. He dropped the boots like a pair of coals. What an arse he was, mooning over a woman's shoes. They'd be carting him off to Bedlam next.

He closed his eyes and clenched his hands. This had to stop. He needed her out of his mind before he lost it. Just an hour, he prayed. Just an hour without this torment. His breath sighed from him as he slowly relaxed his fists. Samson might not know it, but he was about to save his master's life.

The stable was generally clear at midday, while the servants took their meal. Edward was glad for that today. He could saddle Samson as quickly as any groom. Even if he couldn't have, a stretch of solitude was worth the inconvenience. His sex was heavy with longing, his skin a forest of prickling nerves. Mindless, he thought. I need a hard, mindless ride.

Samson whickered at his approach. Regrettably, the big black stallion was not alone.

"Miss Vance," he said.

She turned and smiled—nervously, he thought. He wondered if his temper were that obvious and tried to school his face. She swiped her hand down the outrageous breeches she liked to wear. He would have asked why her maid let her out in that state, except the poor old creature was so nearsighted she probably didn't know.

"Won't you call me Merry?" she said, more serious than was her wont. "I know I'd rather call you Edward."

Since he wasn't sure how to answer this question, he evaded it. "Are you going riding?"

If she was going riding, he wasn't. Edward liked Merry Vance. She was plucky and she amused him, but he wasn't in the mood for her company now: a girl barely out of the schoolroom who didn't know better than to play with fire. Alas, she didn't know better now.

"I'd rather *be* ridden," she said, her voice husky, her freckles lost in a sea of pink. "Maybe you'd care to help me out."

He was not as quick as he should have been. Her words didn't fit together until she stepped to him, wound her arms behind his neck, and pulled his head down for a kiss. His body responded without thought. He was primed for a woman, any woman. His mouth yielded to her pressure. His heart thudded, his cock surged, and before he knew it his shirt was pulled out and pushed up and ten short nails were raking through the hair on his chest.

"Oh," she gasped, pushing back to admire the skin she'd bared. "I knew you'd be like this: too, too perfect for words."

Her head swooped in, catching one of his nipples between her teeth. He yelped. He meant to push her off, but her hands had snaked round his back and were scratching his spine in a manner that made his knees much weaker than he wished. Waves of heat rolled through his body. She was squirming against him like a cat. Her little breasts were soft and bare beneath her cotton shirt. Her nipples were sharp. Her thighs—well, he didn't want to think about her thighs. Those breeches didn't hide the half of what they should.

"Merry," he warned, wondering precisely where it was safe to grab her. "Merry, stop."

"I know I'm not pretty," she said between dangerously descending bites, "or experienced like your usual women, but oh—" Her knees hit the ground as her mouth sucked the skin of his belly. "I'm willing, Edward. Willing to do anything you please."

Her words were whiskey poured on flame. He gasped as her hands found his balls. Where on earth did a girl as young as Merry learn to be so bold? With a muttered curse, he pulled her wrists away. "I said stop, Merry, and I meant it."

Her expression was priceless: part anger, part two-year-old's pout. Any other day, he would have chuckled inside to see it. But she was also hurt, and he knew too well what it was to want what you could not have.

"You like me," she said, stubborn to the last. "I know you do."

"I like you very much, but that doesn't mean I want to sleep with you."

"You want to a little." Hands still trapped, she leaned forward far enough to nudge his erection with her chin.

He rasped out a laugh and moved his hips from harm's way. "Yes, I want you, but you're too young and too well born to be playing this sort of game."

"It's because I'm plain," she huffed. "You're disgusted by the thought of seeing me naked."

"Oh, Lord." Rolling his eyes, he lifted her to her feet. "You're a perfectly nice-looking girl and I'm sure any number of men, myself included, would in many circumstances be delighted to see you without your clothes. How-

ever, I've no intention of paying the price for that delight."
He held up his hand when she started to speak, no doubt
about to swear no one would know but her. "Save that privilege for a man who loves you, Merry. To him you'll be
beautiful. And with him what you're proposing to do will
be beautiful, too."

She made a sound of disgust much truer to her age than
her recent actions. "You sound like my father."

"Good," he said. "I'd much prefer that's how you
thought of me."

Her hands were planted on her hips and her gaze trav-
eled over him from neck to groin. It was an ogle whose
frankness Imogene would have struggled to match. To his
amazement, Edward flushed.

"I could never," she declared, "think of you as my father."

He had to laugh then. Merry Vance wouldn't be a handful; she'd be a plague.

Florence collapsed against the outer wall of the stable
with Nitwit's apple clutched to her heart.

She'd peered in the window to make sure the place was
empty. She preferred giving the mare her treats alone, with
no witnesses to the silly things she said or the kisses she
dropped on her nose. The mare, too, seemed to behave better without an audience, as if she were ashamed to admit
she'd grown to like her awkward rider.

She hadn't expected to see Merry and Edward embrac-
ing, much less in that fashion! Merry had been on her
knees, her arms pushing up Edward's shirt, her mouth nuzzling his belly.

His bare belly.

Muscles had rippled like cobbles at his stomach. Smooth
and powerful, they'd tensed as Merry circled his navel with
her tongue. A line of ink-black hair rose from the curving
indentation, then spread outward over his chest. More muscle swelled there: broad and sun-browned with fans of ten-
don at the side.

And he had nipples. Florence had never thought about men having nipples. Who could have guessed they'd be so fascinating? They were small and coppery and the tips poked through that cloud of hair in tiny rose-kissed peaks.

She pressed the apple to her throat, the tips of her own breasts tightening until they ached. She curled her tongue over her lip. She wanted to kiss his nipples. She wanted to rub her face in his hair. She wanted to run her hands up the long, hard curve of his thighs and cup his secret flesh.

He'd been aroused. His organ had swelled into the space between Merry's chin and neck, distorting the cloth of his trousers just as it had that night at the ball. The light from the stall window had limned the arcing shape. The end was round, ridged at the bottom. Big, she thought, with a deep, hot shudder. Big as a summer pippin. Perhaps it hurt to have one's body part grow so large. His expression might have been pained. His eyes had been closed, his face taut with the longing Merry stirred.

Florence's nails pierced the skin of Nitwit's treat.

The longing Merry stirred.

It was true, then. He did want the duke's daughter. Florence hadn't been special. That night in the Vances' conservatory, when he'd kissed her and changed her life, she'd merely been convenient.

Merry served as easily as she.

Her eyes burned but she did not cry. She pushed away from the stable and walked in stiff, measured steps towards the distant grove. When she'd gotten far enough not to be seen, she ran. When she'd disappeared deep enough into the trees, she stopped. She braced her hands on her knees and panted, her bodice soaked with sweat, her head swimming with exertion.

If she'd been wearing one of her Paris corsets, she'd have fainted. As it was, she had to sit, heedless of the dirt and the bugs and the crackle of last year's leaves. The roots of a gnarled old oak formed the arms of her chair, its trunk her back's support. She shut her eyes and everything she'd seen was there, seared into her memory. With a low cry, she pressed her hands to the damp, hot skin of her face, but even that could not shut the visions out.

Pandora's box had spilled its awful secret.

Bad enough she lusted after the brother of the man she meant to wed. She should have been grateful Merry had made pursuing him impossible.

But she wasn't.

She was sick with envy, sicker than she'd been at the loss of Buttercup. Her stomach was cramped, her throat tight, and her heart ached with the truth she'd feared to face. Her affection for Freddie had not saved her, nor her memory of her father's broken heart, nor the many hurts Edward had inflicted without her having done a thing to earn them. Nothing had saved her. Florence was lost.

Florence was in love with Greystowe's earl.

CHAPTER 10

❧

Mrs. Forster had just helped Freddie with his bed bath. According to the housekeeper, his morning tiff with Nigel had been of a severity to make the steward reluctant to offer aid.

"Grown men," she clucked as she gathered basins and towels. "Tussling like boys."

Freddie had the decency to look abashed. He sat by the window in a purple throne-backed chair, perhaps an indication that he had won the morning's fight. One leg of his silk pyjamas was slit to make room for his cast. A fine lawn shirt hung open at his chest. It was a nice chest, every bit as nice as Edward's. It was paler and not as broad but it had just as many muscles.

When Mrs. Forster saw who'd come in, she moved to button Freddie up.

"Oh, leave it," he said with a languid wave. "It's warm today and it's only Florence. I doubt my betrothed will faint at the sight of my manly glory."

The housekeeper muttered about "modern morals," but Florence could tell she wasn't truly angry. Freddie's voice stopped her at the door.

"Thank you, Mrs. Forster," he said, gentle and serious. "You've been an angel."

Mrs. Forster had saved her parting shot. "Guess I won't faint at the sight of your manly glory, either."

Freddie grinned at her broad, departing bustle, then offered his hand to Florence. "Good morning, sweetheart. To what do I owe this honor? I thought you'd be at your lessons."

Florence obeyed his urging to perch on the arm of his chair. Unwilling to meet his eyes, she stared at his chest where his breastbone divided two smooth curves of muscle. "Merry is gone. She and her maid left at dawn. I think she and Edward had a disagreement."

"Not over you, surely?"

"No," Florence conceded, but couldn't bring herself to explain. She could still see Edward's strained expression as Merry's mouth teased his belly; could still feel the emotions that stormed inside her when Lizzie broke the news. Merry was gone. She had tried to seduce the earl and the earl had sent her away. For too many reasons to count Florence should have been sorry to see her go. To her dismay, she was exultant. None of which she was about to tell Freddie.

Good-natured as ever, he stroked her cheek with the back of his fingers. "Very well. Never mind telling me why. I can guess. Edward must be kicking himself for not discouraging her sooner. I'm sure he didn't enjoy disappointing you."

"I . . . I'm all right," she said, and deliberately trailed her hand down his resting arm.

Freddie inhaled sharply in surprise. Their eyes met. His were wary, but he masked his caution with a smile. "What is it, Florence? What's troubling you?"

She played with the edge of the cotton that draped his chest. "Would you mind if I kissed you, Freddie?"

His jaw dropped. "Of . . . of course not, sweetheart. But—"

She leaned in before he could blather about innocence and honor and what her father would think if he knew. He fell silent as she braced her hand on the violet seatback beside his head. The fabric brought out the blue in his eyes, eyes as lovely as any she'd ever seen. His face was a pleasing arrangement of strong, smooth bones, his lips well cut and sensitive, his brows perfect winging arches. He was more than handsome: he was as comely as a poet's knight.

"Florence," he whispered as his golden lashes drifted down. Gathering her courage, she pressed her lips to his.

His mouth was soft. Remembering Edward, remembering Merry, she touched its seam with the tip of her tongue. Thankfully, Freddie guessed what she was about. He sighed and opened for her and met her wet, gentle stroke with his own. He knew this game better than she did. She was happy to let him take the lead. His arms gathered her closer, turned her, and pulled her onto his lap. Her breasts rested on his chest, her bottom on the top of his thighs. Despite his cast, she fit easily against him.

His kiss was delicate; careful, as if the least bit of force might break her. An angel might have been rocking her in warmth and kindness. The turmoil she'd felt when kissing Edward was absent, but so was the excitement. Nonetheless, the feelings Freddie stirred were pleasant. Her body relaxed as his fingers trailed down her neck, playing over her collarbones in long figure eights, as if he relished the texture of her skin.

Heartened by her progress, she slipped her fingers under the open edge of his shirt. When she brushed her thumb over the point of his nipple, he stiffened and pulled back. His face showed none of the tautness she'd seen in Edward's, only a brotherly sort of calm. Apparently, she did not have Merry's skill at rousing men.

"I'm sorry," she said, hanging her head. "I know I'm not good at this."

He smiled at her, pulled her hand from his chest, and kissed its knuckles. She felt uncomfortably like a child who was being humored.

"You did nothing wrong. But I think these are not matters we should rush. A woman's honor, once lost, can never be regained. What would your father think?"

"I knew you'd say that."

"You see? You don't feel comfortable, either." He

stroked her hair with a warm cupped hand. "Don't be glum, sweetheart. Five months is not so long to wait."

Not for him, perhaps. But a lot could happen in five months. Rather than say so, she snuggled closer. Her movements seemed not to affect him. His manly part did not rise, nor did his heart beat wildly in his chest. Freddie remained what he'd always been: a perfect gentleman.

She wondered what he'd do if he knew his betrothed was not a perfect lady.

Aunt Hypatia's invitation could not have come at a better time. Florence was desperate for distraction from her failure to seduce her fiancé, if only the distraction of a visit to one of the duchess's childhood friends. Oddly enough, the impending reunion seemed to make the duchess nervous. She fidgeted with her skirts and gloves, then draped her lace-ruffled elbow over the side of the open carriage. Her sigh was soft but audible.

"Is something wrong?" Florence asked.

Aunt Hypatia drummed her fingers on the victoria's curving door. "Just an old woman's memories. When you're my age I suspect you, too, will have the dubious pleasure of seeing the changes time can inflict on those one cares for."

"You're not old," Florence assured her.

Aunt Hypatia laughed, a soft, dry echo of her eldest nephew. "It's not the years, my dear. It's the bruises. But the friends of our childhood are the friends we treasure most. They're our link to the past. No one knows us so well or forgives us so much."

With those provocative words, the carriage pulled into a narrow, rutted lane. Low stone walls girded the road, along with pretty two-storied houses. The one at which they stopped stood out from the others by its fresh-scrubbed air. Half-timbered, with a clean thatch roof, it was not much larger than the vicarage in which Florence had grown up. A small garden surrounded the white limed walls. The gravel path to the door was perfectly straight, as were the low, blooming flowerbeds. Marigolds marched like soldiers down its length, in alternating stripes of orange and gold. The compulsively tidy display made Florence smile.

To her surprise, Aunt Hypatia touched her sleeve to stay her.

"Sit for a moment, dear. I believe I should tell you something of the woman you're about to meet. Catherine and I were girls together. Very dear friends. I have never known a creature so loyal, nor so protective of those she loves."

"But?" Florence prompted when the duchess paused.

"But she was disappointed young, by a man, as it happens. It has made her bitter and perhaps a trifle strange. I know you will not judge her. You're a kindly soul. But it might be best if you did not speak too much of your engagement to Freddie, even if she asks. She worries that other women will make the same mistake she did."

"I shall guard my words," Florence promised, her heart going out to this woman she'd never met. How easily might she step into those painful shoes herself! With more than her usual care, she helped the duchess from the carriage. She was the loyal one, Florence thought, to remain this true to a childhood friend.

A servant in brown twill and apron answered their rap on the door. She was as plain a woman as Florence had ever seen: young, but as stolid as a dockworker. Her eyes were dull in her weary face, her arms thick with muscle. Considering Aunt Hypatia's warning, Florence wondered if she'd been hired for her lack of male-attracting traits.

Inside the little house, the comical tidiness of the garden turned oppressive. The servant, probably a maid-of-all-work like Lizzie had been, led them to a small front parlor. The furniture was spotless and plain and completely unwelcoming, in the style of the days before the queen. Modern taste appeared only in the profusion of gewgaws that covered the polished surfaces of the room. The effect would have been friendly but for the regimental precision with which each item had been aligned. The candlesticks and doilies, the gilt-framed photographs and ceramic memento art seemed an army against the forces of disorder. Even the sunbeams that poured through the broad bow window could not diminish the effect of rigidly imposed control.

Interestingly enough, upon entering, their hostess strode briskly to the window and closed the drapes. "The carpets," she murmured over her shoulder, a gentle, mournful scold.

The hulking servant hung her head. "Sorry, ma'am. I thought your guests might like the light."

Her employer's sad little smile did not alter. Since she wasn't looking at them, Florence studied her with interest. Her figure was not as trim as Aunt Hypatia's, but it had not thickened much. Her hair retained a touch of blonde among its gray and her face, now seamed with age, must once have been very pretty. Her features still conveyed a sense of delicacy, like a fine bisque doll. Her house dress, neither fashionable nor noticeably the opposite, was of well-pressed and slightly faded black silk, as if she'd spent much of her life as a widow.

Hypatia's description of her as a woman disappointed by love hadn't struck her as widowlike. Could losing one's spouse to an early death sour one on the institution of marriage? Her father hadn't been that way, but perhaps Florence hadn't seen enough of life to know the forms that grief could take.

She composed herself on the hard green sofa, expecting the duchess's friend to turn and greet them. The woman, however, was not yet finished with her servant.

"Bertha," she said in a voice even softer than before. "Was that the butcher's boy I saw hanging about the back door this morning?"

A dull flush crept up the lowered face. "Jeb was only dropping off the meat."

"You know how I feel about my servants having followers."

"Yes, ma'am. I wouldn't do that to you. Not never."

By this time, Florence was feeling sorry for the embarrassed girl. When her eyes darted towards her mistress's guests, Florence offered a tiny smile. If the maid saw it, it did not abate her misery. "Shall I bring the tea now, ma'am?"

Their hostess patted the slump of the maid's big shoulder. "You know I'm only thinking of you, Bertha. A woman can so easily be led astray."

"Yes, ma'am. The tea?"

"Of course, Bertha. And use the tongs to arrange the cakes. You know I can't abide finger marks." With that, their hostess finally turned. Her smile was lovely; peaceful even, like a nun who had spent her life in prayer. Florence found herself warming to her, despite her peculiar treatment of her servant. She rose from the couch and offered as graceful a curtsey as she could. The woman seemed to appreciate the effort. Her smile curled more deeply into her cheeks.

"You must be Florence Fairleigh. Hypatia has written me of your many virtues. I am Catherine Exeter, the Honorable Miss Exeter until my father died. But that is ancient history. I hope you will call me Catherine, as my dear old friend Hypatia does. From all she has said, I feel as if I know you already."

"It . . . it would be my honor," Florence stammered, darting a startled look at Aunt Hypatia. Just how much had the duchess told her friend? She felt distinctly off balance as she settled back into her seat.

"You're engaged to Freddie Burbrooke, are you not?" Catherine asked, perching like a bird on the edge of a delicate green and white chair. Her demeanor spoke only of interest, polite but genuine.

"Yes," Florence answered, fighting her impulse to turn to the duchess for guidance. She knew she must not appear overly enthusiastic. "I think we shall suit. He is a kind man."

"I'm certain he seems so," Catherine said. "But a woman can never be too careful. The kindest face can hide a heart of stone, especially when that face belongs to a Burbrooke."

This extraordinary speech robbed Florence of hers.

"Catherine," said the duchess in almost as gentle a scold as her friend's.

As if it were a joke, Catherine released a musical laugh,

one that must have charmed her suitors when she was young. "You're right, of course. I must not forget that nest of vipers is your family." Her eyes sparkled with humor as she patted the arm of the couch beside Hypatia. "The Burbrookes brought me you. For that I will always give thanks."

"We can both give thanks," said Hypatia, answering Catherine's smile with one of her own. "Now tell me, old friend, what gossip have I missed since I last stopped at Greystowe?"

The pair had much to catch up on and Florence was happy to relinquish the burden of conversation. Their speech was filled with exclamations like "no" and "indeed, it's true" and "who'd have thought she'd do such a thing?" Florence could tell they were enjoying themselves. As soon as the tea and cakes were comfortably dispersed, she rose to wander the room, taking care not to brush its ornaments.

A lovely fruitwood spinet sat in the farthest corner, with an old Church of England hymn spread open on its stand. She was tempted to sit and play, despite her indifferent skill. Instead, she touched the ornate silver frame of the single photograph on its top. An elegant young woman in rich modern dress gazed serenely out at Florence. The resemblance between her and Catherine Exeter was striking. She had the same sleek fair hair, the same doll-like perfection to her face. The photographer had captured not only her beauty but her confidence. Here was a female secure in her womanly charms. If Catherine Exeter had looked like this when she was young, Florence had a hard time imagining the man who could disappoint her.

"Ah," said Catherine now, "I see you've found the picture of my niece. Pretty, isn't she?"

"Beautiful," Florence agreed.

Her hostess crossed the threadbare carpet to stand behind her. With the tip of her finger, she made an infinitesimal adjustment to the picture Florence had just released. "She writes me every week, you know. Keeps me apprised of the doings of society. Foolishness, most of it. But my Imogene is a sensible girl. Married as well as a woman can, with her head and not her heart. Her husband gives her everything she wants."

"How . . . fortunate," Florence said, not sure how to respond. Despite her words, Catherine Exeter was frowning, as if the beautiful image did not completely satisfy.

"Yes," she said musingly, her lips turned down. "Fortunate. Keeps him wrapped around her finger. Only safe place for a man. My Imogene would never be so foolish as to fall for a Burbrooke."

Florence squinted at her hostess, perplexed by the strangeness of her tone. She seemed to be trying to convince herself of something she knew to be untrue. And what grievance could she have against the Burbrookes? Twice now she had mentioned them disparagingly.

"Catherine," Hypatia warned, but this time her friend did not let the dangerous topic drop.

"No, Hypatia," she said, her eyes remaining on Florence. "The girl has a right to know what she's getting into. Oh, I don't say Freddie is the worst of the Greystowe males. I leave that honor to his brother. But the blood is bad. It chills their hearts and forks their tongues. No one can hold them, neither with beauty nor with charm. By all means, take what you need from them, but do not give them your trust; do not give them your love. If you do, you'll spend your life ruing the day."

Florence's heart beat unevenly in her throat. The woman's claims struck a chord she could not silence. She had given Edward her love and she did indeed rue the day. And Freddie—could he be cold? Was that why he didn't respond to her kisses? But no. She shook herself free of her fear. Freddie liked her; that could not be feigned. As for Edward, if he broke her heart, it would be her fault, not his. He had never promised her anything. He might be moody and brusque, but she'd wager her soul that he was honest.

"I'm sure you must be mistaken," she said, somewhat breathless beneath the intensity of Catherine's gaze. "Edward and . . . and Freddie are very good men."

"The best," Hypatia seconded. She had risen as well and

now laid a soothing hand on Catherine's back. "Neither of them are anything like their father."

Catherine gave a little shudder before her expression cleared.

"Perhaps," she said. "But you must promise me"—she captured Florence's hands—"should they ever hurt you, should you ever need help, you'll do me the honor of turning to me."

Florence hadn't the faintest notion what to say. Luckily, Aunt Hypatia loosened Catherine's grip on her hands. "I'm sure that won't be necessary," she said. "My goddaughter is a sensible girl."

Her friend blinked. "Good. Good. I am gratified to hear it. But should you need me do not hesitate to ask."

The duchess stroked the back of Catherine's neck where it rose above the ruffled black silk of her collar. It was, for her, a gesture of uncommon tenderness. "Perhaps we should be going, my dear. We don't wish to overstay our welcome."

"Never," said her friend with a warm, staunch smile. "You are always welcome here. But I know you must have other calls. Letty Cowles will never forgive me if I keep you to myself. She has two new grandchildren, you know. Boys."

Hypatia's laugh was comfortable. "Indeed, we must not rob her of her chance to crow."

The two women clasped shoulders and exchanged affectionate kisses. Florence could see the shadow of their youth in their smiles; the ease of their lifelong friendship. Abruptly, she regretted the departure of Merry Vance. Would she ever be known by anyone as Catherine and Hypatia knew each other: her flaws forgiven, her foibles understood?

She waited until the coachman flicked the reins across the horses' backs to ask the question that had been pressing on her mind. "Catherine is the woman Edward's father jilted, isn't she?"

"Yes," Hypatia admitted, twisting her palm over the head of her ivory cane. "Just one of his many sins. The odd thing is, I think Stephen truly loved her. He always treated Edward's mother coolly, as if it were her fault she'd been born the daughter of a duke. Poor thing never knew what she'd done wrong. Always fluttering about trying to make it up to him."

Florence shivered in spite of the heat. She prayed she'd never know that kind of pain.

Edward could tell Florence wasn't well. Off her feed, Jenkyns would have said. She didn't ride, didn't laugh, didn't sneak off to the kennel to spoil the dogs. Without a hint of her old anxiety, she followed the duchess on her round of local calls, taking tea with the old ladies as if life held nothing more interesting than grandchildren's antics or the beadle's wife trying to pretend a ten-year-old dress was new. They even went to visit that loony old bat, Catherine Exeter, the one whose door the boys in the village made a dare of touching. Considering her history, Edward knew he ought to make allowances, but she had once pelted three-year-old Freddie with a brace of windfall apples. Called him a spawn of the devil, simply because he'd tumbled over her wall during a game of hide-and-seek. She'd apologized later, and their mother had accepted, but Edward had never been able to forgive her. He didn't care how many socks she knitted for the poor or what a God-fearing Christian she was.

If Florence could visit a woman like that without complaint, there was definitely something wrong.

Even Aunt Hypatia noted her loss of verve.

"Missing your friend?" she probed one night at dinner. "It's a shame she had to leave, but Edward could take over your lessons."

Florence shook her head. "I'm just a bit homesick. Your friends remind me of the ladies I knew in Keswick."

"Hmpf," said Aunt Hypatia.

Edward longed to echo her skepticism. A bit of homesickness didn't put circles under a girl's eyes or cause her to pick at her food like a bird. He couldn't remember the last time Florence had looked directly at him. As uncomfortable as that intimacy could be, he found he missed it. And what did she mean by shaking her head at the suggestion that he help her with her horsemanship? He knew such an arrangement was inadvisable, but that she would dismiss it out of hand pricked him like a nettle. Irritating chit. Did she think he'd sent Merry Vance away to spite her?

His fingers tightened on the stem of his wineglass. Given his behavior in the past, she might believe just that.

"You'll ride with me tomorrow," he announced. "You mustn't forget what you've learned."

She shot him a startled look, her eyes like polished beryl in the rain. He'd forgotten what her gaze could do to him, how it seemed to reach inside and tug directly on his groin. Beneath the shadows of the table, he felt himself start to fill. The head of his cock stretched down his trouser leg. A tide of heat that had nothing to do with the Mulligatawny soup rose threateningly up his neck. He looked away before it could reach his face.

"If you truly wish it," she said, quiet and deferential, "I'd be happy to ride with you."

The deference broke his temper.

"If I didn't wish it, I wouldn't have asked," he snapped.

His aunt lifted her brows but Edward ignored their unspoken question. He'd be damned if he'd explain himself. After a moment, the duchess returned her attention to the curried broth.

"Good," she said her voice both mild and dry. "We wouldn't want Freddie's intended growing bored."

Edward refused to consider what he was doing, though he suspected his restless night had been due to dreams of having Florence to himself. He ignored the quickening of his pulse as he boosted her into the saddle. Nothing was going to happen today. Nothing. This prickle of excitement he felt was mere wishful thinking. But the wishes grew deeper as he noted how flatteringly she had dressed. She wore the same form-fitting blue habit that had dried his throat in

London, the one that made her breast look provokingly like a pigeon's and her waist a circle a man could span in his hands. Her boots were black and laced to the bottom of her calves. He tried not to hold them any longer than it took to place her left foot in the stirrup.

He couldn't say if he was grateful or annoyed that she did not speak except to thank him.

Clicking Samson to a trot, he headed for the northern border of the estate, to the ruins of the original Greystowe Hall. Under the depredations of the eleventh earl, their land had shrunk to a few surrounding acres. When Edward's grandfather restored the family fortunes and rebuilt, he'd raided the tumbled fortress for its stone. Now only its outlines could be seen between the weeds. Edward's father had brought him here many times. *This is the fruit of demon drink,* he'd say. *Succumb to liquor and games of chance and your destruction will be as sure.*

His father would have shuddered to know how romantic young Edward found the site. Oh, the earl's lessons had found their mark but, to Edward, this was a place where fairies might dance or dragons breathe their last breath. No doubt he shouldn't have brought Florence to a spot so meaningful to him, or so isolated, but at present he found it difficult to be sensible.

"My," she marveled in her soft, country voice, "what a wonderful place. I can just picture you and Freddie here, having imaginary sword fights with a pair of sticks."

"Broom handles," he confessed, and swung off his blowing horse. Many women would have dismissed the ruin as a useless pile of rocks. He was gratified by her reaction. He would admit it, he decided. He would enjoy it. This day was a harmless pleasure. For once he would not spoil the delight of her company with thoughts of all he must not do. When he helped her down from Nitwit, he allowed himself to relish the brief, gloved clasp of her hands. His body was alive in every cell, pulsing, humming. The air was sweeter, the ground springier.

He only wished Florence could share a portion of his joy.

She followed his lead as they walked the horses side by side along the old foundation. She'd kept up with him on the ride. He'd barely had to hold Samson back. He wondered if he ought to compliment her on her skill, but that seemed too great a divulgence. No doubt Merry had told her how much she had improved. No doubt she knew it herself.

They stopped before a long vista: checkerboard fields and sheep pasture and, in the misty, rolling distance, the first blue rise of the Peaks. Edward removed the horses' bridles. Samson wouldn't wander far and Nitwit would not leave him. The stallion was the master of the stable, certainly the master of the mares. Like two old friends, the horses began tearing grass from the same patch of ground. Florence watched them bump shoulders as if her thoughts were far away, her expression not so much sad as blank. Consequences be damned, Edward thought. He couldn't stand to see her spirits quashed.

"Won't you tell me what's wrong?" he said. "I know more has been bothering you than missing home."

If his concern surprised her, she did not show it. Instead, she fixed him with as level a gaze as he'd ever seen her use. Florence tended to wear her emotions on her sleeve, but he could not read them now.

"I've been wondering about women," she said. "Women's feelings."

Edward coughed, not sure he was prepared to discover where this led. "Women's feelings?"

"Yes." She folded her hands over her waist, the pose perversely prim. "I've been wondering if they are supposed to have the same needs that men do, or if such feelings are exclusive to the male sex."

The flush Edward had managed to avoid the night before blazed like fire across his skin. Of all the things to ask him! He didn't want to think what had inspired the question, but he could not ignore it, not when it so plainly distressed her. Lord, though—what had she and Freddie been getting up to? Stalling for time, he raked his hair back with his hand.

"Of course women have feelings," he said. "I can't

swear they're the same as men's, but from the evidence I've seen, they're very similar."

Florence's eyes did not leave his. "And they were ordinary, decent women who provided this evidence? Not—" She waved her arm, reluctant to give a name to women who were otherwise.

This sign of her old diffidence reassured him. He put his hand to her shoulder. "Yes. Ordinary, decent women. Well born. Gently bred. Neither depraved in spirit nor sick in their minds. I assure you, it's quite natural for a woman to feel physical desire."

She pressed her lips together and her gaze evaded his. From chin to brow, her face was as pink as a budded rose.

"Florence." Giving in to temptation, he stroked the velvet warmth of her cheek. The sensation made him want to cry with pleasure, but he did nothing to intensify the caress. He gentled his voice. That was his caress. That was the secret expression of his love. "Has someone been telling you decent women don't feel desire?"

She shook her head, quick and definite, but he wasn't sure he believed her. He'd seen tracts himself, written by doctors, claiming that well-bred ladies did not like the marriage bed.

"It's perfectly natural," he repeated. "What's more, a woman is entitled to the same pleasure as a man in the act of love."

The color in her cheeks heightened from rose to scarlet. For a moment, she did nothing but bite her bottom lip. Then her eyes lifted again to his, bravely, determinedly, but with such uncertainty he wished he had the right to embrace her.

"I'm afraid I don't know what you mean," she said. "Oh, not about the act of love. I grew up in the country, after all. But the other, the pleasure part. I don't—I'm not certain I understand."

Edward's groan would have tumbled a few more stones if he'd dared let it out. Any other woman he would have sent to her fiancé. Such matters were best sorted out between man and wife. Unfortunately, Florence's fiancé was Freddie. For all his brother's popularity with the fairer sex, his actual experience with women was a mystery Edward didn't care to plumb. Would Freddie know how to answer Florence's question? Would he wish to if he could? Edward didn't want to think his brother too selfish to enlighten his betrothed, but he was forced to acknowledge he might be too embarrassed.

Oh, Lord, he thought, I shouldn't do this. I shouldn't even consider it.

But it was more than possible he'd be doing Freddie a favor. Freddie cared for Florence. If she came to her conjugal bed with a few hints as to what went on, her wedding night might not be the catastrophe Edward feared. Moreover, Florence deserved to know the answer.

Sighing, he pulled her trembling form against his chest. The way she snuggled against him, trusting and soft, made him want to hold her there forever.

"I'll show you," he said, his throat tight. "But only so you'll know and only if you promise this stays between us."

At last, he had succeeded in shocking her. She tipped her head back to see his face, her eyes round, her rosy mouth agape. "You'll show me?"

He could not help himself. He had wanted her too long, with more than his body, with more even than his heart. She called to the part of him that could not change, that would love her forever, no matter what life brought them both. With a groan of agonized pleasure, he dipped his head and kissed her.

She did not resist. Indeed, she seemed to melt against him: her mouth, her body, all her softness pressing the parts of him that needed pressing most. The unexpected capitulation drove everything but hunger from his mind. He couldn't remember the difference between what he'd intended and what he hadn't. He could only want; could only seize the moment and hold it tight.

He gripped her bottom and lifted her into his groin. The added pressure made his erection throb intensely enough to hurt. He drove deep into her mouth, needing to taste, to claim, to assuage every instant of longing since he'd held her last. When he suckled her tongue she made a sound like a startled dove. His head spun. She was holding him. Her arms clung to his back, her hands to his shoulders. He wanted to rip off her gloves and bite the tips of her fingers. He wanted to toss her habit over her head and sink forever into her sex. Instead, he hugged her so fiercely she gasped.

He could not bring himself to release her mouth, not even to apologize for being rough. Impatient beyond bearing, and knowing they could not stand here in the open, he swept her off her feet and carried her like a child to the half-ruined hulk of the old hearth.

"Wh-what are you doing?" she said as he set her down. Blood burned in her cheeks, in her bee-stung lips. Her hair had fallen, a shining chestnut gleam across her heaving breasts. Her eyes blazed with wants he doubted she could have named. She looked a perfect wanton. An innocent wanton.

He could not answer her question. He didn't know what he was doing. Instead, he kissed her again, deeply, working his mouth into hers until she moaned and went limp. Only his weight held her up against the chimney, his knees bent to align their heights, his hips grinding slowly over hers. His cock was so hard, so sensitive, he seemed to feel each fold of cloth between them. Florence felt it, too: the pressure of his rigid penis against her mons. The flesh between her legs was very warm. It would be wet, he thought. It would be weeping now for him.

With a groan, he burrowed harder. Her nails pricked his nape. Something shifted inside him, dark and forbidden. He pulled her arms away and pressed them, wide and straight, to the sun-warmed stones above her head. He held her wrists as if his hands were shackles, as if she were the prisoner of his desires. The image whipped him like a lash. His body clamored for him to take her, here, like this, until this terrible desire was sated.

"What are you doing?" she said again, tremulous, her breath panting against his jaw.

He eased his head away, still holding her by the wrists. When he spoke, he scarcely recognized his voice. "I'm showing you."

"Sh-showing me?"

"What desire is."

"But—" She bit her lower lip, swollen now from his kisses. "I already know that."

He could have cried from the bolt of lust that speared his loins. He had to ease his hips away from hers for fear of spilling like the greenest boy. He did not, however, give her a chance to escape. Not that she showed any signs of wanting to. Despite her obvious misgivings, she remained as he'd positioned her: her thighs slightly spread, her arms lifted obediently above her head. Her submission, even her fear, was an aphrodisiac he was reluctant to acknowledge. But he could not deny its allure, nor pull himself away. The best he could do was try to gentle the harshness of his voice.

"Desire comes first," he said, the words hoarser than he wished. "Then pleasure. One builds on the other. Depends on the other." He released one wrist to cup the heated fullness of her breast. Its nipple pressed discernibly through her bodice. He turned his palm and it hardened even more. "Do you feel it? The ache of wanting? In your breasts? Between your legs?"

She nodded, shakily, and he kissed her in reward; kissed her until his head pounded in time with his cock, until his passion burst from his chest in a primitive, animal growl. He kneaded her breast, pinching the sensitive tip, raking the swollen areola with his nails. She began to squirm against the trap of his body, not to get away but to get more. He knew how she felt; oh, did he know. He lowered his head to her breast and bit its peak.

"Edward," she gasped, pushing weakly at his shoulders. "I think I understand this part well enough."

He lifted his head to meet her eyes. He could barely catch his breath. "I'll need to touch you to show you what pleasure is. I'll need to put my fingers between your legs and stroke your little pussy."

"M-my pussy?"

In spite of himself, he smiled. What an innocent she was. He nipped the curve of her chin. "I could call it your love garden, if you prefer. Or Cupid's alley. Or perhaps your buttered crumpet?" She pleased him with a giggle. "In any case, you'll know what it is soon enough . . . if you choose to let me go on."

She thought for a moment, then squared her shoulders. "I do. I do choose to let you."

His tension sighed from him. What a brave little darling she was, what a sweet, untouched, juicy plum. He played his lips over hers, letting their breath mingle in increasingly urgent gusts, letting her taste just the tip of his tongue. When she whimpered, he gave her more. When she moaned, he gave her all. Her fears thus distracted, he gathered up her skirts, slowly, taking the petticoats, too, warming her thinly clad legs with his own. When the mass of cloth reached her waist, she broke free of the kiss.

"Shall I hold my skirts?" she whispered.

"Yes," he said, just as softly. "I may want both my hands."

"If you do, you'll have to let go of my other wrist."

He laughed without sound. Even now, Florence could be practical. He pulled her still trapped hand to his mouth. Sweeping his tongue under the edge of her glove, he bit the plump flesh beneath her thumb. When she shuddered, his body did as well, hardening until the pain of wanting her stung in his eyes like tears. When he released her, his hand shook as badly as hers. Gritting his teeth, he took one step back to look at what he'd bared. Her legs, covered by the fine, lacy drawers, were as long and curvy as he remembered, her hands small against the bundle of sea-struck blue. Her boots—he shut his eyes at a spasm of longing—clung to her ankles with loverlike devotion. He hadn't planned on going to his knees, but his legs would not hold him. He fell and she drew a startled breath. A second later his hands wrapped the ankle of her shoes.

"Oh," she said as his fingers kneaded the bone beneath the kid. "Oh, my."

He smiled when he saw her toes curl, then slid his hands higher. She was sensitive, his Florence: a well-tuned violin. He pressed his temple to her hip and blew softly through the lawn that covered her mons. Her shiver delighted him more than another's full-fledged moan.

"Just a little more," he said, drawing a teasing circle on her calf. "Just a little further and you'll know."

Her thighs trembled when he stroked them. He could scent her now, musky and sweet. Heart pounding, he nuzzled the open slit of her drawers. His hands followed, parting the sheer cotton, finding the crisp, tightly gathered curls. She tensed but did not move away. He sensed her waiting with bated breath. He combed her thatch to pet her mound. How wonderful were these secrets, and what a marvel that she would share them with him! Gently, he rubbed the tender cushion, gently, until the soothing strokes convinced her to relax. Then he drew one thumb, light as goosedown, over the shy, warm furrow of her lips. Tense or no, she was wet. Moisture painted his skin and hers, rich and fragrant and slick. That he had the power to call it from her both humbled and aroused.

"This is your pussy," he said, low and husky. "This and the secrets that lay within. I'd like to touch them if you'd let me. I'd like to show you the magic they can do."

"This is the pleasure part?"

He smiled and kissed her tangled curls. "Yes. This is the pleasure part." Hearing no protest, he parted her with his thumbs, rubbing into and up her folds. Her skin was sleek as satin here, oiled with desire. She jumped when he brushed her clitoris. Smiling again, he pressed it lightly, the pad of each thumb compressing either side. This time his reward was a violent shiver. She dropped one hand over his as if to stop him, then just as nervously withdrew.

"Are you sure this is where you're supposed to be?" she asked.

"I'm sure," he laughed, and squeezed more firmly. This time she moaned. "This is the secret to a woman's pleasure. This little pink bud of flesh."

"But it feels so strange. It—oh!" she gasped as his mouth covered the bundle of nerves. Her hips canted forward, innocently eager. Edward's blood roared in his ears. He hadn't known he was going to do this until he did. She tasted of the sea, of spice and heaven. His tongue stroked. His lips suckled. His fingers spread and rubbed her plumping sex.

"Oh," she cried, her head falling back against the ruined wall. "It almost hurts."

He did not heed the words, only the tone, only the hand that fluttered to his hair to press him closer. He drove her up the slope to climax, savoring every gasp of surprise, every moan of longing. He craved her pleasure as a starving man craves food. This was Florence. This was the woman he loved. He used everything his lovers had taught him: when to push, when to tease, when to murmur things he wished to do. Most of all, he listened to her body. Her tremors told him what she liked, the tensing of her thighs, her ever-tightening grip on his head. For that, no other woman could guide him. This act was for her alone. When she died the little death, his soul exulted at her cry. He slid the tip of his finger into her passage, feeling the contractions at her barrier as his mouth swept her over once again. He didn't need to do this. He'd shown her what he promised. But he couldn't let her go. This was all he would have of her. This first knowledge of her body. This first introduction to her bliss.

He wanted to make it as memorable as he could.

At the fifth orgasm, her knees gave way. She fell against him, taking him by surprise and tumbling them both to the grass. His body surged at the pleasant shock of her weight, remembering all at once that it had needs as powerful as hers.

More powerful, he thought, fighting an urge to do more than run his hands down the length of her back. Unlike her, he'd tasted the joys his cock could know. He knew what it was to slide into a woman's warmth when he was hard enough to scream.

Of course, he'd never known what it was to do it with a heart wound tight by love.

He'd thought she would lay there. He'd thought he would hold her as she calmed. Apparently, Florence did not wish to calm. She squirmed up his body and mouthed the bend of his jaw. Her lips brushed a runaway pulse.

"Show me," she said. "Show me how I can pleasure you."

It was a demand he dared not meet. He made a noise, a low, threatening rumble in his chest.

"Show me," she insisted, her hair hanging round them in a lemon-scented fall.

He didn't know how it had happened, but her wrists were in his hands again. He had manacled them; stretched them out from her sides. He knew he ought to release her. He knew, but he could not. His legs were splayed beneath her. Her thighs lay over his sex. He wanted to imprison them as well, to make his legs a second trap.

"Don't ask that of me," he said through gritted teeth.

She kissed his mouth, a girlish press with an intoxicating hint of tongue. "It's only fair, Edward."

The way she said his name undid him: low and throbbing, as if it held a meaning for her heart. He rolled her beneath him, pressing her into the ground with his greater size and weight. Now he had her. Now she could not get away. He cupped her head between his hands and fed his passion through their mouths.

"Oh," she moaned, gasping for air. "It hurts again."

He nearly came. He had to lift his hips and when he did her hand slipped into the space between them. Before he could stop her, she cupped his straining sex. His body flinched, a great, nerve-jolting shock. He could not speak for the effort it took to hold his climax back. Sweat broke out all over his body.

"Does it hurt for you?" she whispered, gently rubbing him up and down. "Does it hurt when you get big like this?"

"Take it out," he rasped. "Jesus-Mary. Open my trousers and take it out."

But he did it before she could, fumbling with the fastenings, nearly ripping his crumpled linen. His cock fell into her hand as if it knew its rightful home. He was thick, hot, pulsing with ungovernable desire. She clasped him lightly. Her hand was damp and warm and so small her fingers barely met around his shaft.

"Florence," he groaned, muscles jumping uncontrollably in his thighs. She was killing him with that light, curious grasp, sliding over him from balls to crown. The caress was almost too much but he was dying for more. She seemed to sense it. She held him harder. She squeezed him in her tender hand and pushed her tightened fist along his length.

The top of his head seemed to lift from his skull. Pressure built in his groin, swelling in his stones, in his shaft. Instinct took over. He cursed, thrust his hand inside her drawers to clear his path. He pushed forward. His crest touched her parted lips. She was at his mercy and he was huge. Desperate. A single stroke from coming. He groaned and squeezed his tip inside her. Nerves fired and screamed. She was wet. Hot. For him. The earth seemed to tremble at her body's silken clasp.

"Edward," she gasped.

There was fear in the sound. He hovered, trembling, yearning to break the fragile barrier and make her his. She would accept him, he knew. Her fluid heat told him that. He wanted to show her the joy men and women could share more than he wanted his next breath. But he could not do it. He could not soil his brother's bride. Not even out of love.

With a tortured groan, he tore himself away. He wrapped his arms around his shins and pressed his forehead to his knees. Only by holding himself could he keep from taking her where she lay. He cursed until he thought he must be frightening her.

She was slower to sit up. When she did she laid her hand on the back of his head.

"Go," he said, stiffening under the touch. "Go now before I hurt you."

No doubt he had already. No doubt the words were bad enough. She pulled away and rose. Heart aching, he listened to her shaking down her skirts. For a moment she stood at his side. She did not argue, merely brushed his hair behind his ear, the gesture sweeter than he deserved. He thought she would speak then, but she walked away in silence and left him to his regrets.

• • •

Ohgod, ohgod, thought Florence, the refrain uncontrollable. She had to pull Nitwit up before she reached the house, so shattered were her nerves. She straightened her hair as well as she could, securing it with what pins she could find among the strands. Her lips burned from Edward's kisses, her breasts from his touch. Indeed, her whole body seemed to vibrate with the pleasure he had shown her.

And when she'd touched him—

His blood had drummed beneath his skin. His organ had lengthened and swelled. And he'd pressed its silken head against her flesh as if it would die without a home.

She cupped the place he'd put his mouth. Her pussy, he'd called it. It was still warm, still pulsing and liquid, as if pleasure were a sound that could echo down the years.

Oh, God, what had she done? Certainly nothing a respectable fiancée should do.

The thought chilled her. Was she wrong to marry Freddie when she had these feelings for his brother and not for him? But Freddie didn't seem to want a wife who had those feelings. No matter what Edward said about them being normal, surely Freddie was a better guide to what a gentlewoman ought to be?

Overcome by confusion, she clutched her hands before her mouth. Her body and, yes, her heart had felt righter with Edward than they ever had before. Which didn't mean she ought to listen to them. Edward didn't offer her safety or affection or anything like a future. Edward only offered heartache. Even if, by some miracle, he were to think of her as a wife, he couldn't be what she needed in a husband, what she'd known she needed since the time she'd found her big, jovial father weeping over a pair of her mother's gloves.

Freddie was what she needed: Freddie's friendship, Freddie's quiet, steady love. He would never break her heart; would never leave her bereft of all that made life worthwhile. And she could be what he needed. She knew she could.

She only had to push these feelings for his brother from her soul.

CHAPTER 11

"*You're treating her* like a nun," Edward said.

Propped against a mound of pillows in his bed, Freddie was trying to scratch beneath his bandages with a billiard cue. On the table beside him two novels lay open, along with a deck of playing cards, a decanter of port, a half-written letter, and a slowly bruising bowl of fruit. Edward recognized the signs of boredom but was not inclined to sympathize. Bored or not, Freddie had responsibilities. Edward intended to see that he upheld them.

If some of his anger was self-directed, that did not lessen Freddie's obligation.

Seemingly unimpressed by Edward's outrage, Freddie squinted at his sibling. "Did Florence tell you she felt like a nun?"

"Never mind what she told me. It's got to stop."

Freddie set down the stick. "Does it, now?"

"Yes, damn it!"

"You know, Edward"—Freddie cocked his head—"when you get angry, there's a big blue vein that ticks at the side of your neck."

Edward swore, then shoved his hands into his pockets. He could feel the vein ticking himself. "You need to take this seriously, Freddie. Florence is a grown woman.

Healthy. Affectionate. With all that implies. She has a right
to be treated with a certain warmth."

"If I understand what you mean by 'a certain warmth,'
I'd rather not."

Edward blinked. "You'd rather not."

Freddie swung his legs over the side of his bed, grimacing when the injured limb took a moment to settle comfortably. "I'd rather not push Florence into a physical
relationship. I want her to be able to back out of this wedding if she changes her mind."

Edward was so overcome with objections he pressed his
fist to the furrow above his brows. If Freddie didn't do
something about Florence, Edward doubted he'd survive
the summer with his sanity intact. Seeing her was too
painful: knowing she had needs Freddie wasn't satisfying,
needs Edward would be all too happy to satisfy himself. At
least once they were married, his oversight would not be
necessary. He could leave the newlyweds to themselves.

He was still shaking his head when Freddie hobbled over
to take his arm. "I can't force her. It wouldn't be fair."

"Nobody's talking about force. Florence is fond of you,
as I assume you are of her. She doesn't disgust you, does
she?"

Freddie looked away. "Of course she doesn't."

"Are you reluctant because you think she'll make you
miserable?"

"No one could think that."

"Then do it, Freddie. Treat her like a woman. You have
to face it someday. You'd like children, wouldn't you?"

"You know I would." Freddie's voice was rough. He
drew a ragged breath and let it out. "Very well. I'll do it. I'll
treat her . . . warmly. But I won't compromise her virtue.
You mustn't ask that."

"I don't," Edward said, his stomach tightening in con-
tradiction to his relief. This was good. Freddie was agreeing. "Just stop treating her like a brother."

"I shall be a perfect Casanova." Freddie's face twisted.
He turned his back. "You can leave now. You've made your
point—though I doubt it's what you really want."

This last was muttered so far beneath Freddie's breath Edward wasn't certain he'd heard. Doubt stopped him at the door. "Of course it's what I want. Your happiness is important to me."

"And hers?"

"And hers," Edward agreed, forcing a lightness he did not feel.

Freddie said nothing to that, simply stood in a shaft of sun, balanced on his one sound leg. A breeze fluttered his shirt around his broad rower's back. Despite his injury, he looked strong: a graceful young man in his prime. His head, however, was bowed in defeat.

Edward gritted his teeth. This arrangement was best for all of them. He could not allow himself to doubt it. Whatever value he personally put on the pleasures of the flesh, by most people's standards, Freddie would make the better husband. Without even straining, Edward could name half a dozen women who'd jump at the chance to marry him, no matter that he was the younger son. Attentive, amusing, even-tempered, were it not for the unfortunate propensities of his past, Freddie would be a paragon. Once he gave Florence's charms a chance to act on him, Edward was certain those other needs would fade. Freddie had no reason to act defeated; this match was the saving of all their dreams.

All their dreams but his.

The thought slipped past his defenses like a thief. Sternly, grimly, he paid it no mind. The earl of Greystowe could not afford to be chasing dreams.

Freddie invited her to dine in the orangery, saying they were due a nice evening alone. Florence was both glad and anxious at the prospect. She welcomed the chance to prove she could put her feelings for Edward behind her, but her guilt interfered with her intention to focus on her betrothed. She'd never done anything as terrible as what she'd done with Edward in the ruins, much less tried to keep it a secret. Her father always said a marriage could not be founded on a lie, but he'd also said one should consider how deeply a truth would wound. If Freddie knew this particular truth, would it shatter his love for his brother? And if it did, what would that do to Edward? Did Freddie have to be told if she promised in her heart it would never happen again?

She could not sort out the right of it, no matter how she tried, and Freddie's arrival did not help. Considering his stated purpose, his mood was decidedly odd. He sniped at Nigel as the steward wheeled him into the small conservatory. The argument was nothing new, but the genuine edge to his anger was. As always, Nigel bore it stoically, wishing Florence a pleasant evening as he withdrew.

"Freddie—" Florence began to chide.

Freddie grimaced, then swatted the air in front of his face as if that would disperse his temper. "I know. I'm a beast. But from now on, I'll behave."

"You always behave with me."

"At least there's that. Ah, sweetheart. Let's forget how we've begun and try to enjoy the night." He surveyed the cloth-covered table that sat among the fruiting trees. A trio of candles scattered light off the crystal and plate, while a centerpiece of deep pink peonies added their perfume to the citrus-scented air. Freddie touched a waxen petal. "How prettily Mrs. Forster has arranged this. We shall dine as if we lived in the land of faerie."

"It was Lizzie," Florence said. "My maid. I'm afraid she has a romantic streak."

Freddie smiled. "Nothing wrong with romance. I could do with more of it myself."

But the meal was not romantic at all. Silence reigned over the lobster bisque and stretched through the pigeon pie. Freddie rallied over the lemon sorbet, sharing an amusing anecdote about a friend who accidentally locked himself in his father's icehouse.

"He was a good fellow," he finished with a wistful sigh. "Had his second child last year."

Florence patted his hand. "You'll be a good father."

Her claim seemed to disturb him. He rubbed a spot between his brows. Behind him, the orangery's glass was a mist-sheened mirror. Darkness had fallen while they ate.

The night hummed with insects, as nights must have hummed since the dawn of time. Florence had the sudden, strange sensation that she and Freddie were alone in all the world. She could not hear the life of Greystowe from where she sat: the hiss of the gaslights, the servants' footsteps going to and fro. Only the crickets kept them company.

Their imaginary solitude weighed on her with a portent she did not understand.

Would she feel this way when they were married? Would she be lonely then, too? Disconcerted, she watched Freddie and his reflection turn a silver spoon through the remains of his melted ice.

"You look tired," she said. "Shall I call Nigel to wheel you back to your room?"

"No!" he said, more sharply than she'd expected. He seemed to hear the sharpness, too, and regret it. "Forgive me, Florence. I didn't mean for our dinner to turn out like this. I meant—" He made a face in which she could decipher only frustration. "I meant something quite different, but it seems I cannot do what I intended."

He wrapped his hands around the edge of the table, fingers on the top, thumbs on the bottom. The pose was that of a man bracing for trouble, and Florence found herself bracing, too.

"Florence," he began. "I've been thinking about yesterday. About our kiss."

Dread fluttered in her breast. Was he angry? Would he berate her for what she'd done?

"I know I shouldn't have been so forward," she said to the napkin in her lap. "I promise it won't happen again."

Freddie touched the side of her lowered head. "Don't apologize. What you did wasn't wrong. Not for a couple who care about each other, who are engaged."

"Then what have I done to upset you?" She did not plan for the question to be a cry, but it came out as it would. "If you'd only tell me, I would stop."

"Oh, Florence." He cupped her chin to press a gentle kiss to her trembling lips. "You are too good, my dear. That's why I have to tell you this."

"Tell me what?"

"That you must not expect— That I'm not—" He filled his lungs with air and began again. "I'm not a greatly physical man. Please believe me when I say I care for you, even love you, and wish you all the happiness in the world. But if what you want from marriage is a close physical relationship, I fear you're doomed to disappointment with me. I fear you'd be better crying off."

Florence felt as if he'd struck her. He wanted her to cry off? To give up everything she'd dreamed of? A home, a family, a little security and a good, kind man to share it with? To be rejected by Edward was one thing. For that she blamed her own stupidity. But to be hurt here, where she'd believed herself safe, where she'd laid her modest hopes in perfect confidence that they'd be met was something she'd never prepared for. Her mind could not encompass her shock, not to mention her shame. Again. Again she was cast aside.

It must be a punishment for what she'd done. She'd made her vow to be true to him too late. Her napkin fell to the floor as she pushed stiffly to her feet. "You don't want to marry me."

"No." He caught her hands and squeezed. "That's not what I meant at all. I'd be honored to marry you. You've no idea how deeply I value your affection. But I've been thinking, perhaps, you should not want to marry me."

Her blood was ice, her eyes searing hot. She knew he was being kind. It was his way: a gentleman to the last. She did not deserve to marry a man like him.

"If you wish it," she said, blinking back tears, "I shall release you from your promise."

Instead, he released her hands. "It's not what *I* wish, Florence."

She could not bear his gentle lies. "Please leave," she said with what dignity she could pull around her. "I wish to be alone."

"Are you sure, sweetheart? I could—"

"Please," she repeated, cutting him off.

She barely noticed the trouble it caused him to turn the

chair. It was an unwieldy thing, meant to be pushed by another. With an effort, he forced the contraption across the
threshold. "I'll speak to you in the morning. Please, Florence, don't decide anything without me."

She nodded, unable to trust her voice.

She did not cry until the crickets drowned out his
wheels.

Edward remained in the library long after his interest in
its contents had palled. His private suite was in the family
wing and the passage outside it led directly past the orangery. He hadn't wanted to hear Freddie and Florence, nor
remind them of his existence. As a result, here he stayed, a
specter by the high French windows, nursing his second
glass of brandy for the night.

He'd ordered the servants not to linger near the courting
pair.

Stomach knotting, he turned his head towards the spot
where the glassed-in structure angled into his line of sight.
He could distinguish nothing through the foliage but a faint
candle glow. They'd been in there an hour. Was Freddie
kissing her? Whispering sweet nothings in her ear? To be
sure, Edward ought to hope he was. He ought to hope Freddie had swept her completely off her feet.

Needless to say, he did not.

He finished his brandy in a single swallow, then glanced
behind him at the long, book-lined room. He could pace as
he'd done earlier. Past the herbals and the Greeks. Up
around the gallery and down the spiral stair. He could glare
at the busts of Plato and Pliny that dignified the doorway to
the drawing room. He could even flip through the duchess's
silly Gothic novels and give himself a laugh.

He did none of these things. Fool that he was, he stood,
nose virtually pressed to glass, watching a distant, flickering glow that told him absolutely nothing, yet managed to
torture him all the same.

Suddenly he straightened, every muscle tensing to alert.

The outer door to the orangery had opened. A figure was emerging. It was Florence. She was alone.

Anyone else would have thought she was taking a meditative stroll. Her pace was measured. Her skirts swept negligently behind her on the grass. Only eyes sharpened by love could perceive the stiffness in her steps, as if a puppet were being tugged by unkind strings.

When she dragged her sleeve across her eyes, he knew she had been crying.

He did not stop to think, not even to wonder what his brother had done. He flung through the French door and across the columned portico. When he gained the lawn, he peered wildly past the reach of the gaslight. She was moving towards the front of the house, towards the lake.

Shorter of breath than his brief exertions should have made him, he hastened in her wake. She was walking faster now. She'd gotten farther ahead of him than he liked. He was aware, in the dimmer recesses of his mind, that he was being ridiculous. A weeping woman didn't necessarily want or need rescuing, nor would many have chosen his services if they'd shared Florence's experience of him. But he couldn't take the chance that she might want his comfort and he wouldn't be there to give it. He had to be there if she needed him. Had to.

He slowed as he saw her step onto the footbridge that connected to lakeshore to the island. His neck tightened. Where was she going? What did she intend? Surely she wouldn't throw herself off the bridge. Whatever had happened couldn't be as bad as that. In spite of this logic, his shoulders did not relax until she crossed the midpoint of the arch. One of the slumbering swans ruffled its wings in complaint. Cursing too quietly to be heard, Edward followed.

He almost lost her on the other side. She must have had the eyes of a cat. If he hadn't been so familiar with the island's paths, he would have missed his way. As it was, twice he had to strain his ears for the drag of her skirt on the gravel before he knew which turn she'd taken. The beeches began to close in, tall dark shapes in the country night. Florence never faltered. He realized she was heading for the summer house, as if drawn there by a beacon he could not see.

Now more curious than alarmed, he drew to the side of the path as she tried the handle of the heavy Moorish door. It didn't budge. She tried again, then pounded the wood beneath the fanciful crescent of glass. This failing to achieve any effect, she slid sobbing to the stoop. That was more than enough to make Edward admit to his presence.

He stepped out of the shadows. Florence didn't seem at all surprised to see him.

"It's locked," she accused, as angry as a thwarted child.

"It's not locked. It's heavy. And the hinges are probably stuck."

"Well, open it, damn you." The curse sounded comical on her lips and he struggled not to smile. She'd pushed to her feet and was loudly sniffing back tears. Edward wondered if she were going to hit him the way she had that night before the Vances' ball. She certainly looked tempted.

So much for offering comfort, he thought, but did as she asked—though he had to brace his foot on the wall and heave. Finally, with a loud squeal of protest, the stubborn door gave way.

A cloud of dust set them both to coughing. This building had been his and Freddie's grandfather's retreat from family life and their father's after him. It was a place of illicit rendezvous, a smoking room, a bastion of male vices. Edward and Freddie had played Crusades in it when they were young, but that had been long ago. Thankfully, a flint and taper still lay on the shelf inside the door. Edward lit the candle, then made a circuit of the large round room.

The oil in the sconces smelled stale, but burned well enough. Soon a buttery glow lit heaps of satin cushions and silk wool carpets and twisted Oriental columns. No thicker than a man's arm, and ornamented with flowers that never grew, the cast-iron pillars had been painted to resemble stone. Low octagonal tables with mirrors set into their wood spoke of meals served lounging on the floor. A greasy hookah sat atop one, its hose wrapped like a sleeping snake around the cylinder of glass. The colors of the room were rich and dark. Sapphire. Crimson. The green of shadowed pine. Dust cloaked the decadent display, dimming the exotic wood and furring the polished green stone that peeped between the rugs. The dust did not, however, inhibit the rounding of Florence's eyes.

Mouth open, cheeks stained with drying tears, she gaped at the filigreed arch above her head. He could almost see visions of harems running through her mind. Before they could run through his, he cleared his throat. "Might I ask why you were so determined to get in here?"

She turned to finger a musty crimson drape. He suspected she was embarrassed. "I suppose I thought I'd spend the night here."

"Because—?"

"Don't take that tone with me," she said, her anger tinged with fatigue, "as if I were a child sniveling over a broken doll."

He couldn't answer at first. He was too taken by the sight of her in his father's old trysting place, her profile glowing in the lamplight, her figure enough to fuel the dreams of a dozen generations. He felt oddly close to her, despite his obviously having put his foot in it.

I even relish her rebukes, he thought, a laugh for his foolishness caught in his throat.

"Forgive me," he said, all humor hidden. "I didn't mean to belittle your troubles. Please tell me what's wrong. Did Freddie do something to offend you?"

The nearest sconce lit the involuntary pursing of her lips. "Freddie doesn't want to marry me."

The answer caught him by surprise. He took a step closer. "He couldn't have said that. He wouldn't."

"Of course he wouldn't. What he actually said was I shouldn't want to marry him. 'Doomed to disappointment' was how he put it." She turned to face him, her back pressing the velvet drapery to the wall. As if her confession refreshed her horror, she covered her face with her hands. A moment later, she dropped them in resignation.

"I don't know what I shall do," she said. "I'd hoped . . . too much, clearly. I'm sinking in debt. I can't afford to hunt another husband, even supposing anyone would want discarded goods. I suppose I can find some sort of position, but that begs the question of what to do for Lizzie." Her lower lip trembled and she caught it in her teeth. "She's been so pleased, Edward. Since Freddie proposed, she's begun to believe she'll have a happy life."

A single tear spilled down her dove-soft cheek. Edward found this more wrenching than a storm of sobs. He knew it was Florence who'd begun to hope for a happy life. Without stopping to count the cost, he opened his arms.

"Come here," he said. As if she'd been waiting a lifetime for the offer, she ran to him with a hiccuping little cry. Her arms clung tightly to his back. Her body shook but it was warm. She fit the harbor of his chest as if God had made her for his hold. Happier than he had any right to be, he rubbed his cheek against her hair. "You'll work it out. I know Freddie didn't mean what you believe."

"He did," she insisted, her face pressed to the front of his shirt. "I know he did. He didn't want me, either. When I kissed him, he—well, let's just say he wasn't looking forward to having me in his bed. Oh, blast it anyway!"

With a furious shove, she pushed back from his hold. "What's wrong with me?" she demanded, arms flung wide to indicate her person. "What fatal flaw do the Greystowe men find so repulsive? Am I too fat? Too thin? Or perhaps my character's too dull? It can't be my boldness because I'm not very and, in any case, you liked when Merry Vance was bold. By God, you even gave her my horse!"

Edward had to smile at this. That had bothered her, had it? Seeing the smile, Florence crossed her arms and looked as dangerous as a peach-sweet vicar's daughter could. He knew it was time to smooth her ruffled pride. "I didn't give her your horse; I allowed her to ride it. Mostly because she assumed I intended to, and I could not for the life of me explain why I'd made such an extravagant purchase for my brother's fiancée."

This, at last, was the right thing to say. Florence hung her head and scuffed her slipper through the dust. "You truly did buy Buttercup for me?"

"Yes, I truly did."

"And you hung that painting in my room, the one you knew I loved."

"Yes."

"I suppose you really aren't an ogre." Her head ducked lower, muffling the admission. "I suppose I'll miss you, too."

She was crying again. His own eyes stung as he folded her against him. No doubt it was reckless, but he didn't care. "Hush." He pressed his lips to her hair. "No one's going to miss anyone. You're going to marry Freddie and stay right here."

She shook her head against his dampened shirt. "I can't make him marry me. Not if he doesn't want to."

"I'm sure he wants to." Of their own will, his lips found the baby-smooth skin of her temple. Florence's arms clutched his back.

"He doesn't. You liked kissing me better than he did."

"I'm sure that's not true," he murmured, though he wasn't certain what he denied. His mouth had drifted to the tender pink lobe of her ear. He tried to convince himself not to bite it.

"It is true," she insisted. "I know he's a gentleman, Edward, but could something be wrong with Freddie?"

That focused his attention. He straightened and drew back in their embrace. "There's nothing wrong with Freddie. Absolutely nothing."

"Then it has to be me. I'm not woman enough to make him want me."

"Oh, Lord," Edward groaned. "You're woman enough and then some."

She narrowed her eyes. "You didn't want me. Not at the very end."

"I wanted you. Just as I've wanted you since we met."

"But you stopped!"

"And nearly killed myself in the process." He pulled her hips to his, to the shocking thrust of his arousal. "Feel that, Florence. Feel how hard I am. How long and thick. You do that to me. Just by breathing. Just by slipping into my mind.

I'm a bloody stag in rut, sweetheart, so don't you tell me you're not woman enough."

A new flush joined the blotches from her tears. The tip of her nose was pink and her lashes stuck together. Even so, he thought her the most delectable creature he'd ever seen. Her hips wriggled in his hold, a devastating little squirm. If she needed further proof of his claims, she certainly got it. His cock leapt like a spawning salmon and his breath rushed from his lungs. His fingers tightened on her bottom, whether to stop her movement or squeeze her closer he couldn't have said. Whatever his intent, she stilled at the increasingly forceful pulsing of his sex. Her gaze met his.

"I want to know," she said, the words all breath and fire. "I know it's wrong of me, but it can't hurt Freddie now. If I'm not going to have a husband, I want to know how it feels to be desired."

For a moment, she thought he would faint. The color drained from his face and he closed his eyes. When he opened them, their blue blazed like flame. She expected an argument, or a polite evasion such as Freddie had offered. Instead he stared at her, blinked, then crashed his mouth down over hers.

After that, it was her turn to feel weak.

"Oh, Florence," he said between deep, devouring kisses. "Don't make me do this."

But she couldn't think of one good reason to stop him. She'd lost everything: her dreams, her future, even her reputation would be ruined when the news of her broken engagement spread. Why shouldn't she, just once, reach for what she truly wanted? Not that she could have stopped Edward. His embrace overwhelmed her, not merely his strength or his size but the blatant ownership of his touch. His hands slid over her, squeezing, rubbing, as if every inch of her were his to claim. He gave no thought to what might embarrass her. He touched her everywhere he wished.

With a low groan, he lifted her off her feet and pressed her back to the wall. Her legs had no place to go but around his waist. He pushed his body between them, eager to rub the hardest part of him against the neediest part of her.

"Wait," she said when he finally let her draw breath.

Panting hard, he dropped his forehead to hers. "Forgive me. I shouldn't have moved so quickly. Or been so rough."

He had misunderstood her. Ignoring the apology, she found the pearl studs that fastened his shirtfront and began to slip them through their holes. His breathing changed course. "What," he asked, "are you doing?"

"I'm touching you the way you wouldn't let me before. I need proof of what I do to you. I need it in my hands."

"You need proof?" The question was strangled. She nodded shyly and hoped he wouldn't stop her. He shuddered. "Proof." He allowed her legs to slide down his sides. He took one step back from her, then another, and then his hands took over the task of divesting his clothes. "Allow me," he said, low and strained.

With a curse of impatience, he shrugged off his satin waistcoat.

Anticipation curled through her like the smoke that hookah must have trailed so long ago. She felt as if more than his body were about to be unveiled. His eyes glittered in the lamplight, color staining his cheeks, brightening his full seducer's lips. He looked beautiful and strange, the victim of a thrall: her thrall. She had asked and he complied. Under his big, capable hands, his shirtfront parted over his chest. He pulled the crisp white garment over his head, his muscles shifting under smooth, sun-browned skin. Her breath seemed trapped in her throat. His shoulders were broad, his nipples two sharp-tipped bronze coins. His build was half laborer, half marble David. But he was so much more exciting than a statue. The sheer cloud of sable hair that trailed invitingly down his center, the warmth of his skin, the way his ribs expanded with his breaths made her feel as if she'd give her very soul to touch his flesh.

"More?" he asked, his fingers resting lightly at the top of his trousers. The swell beneath made a prisoner of her gaze. It was a living, pulsing thing: the object of her unending fascination.

. And he obviously feared she might not want to see it.

"Please," she said, the word choked. "May I do it? I've

been wanting to touch you ever since I lost my nerve at the Vances' ball."

His laugh was half gasp. "And here I was thinking I'd scared the wits out of you."

"No," she murmured. "Not even when I wished you would."

His arms fell to his sides. She reached. Stepped closer. How extraordinary it was to know that all this time they'd been thinking of each other, and that he, too, had desired her touch. His belly moved in and out as she struggled with the metal clasp. The buttons were easier. The pressure behind them nearly pushed them free. Mindful of his rigidly swollen organ, she eased his linens around its jut. His head dropped back as she pulled the gathered cloth to his ankles. Her fingers brushed the hair on his legs, a prickle of goosebumps sweeping in their wake.

"Florence," he moaned, the sound beating like his heart.

She looked up at him from the floor: at his hairy chest and his beautiful limbs, at his towering maleness and the odd little sack that dangled underneath. It had pulled up higher than before and she wondered what that meant. He was watching her reaction now, his gaze searingly intense. Despite the attention, she could not drag her eyes from the part of him that was so changed, so gloriously upright. She remembered how smooth it had felt and yet the veins that twined its pulsing girth did not look smooth at all. Its head reared almost to his waist, seeming to loom in threat above her, as if angry at her presumption.

"What do I call it?" she whispered.

"This?" He gripped the column in his fist, pulling slowly towards the gleaming crimson tip. The flesh that sheathed it moved, looser than she'd expected. Her body jumped inside as if his hand were touching her. His longest finger curled over the tiny slit. "This is my penis. My cock."

"Cock," she whispered, trying the hard, crisp word. The thing leapt as if it recognized its name. Her hand ventured towards the hanging sack. "And this?"

"Ballocks," he said, and released his grip.

She scooted closer, steadying her balance by holding his

knees. She was not going to let fear get the better of her tonight. "May I kiss them? May I kiss all of you as you kissed me?"

For the space of a breath, he did not answer. She feared she had once again overstepped the bounds of what was done. Then his fingertip stroked gently down her cheek. "You may kiss whatever you like. I said you could have proof."

But she did not kiss him first. First she simply pressed her face to his groin, turning her cheeks back and forth, taking his textures through her skin, his scent, his vital, leaping pulse. He sighed at the slow, catlike caress, then tensed when her tongue came out to taste.

"Yes," he gasped. "Lick me. Lick me as if I were sweet."

"You are sweet." She found a spot that made him shiver. "And big."

He lengthened at the words, noticeably, as if the claim were darkly magic.

"Not too big," he whispered. "Not too."

His words tempted her to laugh. He wanted to be big. He liked that she thought he was. She knew this with an instinct that was born into her sex. The bigger the sword, the more powerful the man who wielded it. The more powerful the man, the safer the people he loved.

"I don't know." She touched the strange papery skin of his sack. "I think perhaps I ought to be afraid."

He could only gasp at that because she'd slid her mouth around the ripe, ruddy head. It was sweet, and smooth, the smoothest of all. She curled her tongue over the satiny curve and sucked, a peculiarly childish delight. The little slit was interesting, too. He had touched it himself and she thought it must feel good. When she tried it, he moaned, pain and pleasure mixing in the sound. His hips flexed and the hot blunt tip strove against the pressure of her tongue. Faintly, deliciously, she tasted salt.

His fingers tangled in her hair, then lifted her away.

"Enough." He pulled her to her feet. "You don't know what you're doing."

For an instant, his words stung. "Then teach me," she said.

But he kissed her instead, a slow, thorough plunder. Her knees failed and she was carried, floating really, to be set on a soft pile of pillows that smelled of old perfume. Her clothes peeled away beneath his expert hands: dress, petticoats, corset. She was embarrassed to be so bare before his eyes, as if he'd stripped away her armor.

"No," he said when she tried to cover her secrets. "Don't deny me the pleasure you wanted for yourself."

He certainly seemed to like her naked body. His hands slid over her, his mouth. The tips of her breasts earned kisses that made her moan. When he saw the marks left by her stays, he rubbed them until the red began to fade.

But he did not remove her boots.

"Are you afraid to see my naked feet?" she teased, her confidence restored by his admiration.

"Perhaps," he said, with a small, shuttered smile.

The shock as he pressed their naked fronts together drove the question from her mind.

"Oh," she said, squirming rapturously against him. "Oh, my!"

He laughed, then growled against her neck. "You were made for this, Florence. Made for love."

She liked the sound of that: made for love. Grinning back, she craned upward for his kiss. Her joy was all the giddier for having begun in pain. She gave herself over to it, over to him, as if she'd never in her life known fear.

"Sweetness," he murmured, sensing her surrender.

He slipped his hand down her belly and through her curls, then moaned at the heat that greeted his caress. Clearly seeking more, his fingers slid between her folds. She felt the delightful ache she'd known before and writhed beneath him, wanting what she knew he could give, thrusting with her hips when she could no longer be still.

This time he watched her climb until she had to close her eyes.

"Yes," he praised, rough and heated by her ear. "Come for me, sweetness, come."

The pleasure broke more sharply than before. She cried out at the startling liquid tremor, and again when his fingers worked her harder still. Lovely wavelets rolled over one another, ebbing and building, lapping deep inside her core. When he finally let her go she was boneless, heated through and through with satiation. As if it were a dream, she felt him stretch against her side. His arm jerked quickly, wildly, until he gasped and stiffened and a burst of something warm splashed her hip.

He sighed heavily when the wetness finished spurting, like a man who'd set down a burden.

He spilled his seed, she thought. He brought himself to pleasure with his fist. She touched the sweaty arm he'd draped across her waist.

"Why did you do that?" she asked. "Why didn't you let me?"

Still breathing hard, he nuzzled the crook of her neck. "I'm sorry, Florence. I wasn't sure you'd want to and I couldn't wait. Watching you was too much. I had to come."

"Then you'll have to teach me to do it quicker."

He rose over her on his elbow. Crinkles spread out from his smiling eyes, warm and reassuring, as if he saw every insecurity she'd tried to hide behind her matter-of-fact tone.

"No," he said, his lips whispering incitingly over hers. "I want you to do it slow."

He showed her how, his organ beginning to grow as soon as he wrapped her fingers around it. He showed her the places he liked to be touched: how a lick of the tongue made her palm slide more deliciously; how his cock rooted deep inside him and could be rubbed behind his sack; how a gentle squeeze at the proper moment left him gasping with delight.

She did all he showed her and gloried in his groans. They excited her more than she could have dreamed: the wild chuffing of his breath, the tight, pained twist of his face as he tried to make the pleasure last. The climactic burst of seed was a revelation, not its quantity so much as the suddenness of its appearance. What a marvel men were. She did not protest when he pressed his mouth between her legs, though her nakedness made the act stranger than before, and the climb to pleasure tired her so greatly she could not stay awake.

"Sweet as honey," she heard him murmur as she drifted off. He held her to his warmth, his arms wrapped protectively around her back. In spite of all she'd been through, she slept as peacefully as a child.

He held her as she slept, his heart slowing, his body blissfully at ease, his mind held from the press of reality by force of will. One night, he thought, one night until the dawn. Then he would do what he must. Then he would return her to his brother. He knew it was wrong, maybe even impossible, for this night to be forgotten. But what choice did he have? Marry Florence himself and abandon Freddie to the wolves? The lure of doing precisely that was almost stronger than he could stand. But even if marrying him might make Florence happier, that path was primarily selfish: abominably selfish, in fact. How could he live with himself, knowing he'd destroyed his brother's last chance to be saved?

He could still make this work. He could. None of them would have precisely what they wished, but neither would any of them be ruined. And in the meantime, he would have his night.

What could one night matter when the damage already was done?

Done but not compounded, said his conscience.

He ignored the nagging voice, easing out from under his love to find the bath. He would not regret this night no matter what.

He pushed aside three dusty velvet curtains before he found the hidden door. The marble floor was cool beneath his feet as he looked around, taking in the memories. It was a rich room, shining with Moorish tile and gilt, the crowning luxury of the pavilion. Spiders scuttled in the plunge bath, but water still flowed from the taps. He did his business quickly, splashed his face, then hesitated as his gaze struck an Indian prayer cabinet. The wood was covered in statuettes, each carved to represent the positions of love. Some were only possible for contortionists. Others he and Florence had done tonight. He and Freddie had sniggered over this cabinet when they were boys, but now Edward remembered what it contained: velvet ties, rolls of long velvet ties.

He glanced over his shoulder to the room where Florence slept. He'd said he wanted memories. Why not a memory of the fantasy that had been haunting him since that day at the ruins? He opened the cabinet's folding door. Inside, beneath a smiling cedar Buddha, was a chest he'd never seen. The baroque French coffer was gold, encrusted with ornamental flowers. It was locked, but the key lay beside it. Curious, he opened the lid.

The contents included a collection of brittle letters, the packets bound with red satin cords. Next to these lay a chased gold locket, big enough to fill his palm. Opening it gave him a start. The portrait inside was the spitting image of Imogene Hargreave. For a moment, he suspected someone of playing a nasty joke. Then he realized the picture couldn't be Imogene. For one thing, the clothes were too old-fashioned. The subject's flaxen hair was scraped close to her head, then coaxed into shining coils. Though the face was familiar, the eyes were different from Imogene's: softer, easier to hurt.

How peculiar, he thought, shaken by the coincidence. He teased one yellowed letter from its stack. He opened the final flap. "Yours forever, Catherine," said the girlish signature.

Catherine, he mouthed, his mind working out the puzzle. The writer could only be Catherine Exeter. The letters were not old enough to be his grandfather's and if his father had courted any other Catherine, the people of Greystowe would have known. Old gossip died hard in a town like this.

But what should he make of her curious resemblance to Imogene? They must be related. That was the only reasonable explanation. Perhaps Catherine Exeter was the aunt Imogene spoke of, the one who had warned her about his cold heart. His mouth twisted in a humorless smile. He could guess what Catherine Exeter had to say about Greystowe men. If that bitter old crone were any indication of how Imogene would age, he was lucky to be quit of her.

He didn't feel lucky, though. He felt as if a goose had walked across his grave. The chill trickled unpleasantly down his spine. Maybe he had more in common with his father than he'd thought.

No. He pushed the possibility away. He was his own man with his own sins, one of whom was curled in sleep on a mound of satin pillows. He should not waste this night in dwelling on someone else's dusty past. The present was all that mattered, the present and the memories it could bring. He reached for a more familiar item, a roll of night-black velvet. When he undid the circling ribbon, eight soft quilted ties unfurled across his palm. His breathing quickened. Should he do this? Would Florence mind? Would she even know she ought to?

He didn't think she would and that aroused him most of all. With no mother to guide her, and no married friend her age, she was a stranger to the shapes love could take. She would not know what was ordinary and what was not. Her questions about women's "feelings" had proved that.

But would she enjoy being made his prisoner?

He closed his eyes, picturing the stark black ties against her blushing skin. He could make her enjoy it. If he were gentle and reassuring. If he showed her there was nothing to fear.

He laughed ironically through his nose. Nothing to fear but the overflowing passions of his heart. He was the one who should have been afraid. If she trusted him enough to allow this, he knew it would mark him forever hers.

She woke to a sense of something out of place. Someone . . . someone was kissing her naked feet. She curled her toes against the tickling mouth and smiled without opening her eyes.

"Florence," said a low, beloved voice. "Wake up and see

how beautiful you are, how every part of you is a dream of what a woman should be." The voice drew nearer and the heat of a large male body hovered over her where she lay. "You are my dream of what a woman should be, love, my dream of beauty."

She opened her eyes and thought all the beauty his. His face was close, his cheeks flushed with what she'd come to recognize as desire. His blue eyes burned in their satiny fringe of black. His lips were a curve of heaven. She did not mark his glowering brows or the harshness of his jaw. His haughty nose was perfect. Her love, it seemed, had turned all his flaws to virtues.

"I'm glad I please you," she said, her cheeks heating at the admission. "You are the first man I ever wanted to admire me."

"The first, eh?" He hid a boyish smile by trailing kisses up the stretch of her arm. "I hope you're still pleased when you realize what I've done."

"What you've done?" She tried to sit up and look around, but her arms would not leave their place. They were fastened by the wrist to a pair of columns, spread outward like an X . Her legs were tied as well, not to anything but to each other, at ankle and at knee. The ties did not hurt but they were strong. Goodness, how could she have slept through such an alteration?

"Why have you done this?" she asked, abruptly feeling panicked. "Why am I tied?"

"Hush," he said. He laid one hand atop her breast, cupping it in his warmth. "I will not hurt you."

The way he bit his lip belied his sureness. His eyes, always proud and stern, pleaded for acceptance, but acceptance of what, she didn't know.

"Why?" she said, even as she calmed beneath his touch.

"Because I wish it. Because I have dreamed of doing it. Because"—his finger trailed down the midline of her belly—"because it will make me feel safer."

She had to smile at this admission. "How could I frighten you?"

He lowered his face and rubbed it slowly against her

own. The scrape of his whiskers made her shiver. "You threaten my control, Florence. When you touch me, you push me to the edge. I could love you as I pleased if I knew you would not tempt me past what can be done." His mouth opened near the bend of her jaw, his breath beating warmth against her neck, his tongue slipping out to test her pulse.

" 'What can be done?' " she repeated.

His lips whispered over her brow. "There are limits. Things we must not do. But if you let me love you this once, this way, we will share every drop of pleasure we can know."

What limits? she wanted to cry. What things? But something stopped her, a quiver of superstition. She was the princess in the ogre's castle, free to open any door but one. If she made her prince explain, would she break the magic spell?

"You truly wish this?" she said, nodding at the ties.

He pulled back and straddled her waist on his knees. The long shadow of his sex flickered against his stomach. It seemed immense in the lamplight, almost grotesque, and yet she found it as beautiful as the rest of him. Too big to hold. Too perfect not to. His palms rubbed up and down his muscled thighs, itching perhaps to touch her. His gaze slid from her left wrist to her right, lingering on the velvet ties. His chest rose and fell as if the mere sight of her bonds excited him. When his eyes met hers, they gleamed like jewels, the pupils huge but steady.

"I wish this more than you could know," he said.

"Then I'm sure I shall enjoy it."

He smiled with a fondness that warmed her heart. "I'll do my utmost not to make you a liar."

"See that you do," she teased.

He laughed and pulled her to her velvet-bound knees.

He had not lied. His kisses were different now, freer, lusher, as if her constraints had loosened his own. His moans were louder, his skin more fevered. He rubbed their bodies together with the enthusiasm of a much less civilized being. "Do you like that?" he whispered. "Do you like my cock against your skin?"

She could not deny it. "It's wet," she gasped as he dragged the throbbing crest across her belly.

"It's crying for you, Florence. It wants to fuck your sweet little pussy." He laughed, low and dark, at her involuntary shiver. "Poor little Florence. I don't mean to frighten you with my words."

"I'm not f-frightened."

He laughed again and squeezed her so tightly his penis seemed to burn between their bodies. "I'll tell you a secret, love. I don't mind if you're a little frightened, so long as you enjoy how I make you feel."

He kissed her before she could respond, deep and possessive, driving every thought from her mind but the sweet, drugging bliss of his touch. His hands were her salvation, his cock the brand that made her his. And she was his, entirely, without a scrap of her soul withheld. Willingly, she surrendered to his wishes, loving that what he wanted was hers to give, loving even the tiny spark of fear. He could do anything to her. Anything.

But he would not hurt her. She knew he would not. The trust she felt was a pleasure in itself. That she, who had so long feared her shadow, could trust a man with not only her body but her body's satisfaction filled her with a hot, sharp streak of pride. Even to Freddie she would not have granted this. Only Edward could be trusted to know her deepest need.

Indeed, even as she tensed with a shadow of self-consciousness, he moved behind her. She sighed at the heady rush the change of positions inspired. She could not see him now, and he could not see her face. She was freed to feel, to react, with that small bit of modesty preserved.

"Cat," he teased at her tiny, purring moan.

As if to underscore the words, his nails raked gently up her back, from the curve of her buttocks to the base of her neck. She rolled her spine and stretched her arms against the limits of her bonds. Despite the unorthodox situation, she had never been so easy in her body. Her wrists were tied to the bottom of the columns, pulled out from her sides but not raised. Such a simple containment, but what a difference it wrought in her mind! I am lucky to be beautiful, she thought, if it makes me the woman this man desires.

"I'm moving closer," he warned. "I'm going to rub us together like the butler and his favorite plate."

He planted his knees outside her calves and slipped his arms around her waist. His chin fit neatly over her head. True to his word, he buffed his front to her back, slowly, firmly, the heavy press of muscle and skin a deep, bone-heating pleasure.

Her enjoyment escaped in a long, melodious sigh.

"Like that?" he said, his fingers drawing circles on her breasts.

"It makes me feel drunk."

"And this?" One big hand covered her belly, pressing her bottom to the thick hot thrust of his sex. Her head fell back against his shoulder.

"Yes," she said. "That, too."

He pleasured her as slowly as she'd pleasured him, hands brushing feather-light against the parts of her that felt it most: her nipples, her mouth, the sensitive stretch of bone between her shoulders. He teased the triangle of curls between her legs and drew patterns over the rise of her hips. He touched her until her skin seemed to hum beneath his hands: burning, yearning, straining harder and harder for the next caress. When he finally slipped one finger between the tightly pressed folds of her mound, the contact made her nerves all leap at once.

But even these enticements could not dull her awareness of what he was doing with his cock. He was rubbing it over her: her bottom, the small of her back, the crease where each cheek met her legs. He squeezed it into the tightly bound clasp of her thighs, just far enough to touch her nether lips before he drew it out. She sensed he was exploring her with it, as if his organ were another hand. She could feel the wet, foreign press of the little eye, warm and slick. He was stretched within his skin, hardening like iron as their play drew out.

"Ready?" he said, his voice harsh but still controlled. "Ready to fly over the edge?"

She could barely move for the waves of longing that weighted her limbs. She managed a feeble nod. For him it was enough. Gone was his teasing then, gone the luxuriant rub of skin on skin. Strength replaced it, and determination. The swiftness of her rise was dizzying. In seconds, her body tensed, coiled with heartstopping pleasure, and sprung free with blinding force. He must have known what was happening to her. His hips jerked faster, pressed harder, and an instant later he joined her in the sweet convulsion. Growling softly, his teeth scored her shoulder as his seed jetted hard against her back.

It was a singular experience, feeling him soften as he held her, knowing they had shared that spasm of joy. He sat back and spooned her against him. This is nakedness, she thought. Letting someone see you lose yourself to the madness of your flesh.

He kissed the place he'd set his teeth, then licked it. Her skin tingled beneath his tongue.

"You bit me," she said, as surprised by his action as she was by her own flutters of intrigue. Obviously, she had much to learn about the secrets of the bedchamber.

Misunderstanding her words, he murmured an apology and bent to release her ties. He checked her wrists to make sure they weren't chafed. The right bore a mark where she'd unwittingly tugged it at the end. He kissed the fading redness, then cradled her hand against his chest. "All right, love?" he said, his pretty eyes concerned.

She'd always be all right when he called her that.

"Just tired," she said, her gratification smothered by a yawn.

The response amused him. "Come then," he said. "I'll get us settled for the night."

After what seemed like minutes of fitful sleep, he woke to a patter of rain on the domed wooden roof. A necklace of small round windows circled its gilded rim. They bled a pale silver light that did nothing to lift his heart. He was stiff from sleeping on the floor, stiff and cold. He had turned away from Florence in the night, leaving her to hug the pillows for warmth. He knew he should not linger but he watched her just a little longer: her downy, sleep-flushed skin, her shining spill of chestnut hair.

She was a chick barely out of its shell, a child-woman with her hands curled together beneath her cheek. Could anyone who saw her not wish to protect her sweetness?

He thought of the way she'd taken him in her mouth, all curiosity and accidental skill. He thought of the way she'd let him bind her, the way she'd squirmed and sighed in his arms. Her lust was as clean as the brook that fed the downs. No act could sully her; at least, not the woman she was today.

Lips thinned by a rueful smile, he smoothed the gold satin sheet across her back. Life would change her: disappointments, disillusions, the narrow-minded judgments of the world. One day she'd know enough to be embarrassed by what they'd done. For now, though, she was innocent in the one way that mattered. Freddie Burbrooke would take a virgin to his bed.

Edward didn't credit her tale about Freddie not wanting to marry her. That was just a foolish pang of conscience. In the end, his brother would act as wisdom required. He would marry Florence Fairleigh. He would safeguard his future and the future of the Greystowe name.

With eyes gone hot, Edward turned from his brother's bride-to-be. He told himself Freddie would take care of her. Freddie would be kinder than a thousand husbands he could name. He swallowed against the painful thickness in his throat.

One thing only Freddie would not do.

He would not cherish the pure, bright flame that burned within her flesh.

CHAPTER 12

Florence cuddled her pillow, hugging the last of her dreams to her breast. She felt quite happily a fool. All this time she'd been afraid of Edward. Perhaps he *was* intimidating, even now when she knew he must care for her. It was a good kind of intimidating, though, an exciting kind.

What an adventure being married to him would be! She was a little sorry to be breaking her promise to Freddie, but it wasn't as if he wanted to marry her himself. She was sure a charming man like him would have no trouble finding a more suitable, less passionate bride.

Poor Freddie, she thought. He had no idea what he was missing. Then again, who was she to judge his nature? No doubt he thought her the unfortunate one.

She extended her arms in a supremely satisfied stretch. Despite her moments of anguish, everything had turned out for the best. She could hardly wait to start making Edward happy.

She would have to wait, though, because her lover was nowhere in sight.

He must have left early to preserve her reputation. It wouldn't do for the servants to witness their licentiousness. Never mind that servants could be as bad; Florence understood what was expected. Why force people to know what would make them uncomfortable, even if they did the same themselves? She nodded in agreement to the empty room. Yes, Edward had demonstrated great discretion in leaving the pavilion first.

And, look! He had left her a token. Eyes caught by something shiny, she retrieved his gold signet from between a pair of pillows. It must have rolled off the cushion while she slept.

The ring fit tolerably well on her forefinger, its ruby winking darkly in the rain-dimmed light. Freddie had not given her an engagement ring, an omission she had not thought about till now. Moved to the edge of tears, she brought the gem to her lips and kissed it.

"I love you," she whispered, trying out the words. "I love you, Edward Burbrooke."

She shivered suddenly, chilled by an errant draft. The room seemed empty with only herself to warm it, as much a ruin as the former Greystowe Hall.

I should dress, she told herself, and return to the house. If Edward could be discreet, then so could she.

When she arrived, more or less dry thanks to an umbrella she'd found in a big brass pot beside the door, the front hall was empty. Her pulse beat frantically in her throat as she managed to slip back to her room without encountering any servants, though they had, of course, begun the day's work already. Relieved though she was, sneaking around gave her a sense of wrongdoing she did not like. She wished she could simply declare the truth to everyone.

She and Edward were going to be together. The thought was miraculous to the point of being frightening. Even as she longed to get the announcement over with, she dreaded telling Edward's family. She'd been intimate with him, after all, hardly a cause for pride—especially when she hadn't officially broken off with Freddie.

But, oh, it had been worth any amount of awkwardness to share that night! Her cheeks warmed with a particularly potent memory and suddenly she had to see him, immediately and alone, if only to reassure herself she hadn't dreamed it all.

Her heart tripped thrillingly against her ribs as she slipped down the corridor to his office, darting to the shadows whenever she thought she heard a maid. Thankfully, the carpets muffled her eager footsteps. The day was so dark even gaslight could not dispel the gloom. One of the doors she passed—giving access to the cellar, she imagined—was actually seeping curls of mist beneath its planks. She felt as if she'd stepped into another time; or perhaps a fairy tale, where she was the intrepid princess and Edward the dark, enchanted prince. She almost giggled as she passed a niche with a suit of armor.

Edward was prince and dragon both, but she had just the spell to soothe him. Inside her pocket, coiled like a nesting mouse, were four quilted velvet ties. She could hardly wait to see how Edward liked them; how they'd look twining his strong, masculine wrists.

The door to his office was open a crack. A golden glow spilled out, lamplight rather than gas. Body humming with excitement, she peeped inside. She smiled. Edward was sound asleep, stretched on a leather sofa, his long legs propped and crossed on the brass-studded end. One hand rested on his chest while the other dangled limply to the floor. Last night must have tired him. She considered leaving him to rest, but temptation had her in its grip. That dangling arm was perfectly positioned. If she snuck in now, she could tie him the same way he'd tied her.

To her dismay, he was a much lighter sleeper than she was. He snorted and bolted up before she'd finished the first wrist. He looked at where she'd bound it to the sofa's central leg. "What the hell do you think you're doing?"

Florence trembled. This was not the reaction she'd expected. "I'm s-sorry. Did I make a mistake? Is this something a woman shouldn't do?"

"It's certainly something no woman should do to me."

She backed away, leaving him to wrench the tie loose. "I'm sorry. I shouldn't have woken you. You're in a bad mood."

"There's nothing wrong with my mood!" He glared at her until her cheeks felt boiled, then blew out his breath. "Look, Florence, I'm sorry for growling at you, but you seem to have misunderstood what happened last night."

"Misunderstood?" she said, the word small and cracked.

"I'm not saying it's your fault. I take full responsibility. You're inexperienced and I, well, I needed a woman. I'm aware that's no excuse. It's just the way life is." He spread his hands, a clearer denial of responsibility than his words. Florence watched the gesture with a sense of unreality. He seemed to mean what he was saying. His tone was quite businesslike. "The important thing is," he continued coolly, "I've spoken to Freddie. As I suspected, he didn't mean to give the impression that he'd lost interest in marrying you. On the contrary, he's fully prepared to go through with the wedding."

To go through with it, Florence thought. There's a flattering construction. But Edward wasn't done.

"I'm leaving tomorrow," he said. "I have business at the mill. I trust you and Freddie will use this time to sort matters out between you. By the time I get back, I expect you'll have forgotten all about, well, everything." Lowering his brows, he gave her his steeliest look. "What happened last night must never happen again."

The finger he shook in her face broke through her shock.

"Then what," she said, thrusting out her hand in accusation, "did you mean by giving me this?"

He stared at his father's ring as if he'd never laid eyes on it before. "Where did you get that?"

"You left it on my pillow."

"Why would I do that? Hell." He scrubbed his face with both hands. "It must have fallen off during the night. It does that when I get cold."

"Then I marvel it ever stays on."

The scrubbing stopped. He peered at her between his fingers, then dropped his hands. He looked so weary she wanted to call back her words. How could he be so cruel, yet look as if he were the one whose heart was breaking?

Stupid Florence, she thought, feeling as weary as he

looked. Stupid, gullible Florence. She squared her shoulders and clenched her hands. "You're telling me last night meant nothing to you. Nothing at all."

He hung his hands over his knees, his fingers limp, his shoulders bowed by an invisible weight. "I enjoyed what we did," he said, "but it meant no more than that."

She stared at his face, trying to find the mark of evil, the sign she should have read. All she found was what she'd grown to love: the proud, sharp nose, the scowling brows, the eyes like a summer sky.

"You didn't deserve to enjoy it," she said, her voice shaking with anger. "Men like you don't deserve to enjoy anything."

He dropped his gaze but did not speak; did not try to explain or beg forgiveness or say any of the things she was praying with all her might to hear. It's a mistake, she wanted to cry. You love me. I know you do. She watched a vein tick unevenly in his neck.

And then she turned away.

Florence trod the second floor corridor like a sleepwalker, blind to the fading portraits, deaf to the quiet passage of a maid. She'd wanted so badly to believe Edward loved her she'd convinced herself it was true. Catherine Exeter was right. Women were easy to lead astray. With the slightest encouragement, they stuck their necks in the bridle and handed the men they loved a whip.

Lord. Her steps faltered as she pressed her jumping heart. What was she going to do now?

Part of her, the weak part, wanted to throw herself on Freddie's mercy. Marry me, the weak part whimpered. Keep me safe.

But no matter what Edward said, she knew Freddie didn't want her for his wife. She'd seen it in his eyes. She'd read it in his kiss. No doubt, he'd said he did want her because Edward was too forceful to defy.

She knew from experience how difficult opposing him could be.

Continuing her journey, she dragged her fingers along the smooth curry-gold wall. She'd have to speak to Freddie. She wasn't sure what she ought to tell him. That his brother had compromised her virtue, then treated her like something he'd stepped in at the stable? Freddie looked up to his brother. It didn't seem fair to undermine his love. But she had to tell him something to explain why she couldn't spend another minute in this house.

Lost in thought, her hand skimmed the gleaming mahogany rail that marked the turn of the grand stairway towards the ground floor. She descended the first tread. Would Freddie take her back to Keswick? London was out of the question. Even if Florence could have faced it, she couldn't afford to return. Aunt Hypatia certainly didn't owe her more support. Plus, she doubted even the duchess could repair the damage a broken engagement would do to her reputation.

It was all too much to decide. She would put it to Freddie as delicately as she could. He was clever. And he did care for her. Perhaps he would see some solution she could not.

Her panic eased as she drew closer to his rooms. The thought of being held with affection, if only for a while, was a ray of sunshine in a storm. She quickened her step, hurrying through the billiard room to the family's private wing. She rapped lightly on his door, then opened it, too impatient to wait for his acknowledgment.

At first she didn't understand what she was seeing. Oh, she knew the two tall figures by the window were kissing. Their mouths were plastered together, after all, and their hands gripped each others' backsides. One of the figure's shirts had all three buttons undone, with the ensuing V fallen over his shoulder. The cloth hung to his elbow, baring a strong upper arm and a beautifully muscled wedge of back. Her brain took a moment to admit that the back belonged to Freddie, and an even longer one to identify his partner as Nigel West.

Edward's steward was moaning into Freddie's mouth as if he'd rather die than stop. And Freddie was kissing him back with all the hunger he'd claimed he couldn't feel. She saw tongues and teeth. She saw whitened knuckles and sweat-streaked necks. They were grinding their hips together like cats in heat. From what she glimpsed between those hips, both were thoroughly aroused.

She gasped for air as if a huge hand had been holding her underwater and had just then let her up. At the sound, the two men sprang guiltily apart. Freddie hissed out a curse. Nigel went white.

"Florence," Freddie said, raking back his wildly tousled hair.

Florence couldn't meet his eyes. He looked just like Edward had after she'd taken him in her mouth, lust pouring off him in waves. Her mind turned in a stupefied circle. Freddie and Nigel. Nigel and Freddie. It was too extraordinary to comprehend.

"Forgive me," she said, beginning to retreat. "I should have waited until you answered my knock."

Freddie and Nigel exchanged glances. "Knock?" Freddie said. "We didn't hear— Hell. Don't go, Florence. We need to talk. Please."

The sharpness of the plea stopped her. She pressed her hands together beneath her breast, as if she could by that means protect herself from further wounds. "I don't know what there is to say, except that now I think I understand why you don't want to marry me."

"You couldn't understand. Not all of it." With a growl of annoyance that reminded her painfully of his brother, Freddie tugged his shirt back over his shoulder. "Damn Edward and his tidy little plans."

"Edward?" Her heart stalled. "What does Edward have to do with this?"

Freddie lowered himself to the edge of his bed, his legs stretched gingerly out, his face filled with a compassion so deep it scared her. "Come in, Florence. I'll tell you everything."

"I should go," said Nigel.

Freddie nodded at him and in that nod lay a secret history. For one odd moment, despite everything that had passed, Florence experienced a pang of envy. These two shared a bond no one else could know.

"Don't do anything," Freddie said.

"No," Nigel agreed, his voice calm but heavy. "I won't do anything until I speak to you again." His step hesitated in front of Florence, then stopped. "I can't say how sorry I am about all this, Miss Fairleigh. Neither of us meant to— well, let's just say I'm aware that what I did was a profound betrayal of your trust. If there's anything I can do to help, anything at all, I would gladly make the attempt."

He might as well have been speaking Sanskrit. Seeming to realize this, he continued to the door. Florence watched him go, her brain refusing to do anything but spin. She watched his long elegant legs, the proud set of his shoulders and head. It was a small head, beautifully shaped beneath its clipped silvering hair. The hand with which he closed the door had graceful, tapered fingers. When it disappeared, she turned back to Freddie.

"He is a man, isn't he?" she asked, more confused than she'd been in her life.

Freddie laughed, a dry brush of sound. "Yes, he's a man. If he weren't, I wouldn't have been kissing him that way."

"You only like to kiss men?"

Freddie's smile was sad. He brushed back a lock that had fallen from her chignon. "I didn't mind kissing you, sweetheart, but I'm afraid it's true. I only really like kissing men. Born that way, as far as I know."

"But how could you know?"

He shrugged. "Edward thinks Eton did it to me. Blames himself for sending me. There's a tradition there of older boys bullying the younger. Making them personal servants. Giving them forty whacks for imaginary infractions. Part of the servitude sometimes involves more intimate favors."

"Kissing," she said, trying to face it.

Freddie held her gaze. "More than kissing. Boys learn to take their pleasures young, and some don't mind who offers a helping hand. A few, like me, like a male hand best. The first time a boy asked me to do him, I felt as if a pair of blinders had fallen from my eyes. Suddenly what I'd wanted all along was clear."

He took her hands and squeezed them, his eyes filled with a bright, glimmering fire. "I know people say it's unnatural, Florence. I know they say it's a sin. But it doesn't feel like a sin to me. It feels like the way God made me."

"I don't think you're a sinner," she said. The words came slowly as she searched through the tangle of her emotions. "Maybe if I didn't know you, I would, but I've always thought you a good, kind man. My father used to say God weighs each man's sins in private. We can't presume to know what's on the scales."

"Your father sounds wise."

A smile of memory touched her lips. "When it came to other people's hearts, he was."

"So I can hope for forgiveness from the vicar's daughter?"

"I'm not sure you need my forgiveness."

Sighing, he lifted her hands to his mouth. "I'm afraid there's more, Florence, more you deserve to know."

Given what she'd just seen, the story of the footman did not shock her. More disturbing was discovering that Mr. Mowbry was also Edward's solicitor. That her father's old friend would help Edward save Freddie's reputation by engineering a match with her quite stole her breath. Then, when she thought she couldn't bear another blow, Freddie revealed how Aunt Hypatia agreed to help.

"They knew?" she said, her face going hot and cold by turns. Amazement warred with fury in her breast. "Aunt Hypatia *and* Edward? They knew what you were and they still wanted me to marry you?"

"They didn't think of it that way. They thought I'd get over it. They knew you needed a husband, and thought I'd be as good to you as anyone."

"But they tricked me! They let me believe you truly cared."

He cupped her face. "I do care. That's never been a lie. If Nigel and I hadn't—that is, if we hadn't—"

"Oh, go ahead," she snapped with a temper worthy of

the duchess. "If you and Nigel hadn't fallen in love, you could have spent a lifetime deceiving me."

Freddie blanched as if she'd told him a truth he wasn't ready to acknowledge. He dropped his arm. "Florence—"

She didn't care what he meant to say. "You're liars, all of you. Liars and cheats. And Edward's the worst of the lot. By God!" Her voice rose out of control and her hands fisted in her skirts as if she meant to rip them from her legs. "I can't believe I actually worried what he thought of me. I can't believe I tried to earn his respect. He's a bug. An insect who isn't worth the energy it would take to squash him!"

"Florence," Freddie chided, a smile flirting with the corners of his mouth.

She jabbed her forefinger into his chest. "He's a slimy, slithering fiend!"

Freddie grabbed her hand and tried to soothe it. To her dismay, she saw she still wore Edward's signet. Before he could see it, she yanked her hand away. Her chin quivered but she positively refused to cry.

"Don't judge him too harshly," Freddie said, the flash of amusement gone. "I don't say his methods were perfect, but he did what he did out of love. He'd protect anyone he cared about that way. Including you."

"Hah!" Florence barked. She swiped her eyes with her sleeve before they could overflow. "There's a pretty bedtime story. Edward protect me? He'd be the first to hammer in the nail."

Freddie protested, but she'd already heard enough. Half blinded by emotion, she spun and left the room. She didn't have to run. Freddie's injury prevented him from following.

Snake, she thought, her skirts kicking fore and aft. What an idiot she'd been to imagine he had a heart. She took the stairs two at a time, panting for breath through her anger and her shame.

They'd all made fools of her, but only Edward had made her a fool for love.

CHAPTER 13

"*I don't see* why we have to leave," Lizzie muttered for the umpteenth time since Florence had told her to pack. "'Least not right away. If your heart is set on going back to Keswick, Viscount Burbrooke will see you get there."

Deliberately ignoring her, Florence frowned at the contents of her wardrobe. Per the duchess's orders, most of her old clothes had been destroyed. Too few remained to pack only what she'd brought with her to London. With a grimace, she pulled out the simplest of her new dresses. If worse came to worst, she could sell them for the price of a railway ticket. Not that she was comfortable with the idea. Strictly speaking, these gowns belonged to Aunt Hypatia.

Lizzie accepted the first, a pale yellow muslin. She smoothed it flat across the bed, then folded it carefully around a length of tissue. Florence had already warned her they'd be taking no trunks; only what the two of them could carry in their portmanteaus.

"Don't know what you think you're going to do in Keswick," Lizzie grumped, her annoyance still sharp.

"I shall hire out as a companion," Florence said with more confidence than she felt.

"Hah." Lizzie fussed over the lay of a hem. "Those old biddies don't have any more money than we do."

"Then I must convince more than one of them to hire me. I shall collect a perfect harem of old biddies."

Taken by surprise, Lizzie puffed out a laugh. But she turned serious quickly enough. "It isn't right: you and Master Freddie parting ways. Whatever you fought about, I'm sure you can work it out. Besides—" Her look grew dark. "I don't like the idea of us going to stay with that friend of the duchess. I've heard the servants talk about her. They say she's barmy."

"She's not barmy," Florence said, fighting for patience. "She's a woman who's seen her share of trouble. Just like us."

"But—"

Guilt at forcing Lizzie to leave her comfortable place, and anguish at having to leave it herself, shortened Florence's temper. "Stay then," she said. "I'm sure the earl will find a position for you. There's always openings in the scullery."

All the blood drained from Lizzie's face. Florence was instantly contrite.

"Blast," she said. "I didn't mean that. Edward wouldn't set you to scrubbing pots. I'm sure if you asked he'd seek out another lady's maid position among his friends."

"B-but—" Lizzie was weeping now. "I don't want to be anyone's lady's maid but yours."

"Well," said Florence, with a humor she thought she'd lost, "it doesn't look as if I'm going to be a lady now."

"You will!" Lizzie declared, flinging herself into her arms. "I know you will."

Florence patted her back. She took a peculiar comfort in consoling the little maid. Poor Lizzie. Deprived of her gaslights and her running water. She resolved that, however events fell out for herself, she would request that Edward help her. She was certain he would, though she couldn't have said from whence that certainty came.

"Maybe you could marry the earl instead," Lizzie mumbled wetly against her neck.

Oh, Lord, thought Florence. God save her from such a fate.

• • • •

The door to Catherine's house was opened by a vision in lavender silk and ecru lace. Coolly blonde, flawlessly feminine, Catherine's niece was even lovelier in person than in her picture. "My, my," she said with slumberous eyes and curving lips, "if it isn't the fabulous Florence Fairleigh."

In Florence's shaken state, this condescending greeting was more than enough to cow her. "I'm sorry," she said, backing away. "I've come at a bad time."

At once, Imogene sprang into motion. "Nonsense," she said, catching Florence's arm. "My aunt would never forgive me if I let you get away. Clearly, you're in distress. If you could see your way to forgiving my atrocious manners, I'd be happy to help however I may."

With this pretty speech, she drew her guest inside. Florence hardly knew what to make of this changeable creature and her dulcet exclamations of concern. Whatever Imogene's motives, Florence had not the will to resist her welcome. Somewhat less happily, Lizzie shuffled in behind.

Catherine came into the hall at the sound of their entrance. As soon as she saw Florence, she folded her into her arms. "Poor dear," she said, her tone so maternal it tightened Florence's throat. "I feared this would happen. No woman who loved a Greystowe ever failed to come to grief."

"Surely *Freddie* didn't jilt you?" Imogene murmured. Briefly, Florence wondered at the familiarity of the question, but it was hard to take offense. Imogene's curiosity was as delicate as the rest of her. It hung in the air like spider's silk, barely there at all.

She pulled back from Catherine's embrace and wiped her eyes. The two women peered at her in gentle inquiry, their brows—one set gold, one silver—raised in identical slender arches. Despite their kindness, Florence could not answer. Even now, she could not bring herself to speak harshly of the Burbrookes.

"No," Imogene mused, her lambent gray eyes taking the measure of her expression. "Freddie Burbrooke is no heartbreaker, but perhaps the elder . . . ?"

"Tush," scolded Catherine before Florence could do more than bite her lip. "The girl is clearly grieving. We must not pester her with questions. It is enough that you are here, my dear. We ask no more than that."

She would not hear of Florence leaving, though her presence, on top of Imogene's, would make more work for the tiny household. "Your girl can stay with mine in the attic. I'm sure they'll find it perfectly cozy."

Florence would have preferred to keep Lizzie with her but, bereft of support—even her own, it seemed—she hadn't the nerve to object to the arrangement. "You're too kind," she said, her vision shimmering with tears.

Continuing to cluck, Catherine led her to a guest room on the second floor. More grateful than she could express, Florence relinquished her rain-dampened clothes and allowed herself to be bundled into bed.

"Rest," Catherine said, her cool hand stroking Florence's brow. "Sleep is the best remedy for a broken heart."

The hour wasn't even noon, but Florence was exhausted. Bertha, the big, sad-faced maid, brought a beautiful white quilt to tuck around her. She glanced back over her shoulder before she spoke. "Things might look better in the morning," she said in a low, hurried tone, as if she were afraid of being heard. "Men aren't as bad as . . . as some people like to make out."

Florence smiled, touched by her advice. She only wished it were true. She waved at the maid as she left. Then, with a weary sigh, she curled around her starchy pillow like a wounded animal in a burrow. She was safe, at least for now. More than that a woman in her position could not ask.

For the first time in too many years to remember, Edward drank with the intention of getting drunk. The library's shelves stretched around him, above him, the wisdom of centuries held within their tomes. None seemed likely to help him—no more than the liquor. By the fourth whiskey, his head was spinning, his mouth tasted foul, and he could still remember every damn word he'd said.

I enjoyed what we did, but it meant no more than that.

Bloody bastard, he thought, nerves stretched by memory and by the infernal droning of the rain. He had half a mind to shatter the decanter against the wall, just to interrupt the noise. His fingers curled to do it. Fortunately, though—or unfortunately—Edward wasn't a man who easily lost control. With exaggerated care, he pressed the cut-glass stopper into the bottle's throat.

He knew as soon as Florence left that he'd made a terrible mistake: the worst of his life, one that would stain his soul until he died. He'd convinced himself it was better all around that she cease to care for him. In the end, though, all he'd done was wound them both. His heart tore from his chest with each step she took. His brain screamed for him to follow, to tell her something, anything, that would bring back the adoration he'd seen the night before.

He wanted to go after her so badly his body ached in its bones.

But he couldn't do it. He couldn't abandon Freddie. Edward didn't delude himself. Florence was Freddie's last chance for respectability. Only marriage to her could restore his place in their world. Even if some people doubted the sincerity of his brother's vows, they'd know he meant to maintain—at least on the surface—the image society strove to project. If Freddie refused to toe the line, they'd push him forever beyond the pale.

Oh, God, he thought, his head falling back in the wing-backed chair. He could still see Florence's expression as she thrust out his father's ring. *What did you mean by giving me this?* she'd demanded, and all he could think was how right that circle of gold looked on her finger. If only he had given it to her! If only he could have loved her as he wished.

His hands gripped the arms of the chair until the wood creaked with the strain.

He couldn't leave it like this. Whatever the cost, he couldn't let her hate him.

He pushed to his feet, groaning as if his limbs were leaden weights. Unsteadily, he wove through the empty corridors to his rooms. He would change the clothes he'd been wearing since last night. He would brush his teeth and tame his hair. Then he'd speak to Florence. He didn't know what he'd say, only that he ought to look human first.

His valet, Lewis, was waiting in his chamber. He appeared both grim and worried.

"What?" said Edward, already pulling off his collar.

Lewis drew himself up with military straightness. "Your brother has left, my lord. Along with Nigel West."

"Left?" Edward's hands paused.

"Yes, your lordship. They've gone to settle the workers' dispute at the mill."

"But I was going to take care of that. I wanted Freddie and Florence to—" He stopped himself and dropped a cufflink onto the top of his chest of drawers. The onyx gleamed dully in the murky light. "You say Nigel went with him?"

"Yes, sir. Your brother left this note for you. Said I was to place it in your hands." Lewis looked as if he disapproved. Edward barely noticed. If Nigel was with Freddie, perhaps he needn't worry. Edward had known his steward for donkey's years, ever since the old earl had taken him under his wing. Nigel, the son of Greystowe's gamekeeper, had been the brightest of the lads at the village school. Too smart for the army, the old earl had declared, then sent him off to Oxford. He and Edward hadn't been close, of course; Nigel was older and of common birth, but Edward knew him to be a paragon of rectitude, punctilious in his sense of right and wrong, and nearly as loyal to the family as Edward was himself. With him along, at least Freddie wouldn't stumble into another scandal.

Then he broke the old-fashioned wafer seal.

"Good Lord!" he exploded as part of the contents caught his eye.

"Sir?" said Lewis.

Edward waved him off and sank onto the edge of the bed. Heart thundering in his chest, hands shaking, he read Freddie's note from the start.

"Dear Edward," it began. "I've come to realize you

aren't likely to relinquish your plan to have me marry Florence unless you are forced to do so. I suspect this ambition lies behind your sudden desire to hie off to Manchester. Consequently, Nigel and I have decided to settle the 'crisis' ourselves. We have become friends during my convalescence, perhaps—as Florence was kind enough to remark— more than friends."

"Florence!" Edward exclaimed, letting the letter slap his thigh. What had his brother been telling Florence? And since when were Nigel and Freddie friends? Whenever Edward saw them, they were snapping at each like mongrels over a bone. Muttering to himself, he lifted the page and continued to read.

"In any case," Freddie wrote, "only time will tell what we can be to each other." (*Be* to each other, Edward snorted.) "Meanwhile, I beg you, be good to Florence. I know you have feelings for her and that she has them for you. It may be that all our happiness rests on taking chances you have thus far refused to consider."

"All our happiness!" Edward spluttered. "He's insane!"

He sprang to his feet but did not move except to press the fist that held the note between his eyes. Damn him. *Damn* him for a misbegotten fool. So. He and Nigel were taking some lovebirds' journey to Manchester. Did Freddie think no one would notice? Was he determined to throw his life into the gutter? No matter what Edward did? No matter what he sacrificed?

Well, fuck it, Edward thought, the whiskey stoking his rage. He was done trying to rescue his little brother. Done, done, done.

"Bloody hell," he swore, and smashed his fist into the wall.

The plaster split, along with the skin over three of his knuckles.

"Sir!" Lewis protested, still hovering nearby.

Edward allowed him to wrap a strip of cotton around the wound.

"Where's Florence?" he said once the cut had been

dressed. Seeing her was suddenly all he could think of. Something must be salvaged from this day.

"Miss Fairleigh?" said Lewis, clearly startled by his tone. "I don't know. In her rooms, I imagine."

But Florence wasn't in her rooms. She was gone, along with half her clothes. Her little maid, Lizzie, had also cleared out her belongings. Edward stood, as if rooted, among the scattered signs of their departure: boots left lying on the carpet, a sprinkling of silver hairpins, a small pink glove. His blood beat through his body as if it were a death knell.

She was gone. Too hastily to say good-bye. While he'd been drinking himself stupid, she'd been slipping out the door.

He'd driven her away. He'd driven them both away.

Edward threw back his head and roared.

By the following morning, the rain had settled to a surly drizzle. Though Edward had discovered where Florence was, any triumph he felt at the success of his detective work was obliterated by the nature of her refuge.

The odds were even as to whether he'd have preferred her to run to the devil.

But the obstacle had to be faced. Florence could not be allowed to remain in such uncaring hands. The witch must be bearded in her den—or whatever the metaphor was for bitter old spinster crones.

He dressed carefully in riding clothes and freshly polished boots. His linen was immaculate, his demeanor as cool as he could make it. Perhaps it was his imagination, but Samson seemed reluctant to stop at Catherine Exeter's house. While the stallion shook his head up and down, Edward threaded his reins through the hitching post ring.

"Wise horse," he muttered, patting his glossy neck.

Lucky horse, in fact, to be able to remain out here.

With a dour smile, Edward strode decisively up the pebbled path. Catherine Exeter herself answered the door. She didn't pretend not to know him, though they hadn't exchanged two words since the incident with Freddie and the apples. Edward's animosity towards the woman seethed in his veins. Only Florence could have brought him within her sphere.

His nemesis stood firmly between the entryway and him. "Little early for a call," she said.

"You know why I'm here."

"Actually"—Catherine smiled like an evil seraph—"if you were Freddie, I would know why you were here. Oh, but I must have forgotten. My niece told me you'd developed a tendre for your brother's fiancée. Tut, tut. Quite incautious of you, Lord Greystowe."

Edward was grinding his teeth so hard his jaw ached. He relaxed it enough to speak. "I want to see her."

"I'm sure you do. She, however, doesn't want to see you. That's what happens when you treat a woman like a dog. She develops an aversion to being kicked."

"I did not treat—" he began, but a movement on the narrow stairs drove the thread of argument from his mind. Florence was coming down in one of her old gowns, this one a medley of pink and yellow flowers. The cotton was faded, the sleeves too wide for fashion, but to him the dress was as joyous a sight as the finest silk. He ran his eyes to her hem and back. How lovely she was, how womanly in every way.

"It's all right, Catherine," she said, her voice calm and soft. "I'll speak to him."

"But dearest—"

Florence squeezed Catherine's small bony shoulder. "Best to get it over with."

After a slight hesitation, Catherine agreed. "As you wish. I'll be in the parlor should you need me."

Florence took her place at the door. Apparently, neither woman intended to let him in. But that was fine with Edward. He had no desire to enter Catherine Exeter's home—as long as Florence returned to his.

For a few slow breaths, he simply looked at her, taking in the soft flushed curve of her cheeks, the sheen of her upswept hair, the uncustomary pallor of her brow. Her lashes dipped, shadowing her grass-green eyes with glistening sable fans. Her mouth was a curve of cherry blossom pink, infinitely sweet. When she bit her lower lip, a shiver of pleasure touched his nape. If it weren't for Catherine, he'd have kissed her then and there.

"You don't know who you've run to," he said.

She lifted her head. "I do. And I've no intention of listening to you malign her. Tell me what you want and be done with it."

With an effort, Edward uncurled his fists. "I want you to return to Greystowe."

"Why?" She crossed her arms beneath her breasts. "So I can marry your brother?"

He thought he knew what she wished him to say, but he could not form the words. He wanted to, but then he thought of Freddie: of Freddie's future as an outcast. Even now he could not claim her as his own.

"I don't want you to hate me," he said, the statement sounding inadequate even to him.

"I don't hate you," she said. "I pity you."

But what he heard in her voice wasn't pity, just as what he saw in Catherine Exeter's eyes wasn't the milk of human kindness.

"I care for you," he said. "I know that's hard for you to believe, but—"

"For pity's sake." Clearly scornful, she cut him off. "If you care for me, I'd hate to see how you'd treat someone you hate. You took my innocence, Edward, and you trampled it in the mud."

"I didn't take your innocence," he hissed, low enough to frustrate listening ears. "You're still a virgin."

"Yes, indeed," she said. "We couldn't have your brother taking a fallen woman to his bed."

Her thrust struck so directly home a tide of shame crept up his neck. Naturally, Florence saw it. "You're despicable," she said, spitting out the words. "If I never see you again, it will be too soon."

Before he could devise an answer, she slammed the door in his face. If Catherine Exeter had done it, he probably would have broken the barrier down. But Florence—Florence's rejection left him gasping for air. He swayed on his feet, his ears ringing from the thud of the heavy wood.

She did hate him. She hated him just as Catherine Exeter had hated his father.

He couldn't handle this. He had to think. He stumbled twice on his way back down the path, his very muscles thrown into shock. Samson lipped his hand as he fumbled with the reins, then stood patiently while he mounted. Secure in the saddle, Edward turned one last time towards the house.

At first he thought he was seeing things: some nightmarish projection of his guilt. When he blinked, however, the image refused to disappear. Imogene Hargreave was gazing out the parlor window, her pale eyes lit by the darkest sort of glee. Oh, Lord, he thought. Florence was in more danger than he'd dreamed.

Florence had removed his ring. It lay now in the pocket of her skirt. Over and over she turned the circle of gold—seeing his face, hearing his words—while Catherine knitted stockings for the poor. Her niece carried the burden of conversation, chattering amusingly of her many London conquests. Half the city had fallen at her feet, it seemed, a claim Florence could not doubt with her wit and her elegance and her cat-sleek beauty spread like a feast before her miserable country self.

I care for you, Edward had said. *I don't want you to hate me.*

Why had he said those things? Was this a game for him? To see how cruelly he could treat her and still keep her dangling on his string?

I care for you, Florence.

Even now she wanted to believe him. She clucked her tongue in self-disgust. If she wasn't careful, Edward's string would choke her.

Catherine looked up at the tiny exclamation. She sat in her plain green chair like a roosting sparrow, the click of her needles as familiar to Florence as the beating of her heart. Just so did the ladies of Keswick occupy their time. "Are you sure you wouldn't like to help? It might take your mind from your troubles."

She removed her hand from her pocket and straightened her skirt. "I'm afraid I can't keep my mind on anything today."

"As you wish," Catherine said in her soothing way. The needles clicked pensively before she spoke again. "You may not believe this, dear, but once upon a time I had more than socks to offer. When Papa was alive, before my loathsome cousin, if you'll pardon the expression, took over the Grange—nothing so fancy as Greystowe, mind, but a good thriving property—ah, then we carried such riches to the poor! Smoked hams and preserves and, oh, my, all manner of lovely things, some of which you may believe I'd be grateful to have today. But such is life. The Lord gives and the Lord takes, though why He had to give so much to silly old Jeffrey I'm sure I couldn't say. *He* had money from his father. But this is how men arrange the world. A girl may not inherit her father's home but must be kicked out willy-nilly to fend as best she can. And if she doesn't find a husband—well! But I'm sure it's for the best. Women are stronger than men, you know. We can carry these burdens. And far better to scrimp beneath one's own roof than to share one with a bully."

"Indeed," Imogene agreed, her tapering fingers stroking her swanlike neck. "One must teach a man his place or avoid him altogether. A man one hasn't the ability to control is a danger too great to suffer."

Since Florence had heard much on these themes already, she knew she needn't answer, only nod occasionally and hum. Humming now, she turned sideways on the couch and propped her chin against its back. Ever since she'd left Greystowe, she'd felt as if she were dragging a ball and chain behind her. Heavy. Hopeless. All her dreams come to grief. Catherine's gentle litany of complaints seemed a vision of her future, as dreary as the day outside. She'd seen a wider world now and she would miss it. With the tips of her fingers, she touched one of the window's rippled panes. The lane beyond was cloaked in swirling gray. As bad as London. And the interior was no brighter. Catherine couldn't afford to waste pennies burning candles.

And here she was wasting pennies feeding Florence.

"I'm sorry Freddie left," Florence said, a bit of intelligence Lizzie had managed to ferret out. "I know he would have escorted me back to Keswick."

"You mustn't worry about that," said Catherine. "A spot of company is a treat for an old woman like me. And for Imogene as well. As kind as she is to visit me, I know you—who have so lately been to London—are a better audience for her tales."

Imogene murmured something agreeable and untrue. Florence had never been a part of society the way Imogene was. Florence was not that sort of woman. Florence was simple and dull and pitifully forgettable. She sighed, a soft, mournful sound she could not repress.

"Now, now," Catherine chided. "Hold firm, dear. Time heals. Before you know it, you'll be free of the Burbrooke curse."

Would she, though? It seemed to her as if her heart would never be light again.

CHAPTER 14

❧

Edward halted a cautious distance from the shepherd's hut. The construction was simple stone and thatch but it was sound. The garden was groomed, the flowers bright, and a flock of fat white chickens pecked the ground outside their coop. Edward wasn't sure the inhabitants of the house would appreciate being the object of charity, but Lizzie had informed him of Catherine Exeter's intent to visit them today.

"If you're interested like," she'd said in a secretive tone, though no one but he was near.

She'd accosted him on the terrace on his way to his morning ride. Despite the heat, she'd pulled her hood over her face like a character in a sensation novel. The market basket dangling from her arm told the excuse she'd used to slip away from the Exeter home. Edward would have chuckled at her melodrama if he hadn't been desperate for word of Florence. Three days running he'd been turned away without a chance to see her. He was beginning to fear he'd have to abduct her to say hello.

Somehow, he didn't think that would improve Florence's opinion of his character.

Now, however, he had another chance because of Lizzie.

"That servant of hers, that Bertha, don't like her one

bit," she'd confided. "She told me Miss Exeter flutters in
and out when she plays the grand patroness. And that Lady
Hargreave won't go at all. Too busy with her beauty sleep.
I know Florence, though. She'll stay to dandle the babies.
She pretends to be embarrassed when they like her, but she
won't be able to resist. Then you can talk to her."

Edward hoped this would be the case. At least the damn
rain had stopped. He felt a fool lurking behind a thicket
while he waited for Catherine to leave. When she did leave,
though, and alone, he knew the wait had been worthwhile.
He straightened his collar, smoothed his hair, and told himself not to act like a schoolboy with a crush. The lecture
didn't help. His palms were clammy as he knocked on the
weather-grayed planks of the door.

Bartle's wife blinked to find him behind it, then smiled,
slow and broad, as if she knew precisely why he was there.

Perhaps she did. Perhaps his lovesick yearning was written large across his face.

"Lord Greystowe," she exclaimed, pushing the door
wider in welcome. "How kind of you to come. I was just
making tea."

Edward stepped inside, his hat in hand. The Bartles' cottage consisted of three rooms: a large main room where the
family cooked and lived and washed, a larder for storage,
and a small curtained nook where Mr. and Mrs. Bartle slept.
The floor was well-swept paving stone, the walls age-
yellowed plaster. Wooden pegs for hanging clothes made an
orderly circuit around the room. The clothing ranged in size
from infant to adult, much of it displaying Mrs. Bartle's gift
with needle and yarn. Her husband took part of his pay in
wool and Mrs. Bartle spun it into gold.

Shining her own sort of gold, Florence sat in a sunny
corner with a chubby baby in her lap. A young girl, no more
than six, carded wool at her feet, her shoulder brushing Florence's knee as if she'd known her all her life. Edward was
careful not to look directly at the reason for his visit.

"I, uh, came to see how your husband is faring," he said.
"I heard he caught a bad cough."

He had indeed heard this, though it had been weeks ago.

"Oh, he's much better," said Mrs. Bartle. "Please thank Mrs. Forster for her tea."

"I will," he said and, for the life of him, could not think of anything further to say. Florence's presence was a weight behind his back. He was afraid to turn and meet the censure in her eyes, but even more afraid of being asked to leave.

Thankfully, Mrs. Bartle took pity on him. She was a fine, fair woman, as Angus Bartle liked to say; broad and blonde, though not as blonde as her four young offspring. She had the calm, capable air some women gain as their families grow.

"I'm sure you know your cousin," she said, turning him gently to face her.

"Florence," he said, eyes drinking her in. She looked a madonna with that child in her lap. His madonna. At that moment, he would have given his right arm for that baby to be theirs.

Her gaze remained on the bundled infant. "Edward," she answered, his name a mere whisper. Her face was pink, her breathing quick. Both could have been the effect of embarrassment, but Edward's body came so swiftly to attention his linens should have caught fire. That he had touched her most intimate parts, that he had heard her sigh with pleasure and could no more seemed utterly intolerable.

He barely heard Mrs. Bartle murmur something about the tea. He was crossing the room towards Florence. He was sitting in the pool of sunshine by her side. The window seat was just big enough for the two of them. Florence's leg pressed his through her flowered skirts. At the contact he felt not an increase in lust, but a comfort so deep it scared him.

He wanted to sit in the sun with her all his life.

The baby fussed as Florence tensed.

"Let me have him." Wanting only to calm her, Edward eased the heavy bundle from her arms. The baby widened his eyes at him, then tried to bat his face. Charmed by his energy, Edward pretended to eat the dimpled fist.

"How's little Ivan?" he growled. "As terrible as ever?"

Ivan wriggled excitedly at the teasing, his baby-chuckle throaty and full out.

"You know him?" Florence said, her gaze finally on him.

"Of course I know Ivan. The Bartles are my tenants."

"And a fine landlord he is," Mrs. Bartle put in, approaching with two steaming dishes of tea. "You couldn't wish for better." The tea dispensed, she handed her daughter a small sweet biscuit. Still leaning into Florence's knee, the girl looked curiously up at Edward.

"Did you bring socks?" she said.

"No-o," Edward answered, the question confusing him.

"Good," said the girl. "'Cause nobody's socks are as nice as Mama's."

"Hush," scolded Mrs. Bartle, though Edward could tell she was fighting a smile.

He wasn't sure he should ask for an explanation. Instead, he hitched young Ivan to a sitting position and anchored him to his chest with the bend of his arm. "Now I've got you, little man. We'll see if you can get at my tea from there."

The baby squealed with pleasure and flapped his pudgy hands. His little feet pummeled Edward's thigh. He was strong, this boy, strong and full of life.

"What a bruiser." Edward chuckled.

"Like his father," Mrs. Bartle agreed, seeming pleased not to have to wrestle for once with her youngest child. She smiled cagily over the rim of her cup. "You're good with babies, your lordship. Almost as good as Miss Fairleigh."

"I suppose I remember when Freddie was this age." He set his cup on the floor so he could mop a bit of drool from Ivan's chin. "He was better than a new pony to me. A happy baby, just like this fellow."

Florence popped up from the seat as if something had bitten her. "I really should be going," she said, her voice strained. "Catherine will wonder what happened to me."

"I'll walk you back," Edward said, rising just as quickly.

"Oh, yes," Mrs. Bartle agreed, already reaching for her son. "You shouldn't go unescorted."

Florence didn't look happy with this arrangement but, as

he'd hoped, she was too polite to put up a fight with Mrs. Bartle looking on. After assuring the shepherd's wife he'd need "the lads" at harvest just like always, he and Florence took their leave. Side by side, they trod the grassy, rock-strewn land, Edward with his hands clasped behind him, Florence with them folded at her waist.

"Are you well?" he asked when she maintained her stubborn silence.

She pressed her lips together and walked faster. Edward was amazed a little thing like her could cover the ground so quickly. Apparently, country living had done more than pink her cheeks. In what seemed like no time at all, they reached the edge of the copse of beeches that led to Catherine Exeter's lane. Edward racked his brains. He had to say something. He didn't know when he'd get another chance.

He cleared his throat. "That's a handsome family Mrs. Bartle has."

Florence came to a standstill. "Stop," she said, as if he'd covered her in curses. "You're not being fair."

"How am I not being fair?" he asked, glad they'd halted but confused.

"You were dandling that baby as if you liked it, as if it were your own."

"I do like it . . . him. Ivan is a nice baby and I've known Angus Bartle since I was small."

This explanation did not satisfy Florence. She brushed impatiently at a fallen wisp of hair. "I know what you're thinking," she said. "You're thinking I can marry Freddie and have babies with you. Well, I won't do it. I won't!"

Edward hadn't been thinking anything of the sort. That she would accuse him of it intrigued him. Despite her fierce denial, Florence didn't sound as sure as she might have liked. Heartened, he ventured to stroke her arm. She yanked her hand away before his fingers could catch it up.

"Don't," she said, and pressed her fist to her mouth. Her eyes glittered with pent emotion, their color richer than the summer trees.

The glitter told him she was weakening; told him she yearned for the comfort he could give. Breath held, he stepped closer and coaxed her head against his chest. His heart sighed with silent pleasure as she yielded, as her hands tightened on the sides of his back. The subtle motion of her fingers on his ribs, a soft, catlike kneading, sent a shiver of sensual enjoyment to his groin. His sex lifted, helplessly, deliciously, as he let his own arms circle her back—not tightly, just enough to hold her near.

"Don't be angry, Florence," he whispered. "I'm only trying to make amends."

"There are no amends for what you've done."

Her words were muffled, hovering on the edge of tears. He murmured her name and pressed his lips to the smooth warm skin of her temple. Longing shot through him like a knife: longing and a pleasure too deep for words. He wanted to take her mouth with his until the wanting melted like wax and drowned them both. Unfortunately, the kiss he did take, gentle though it was, seemed to remind her of what had gone before. With a cry of impatience, she pushed at his chest until he freed her.

"Stay away from me," she said, the warning shaking like a leaf. She backed away, her skirts swishing in the bracken beside the path. She put the length of two men between them before she turned. Edward wanted to follow, but instinct told him to let her go. He watched until she disappeared among the dancing shadows of the trees. He remained where he was, rooted to the damp earth-scented ground.

Something was happening inside him, a subtle shifting, like the changing of a tide. Her accusation had turned his imagination down a frightening path.

Florence thought he wanted her to marry Freddie but sleep with him.

He didn't understand how she could let such an arrangement cross her mind. Couldn't she see it would make a travesty of what they felt? They had cared for each other; still did, he was certain, not just with their bodies but with their hearts. Florence would never have been intimate with him if that were not the case. She was no jaded daughter of the peerage. She was a vicar's child, and a good, sweet woman in her own right. That she could consider a duplicity of this magnitude, even for a moment, meant she must love him very much.

Perhaps as much as he loved her.

The possibility sent a tingle of shock across his scalp. If it was true . . . If he had become as necessary to her happiness as she was to his, how could he offer her less than his all? How could he *not* marry her?

The question dizzied him, rocking foundations he'd thought were granite firm. Marrying Florence would mean putting her first, ahead of Freddie. He'd never set a woman ahead of his brother. He'd never even set one ahead of his holdings. The thought of taking a wife had always made him feel impatient, boxed in. But Florence . . .

He couldn't live without her, not with any ease of heart or mind.

And he no longer believed Freddie would make her happy.

But perhaps Edward could. Perhaps, of all the men in the world, only Edward could. Her tears said she thought so, even if she wasn't willing to admit it.

Freddie wanted to be free to love where he pleased. Maybe Edward should finally let him. Maybe, in spite of all the arguments against it, Freddie knew what was best for him. Edward's heart thudded his ribs as if he'd run a race. Fear was part of what drove its swift percussion, fear and something he thought was hope.

"I will," he whispered to the cloud-flecked sky, to the wind-ruffled leaves and the birds that chittered busily in the trees. "I will marry her."

A whoosh of lightness swept his body. Once he'd made the decision, it seemed inevitable, as if he'd been moving towards it from the moment he saw her at Madame Victoire's. He would marry Florence. He, Edward Arthur Burbrooke, earl of Greystowe, would take the vicar's daughter for his bride. He remembered the way the Bartles' girl had leaned against her knee. The vision made him grin. He and Florence would have beautiful children together.

And all he had to do was bring her to the same conclusion.

Florence hurried up the narrow stairs as if she were being chased. Her room was a snug little nest on the second floor, small but bright. It had a bed, a chair, a chest of drawers, and a washstand and basin so like the one she'd had at home it might have been its twin. Simple things for a simple life. Her shoulders did not relax until she shut herself among them.

She'd been wrong to want to escape this, to aim any higher than what she had. A simple girl like her could not navigate the snares of the upper class.

It was just as Catherine said. The Burbrookes had a fatal charm.

She sagged back against the door, her hands pressed flat to the wood as if to bar her fears from entry. It was far too late for that. The danger lurked within. Seeing Edward had brought it back: not just the erotic things he'd done, but the sweet ones.

She remembered how protective he was of Freddie. How he'd pulled her by the hand through the Royal Academy of Art, flaunting propriety just to show her a picture he admired. She remembered his rare smiles. His common frowns. The way he'd held her tucked against him in the night. The way they'd danced at the Vances' ball like angels twirling on a cloud. She missed his company with an intensity that made her ache.

Disgusted, she thumped the wood behind her with her fists. Those memories were lies. The real Edward had ice water in his veins. The real Edward cared for nothing except his family name. He was a devil in noble clothes.

But the baby, her torn heart cried. A devil couldn't make a baby laugh!

She swallowed hard and pushed herself from the door. Edward wasn't a devil. He was a man, a man who might well find entertainment in bouncing a baby and still not give a fig for her. He wouldn't have been dreaming of having a child himself. He wouldn't have thought: what a good mother she'd be, or how I'd love to have a daughter with her eyes. No. His only concern had been tricking her into saving his brother, a brother who—quite obviously—didn't want to be saved.

Be firm, she thought, taking Catherine's advice for her own. Be firm, be firm, be firm.

When her legs crumpled beneath her, Edward's ring, still hidden in her pocket, hit the floor with a fateful clink.

Though Lizzie kept Edward informed of Florence's schedule, he hadn't been able to catch her alone since that day at the Bartles' cottage. She clung to Catherine Exeter as if the woman were a lifeline in a storm.

From what Edward could see, she was the opposite. Day by day, the duchess's friend was sucking the life from his beloved: stealing her glow, her smiles, her very spirit. And who knew what tales Imogene had been telling? Each time he engineered the crossing of their paths, Florence looked paler and thinner. Haunted, he would have said if he'd had a romantic turn of mind.

He worried for her. He would have done anything to help and yet he could do nothing. Nothing but wait, that is, for another chance to speak, to touch, to somehow convince her of his care.

He began to wonder if it was he, by his pursuit, who had put those shadows beneath her eyes. The thought hurt but did not sway him. If it were true, it was only because Catherine Bloody Exeter and her viper of a niece were dripping poison in Florence's ear. He could cleanse her of it, if only she'd give him a chance.

Assuming he didn't lose his mind before he got one.

For the first time in years he attended Sunday service at the village church. He sat in the last row, watching the dip of Florence's hat over the prayer book, feeling his throat tighten as the child behind her tried to climb the wooden pew. The parents scolded and Catherine Exeter shooed, but Florence reached back to brush the little nose with her thumb. Her sheepish smile for the parents nearly broke his heart.

Edward wished it were as easy to make her smile at him.

He positioned himself carefully as the congregation filed out. People whispered when they saw him. Greystowe was not so large they didn't know him by sight. A few of the men nodded and a few of the women smiled, but mostly they were curious. If the earl felt a need to worship, he had a chapel on his land. They couldn't imagine what he was doing here. With them. In the back of their simple church.

Edward didn't care what they thought. Florence was drawing closer, her head averted in a manner that suggested she had seen him. Her arm tightened on Catherine Exeter's and then she was there, in front of him. Gently, he caught her elbow. She yanked away as if he'd burned her.

"Florence," he said, fighting through hurt for calm, "you must speak to me."

"She must do nothing of the kind," said Catherine Exeter.

Edward ignored her. The crowd had bottled up in front of them at the door. He had a few precious seconds before Catherine hastened her away.

"Florence, please." He stroked one finger around her down-turned cheek, the soft still heat of her causing his eyes to sting. "You're breaking my heart, Florence."

"You have no heart to break," snapped Catherine Exeter, but Florence lifted her head. Tears streaked her skin in glistening crisscrossed trails. Her face had hollows he'd never seen before.

"Leave me alone," she said. "I can't bear this anymore."

He fell back, shocked by her appearance, by the dull misery in her voice. Had he done that to her? Had he? Before he could gather his wits, Catherine pulled her briskly through the door and down the steps. Edward could only stare and catch his breath.

"There, there," said a plump older woman, giving his arm a pat. "She'll come around, your lordship. Girls that age don't know what's good for 'em."

It was proof of his distress that he took comfort in a stranger's touch.

• • •

He retreated to Greystowe, to pace his study and write a thousand letters in his head. Finally he sent one, then half a dozen in quick succession. They all came back in pieces and he honestly didn't know whether Florence had torn them up herself. He imagined Imogene reading them, and laughing, and couldn't even bring himself to care. No one's opinion mattered except for Florence's.

He missed Freddie, then was glad his brother could not see him in this state. Hypatia he avoided like the plague. He grew disheveled. He did not drink, but looked as though he had. His eyes were red from lack of sleep, his jaw shadowed with the beard he could not be troubled to let Lewis shave. He could not read; he could not sit; he could not follow a train of thought for more than a minute. At night, he walked to town and stood in the lane beneath her darkened window, yearning for her with all his blood and bone.

A different man would have climbed the trellis and carried her away. Edward wished he were that man; wished he didn't fear Florence would scream for help. And what if she were right to do so? What if he were the danger Catherine claimed? He didn't know who he was anymore. All the rules by which he'd lived were gone.

He only knew he loved her to the point of madness.

One sultry gray morning, when the clouds hung as heavy as his spirit, Lewis and his aunt came together to his study. Lewis thumped a mug of cider on his desk, Hypatia a platter of roast and bread. Edward doubted she'd carried anyone a meal before in her life.

"Enough of this self-pitying nonsense," she said. "I'm not leaving until you eat."

"And I'm not leaving until you shave."

Edward looked at them, his aunt and his valet. Worry and anger mixed in their expressions; a bit of fear as to how he'd react, but even more concern. They knew, he thought, his own eyes burning. Everyone knew he loved her.

"You can't go on this way," said the duchess. "You've done that girl wrong. We all have. But you won't begin to undo it unless you pull yourself together."

Edward stared at his hands, spread wide across his desk, and tried to breathe.

"She's just skittish," Lewis added. "Women get that way. You wouldn't let a horse hide in the brambles if it was scared. You'd catch it and you'd gentle it and then you'd lead it home."

"I don't know how," he said, the words a gasp. "She won't—she won't let me."

"Eat," said his aunt, nudging the plate within reach. "Nobody thinks well on an empty stomach."

He stared at the meat, red and glistening with juice, just the way he liked it. Cook had outdone herself. His mouth watered. He cut a piece and took a bite. Amazingly, it tasted good. After the second bite, his head began to clear. "You don't have to stay," he said. "I'll be all right."

His aunt narrowed her eyes. "I want that plate cleaned, Edward. I am not going to tolerate two idiots in one family."

To his surprise, he smiled. "This was very kind," he said. "Thank you."

"Hmpf," said the duchess. "You can thank me when that girl is back where she belongs."

"There's still the matter of a shave," said Lewis, and Edward smiled at him, too.

He wasn't any wiser than he'd been before, but at least he didn't feel alone.

Fed and shaved and bathed, Edward put his mind to work. He had to find the key to coaxing Florence back. He had to remember everything he knew of her. Then he'd be able to formulate a plan. Hoping for inspiration, he returned to her rooms. He touched her remaining dresses, recalling how she'd looked and what she'd done in every one. He took her novels and read them. He dipped his handkerchief in her perfume. He visited her favorite corners of the garden and drank her favorite tea. He steeped himself in memories, letting himself miss her until it hurt. He took a perverse but definite pleasure in the pain.

He'd made up his mind. Nothing and no one could stop him.

Not even her.

Finally, he returned to the pavilion. There he relived their one forbidden night: her kisses and her sighs, her trust and her bravery. Again, he tied her between the columns. Again, he took his pleasure against her velvet curves. His lips remembered, and his sex. He took the lingering scent of her arousal through his skin. He opened himself to feeling as he never had before. Even the last he faced: the moment of his shame when he slipped from her sleeping hold and crept out like a thief. Loving her had not been his error. His error had been letting her go.

Drained but calm, he padded to the bath. As he'd done before, he opened the carved Indian cabinet and removed his father's letters from the chest. One by one he read them and bit by bit he found a compassion for Catherine Exeter he'd never thought to know. She'd loved the former earl, foolishly, recklessly, with the wholehearted innocence of youth. Then, halfway through the second stack, he discovered something unexpected. He groaned when he realized what it was.

Poor bastard, he thought, both awed and aghast. Poor stupid, selfish bastard.

Stephen Burbrooke had loved Catherine Exeter. He hadn't shoved her in a box and forgotten her. He'd written her, every year, on the anniversary of their parting. He'd poured out his heart, expressing a depth of emotion Edward had never glimpsed. He said he was lost without her; said he felt like half a man. She was his soul. She was all of him that had been true and good.

But he never sent the letters. Not one. He'd made his choice. He married Edward's mother, the daughter of the duke. He raised two sons and polished the family name. He suffered in rancorous silence, keeping everyone at arm's length, hoarding his love for a woman who thought he'd ripped it from his chest. How many lives had he damaged when he put his honor above his heart? His wife's, certainly. His sons, without a doubt. Hypatia's, he suspected.

Catherine's. His own. Who knew how long the list had grown? And for what? A nod from a duke? A yearly invitation to court?

Edward shuddered, the cold slithering down his spine.

His father's sins could so easily have been his.

CHAPTER 15

Believing he'd found the key didn't make Edward eager to turn it. Catherine and her niece had done his family too much harm for that. He toyed with his breakfast while possible outcomes ran through his mind. Finally, too nervous to eat, he readied himself to go. He felt as if his future rested on this day; one wrong step and his life would crumble.

The sky stretched clear and blue over the familiar paths to town. Edward swung his leg over low stone walls and vaulted stiles, the exertion a necessity to nerves stretched taut by dread. Fields ripened in the distance, watered by the rains, their growth so vigorous they must have been eager to fall to the harvester's blade. Willing the warmth to calm his nerves, he turned his face to the sun. His father's letters lay in the pocket of his summer coat, a crumpled garment he wore when he lent a hand at calving or in the stables. The cloth was the color of bleached tobacco, so old he couldn't remember when he'd bought it. His shirt was plain and collarless, his trousers nearly out at the knees.

He intended to present his suit as humbly as he could, as man and not as earl.

When he reached the cottage, Catherine was in the garden weeding. Unlike Florence, the marigolds seemed to be thriving in her care.

She looked up from under the brim of a battered straw hat, her mouth pursed with disapproval, her skin showing its years in the brilliant light. He fought a surge of old dislike. Those lines were not all Catherine's making. She'd had cause for bitterness—at least at first. When she chose to nurture her resentment, the responsibility for its effects became hers.

"Well?" she said, her gaze traveling scornfully over his clothes. "You're certainly dressed to shovel shit. Not that Florence needs to hear any more of that."

With an effort, he held his temper. "It's you I came to speak to. About my father."

"Your father." She chocked her trowel in the dirt and stood with the stiffness of age. Both her gloves and her apron were stained with soil. "There's nothing you could tell me about Stephen Burbrooke that I would care to hear."

"What if I could prove he'd never forgotten you? That he loved you all his life?"

Catherine's face tightened. "That would be a clever trick, but patently untrue. Now, if you'll excuse me, my lord, I have laundry to see to."

In two bounding strides he put himself between her and the door.

"I have proof," he said. "I have letters he wrote to you every year until he died. Love letters, Catherine. He wasn't the man you thought he was. His heart was never cold."

Her eyes narrowed to slits of cloudy ice. "I've no doubt you've concocted some fiction you think will convince me to let you have another go at Florence. The fact remains, however, that she has no desire to speak to you and neither do I. Now step aside or I shall be forced to call the watch."

Since Greystowe's constabulary was funded in large part by its earl, the threat was not a good one. Paying it no mind, Edward withdrew one of the letters and spread it, facing Catherine, across his chest. "You'll recognize his hand, I wager. And perhaps his pet name for you: 'Dearest Angel'?"

"Lies," she spat. Her face turned from the letter as if it

were Medusa's hair. "Your tongue is as forked as your father's."

"Perhaps you'd like me to read it?" he suggested. From the way she flinched, he knew his offer was no kindness. It did not matter. However worthy of being discarded he might feel her, and however comfortable she may have grown with her beliefs about his family, he could not allow her misconceptions to survive. They stood between him and Florence. They would have to be destroyed. He turned the letter around to read, hearing in every flowery phrase the ghost of a father he'd never known.

"'Yesterday,'" he began, "'I walked to the well—remember our well?—and thought of you; how you scratched our initials in the stone when we were twelve. You were an elfin creature, beauty and mischief, like sunlight dancing on the water far below. My heart barely knew desire and yet, for you, I felt it. I wanted to wrap myself around you, to carry you inside me through the dark. Dearest Angel, I fear you have forgotten those days, but I never shall. That innocent time was all I have ever known of joy.'"

As he read, Catherine drew her hands to her breast and curved her shoulders forward, as if shielding from a blow. He thought his words were getting through, but as soon as he lowered the letter, she exploded.

"Bastard!" she cried, hands lashing at his face. "I won't let you have her. I won't!"

The attack surprised him so much he stumbled back into a boxwood hedge. In a flash, she was in the door. He leapt to push in behind her but her body slammed it shut before he could. He heard the frantic turning of a key, then the dropping of a bolt.

Bloody hell, he thought. He was not going to be bested, not by her, not this time.

Without stopping to think, he ran to the parlor window and drove his elbow through the pane. The glass shattered on the first try. He heard a female shriek, then running feet: Catherine, trying to escape his rage.

Let her run, he thought, his will like fresh-forged iron. Removing his boot, he used the sole to widen the hole.

More glass broke, and wood. The truth would find her if he had to shove it down her throat.

Grim as death, elbow throbbing, he shoved his foot back in his boot, wrapped his coat around his hand, and climbed through the broken window. Then, tossing the coat impatiently before him, he stepped onto an ugly puce-green settee, not the least bit sorry to be muddying it as he went. A second shriek greeted his entrance. This voice did not belong to Catherine. As his eyes adjusted to the dimness of the curtained room, he saw a large pale maid huddled like a frightened calf behind the chancy shelter of a spinet.

"Where's Florence?" he said, his tolerance for feminine vapors gone.

The terrified girl pointed towards the ceiling. "Sh-she didn't come down from her room this morning. Nor yesterday, neither."

Edward gritted his teeth and stumped up the stairs. Yet another sin to lay at Catherine's feet: that she had undone Florence's hard-won quest for courage.

"Florence!" he roared, not knowing which door to pound. "Florence, get out here now!"

She appeared with a strangled gasp. He'd obviously caught her combing her hair. The rich brown locks lay over her shoulders and back, falling clear to her waist, as smooth as burnished silk. Her face was pale and puffy, but she was dressed.

"Edward," she said. The hand that held the brush drew inward to cover the skin above her collar. "What are you doing?"

He didn't waste time, but immediately cupped her pallid cheeks between his palms. Her skin was cold. Worried anew, he pressed his lips to the curve of one brow.

"Florence," he said, her name made gruff by the intensity of his feelings. "I love you so much it shames me. I want you to come home. I want to make you happy."

Her brow puckered. She drew a breath to speak, but doubt seemed to silence her. Aching for her confusion, Edward stroked her baby-soft face with his thumbs. Trust me, love, he thought. Trust me.

"Well, well, well," interrupted a voice he'd been praying to avoid. "Look who's come to claim his latest prize." Flushed with sleep and slyness, his former mistress emerged from the second bedroom, draped in a nightdress of filmy, glacier pink.

Edward growled at her. "You stay out of this, Imogene."

"You know her?" Florence gasped.

He cursed his incautious tongue. He'd assumed Imogene had already revealed their sordid past. Apparently, she'd been saving the disclosure for a special occasion: one that had arrived. She folded her arms and smiled.

"Edward knows lots of women," she said, her eyes half closed with pleasure. "Strictly in the biblical sense, mind you. Go all night if you let him. Yes, indeed. Quite the cocksman, our Edward. Knows how to whisper those sweet nothings, then fuck a lady till she screams."

"Hold your tongue," he warned, though he knew she would ignore him. Florence was staring from one to the other with rounded eyes. Noting this, and obviously enjoying it, Imogene flashed her teeth at her.

"Has he gotten masterful yet?" she asked, one long nail brushing Florence's trembling sleeve. "He's good at that. Very top wolf." She assumed a mocking, masculine voice. " 'I must have you, darling. Don't even think of resisting me!' "

It was a canny guess, considering Edward had only behaved that way with her once. She must have added up the dates and realized he was thinking of Florence when he did it. None of which Florence knew, of course. Her face looked as hot as his felt. Nervously, she rubbed her wrists and he knew she was remembering the velvet ties. Damn Imogene for making her think of that as anything but special.

"No," he said. "Never with anyone but you. You're the only woman I've ever loved."

Imogene's laugh was lemon sharp. "My goodness, darling. You must be randy to say a thing like that! The thrill of stealing a march on your little brother must be more seductive than I'd thought."

Edward refused to acknowledge the implication. Instead, he took Florence's shoulders in his hands. He didn't care who heard him or what they thought. He'd get through to Florence if he had to beg her on his knees.

"I love you," he said, low and rough. "I want to marry you if you'll have me. I want us to share the future side by side."

"M-marry me?" Florence stammered just as Catherine came up the stairs. Edward tensed. The old bat must have recovered from the shock of him breaking in. Or perhaps she thought her niece needed reinforcement.

"You see," she said, stealing Florence's gaze from his. "You see what he is? My Imogene is clever. A diamond on a heap of coal. Men turn to puppies when she walks into a room. If he could lie to her—to *her*—why wouldn't he lie to you?"

Even as he consigned her to perdition in his head, Edward struggled to rein in his temper. Abusing an elderly lady would not aid his cause.

"I never lied to Imogene," he said. "And I'm not lying to you. Read the letters, Catherine. My father loved you. Just as I love Florence. The only difference is I'm not fool enough to let her slip away."

The hall fell silent then, the three of them gathering their wits for the next sally in the war for Florence's trust. To everyone's surprise, she was the first to speak.

"You lied to me," she said. "And you started the day we met."

She watched Edward blanch at her quavering words and wondered where she'd found the strength to speak them. Her heart was a tumult of anger and confusion. Despite her accusation, she did believe he loved her. He was not the sort of man to expose his feelings unless he meant them, certainly not in public. Even if she'd doubted that, his obvious misery would have convinced her.

But she also believed he'd slept with Imogene: beautiful,

polished Imogene, whose charms she could not match in a thousand years.

Maybe Edward *would* marry her, but Florence didn't delude herself that she could keep him. One day, sooner or later, another Imogene would slink into his bed.

Her heart felt as if it were breaking already.

"Florence," he whispered, his expression tortured, "I wish I could take it back. I didn't know how much my lies would hurt you. I swear, though, swear on my mother's grave that I'll do everything I can to make it up to you."

The words were as sweet as a poppy-smoker's dream.

"What—" she croaked, then swallowed and tried again. "What about Freddie?"

At that, his lashes lowered, as if this were a source of shame. "Freddie will have to find his own way. You were meant for me. We both know that."

Before she could respond, Imogene clapped, slow and scornful. "Bravo, darling. You should have been on the stage."

"Pure nonsense," snapped her aunt. "Come away, Florence. You don't have to listen to this scoundrel's lies. We can protect you. We know what's best."

Florence looked at her, then at Imogene, and a veil seemed to fall away from her vision. Neither of them cared about protecting her; they only cared about hurting Edward. Catherine wanted revenge for Edward's father and Imogene for the breakup of their affair. Of the pair, Catherine might possess a modicum of sincerity but, truth be told, they were two of a kind: both preferred to see the world through bitter eyes.

If Florence accepted Catherine's offer of protection, would she end up as cynical as her niece? Would she refuse to believe in love when it was staring her in the face?

"Florence," Edward begged, calling her back, "all I ask is a chance."

A chance. A chance to love and lose like the man who raised her. She closed her eyes. She knew what her father would have chosen; knew he wouldn't have given up the happiness to avoid the pain. For all his sadness, he had loved his life, loved his work, loved her with all his soul. Before her stood the price of living safely, of guarding oneself with vitriol and mistrust. Catherine and Imogene had half the life they might and less than half the joy. Her father would have wanted better for his daughter, even at the risk of being hurt.

She looked at Edward, her heart beating harder, her faith struggling to rise.

"Yes," she said, sliding her arms around his neck. "Yes, please take me home."

He hugged her hard enough to squeak, hard enough to warm her through and through.

"Yea," cheered a little voice from the bottom of the stairs. Florence peeked over Edward's shoulder. Lizzie had been eavesdropping, along with Catherine's servant, Bertha.

"I'll start packing," Lizzie said, scurrying eagerly up the stairs.

"I'll help," Bertha seconded, thumping up behind her. Her eyes held a glint Florence had never seen in them, a rather defiant glint. Florence hid her smile against Edward's neck and hoped Greystowe had room for an extra maid. She suspected Bertha would soon require another post.

"You'll be sorry," Catherine predicted as the four of them trooped down with their belongings. "And next time I won't be here to take you in."

A cooler shadow of her aunt, Imogene watched from the door of her room. "Give my regards to Freddie," she purred.

Florence could not help but shudder at the sweetness of the threat.

Edward didn't remember his father's letters until they'd walked a score of paces down the lane. The bundle was still in his jacket, which lay in a scatter of glass on the parlor floor. He hesitated a moment, then continued doggedly on. He'd brought those letters for Catherine. They might as well stay where they were. Maybe she'd read them. Maybe she'd throw them on the fire. He didn't give a damn as long as he never saw her again.

Not that he counted on being so lucky.

He looked around at his companions. Considering what they'd escaped, they were surprisingly subdued, blinking in the sunshine like a bunch of prisoners let out from the Tower. Shock, he supposed. It wasn't every day the underside of human nature got exposed. For her part, Florence walked a wagon's rut apart from him, not far enough to insult, but not close enough to touch. The two maids trailed behind, whispering furiously behind their hands, as mismatched a pair as Edward had ever seen, though they seemed to be bosom friends.

"Yes, Bertha can work for me," he called over his shoulder.

The whispering dissolved into giggles. Edward smiled. That was more like it.

"Thank you, Lord Greystowe," chorused the girls.

Buoyed by the change in mood, he reached for Florence's hand. She jumped at his touch but let him hold it. Her warmth was sweeter than sunshine, her closeness a tonic for his soul. He wondered that anyone could take such joys for granted. But Florence wasn't quite as happy as he.

"I feel horribly foolish," she said, low and shamed. "I didn't believe you when you warned me about Catherine Exeter."

"You had no reason to believe me," he said. "And quite a few reasons not to."

"But I should have seen—"

"What her oldest friend could not? Hypatia is no one's fool, you know." Knowing she needed reassurance, he led her across the ditch to sit on a low stone wall. Pasture spread around them, and sheep grazed in huddles. Fields of grain rippled like water in the summer breeze. The girls exchanged knowing grins as Edward waved them on. When Florence was settled beside him, he stroked the full length of her unbound hair: a husband's privilege, one he hoped would soon be his.

"Was it true?" she asked. "About the letters from your father?"

"Yes."

She folded her hands between her knees. "How very sad."

"Mm," he said dryly. "A cautionary tale."

Florence did not smile. "Do you suppose she'll ever read them?"

He wondered why this worried her but he answered. "I don't know. She might not be able to face the truth. Her hatred for my father may be all that gives her life its shape."

"She taught Imogene to hate men, too, you know. Or at least to think she's better than they are."

Edward smiled. "I imagine that's a lesson Imogene's vanity predisposed her to believe." He smoothed Florence's hair behind her ear. "Must we talk about them? I'd far rather talk about us. For instance, you haven't said whether you'll marry me."

"I want to," she whispered, her gaze evading his.

"But?" he said as gently as he could. When he tried to look into her face, she hunched her shoulders. "You can't tell me you don't love me, Florence. I've seen it in your eyes."

"I do," she said. "I do love you."

His heart swelled to hear her say it even though he'd known it to be true. "But?" he repeated.

"But it's so new. So much has happened in the last few months. Leaving Keswick and Freddie and Catherine and, well, it's hard to sort everything out. I believe you when you say you love me, but I wonder—" She drew breath to gather her courage. "I have to wonder just how long that will be true."

"I see," said Edward. And he did see all too well. It was going to take more than pretty words and promises to undo the damage he had done.

Aware that she'd pricked his feelings, Florence wound her fingers into a knot between her knees. She didn't like hurting him but she couldn't call back the words. She would not lie anymore, not to herself and not to him. Imogene might have stretched the truth, but Florence knew she'd told a part of it. Edward was a man accustomed to taking his pleasures. Florence had seen that for herself. Given that she'd done the same, she could not judge him for it. She could, however, fear.

They sat in silence while a wagon full of chickens plodded past them towards the town. The horse wore a hat on its nodding head, its balding owner none. The driver offered a hail which Edward returned with a lift of his hand. From the ease of the exchange, Florence knew the man had not recognized his earl. Not seeming the least insulted, Edward rested his forearms on his knees.

"Florence," he said once the last squawk and rumble had disappeared, "I know I haven't been what I should to you, neither as brother-in-law nor as lover. I lied when I should have been honest. I was a storm when I should have been a shield. If you'll let me, though, from now on I should like to be your friend. I should like the chance to win your trust."

Without turning his head, he extended his hand to her, palm up, fingers gently curved. She knew he did not make this offer lightly. His arm was tense and he watched her from the corner of his eye. She suspected if she turned him down, he might not try again.

She held her breath even as he held his. She was almost certain she could give him what he wished. She knew she couldn't refuse to try, not when he asked so humbly for her pardon. With the sense of leaping into a gulf, she placed her small hand in his large one. His fingers curled around her own, warm and sure and slightly damp. His grip spoke of both strength and vulnerability. An honest hold. A loving hold. The sensations it inspired were so powerful she had to close her eyes. Slowly, as if she might shy, Edward pulled her hand onto his knee.

"So small," he murmured, reverently stroking its back. "And yet within this little hand she holds my heart."

The words startled her, as did the sentiment behind them. Her eyes blinked open to search his face, but he merely smiled and looked away. He seemed no more able than she to get used to this kinder earl.

"Come," he said, gently tugging her to her feet. "I want to take you home."

What to expect when she got there, she had not the faintest clue.

CHAPTER 16

The grandfather clock ticked in the corner of the dining room, measuring out the silence a second at a time. With nerves as tight as the pendulum's spring, Edward watched Florence push her lamb and peas around her plate. Though her head was studiously lowered, he doubted she'd taken a dozen bites. He wasn't particularly hungry himself. He forced himself to swallow to set a good example.

She was pale yet from her ordeal. If Edward had his way—indeed, if Mrs. Forster had hers—she would have taken this meal in bed. Florence had resisted with the stubborn lift of her chin he'd come to admire as well as dread. "I'm not completely spineless," she'd said. "I think I can manage to dress and come down for dinner."

None of his assurances that he didn't think her spineless had turned her from her intent. Her attitude alarmed him. He was afraid that, in her desire to redeem herself for taking refuge with Catherine Exeter, she might refuse to take refuge with him.

He'd already spoken to Aunt Hypatia; consulted her, actually, on the grounds that she must know more about women than he did. She'd smiled and patted his hand as if she did possess a secret. "It isn't merely you she doesn't trust," she said. "It's herself, her own judgment. If you want her to feel less vulnerable, you have to make yourself more so."

But Edward didn't know how a man could be more vulnerable than to ask the woman he loved to marry him.

"Give it time," his aunt soothed. "You'll think of something."

Because of this exchange, he and Florence sat alone at the long mahogany table—his aunt having developed a convenient headache. Their plates were set properly at either end, so as not to make Florence feel pressed. Despite the distance between them, he'd never been more aware of her. Every flutter of her lashes stirred a ripple in his heart. The motions of her hands were more erotic than a naked *tableau vivant.* She wore one of the dresses Aunt Hypatia had bought, a pale blue silk with ruffles of ivory lace. The candles in the huge epergne sent shadows dancing across her cleavage, shadows that filled the aching tissues of his groin.

He wished he knew what caused that quick rise and fall of creamy flesh. Nerves? Fear? Or was she, too, thinking of the night to come?

He'd declared his love. He'd asked her to marry him. Those things ought not to have sent her back into her shell. They ought to have set their relationship right. They ought to have brought them closer.

Impatient with their impasse, Edward rose. Florence looked up. As always, her beauty squeezed his heart, more so now because she looked so thin and breakable. Gritting his teeth, he held his wineglass and plate before him.

"I'm coming down there," he said, more aggressively than he'd intended.

Florence merely nodded and continued chasing peas with the tines of her fork.

Muttering under his breath, he took the chair beside her. He gestured to her laden plate. "Cook will be upset if you don't eat."

Florence grimaced and took a single bite. Edward was not satisfied.

"You need to build your strength," he insisted. "You don't look well at all."

For some reason, this made her smile. To his surprise, she reached out to smooth his hair, one finger combing it gently around his ear. Edward could count on his hand the times she'd touched him on her own. His body tensed, his breath caught in his lungs. A tingle shivered outward from the passage of her hand. The effect of the simple caress was devastating. He wanted to tip her across the table, to toss up her skirts and shove his aching prick between her legs. He wanted to sink his teeth into her flesh. He wanted to possess her.

But if he did, he'd surely scare her off.

"There's my Edward," she said, light and wry. "Always diplomatic."

Her hand fell from his head to his shoulder, then patted his forearm through the sleeve of his coat. He caught her fingers before she could completely pull away. Her arm stiffened, but he didn't let go. Desire beat at him from inside, so insistent he knew he could not court her as he should. He had touched her secrets; had tasted the honey of her need. He could not remain a gentleman, not when he remembered the pleasures they could share.

"I want you," he said, the words husky. When her lashes rose, her eyes were starred and wide. Fearing what he'd read within them, he shifted his gaze to the satiny curve of her lower lip. A pulse beat in his temple, almost as strong as the throbbing in his groin. He wasn't sure he ought to make this confession, but the words seemed to press out on their own. "There's an ache inside me, Florence. A hunger no one but you can ease. I'm not sure how long I can wait for you to accept my suit."

He could have cursed himself when he saw his words sink in. Her mouth drew up in a troubled little pucker.

"You don't have to marry me," she said, "just to get me into bed."

He sat back in his chair, still holding her hand, his mind working furiously to clear. This was the last response he'd expected. Hadn't she run away because he *wouldn't* marry her?

"Florence," he said, "I wouldn't do that to you. I would like us to marry quickly, yes, as quickly as possible, but I wouldn't treat you like a lightskirt. I mean, I know we—" His voice dropped as he recalled their night in the pavilion. "I know we've shared experiences that perhaps we shouldn't, but things are different now."

She was shaking her head. "You don't understand."

"Then tell me, love." He brushed a kiss across her knuckles. "Tell me."

As if she couldn't both answer and meet his eye, she stared at the hand that lay in her lap. Her breasts rose enticingly with her breath.

"That night," she said, "when you ran after me, when we showed each other pleasure, I told myself I only wanted to know how it felt to be desired. I hoped—" She gave herself a little shake. "Afterwards, I hoped I'd become more to you, that you would ask me to be your wife."

"You weren't wrong to think that. I should have asked."

"No." The hand that lay in her lap rose to join the one he held. Her fingers stroked the tiny hairs on the back of his wrist, raising goosebumps and stilling further words. Then she pulled both hands away. "That isn't what I'm trying to say. I'm trying to say that before we . . . did what we did, I wasn't thinking of what was proper. I genuinely didn't care. I've seen the harm that living up to society's expectations can do: to Freddie, to your father. Then I was too timid to break the rules. Now I'm no longer sure they matter."

Edward cupped the side of her neck and tipped her chin up with his thumb. "They matter, love. Those rules are the way we honor each other. The way we show respect."

Her chin evaded his hold. "You said you were ashamed of loving me."

For a moment, her words robbed him of the power to speak. "I didn't say that. I couldn't have."

"You did. When you came to get me at Catherine's, you said you loved me so much it shamed you." When her eyes met his, they brimmed with tears, like emeralds in the flickering light. "I'm still the vicar's daughter, Edward. Not glamorous. Not rich. Just simple and shy and poor. Marrying me won't polish the Burbrooke name. Marrying me won't earn you anyone's respect. I know you want me tonight, but once you tire of me, wouldn't you rather not be married?"

"Good Lord," he exclaimed, completely thrown aback. "Didn't you hear me today? Do you think I've learned nothing from my father's mistakes?"

Her eyes flashed fire. "I think you want to sleep with me, and your blasted sense of honor demands we be man and wife."

"My blasted sense of honor has nothing to do with it. Lord, Florence, a few days ago you thought I wanted you to marry Freddie and sleep with me."

"Well," she said grudgingly, "I admit I was wrong about that."

"You're wrong about this, as well." He clasped her shoulders, tempted to shake some sense into her. "I want to marry you because I love you. Because you fill a space inside me I didn't know was empty. You make me happy. Holding your hand. Watching you charm a puppy or a little boy. Those things bring me the greatest satisfaction I've ever known. I can't imagine my life without them. I don't *want* to imagine my life without them. What's more, I'm not going to stop loving you. You can get that nonsense out of your head right now."

Her face flushed, but the way she bit her lip told him she still resisted. "Those words are beautiful," she said. "But it's hard for me to believe you really mean them."

Frustration curled inside him in a tight, despairing snarl. "You don't believe me because I lied to you before."

"Maybe I don't believe you because I'm really no one special."

"Oh, Florence." He released her shoulders to stroke her face. "You're incredibly special."

Her chin wobbled, then firmed with challenge. "I'm a pretty country girl is all. A brief, animal attraction. I'm no diamond. I couldn't wrap a man around my finger if I tried."

Edward cursed Catherine's adder tongue, then pressed a kiss to her furrowed brow. "Catherine twisted the facts to suit herself. The truth is I left Imogene because she wasn't you, because I knew she would never move my heart as you have. There's nothing brief about what I feel. And if anyone has me wrapped around her finger, that person is you."

A tear clung to the spikes of her lower lashes. "I want to believe you," she whispered. "I want to so badly it hurts."

"Then do," he said. "Do believe me." Spurred by a sudden impulse, he rose and coaxed her from her seat. "Come with me."

Her confusion was evident, but she complied. "Where are we going?"

He barely knew himself. An idea was forming, rash and nebulous, one act that might prove how committed he was to sharing his life with her. *Make yourself vulnerable,* Hypatia had said, and now he'd thought of a way to do it. He tugged her backward across the parquet floor.

"I asked you to trust me before," he said. "Now I'm going to show you how much I trust you."

She resisted, her arms stretched taut. "You don't have to—"

"Yes, I do, my love. Yes, I truly do."

Walking backwards with both her hands in his, Edward pulled her past the grand stairway in the hall, past ancestral portraits and busts and faded tapestries that smelled of must and spice. Florence knew these objects must have been saved from the old Greystowe Hall, tangible symbols of his family's ancient power.

I don't belong here, she thought, but the words were more habit than conviction. Edward made it easier to believe she might belong, with his iron grip and his eyes like burning flames. Those eyes were willing her to follow, willing her to do everything he asked.

When they reached the arch that led to the billiard room, he turned, releasing her hands to drape his arm around her back. Florence found herself trembling with anticipation.

His arm was heavy, knotted with muscle. Its strength made her feel feminine and small.

He guided her down the family hall. Here the carpet was new and soft, a swirl of navy and cream. They passed Freddie's suite, empty now, since he and Nigel had not yet returned from their business at the mill. Finally, two doors from the orangery, he stopped. This close to the greenhouse, the air was citrus sweet.

"These are my rooms," he said, and opened the door to admit her.

She waited just inside while he struck a match and lit a twisting silver branch of candles. The drapes were tied back, the French doors gapped to admit a velvety evening breeze. The doors opened onto the front lawn. Outside, the sky swept from star-dotted sapphire at its peak, to glowing lime, to a glimmer of crimson beyond the ruffled lake. The colors melted into each other as if the heavens were an exotic cordial. Florence could practically taste the last of the sunset, as if it, too, were a scent that hung in the air.

She had an unexpected urge to peel off her clothes and bathe in the vibrant light.

"This way," Edward said, preceding her through the sitting room to another door.

This led to his bedroom. He lit a second branch of candles and set both on tables beside a massive four-poster bed. Her body tightened, helpless to resist the connotations of her surroundings. This was Edward's private chamber, where he slept, where he dressed, where he dreamed whatever it was he dreamed. The bed's carved posts were thick and twisting, the hangings fit for a king. Their bloodred damask folds glittered with gold embroidery, old but well preserved. The rest of the room was equally dark and rich: glossy wood, heavy, overstuffed chairs, and here and there the glint of precious metal. The walls were painted the same earthy red as the bed.

Above the brown marble mantel hung a small icon of a madonna, her halo thick with gold leaf, her robes so realistically rendered Florence almost reached up to touch them. The Mary was plump and smiling and kind, curiously human, despite the painter's mannered Russian style. The mere sight of her brought tears to Florence's eyes.

She turned to Edward, knowing her awe shone in her face.

"No," he laughed, reading her expression. "She isn't what I brought you here to see."

Turning, he crouched to open one of the low teak cabinets beside his bed. Fighting a sigh, Florence watched the seams of his elegant frock coat strain across his shoulders. Only Edward could make this lavish room seem small.

He rose with something in his hand, a ball of black cloth. He extended it towards her, his face serious and perhaps a bit unsure.

"I believe you wanted to use these," he said. "On me."

Curiosity rose from her chest to flutter softly in her throat. She tiptoed across the Oriental carpet, then gasped when she saw what he held: the ties, the black velvet ties he'd used to bind her that night in the pavilion.

Her hand flew back to her breast before she could touch them. "I thought women weren't supposed to—that you didn't like—"

Edward saved her from her confusion. "It's because I trust you. I'm giving you the power to put me at your mercy. You still want it, don't you?"

Her mouth watered at the thought of him stripped and bound. All that male strength hers to explore, to command. Her body went heavy and soft, as if her sex were a ripening plum. She swallowed hard.

"I—" she said, then had to start again. "I wouldn't want to do it if I thought it would displease you."

His laugh was not entirely steady. "Look at me," he said. "I'm as hard as my great-great-grandfather's pike. I'm not sure anything you do could displease me."

The bulge that pressed his trousers forward argued on his behalf. It was indeed large; forceful, with a throbbing shimmer of movement that must have echoed his beating heart. His bemusement urged her to believe him, but before she proceeded she had to understand precisely what he was offering. She couldn't bear to mistake him again.

"I could do anything I wished?" she asked. "Give or take any pleasure I desired?"

Blood climbed his face in a swarthy tide. "Any pleasure at all." The confirmation was rough, as if her question had aroused him. "My will would be yours to command."

She smiled, helpless to conceal her amusement. That the earl of Greystowe, the dour, stone-faced grump, would cede this power to her was almost too much to credit. Amusement, of course, was not the half of what she felt. Her body burned to accept his offer. She dropped her lashes, shielding the fire she knew must glow within her eyes.

"I believe I should like that," she said.

Edward shuddered, then thrust out the hand that held the ties. "Take them, then," he ordered. "Before I change my mind."

She took them, carefully unrolling each quilted strip and laying it on the bed, one for each of the big posts. Edward would reach, she thought, with a shiver for the picture in her mind. Edward was large enough to reach. When she returned to him, he was watching her like a hawk. She touched the lapels of his coat, then stopped.

"I would like to remove your clothes," she said.

This time the shiver moved through him. "You don't have to ask permission, love. Not tonight. Tonight you may do with me as you please."

At last, she began to trust.

Edward thought he'd die of lust before she finished stripping off his clothes. Piece by piece, she disrobed him. His frock coat and his vest. His cufflinks and his gray silk necktie. The removal of his shoes and socks was mysteriously—almost unbearably—intimate. When they were gone, she skimmed the tops his feet with the pads of her fingers, sending strange, sensual chills along his legs.

"My, what big long toes you have," she said with a fey, half-hidden smile.

His cock nearly burst through his trousers at her words. He felt like the wolf in the story: a beast with a primitive urge to claim its mate. He trembled under the onslaught of instinctive need, but did not move. She had chained him with the metal of his love. He had to bow his will to hers until he knew she was reassured.

As he did, her confidence grew. He could see it in the way she tossed her hair, in the taunting sway of her hips as she circled his increasingly unclothed body. He loved watching the change; loved the way she ran her hands over his back and shoulders, greedily, leaving fire in her wake, seeming to measure every muscle and bead of sweat. When her fingers drifted lower, over his trousered rump, his buttocks tightened without his will.

"You're hard here," she said, her touch roaming unchecked over tensing curves.

His jaw clenched in an agony of desire. "I'm harder than that in front."

It was a hint she could not miss. She laughed, a womanly sound, sweet and sultry. Her arms wrapped him from behind, hands shaping the heavy muscles of his chest. When they slipped still lower, he gasped. Her fingers had dipped beneath his waistband, teasing the smooth, sweat-dewed skin of his upper belly. His shaft strained upward, outward, desperate for its share of her caresses.

"If I finish undressing you," she said, her face brushing back and forth across his spine, "if I take your hardness in my hand, will you still do as I ask?"

He hesitated, then rasped his answer. "Yes, love. Tonight the power is yours."

She kissed the center of his back, then carefully opened his trousers. Because she stood behind him, her hands moved almost as his would have. He watched them work the buttons, her fingers slim and white. He felt deliciously unmanned, rousingly unmanned, in a way he would not have thought possible. His organ surged at the release of the cloth that constrained it, and at the peculiar sense that it belonged to her now, not to him.

When she pushed his remaining garments to his ankles, her cheek rested lightly on his haunch. Her skin was hot, a flush he could not help but feel. She was excited. This aroused her. A growl threatened to rumble from his chest. His self-control was a thread stretched to breaking.

"Florence," he said, the sound choked, "perhaps you ought to tie me now."

To his complete astonishment, he felt her teeth nip the meat of his buttock. Before he could stop himself, he yelped.

"Oh!" she gasped. "I'm ever so sorry. Did I hurt you?"

"No." His muscles clenched even tighter at the way her hand was rubbing the injured flesh. "You just surprised me."

"I don't know what came over me," she said, still rubbing, still contrite. "You're just so pretty back here. So small compared to the rest of you. Your . . . your bottom is like an apple. I had to take a bite."

He was caught between a laugh and a groan. Her thumbs had curled a little way between his cheeks and now drew arcs towards his tailbone in a manner that was not the least bit soothing—assuming that soothing him was her intent.

"It's all right," he said. "You didn't hurt me." His voice sank. "Actually, what you did was rather sexy."

"Oh," she said, breathless now. "Well . . . good. I'm glad."

He fought the laugh until she slipped around him to his front. Then he could not even smile. He was too busy trying not to groan. Her fingers scratched lightly through his chest hair, then teased the beaded coppery nipples she found within. New sensations sang along his nerves, incendiary twinges that arrowed through his body to his sex. They pulsed in its tip, tapping the sensitive skin like drops of oil. Her fingers had a power no other woman's had possessed. He was drowning in lust, fighting with all his strength to keep control, to keep from frightening her with his need. She bit her lip as she watched his penis bob and darken.

"You like this," she said, still feathering her thumbs across his nipples.

What breath he might have used to admit it disappeared

when she sank to her knees. Unable to resist, his hands moved to spear her shining upswept hair.

"Don't touch me," she said. "I want to do this by myself."

"Tie me, then," he groaned. "Because if you take me in your mouth, I'll have to touch you. I won't be able to stop."

After a moment's hesitation, she pushed to her feet. She looked at his straining shaft, then at the bed. "I've changed my mind," she said.

His heart lurched, the reaction violent and confused. Did she mean she released him from his promise to let her do with him as she pleased? He wanted to take her, it was true. He wanted to drag her to the floor, to rip her clothes from her silky skin and drive so deep and hard between her legs she would feel him pounding there for days. He craved that triumph with everything that made him male. And yet, despite his compulsion to conquer and subdue, part of him wanted her to take him first.

He waited for her to explain, his contrary longings at war within his breast. She pressed two fingers to her lips in contemplation, unwittingly drawing the tension out.

"Yes," she finally said, the word decisive. "I want to tie you standing up."

His heart gave a second galvanic pump, this one unmistakably excited.

"If you're lying down," she explained. "I won't be able to touch as much of you."

"Perfectly all right," he rasped. "I quite understand."

She grinned, a sudden flash of humor. "Do you?" Her tone was knowing, seductive. She put one hand on her hip and pointed with the other to the end of the bed. He could see the teacher in her then, the little general who expected to be obeyed. "Please stand in front of those posts so I can tie you."

His skin heated as he complied. His reach was just sufficient to grip the polished turns of wood. She bound his wrists with endearing concentration, more firmly than he expected, and with a great many knots. She would never make a sailor but they would hold.

"That isn't too tight, is it?" she said. He shook his head and she patted the center of his chest. "Just tell me if you want them taken off."

But he didn't. To his amazement, he liked being at her mercy, liked wondering what she'd do next. Whatever she chose would be her idea: no coaxing, no intimidation, just precisely what she wished. He would know what she wanted to give. He would learn what she enjoyed. He looked from the hand that pressed his breastbone to her eyes. They shone with the same excitement that was building in his bones. He didn't want to shatter the magic with a word.

She smiled and took a long step back.

"I'm going to remove my clothes," she said, wonderingly, as if the announcement surprised her, too. "And you're going to watch. You're going to be the first man I ever wanted to see."

His breath rushed out, hollowing his ribs. He couldn't have spoken to save his life. He had an inkling what this meant. Florence had never been comfortable with people's admiration of her looks; she'd always been too shy. But if she wanted him to watch . . .

She must love him, must truly, truly care.

She removed her dress without posturing or flirtation, merely the caution a woman of modest means would use with a valuable garment. She laughed as she struggled with some of the hooks, a little nervously, but not as if she wished to stop. She wore no corset. He supposed the weight she'd lost made it unnecessary. The removal of her gown left her in chemise and drawers, a pretty concoction of lace and tucks and sheer, sheer lawn. He could see her budded nipples through the top, and the triangle of sable curls between her legs. The image drew him back to the day he'd seen her at Madame Victoire's. The arousal he'd felt then was nothing to the yearning that gripped him now. His body trembled with it, and his heart. More than his cock craved her body's tight embrace.

Florence didn't see the tremor that swept his limbs. She was too caught up in squirming out of her underthings before she lost her nerve. The chemise had tugged her chignon halfway off her head. She had to hop on one foot to remove the second leg of her drawers. She seemed the perfect opposite of a coquette and Edward had never loved her more.

"There," she said with nervous, breathless pride as she threw the drawers into a corner.

His grin threatened to split his face. Another woman would have stroked those creamy breasts or palmed that luscious swatch of curls. Florence merely stood, biting her lip and smiling, looking as if she wished she could wring the lovely hands she'd clasped before her belly. He suspected those hands were shaking more than his.

Her courage moved him beyond belief.

"You," he said, "are the most beautiful woman I've ever seen."

She smiled and ducked her head. "Now you're being foolish."

"No," he said, perfectly serious. "No one has ever seemed more beautiful to me."

"Oh. Well . . . well, thank you," she said, her chin still tucked. "You're rather beautiful yourself."

He laughed at that, but then she set out to prove it.

She kissed every part of him her lips could reach, standing on tiptoe to mouth the arch of his neck, kneeling down to kiss his curling toes. Her hands were pure seduction, feathering touches from his legs to his hips to the curves of his supposedly apple-like arse.

"Oh, Edward," she sighed as she tickled the hair beneath his outstretched arms. "Everything about you is so interesting."

Apparently, she thought his sex was interesting, too. She cupped and jiggled and stroked and squeezed until his every exhalation became a groan.

When she bent to taste, he gripped the posts so hard, his fingers went briefly numb.

Her mouth was heaven, sheer soft, warm, wet, silky heaven. Steadying his shaft with one hand, she cupped his testicles with the other and sucked him to the brink of climax. Her tongue laved the cluster of nerves beneath his crown. Her lips pulled his foreskin over the head. She sucked him as if she loved his taste and feel, as if there was nothing about him she couldn't accept.

He felt himself swell to bursting; felt the sweet, throbbing ache gather at his base. "Florence," he moaned, knowing he should stop her. Instead, his hips thrust towards the strong, clinging heat of her mouth.

One more, he thought, his nails scoring the bedposts. One more heavenly drag and he would stop.

She seemed to sense what his body wanted. Her hands tightened, then her mouth, cajoling him to succumb to the killing urge. Sparks danced before his eyes and reddened and then his cock turned inside out. He bent forward at the waist as if someone had punched him, hips jamming forward, muscles convulsing all at once. The orgasm was a tight, throbbing blaze of feeling, endless, intense. He gasped with shock as the pleasure poured from him into her. He couldn't even groan until it finished, until his stolen breath returned. His legs sagged back onto the mattress, no longer able to hold his weight.

"Florence," he panted. "My God."

She giggled against his chest and he discovered he was holding her. His hands were free. He hadn't even felt her untie him. Still breathing hard, he spread her glorious hair across her shoulders. One last pin scattered to the floor.

"That," she said, hugging him back, "was wonderfully entertaining. I can't imagine why women aren't supposed to do that."

He tipped her head to kiss her, deeply, wetly, his cock going weighty as he realized he could taste himself in her mouth. His seed was salty, bittersweet. That they were sharing it was alarmingly erotic. A sound broke in his throat, helpless and sharp. The noise did something to Florence. Her hands clutched the back of his neck and her soft bare breasts wriggled deliciously against his chest. Abruptly short of breath, he broke the kiss. Her weight was nestled against him, between his legs. From the way she squirmed, he knew she was hoping for a quick recovery.

With a low, easy laugh, he swung her into his arms and tossed her on the bed. She shrieked as she landed, then smiled through tousled hair. To see her naked, in his bed, was a pleasure he had not thought to know.

He crawled up after her, slowly, predatorily, feeling very much the animal he sometimes feared he was. He loomed above her on all fours, his shaft hanging, beginning to thicken even as it swayed.

"Edward?" Florence said, tentatively touching his belly with the back of her hand. Her voice shook as if she were afraid, but her face was deeply flushed.

Edward bared his big sharp teeth with great enjoyment.

"Now, Little Red Riding Hood," he said, "let's see how entertaining *you* can be."

As it happened, she was quite.

CHAPTER 17

Florence trembled on the verge of an almost terrifying happiness. Edward loved her. Edward trusted her. Edward smiled each time his eyes met hers.

Like children, they had raided the kitchen for a midnight snack. "I need my strength," he'd said, goosing her through the shirt—his shirt—which was all he'd let her wear.

This playful Edward delighted her: the softness of his smiles, the ease of his wolfish chuckles. He seized on any excuse to touch her, playing with her fingers and her hair, squeezing her knee, touching his mouth to the tip of her nose. Having restrained himself so long, he could not seem to keep his hands to himself.

Now they sat cross-legged in the shelter of his bed, the hangings pulled around them, picking at their pilfered tray of fruit and cheese and honey-slathered bread. Edward fed her a slice of apple, eyes glowing as he eased it past her lips. "I have a sudden hunger," he said, "to know everything about you."

She blushed at his tone and let her teeth scrape gently, daringly, down his thumb. "Everything?"

His lashes drifted a fraction lower.

"Everything," he insisted, his hands sliding languorously down her neck. "First word. Favorite color. The name of your very best friend when you were twelve."

The warmth of his touch was wine pouring through her veins. He seemed to like the look of her swimming in his shirt. He clasped her upper arms, forcing the starched white cloth to bunch around his fingers. She had to struggle to think past the pleasure of his nearness.

"My first word was kitty," she said. "Blue is my favorite color. And Papa was always my best friend. He had the silliest sense of humor. Puns and practical jokes. No one could make me laugh the way he did."

Edward's mouth twitched as if the mention of her laughter called to his. "Ball," he said. "Cherry red. And Freddie, though Plunket my pony came close."

"Plunket?"

"Named him myself. Looked just like one of our tutors." He smiled at her then, his eyes as kind as the icon on his wall. "Would you mind, Florence, if I asked how you lost your mother?"

"I was three," she said, covering his hand to reassure him the question had not hurt. "She died in childbed and the baby, too. It would have been a boy. I don't remember her except for Papa's stories. They were born in the same little town. Never loved anyone else, either one. Papa said she was the sweetest, wisest woman he'd ever known and she could never get anywhere on time. He never really recovered when she died. He didn't say so, but sometimes—when he thought I wasn't watching—his eyes grew terribly sad." She looked away, not wanting to dwell on that now, not with Edward so near and dear. She forced a smile. "When I met Freddie, I thought, 'Here's the brother I never got a chance to have.'"

It occurred to her then, and perhaps to Edward, that if she accepted his proposal, she could have Freddie for a brother. Whatever his thoughts, Edward gathered her hands into the dip of silk and skin where his ankles crossed. His fingers rubbed comfort into the hollows of her palms. "I'm sorry you lost your mother so young."

"I was sorry, too," she said as the furrow between his

brows melted what was left of her heart. "But Papa was good to me. Our parishioners used to call him Father Fairleigh: the mother hen. He was forever fussing over his flock, making sure the little old ladies had someone to look out for them." *

"Little old ladies?"

"We had quite a few in Keswick. Papa liked to call them our first, best crop." The memory warmed her, her father's voice suddenly as clear in her mind as Edward's. How could she have forgotten how optimistic he was, and how little of his life was lost to mourning? "He was a kind man," she said firmly, "and a wonderful father, just not very clever with money."

"Thought God would provide?"

"Well, He did!" she said, laughing at the quirk of Edward's mouth. "He simply didn't provide extra."

"And this attraction you hold for animals—"

"Just cats," she interposed.

"Oh, yes, just cats," he agreed, an entirely unexpected dimple appearing in his cheek. "You always had that effect? Even as a girl?"

"I'm afraid so. The children at school used to call me Little Miss Sardine because, well, sometimes the village cats would follow me home en masse."

"A great embarrassment, I presume."

"Quite. When the local toddlers took to trailing after me as well, I nearly refused to leave the house."

Edward was unable to keep his mirth inside. It escaped in snorts from his aristocratic nose. "Poor Florence!" he cried. "What a trial! Unable to walk down the street without her retinue of small, adoring subjects."

"It was a trial," she protested even as she grinned. She hadn't felt this easy telling a story since she'd had Freddie for a listener. "You can't imagine how mortifying it was."

Edward reached out to tweak her nose. "You're a dear, Florence, but I must admit my sympathies lie with the cats and toddlers."

He grew contemplative then, his smile fading to a gentle curve as he ran his hand along her lower leg. The gesture was absentminded but oddly comforting. Possessive. His hand belonged there, she thought: close and easy and warm.

"Your childhood sounds very rich," he said, his expression hidden from her gaze. She knew his own must have been different. A cold father, a fragile mother, and probably more servants than friends, at least while he lived at Greystowe. She knew he wouldn't want her to feel sorry for him and yet she did. One person to love you unconditionally was more important than any amount of privilege. Of course, Freddie had loved Edward that way but, being much younger, he could not have made Edward feel safe.

She stroked the silky top of his head. "What about your childhood? Freddie told me a little, but not everything."

He shrugged one shoulder. "There's not much to tell. Freddie was the best thing about growing up. Tormenting our tutors—"

"Teaching him to swim."

"He told you about that, then." He squeezed her ankle. "Yes, that's a happy memory. At the time, of course, we were both quite miserable. Not to mention half drowned. Here." With unconscious grace, he rolled from the bed. "I think I still have his first trophy."

He rummaged in the bedside cabinet, then emerged with a triumphant "Ha!" He handed her a round medal, most of the gold worn off, which hung from a frayed blue ribbon. Florence ran her finger around the burnished laurel wreath, wishing—as she had with Freddie—that she could have known Edward then, not as a girl but as a woman. She would have liked to protect the boy he'd been from a father who could only love a memory.

"You really kept it," she said, her eyes filling. "All this time."

Edward had returned to his seat on the bed. He laid his fingertip next to hers. "Yes. Young as I was, I knew that was a day I would want to remember."

"You were a good brother."

A shadow crossed his face, but he covered it with a smile. "Freddie was a good brother." He brushed her hair behind her shoulder. "I imagine our upbringing was different from yours, but Father made sure we never lacked for anything. Anything material, at least." He paused to gather his thoughts, his gaze distant but calm. "I suppose that was the only way he knew to show he cared. He kept the estate together. Made sure we'd never have to struggle to get out of debt, the way his father had to."

"You needn't feel guilty for admiring what was good in him."

Again, one shoulder lifted. "He taught me the value of responsibility. And discipline." His mouth slanted with sudden humor. "Though I fear I've shown precious little of that with you."

"Perhaps not tonight," she said, and they exchanged a smile.

"Oh, Florence." Impulsively, he clasped her hands. "I love you so much. I'm sorry I ever gave you reason to doubt me."

"I love you, too," she said, the words new enough to call a flush to the surface of her skin.

He made a sound, low and hungry, then leaned forward to brush his lips across that building warmth. "I want to finish what we've begun," he said against her cheek. "I want to lie with you, to come inside you, to make our bodies one."

Heat spread through her in a pulsing wave, pooling in her breasts and belly. The reaction was so intense she had to drop her eyes.

"Please," he said, his grip tightening on her shoulders. "Tell me you want that, too."

She slid her own hands up his chest, over his robe, feeling through silk and muscle the hard, swift beat of his heart. It pounded as if he feared what she would say, as if her agreement were a matter of grave importance. Her fingers curled into the cloth.

The answer hung in her mind like an apple about to drop.

She knew if she accepted, she'd be giving herself to him in every sense of the word: all she was and all she would be, till death did them part. Yes, he'd asked her to marry him, but a promise was not a deed. He could change his mind or fall tomorrow for the butcher's daughter.

And Florence would be left with nothing but the memory of this night.

It was enough. She wanted the risk; wanted to leap into the void. Her heart was his already. She had no wish to take it back.

She might be afraid, but she would not be a coward.

"Yes," she said, her answer almost steady. "I should like that very much."

His breath sighed from him. He cupped her jaw, his fingers stroking her neck beneath her hair. "I hope you like it," he said, with a tinge of wryness. "But the only promise I can make is to be careful."

Her hand moved beyond her control, sliding beneath the lapel of his robe to find the warm, hard curve of his ribs. "I don't mind when you're a little wild."

He laughed, the sound all breath. "Not this time, love. I might hurt you. But perhaps you're not familiar with the logistics?"

Her smile curled into his neck. He'd forgotten how much a simple country girl could learn. "I'm familiar with them, though I doubt I've sufficient experience to conduct myself very well after we, er, after we . . ."

"Achieve the desired union of our parts?" he said, saving her from her sudden loss of nerve. His chuckle rumbled in her ear and she knew he liked her shyness. "You needn't worry about the after. After has a way of taking care of itself and, as I said, I'll be careful."

Something in his voice caught her attention, a deeper arousal, a tension that was more anticipation than concern. Wondering what had triggered it, her hand slipped down his gaping robe, over skin and bone and muscle. His stomach tightened as her thumb crossed his navel and then she found him, rising thick and hard from the tight black nest of curls. The base of his cock more than filled the circle her fingers made. He cradled her forearm, gently encouraging her touch.

"I'll be careful," he whispered, the words shaking. "I won't hurt you."

She smiled where he could not see and vowed she'd never let him know she'd guessed his secret. Part of him, the part that would have made a fine Crusader, relished the thought of deflowering her with his symbolic sword. Marauder and protector. Primitive beast and courtly knight. Both were part of Edward's soul. Relaxing her grip, she trailed her fingers lightly up his shaft. The mighty column quivered at her touch. Like a puppy, she thought as she traced the net of swollen veins, wriggling for a treat.

"There is the matter of size," she said as seriously as she could. To her delight, the quiver grew violent.

"Sh." He covered her hand, molding it to his silky, pulsing skin. "I am convinced you shall take me." His second hand slipped beneath her shirt to stroke the lush curve of her hip. "You were made to take me."

"It's true, I'm not delicate, but you must admit your equipment is formidable."

His palm gripped hers, a brief, involuntary spasm. His shaft lengthened in their mutual hold. Oh, how she enjoyed this. What power people's secret wishes had! When he spoke, his voice was whiskey rough. "I know you can't truly be afraid. You aren't even shaking."

"No, but perhaps in my ignorance, I haven't fully appreciated the challenge of—"

He silenced her with a kiss that drove from her mind her intent to tease him. Abruptly urgent, he rolled her beneath him, pressing her down with his weight. The kiss stole her breath and fired her blood. He released her long enough to pant for air, then ripped the shirt she wore down her front. With a whispered curse, he tore off his robe and sank back over her, fitting his hardness to her curves, rubbing them together until every inch of her thrummed with excitement. For long minutes, her mind was filled with nothing but the feel of him under her roving hands, the rush of his breath, the wet, greedy tug of his mouth. She could not get close enough to him, nor he, it seemed, to her. They grappled and writhed and clutched each other's backs. His erection was a brand against her thigh, her hip, her belly. She spread her legs to wrap them around him, and even that embrace was not enough. She wanted him: all his size, all his passion, all his hidden desires.

"You'll have to tell me," she said, gasping as his kiss moved towards her breast. "You'll have to tell me what to do."

"I'll show you," he said, and captured her nipple with lips and tongue. He pulled her into his mouth with shocking strength. Feeling speared through her, turning molten in her sex. She was melting, desire running from her like liquid gold. He turned to the other breast and drew that just as hungrily against his tongue.

Florence groaned and arched her back. "I wish you would show me soon."

He chuckled and cupped his hand around her curls, squeezing the soft, aching cushion within his palm. She groaned again, louder than before. His fingers—so strong, so hard—pressed between her plumping lips but did nothing to ease her need. She whimpered when he let go.

"Put your hand on my cock," he said, the words a smoky rasp. "Take me up against you. Put me where you want me to be."

Now she did shake, though she did not think she shook with fear. She slid her hand down his back, around his hip, her breath coming quick and shallow. They both jumped when she touched him. His organ was heat in her hands, hard, throbbing fire. She drew it closer to her sexual heart.

"Lift your knees," he said, coaxing one leg into position with his hand. He balanced his weight on the other elbow, his hips canting forward as she guided his approach. He had to bow his back to look into her face, and suddenly the disparity in their sizes was very real. He overshadowed her, overwhelmed her, and yet she did not wish him any other way. She knew he would be careful with her. She knew she would be safe.

His eyes squeezed shut for a moment when the crown of him slipped between her lips. He was big and eager, dripping with it as he tried to find his place. She wasn't quite sure how to manage, but his fingers soon joined hers, adjusting, easing, with an intimacy that made her blush. A second later, the hot round tip was pressed inside her, the sensation of pulsing, stretching heat making her sigh and fight a squirm. When he opened his eyes, his pupils had nearly swallowed up the blue.

"There," he whispered. "How does that feel?"

It felt like her soul was tearing down the middle, not with pain but gladness. With this act, her whole being made room for him.

"Silky," she said, afraid to push but wanting to immensely. "And hot. And very, very good." His cock bucked at the words. She could not quell her body's reaction. Her longing flowed out against him. "Oh, Edward, I'm all awash."

He growled against her neck and nipped her lightly with his teeth. "I like you all awash. It tells me you're ready to take me."

But he did not move, not even when she locked her arms behind his waist and urged him in. Instead, he stroked her hair from her brow and kissed it. His lips were hot, his breath harried. She didn't understand his inaction. Didn't he want to take her? Didn't he want to make them one? A niggle of worry began to rise.

"You came this far before," she said, "that first time at the ruins."

"Yes." His face tightened as if the memory hurt. "I did."

"You're not going to pull back this time, are you?"

He shuddered and his hips moved, pressing a tormenting fraction deeper. "You're the only person who could make me."

"I don't want to make you. I want you to—" She bit her lip.

"Tell me," he said and ran his tongue across the place her teeth had sunk.

She let go with a gasp. "I want you to push. I want you all the way inside me."

"Even if it hurts?"

"I don't care." She squeezed his hips with her thighs. "It hurts too much to wait."

"Oh, Florence," he said, her name a moan. "Brave, sweet Florence."

He kissed her, deeply, and began to press gently forward and back against her barrier, nudge and release, nudge and release, until her fingers curled into claws behind his shoulders. What he was doing felt terribly good, but not quite good enough.

"Please, Edward," she breathed, unable to bear it. "Please, please take me now."

She felt him gather; felt a sting of pressure. Then, with a quick forward thrust and a helpless grunt of pleasure, he rent the obstacle between them. He pushed once more, sighed, and forced himself to stop. His shoulders were suddenly slick beneath her hands, his head bowed on his neck. Already, the pain of his entry was fading; was melting into need. She knew she had not taken much of him, not even half. A distance remained between their hips.

"I'm all right," she said, kissing the ball of his shoulder, stroking the clenched and quivering muscle of his rear. "I want the rest."

"Florence." He raised his head, his voice so deep it was nearly hollow. "I want to watch your face when I make you mine."

Their eyes locked. She'd never seen such vulnerability—or such love. He slid one big warm hand beneath her hips, his fingers spread from the small of her back to the lowest swell of her bottom. At last he pushed, slowly, firmly, forcing the walls of her sheath to part for his penetration. Nothing stopped him. She experienced no pain, no fear, no limitation of flesh that would not ease. She *was* made for him. Her body gave before his slow, sleek drive, oiling his way, hugging his pounding length. She sighed when his hips pressed hers, filled to satiation, joined to him by that hot tensile shaft and by the luxuriant pleasure of a close and perfect fit.

He moaned her name, dropping kisses across her face. "Oh, Lord," he breathed. "That's good."

Now that he was seated, he drew her hands from his waist and pressed them above her head, twining their fingers in a tight, sweaty grip. She didn't mind. If she was captured, so was he. Both of them were trembling, both smiling into each other's eyes.

"Love," he said, and began to draw and thrust. Nothing moved except his hips and his expression: like a man seeing a vision he did not want to end. Straight in he stroked. Straight out he pulled. Thick and strong and simple. The way it made her feel, however, was anything but simple. She was conquered and powerful, needy and generous, a pauper and queen of the world. He was making her a woman in the most primitive sense of the word.

He whispered of his pleasure: hot, forbidden words that made her tighten deep inside. He was on fire, he said. Ablaze to feel her spend. He murmured praise to her breasts, to her small, white feet, to the damp, dimpled backs of her knees. He told her how hard he was, how badly he ached. He urged her to rock with him, then swore when she obeyed. It seemed a blessing when he slid like satin inside her, strong as a bull, gentle as a lamb.

Each thrust drove him to his limit, hard but slow, so slow she could scarcely bear his long withdrawals. He seemed to be entering her anew each time, ravishing her anew, as if his cock adored that claiming stroke.

"Don't rush," he pleaded when her body grew impatient. "We'll only have one first time."

He released her hands and curled his thumb between their hips. She shattered at his touch, her body clenching uncontrollably, her throat burning with a helpless cry.

He laughed when she apologized. "Again," he demanded. "Quick, love, do it again."

She couldn't have resisted if she'd tried. He seemed to know what her body wanted before she did; when it needed a pinch, or a stroke, or a greedy, grinding push. She came until her body was limp with joy. At last, though, his own needs rode him too hard to be denied.

"I can still pull out," he said, his arms trembling, his body dripping sweat. "You don't have to take my seed."

Her head rolled back and forth against the bed. "I want it," she said, hands urging his hips. "I want everything."

He winced. His movements were heavier now, less controlled. He was not drawing out as far. He could not seem to bear to.

"If you take it," he growled, "you'd better consider yourself my wife. If I spill inside you, this will be our wedding night."

She smiled, amazed he could doubt she'd already surrendered. "You're the husband of my heart. There will never be another."

He paused long enough to search her eyes. His were narrowed, searching for the truth. She grinned at his seriousness, unable to help herself: he had filled her so with bliss. He must have seen this because he finally nodded, the same curt acknowledgment that had piqued her in the past.

"Good," he said briskly, all Edward, all beloved. "There will never be anyone else for me."

"Come then." Still grinning, she dragged her nails down the long, sweaty curve of his spine. "Make me yours."

He flinched, then darkened, then exploded into motion between her legs. She had unleashed something even he could not control; his release had waited too long on hers. Now he would not take his pleasure, it would take him. His body jolted hers, harder, faster, his sex a piston of throbbing need. She grabbed the side of the bed to keep from sliding and even with this, he'd soon thrust her up against the headboard.

"Hold on," he ordered, bracing his arm on the polished wood. "Hold . . . on . . . to . . . me."

She held, curling her hands behind his shoulders, keening at the pounding wonder of his wildness. He was grunting as he thrust: broken phrases, endearments. *Deeper,* he begged. *Oh, God, sweetheart, deeper.* She tried to help but his skin slipped under her hands. She dug her heels into the mattress. She pushed. The added force unraveled him. He cursed and swelled and drove so far he seemed to breach her womb. His body held, trembled, then shuddered with the first unstoppable wave of climax. His fists were clenched, his eyes screwed tightly shut. Veins stood out on his neck as he strove to hold his place while his cock gushed hot and hard. He gasped at the end, and moaned and then, as his muscles relaxed, her peak unfurled like the petals of a flower. Still couched inside her, his penis twitched at the fluttering pulses, in perfect sympathy with her pleasure.

She was glad her body had waited. She wouldn't have wanted to miss the drama of his peak.

"My," she sighed, stroking his hair as he collapsed onto her breast. "That was wonderful. I can't wait to do it again."

His shoulders shook and she realized he was laughing, silently, but he was. His shaft slipped from her with the motion, heavy and limp and wet, an effect she found peculiarly erotic.

"Florence," he groaned, nuzzling the bend of her neck. "I'm afraid you'll have to wait a bit."

He felt as if the earth had stopped turning. For the first time in his life, his spirit was at peace. The air was hushed and fragrant, and his heart so full of love he thought it must overflow.

Florence lay against him, nestled in the curve of his arm. She was drowsy and soft and her hand played gently up and down his side. She was easy with him now—as well she should be. This night had been one in a million. Nothing could have prepared him for the ecstasy they'd shared, for the closeness, the profound sense of change he felt within his soul.

She'd called him the husband of her heart.

She'd given herself to him, without reserve.

And this was only the beginning. A lifetime of pleasures opened in his mind, holding her, loving her. She would be his bride. They would walk into the future hand in hand.

He thought he could live on this happiness for years. As it happened, though, he only had a day.

CHAPTER 18

They bathed together in Edward's private plunge bath. The tile was garnet and gold, the tub white-veined black marble. The water flowed hot from the silver tap in a seemingly endless stream. The tub was so deep Florence could sink in it to her neck. She had never seen a marvel like it and yet the greatest luxury of all was the freedom to touch the man she loved. He seemed to feel the same for he teased her and tickled her, whispering foolish endearments as he drew the soapy sponge along her skin. Florence purred under the attention, so weak with pleasure she could barely caress him back.

"You are the queen of the cats," he whispered as he slid inside her once again.

As breath-stopping as their first time had been, this wet, languorous coupling was even better. He taught her what a truly clever cock could do. How it could probe and rub. How it could weep with desire and find tender, hidden places that made her want to weep herself.

"That's the way," he praised as she cried out and clung. "Teach me what you like."

That an organ so inherently selfish could be made so generous she found amazing, almost as amazing as the pleasure she took in its gratification. Awed by the magic they could make together, she cradled him gently in her palm.

"When you touch me like this," he said, his hand lightly stroking hers. "I know how weak a man can be."

Such weakness she could learn to love.

He followed when she slipped back to her room to change. He insisted on dressing her himself, instructing Lizzie through the closed door to take the day off. Far from being scandalized, the maid giggled and pattered off. Florence was certain Edward's sword had reached the limits of its strength but somehow, during the process of lacing her new French corset, it found the wherewithal to rise again.

His fingertips roved the stays that bound her, the lace and satin, the nip of her waist and the swell of her lifted breasts. "Jesus," he said as if the awe of it overwhelmed him. "I can't get enough of you."

As if there weren't a second to lose, he turned her, bending her forward over the end of the bed and tearing her drawers out of the way. His actions were so frantic she could hardly believe they'd been making love for hours. His fingers spread her, his chest cupped her and, with a long, heartfelt groan of relief, he drove into her from behind. He felt huge from that angle, a stranger almost. He did not wait but began thrusting like a man possessed, his expression hidden, his grip desperate on her hips. In seconds his erection stretched to bursting inside her, fevered and thick as he begged her to open, to let him all the way in. *Let me,* he moaned, *let me* with strokes so long and fierce she could only stand and brace. He came so quickly she barely had time to follow, despite the knowing motions of his hands. His hoarse cry of completion pushed her over the trembling edge. When they'd both settled, he apologized for his roughness, but Florence had never found him more exciting.

Shaking her head, she stroked his sweat-sheened face between her palms. "It doesn't matter what you do. Your touch will always move me because it's yours."

He flushed at that and muttered something like "Only time will tell." Florence was prepared to prove her claim,

more than prepared. First, however—she stifled a prodi-
gious yawn—she really had to rest. They tumbled together
into her bed, fully intending to sleep till dinner.

A low, persistent knocking woke them both.

"Miss Florence," Lizzie called through the door, "Lord
Greystowe. Viscount Burbrooke has returned."

Edward bolted up so quickly her head bounced from his
chest. In the dying daylight, his face was as pale as the
sheets. "Freddie," he panted, his fist pressed to his heart.

It seemed a part of him was not at peace with what
they'd done.

Freddie had changed. Edward noticed it the moment his
brother answered his summons to the library. His cast had
been removed, for one thing, but the difference ran deeper
than that. Though his eyes held the same amusement at the
world, their gleam was happier. He seemed more self-
possessed; taller, if that were possible. Most of all, despite
a slight limp, he had the loose-limbed, loose-hipped stride
of a man who'd spent the last few weeks with someone very
skilled at exorcizing lust.

Not that Edward wanted to dwell on that.

He turned his attention to the whiskey decanter and the
finger of Irish gold he'd poured into Freddie's glass.

"Heavens," said his brother, strolling across the room to
where he stood. "This must be serious if you're breaking
out the single malt."

"Serious enough," said Edward. He handed Freddie the
crystal tumbler, then looked out the window through the
colonnade. Torches lit the grounds as if there were going to
be a party. Edward had a feeling Lizzie had spread the news
about him and Florence to the staff. No doubt this was Mrs.
Forster's idea of encouraging romantic midnight walks.
Under other circumstances, he would have appreciated the
hint. Tonight, however, the reminder of the news he had to
break to his little brother made his stomach sink. The fact
that Freddie was likely to welcome it did not help.

Unaware of what was coming, Freddie sipped the

whiskey and peered at him with half-lidded, ironic eyes. "If you intend to scold me," he said, "you may as well save your breath."

Edward's hand tightened on his glass. "It's not you who needs scolding."

"Do tell," said Freddie in a rakish, mocking drawl.

Unfortunately, what Edward had to say was no laughing matter. He tossed back the drink and set it deliberately down. When he turned, his brother was waiting with one raised brow.

"I'm marrying Florence," Edward said.

The announcement was clipped and challenging. He knew he was glaring, but couldn't quite make himself stop. Freddie was not going to change his mind, not for anything. To be sure, the chance that Freddie would want to was very slim. But rationality had no part in Edward's behavior. Florence was his. He was going to stake his claim.

Given Edward's manner, Freddie's response was mild. He toyed with the edge of the ebony console table where Grimby had left the liquor, then looked up with a smile.

"Well," he said, "as this is something I know you've wanted since before you knew you wanted it, I have to wonder why you're so dour. If you're feeling guilty, I assure you it's misplaced. Any idiot could see your marrying Florence will make us both much happier."

"Will it?" Edward studied his brother. Freddie was dressed casually in a crisp white shirt and summer trousers. His vest was a subtle medley of ivory silk and gold embroidery, colors that called attention to the sun he must have gotten since he'd left. He was the flower of English manhood: kind, witty, brimming with health and life and far handsomer than Edward would ever be. A man with Freddie's gifts could make anything he chose of his life, any dazzling thing at all. He wondered if his brother understood what he was giving up.

"Freddie," he said, "do you realize how cruel the world can be? Imogene Hargreave, for one, will never let this pass. When news of my marriage gets out and the inevitable conclusions are drawn, a great many of your friends will no longer be your friends. Whether they empathize or not, their sense of propriety will oblige them to drop you. You won't be welcome in their homes. They'll cut you on the street. Your life as you've known it will cease to exist."

"Do you believe that's all I care about?" Freddie said. "The cut of my coat and the social round? Unpleasant as becoming a pariah may be, I suspect my fall from grace will mean more to you and the duchess than it will to me."

Edward strove for a reasonable tone. "Hypatia can weather any storm. She's been a social force too long for that to change. As for me, if people cut me, so be it. But you . . . You can't deny you've enjoyed being society's darling, because I know you have. Look." He undid the button that seemed to be choking his neck. "Maybe we could find another woman to marry you. Someone older. A widow, perhaps."

Freddie lifted his hands but not in surrender. "No," he said, with a steeliness Edward had never heard from him before. "No more lies. Nigel and I have discussed this at length and we've both made up our minds."

"Nigel and you."

"Nigel and I," Freddie said, as if to make Edward acknowledge their pairing by force of repetition. "Whether you believe it or not, Nigel and I are in love."

The declaration held an unmistakable tinge of pride; wonder, too, and the same gratitude any new-minted lover might feel. Struggling to understand, to accept, Edward sagged back against the table. He pressed the heel of his palm to the megrim blooming slowly behind his eyes. "This is going to be so hard for you, Freddie. So very, very hard."

"We know that," Freddie said, the softness of his voice clearly meant to reassure. "Perhaps we know it better than you. You love me more than anyone. More than Nigel, I expect, for his is a sentiment only time will prove. In any case, I can hardly harbor illusions as to how the rest of the world will react when you, who love me best, cannot accept me as I am."

"I'm trying," Edward said. "Truly, I am."

"You're trying to protect me. But you can't choose my

path this time. You have to let me run ahead and stumble. Otherwise, I'll never have any sort of life at all."

Edward found it difficult to swallow. His stomach had tightened into a knot and his hands were trembling with distress. Every instinct he possessed urged him not to let Freddie do this. There must be some argument he'd neglected, some way he could compel his brother to show some sense.

Alas, he doubted Freddie would forgive him if he found it.

"Do you—do you know what you'll do?" he said, forcing the question past the resistance in his throat.

"We're leaving for France," his brother responded, his gentlest announcement yet. "Probably very soon."

"France. Well." Edward shoved his shaking hands into his pockets. "I know the provinces are beautiful and the political situation does seem to be settling down. I suppose you could reopen the property Mother left you."

"That was our plan. It's in Bordeaux, you know. Nigel and I thought we'd try our hand at growing grapes."

"That . . . well, that sounds . . . Freddie, France is very far away."

"A train to Dover and a ferry to Calais."

"You know what I mean. It's a different country. A different continent. You don't know anyone. You don't even speak French."

"Nigel does," said Freddie with a crooked smile of understanding. "And I shall learn. This is what we need, Eddie. A clean break. A place where no one knows us, where we can live as we please so long as we're discreet."

The knot in Edward's stomach seemed to grow. "You'll tell me if you need anything? Money, letters of introduction?"

"We'll let you know. I suspect we'll be fine." His mouth quirked a little higher. "As you know, Nigel's business skills are formidable."

Edward did know it, but the comfort the knowledge might have brought was tempered by dismay. He and Freddie had spent the better part of their lives together. Freddie was more than a brother; he was the goodness that leavened Edward's soul.

"France," he said, unable to let it go. "I don't know what to say."

"Say you wish me happy."

"I do, Freddie! With all my heart."

Freddie must have heard his reservations. He reached out to clasp Edward's neck, his thumb on the bend of his jaw, his fingers curling warmly behind. It was a gesture of support, a gesture a father might have made. Edward's throat constricted at the strange reversal of their roles.

"I'll miss you," he said, not even trying to hide his pain. "And Florence! I don't know how I'll break the news to her. She was looking forward to being your sister."

Freddie laughed, a soft, bright sound. "Wherever I am, I shall always cherish her as such."

He hugged Edward then, a tight embrace that said far more than words. Edward slapped his back and held tight, wishing Freddie were small again, wishing he could keep him safe. When they let go, they both had to wipe their eyes.

"I love you," Edward said, and there was more in the words than the emotion.

Freddie nodded and backed away, his eyes dazzling bright. He must have known that if he stayed Edward would feel obliged to make another plea.

His retreat left the library very quiet. A clock ticked on one of the mantels. The gas hissed within its painted globes, a breath more even than Edward's own. Exhausted, he tipped back his head and stared at the shadow-haunted gloom of the vaulted ceiling. Angels flew across its mural, their wings as muscular as their limbs. Tonight, in the weak yellow light, they looked to Edward as if they were flying straight to hell.

His little brother was in love with Nigel West. He was leaving the country, leaving everything and everyone he knew.

And Edward was letting him do it.

He clenched his hands to sweating fists, but his stomach

had made up its mind. Heat rising queasily in his throat, he ran for the terrace. The air outside was sweet, the breeze a cooling ribbon. Nonetheless, as soon as he gained the lawn, he was violently, miserably ill. Only his hold on the marble column kept him from falling to his knees.

Florence found him after the sickness had passed. He was rocking back and forth at the edge of the colonnade, his boots in the dewy grass, his head pressed to his knees. He did not have to look up to know who sat beside him.

"I don't know how to let him go," he said. "I've tried but it's so hard."

Florence wrapped herself around him. "You're not letting him go. You're letting him be himself."

"The world will do its best to hurt him."

Florence soothed his head with a stroke of her hand. "Maybe losing Nigel would hurt him more. He deserves a chance to be happy, to love and be loved like anyone else. Maybe this is the only way."

"Maybe," Edward moaned. "I'm supposed to let him risk everything for a maybe?"

"Maybe is all anyone has. You have to let him make the choice."

Edward knew she was right, but knowing didn't make it easy. He turned in her arms and clung. He felt utterly helpless, more helpless than he'd been since the days he'd tried to protect his rambunctious little brother from their father's ire. Florence petted his hair and rocked him—the way any woman might comfort a man she loved. Her words, however, were not those of any woman.

"Love him as he is," she said. "That will give him the strength he needs to face the world."

Though Aunt Hypatia had been suspiciously scarce of late, soon after Freddie's return she sent for Florence to meet her in the drawing room. She nodded as Florence entered but did not speak until she'd poured them both a cup of tea.

"I have put this discussion off," she began, "because I felt I owed you the chance to concentrate on working things

out with Edward. Since you have obviously done so"—her
brows rose with worldly humor—"I feel the two of us
should clear the air. First"—she lifted her hand to stall Florence's speech—"I should like to apologize, both for my
part in deceiving you and for failing to realize Catherine
Exeter was so vindictive. I had no idea she would use you
in that fashion. I consider it most unfortunate, and entirely
my fault, that you did not feel you could turn to me in your
distress."

"It . . . it turned out for the best," Florence said, her
hands clutched nervously on her cup.

"Liked having Edward rescue you, eh?"

"Yes, your Grace."

"Hmpf, well." The duchess shot her a knowing glance.
"Good for him to have to rouse himself. That boy has always been too stolid. You, at any rate, will keep his blood
pumping."

At her blush, Hypatia unbent enough to pat her knee.
Then, with a sigh of resignation, she dug her walking stick
into the carpet and pushed to her feet. The drawing room
windows overlooked the rose garden, now a riot of late-
summer blooms. In the bright gold light, the seams of her
face showed the struggles she had passed through in her
time.

"The Burbrookes have much to answer for," she said. "I
wonder you are able to forgive any of us."

"My own actions have hardly been above reproach,"
Florence cried, distress bringing her off the couch. "I would
not blame you for thinking me the worst sort of fortune
hunter."

"Piffle," said Hypatia. "I know very well Edward's fortune had nothing to do with it. The point is we lied to you,
deliberately and with intent to deceive. The only argument
I can offer in my defense is that I honestly thought Freddie
would change for you. I thought you would make each
other happy."

"We might have," Florence said, "if we hadn't fallen in
love with other people."

The duchess sighed and turned her gaze to the garden.

"As much as I've seen of life, as much as I've done, you'd think this wouldn't bother me. You'd think I'd say Freddie was entitled to love where he pleased. But I suppose everything's different when it affects your family." She hunched her shoulders, then forced them down. "We should be grateful he didn't fall for that footman, I suppose. At least this Nigel person will know which fork to use. Decent manners and all that."

"Perfectly decent," Florence assured her.

"France, though," said the duchess, shaking her head. "Filthy people. Spend all their time lopping off each other's heads or pinching women's bottoms."

Florence could not stifle a giggle.

"Yes," Hypatia agreed, her face lifting naughtily. "At least Freddie and Nigel won't be compounding that problem!"

She thumped her stick on the floor in enjoyment of her own wit. Florence's heart eased as she laughed along. If the duchess was making jokes about pinching bottoms, Florence knew the worst was past.

Edward prowled the library late into the night. His brother was leaving in the morning. His brother and his lover. He simply couldn't get used to the idea, though he'd never seen Freddie this content. A weight had been lifted from his spirit, a weight Edward hadn't known was there.

Nigel had convinced Freddie to stay through harvest, so as not to deprive Edward of his steward at the busiest time of year. He even coaxed him into helping get the corn into the ricks, a back-breaking, filthy job. "If you're going to be a farmer," Nigel had teased, "you have to be willing to sweat."

The harvest home party they'd held for the laborers was the finest Greystowe had ever seen, a true fête, according to Mrs. Forster, it being in addition to the celebration of Edward and Florence's betrothal. The revels had stretched well into the wee hours. Every man in the county had begged Florence for a dance, including Freddie and Nigel.

For once her shyness was forgotten. She read stories to the workers' children, and served up slices of pie she'd baked herself. With every smile, she proved she was at home here, among his people, literally laughing until she cried.

Edward had never known joy could be bittersweet.

He was pacing towards the bust of Plato when the object of his ruminations poked her head past the double door. She was wearing her nightshift and robe, a filmy, flowy combination that sent an immediate surge of heat to his neglected sex. Ever since Freddie's return, he and Florence had observed the proprieties. Edward meant the premarital abstinence as a demonstration of respect, both for his aunt and for Florence. Not so much as a kiss had been stolen behind a door. No doubt that, as much as anything else, was contributing to the foulness of his mood.

"Don't come in here," he warned, his resolve pushed to the limit, "unless you want your skirts tossed over your head."

"I'm not wearing skirts," she said as she padded softly in. Her pretty white feet were bare, twinkling toes and all. Clearly the woman had no sense. As if to prove it, she cocked her head at him and smiled. "I came to make sure you didn't pace straight through the carpet."

"You're playing with fire," he warned, but she ran to him as if fire was what she most desired.

His good intentions disintegrated on the spot. He had his trousers open before she reached him; had her down on the floor before her first laughing kiss brushed his lips. He cursed at the tangle of her gown, and again at the eager encouragement of her hands.

"I'm trying to behave," he protested as she spread her legs beneath his weight.

She muttered something that sounded very much like "To hell with behaving" and then the folds of lawn and lace seemed magically to give way. His nerves spangled like shooting stars. He felt her body's welcome against his crown and entered her before he could think of stopping. The first stroke was pure, tooth-grinding bliss. She was hot and tight and wet, and her tiny cry of pleasure made him groan like a dying man.

"I missed this," she said, hugging him close with arms and thighs. "I missed this so much."

Edward had no control at all. Their coupling was so fast and hard it had both of them gasping for air. He was thumping her into the carpet and she was drumming him deeper with her heels. Nothing mattered but racing to the finish, but reaffirming his ownership of her sex. His climax broke like glittering golden fire, explosively good, blinding him to everything but the long, gushing convulsion. He wouldn't have known she followed but for her sharp orgasmic cry.

Once he'd rolled her above him, he never wanted to move again.

"Now," she said as she sprawled atop his chest with his shaft still pulsing lightly in her sheath. "Tell me what you and Nigel discussed at your oh-so-serious talk."

Edward's breath came out on a sigh. Leave it to Florence to guess what had upset him, and to make it easier for him to share it.

"He apologized for abusing the family's trust," he said. "As if that mattered at this point. He advised me on replacements, gave me the key to his files. Ah, and he assured me he'd take the 'best possible care' of my brother. I felt like the bloody father of the bride."

"Mm," said Florence. "And what did you say in return?"

"Gave him a bank draft," he muttered. "Just in case."

He could feel her smiling against his skin. "I'm sure he appreciated that."

"Of course he did. Unlike Freddie, Nigel is a practical man."

Florence rubbed her face across his chest. At some point during their encounter, she had opened his waistcoat and pulled up his shirt. Now her arm slid under the hem to hug his ribs.

"I'm proud of you," she said, kissing the tender spot above his heart.

"Don't be proud until tomorrow," he huffed. "They'll be lucky if I don't stop the bloody train."

• • •

The train sat at Greystowe Station, a dusty black denizen of the modern world. Steam puffed from its stack as it took on water and coal. Every now and then its whistle sounded a mournful double toot. *Good-bye,* it seemed to say. *Good-bye. Good-bye.* Florence longed most heartily for it to stop.

"I still wish you'd stay for the wedding," she said, hugging Freddie so tightly he pretended to choke. Edward waited a few steps behind her, giving them room for their farewells.

"I know you wouldn't mind," Freddie said. "I, however, shouldn't like the scandal of my presence to distract from your day."

"But I'd far rather you gave me away—instead of my father's old lawyer."

Freddie pushed her back by the shoulders. "Now, now. Mr. Mowbry brought you and Edward together. What could be more appropriate?"

"But I'll miss you," she said, feeling his absence already. Freddie hushed her with two fingers of his neatly gloved hand. He smiled affectionately at her pout.

"Remember what I told you, dearest. You and Edward must get to the business of siring heirs. I expect no less than half a dozen named after me."

"Half a dozen!"

"Oh, yes," he said airily. "Freddie, Frederica, Fredwina, Fredward—and I'll leave the other two to you."

"You are too foolish for words," she said, smiling past her heavy heart.

He straightened the brim of her feathered hat. "I'm counting on you to be foolish in my stead. My brother mustn't be allowed to sink into dourness while I'm gone. Of course, since his sense of humor is extremely primitive, that shouldn't prove too great a trial."

Edward snorted behind her, but neither Florence nor Freddie paid him any mind.

"I shall do my best to cultivate some silliness," she said.

"Good," Freddie responded, his eyes abruptly brimming. Rather than let himself spill over, he blinked hard and squared his shoulders like a soldier on review. "I shall look forward to hearing of your progress. If you like, I'll send explicit instructions on filling his slippers with jam."

This was enough for Edward.

"You're filling her head with nonsense," he said, his voice gruff, his arm dropping warmly around her shoulders.

Freddie chucked her chin before turning to him. "Take care of her," he said. "Remember, she was my sweetheart first."

The brothers exchanged a long, memorizing look. Edward's eyes were serious and Freddie's twinkled, but Florence knew each was recalling what the other had meant to his life. Finally, Edward thrust his hand into his pocket.

"I have something for you," he said, and brought out a familiar disk of gold. "Your first swimming prize. I've kept it all this time. I thought you might like to have it."

Freddie opened both hands so that Edward could lay the medal and ribbon across his palms. "Edward!" he exclaimed, caught between shock and laughter. "If I weren't already, your gift would completely unman me."

"You'll always be a man," Edward said in his gravest voice. "You've proved that more times than I can count."

Freddie covered his eyes and shook his head, more than male enough not to want to cry in front of his sibling. Obviously embarrassed, Edward squeezed his shoulder and stepped back to make room for Aunt Hypatia. Her farewell was punctuated by hugs and barks of laughter. At last, Freddie tore himself away and joined Nigel on the steps of the first-class carriage.

Edward shook hands with his former steward and again with his brother, and then the train chuffed slowly away.

Florence broke into a run before the car could leave the platform. "Winifred!" she shouted, waving her handkerchief wildly at Freddie's window.

"Fredalia," he countered, waving wildly back.

At that, she gave in to tears. She cried all the way home, cuddled close to Edward's chest. She cried at dinner at the sight of Freddie's empty place. She cried when she found the rose he'd left on her pillow, and again when Edward snuck into her room in the middle of the night.

"What a watering pot!" he declared, gathering her in his arms. "Keep this up and I shall leave you in the garden for the flowers."

But Florence knew better than to believe he was annoyed. Freddie was worth the tears. Besides which, she suspected comforting her kept Edward from crying himself. Throwing himself into this very important duty, he rocked her in his lap and crooned under his breath and finally kissed the last tears from her eyes.

"We've been given a gift," he said. "One few people are privileged to know. Freddie wouldn't want us to be sad."

"No," she agreed, dabbing her nose with his best silk handkerchief, the one that had mere minutes ago peeped neatly from the pocket of his robe. The sentiment was so sweet, and the mention of gifts so unwittingly apropos, she almost welled over again.

Edward laughed at her sniffle and hugged her closer. "Florence, Florence, Florence. Where would I be without you to melt my heart?"

Florence didn't know, nor did she care to find out. With an extra flutter to her pulse, she pressed her hand to her belly and lifted her gaze to his. What she found there made her smile even more than the secret she'd been cradling to herself all week.

"Edward," she said, her grin breaking free, "I've been wondering if you'd mind very much if we'd started a little Frederica already."

He blinked at her, then let out a whoop that probably jolted half the staff out of their beds. "Mind?" he said, tossing her into the air until she shrieked herself. "No, I don't mind, Florence. Not at all."

She hadn't caught her breath from landing before he was kissing her senseless, murmuring love words and stroking her belly with a reverence that made her think motherhood might be very nice indeed.

She had taken the greatest risk a woman could and was now facing the consequences, despite which she had not felt a shred of fear since the day the possibility had crept into her mind. She had hoped, she had bubbled with suppressed excitement, but she had not feared what would become of her. Married or not, no woman would be as cosseted as the woman who bore Edward's child. Add to that the love that glowed so steadily in his eyes, and Florence knew this baby would be infinitely more than a seven-month surprise.

This baby would be a gift, a gift they gave and a gift they received; full no doubt of mystery, but wrapped in adoration.

"Are you well?" Edward asked, suddenly stiffening with concern. His big warm hand spread protectively across her womb. "No sickness? No fatigue?"

"I was only sick once," she said with a quiet laugh for his alarm. "Which gave me the notion I might want to start counting days."

"And your tears," he eagerly put in. "They say women are more emotional when they're with child."

"That they do."

He didn't see her amusement. He was too busy examining the unchanged curves of her body. Or almost unchanged. When he cupped her breast, a deeper pang of sweetness streaked through her flesh.

"Just imagine," he mused, his fingers strumming the sensitive peak. "A little Frederica we can cradle in our arms."

Florence's toes curled pleasantly at his caress.

"I don't know," she said, her own hand beginning to wander. "For myself, I'm rather partial to Fredward. . . ."

EPILOGUE

❧

Traveling with the earl was an education. Florence knew her husband possessed many admirable traits, but she'd never guessed he had the patience of a saint. One of them certainly needed it, for Frederica was their companion on the trip. At two, she had her mother's green eyes, her uncle's charm, and her father's stubbornness of mind. Today she seemed convinced she could hasten the horses by bouncing more vigorously on her father's knees. Edward winced but grinned, as if nothing could be more delightful than a pummeling by one's child.

"Settle down," Florence urged, stroking her daughter's wispy golden hair. "Your papa needs his knees for later on."

"Papa, Papa, Papa!" Fredi shrieked, not calming in the least. This chortle was followed by a new bit of intelligence. "Gween," she announced, pointing out the window of their big rented coach. "Look, Mama. Pwetty gween!"

"Yes," said Florence. "Very pretty green."

Her daughter was correct in her judgment, if not her pronunciation. This area of Bordeaux was indeed beautiful: lush in its late spring growth, picturesque in its rambling village, and pure magic in its old châteaux. The coach's high wheels rumbled down a sandy road where glimpses of the Garonne River alternated with crumbling stone gates and workers moving slowly down rows of vines. The scene was timeless and peaceful. With a sigh of pleasure, Florence pulled her daughter back into her lap.

"Soon?" said Frederica, cuddling close in one of her quicksilver changes of moods. "Soon we see Uncle Fweddie?"

"Yes," Florence assured her, kissing her warm, round cheek. "And then you, Madame Stickyfingers, will get a good wash."

"Stickyfinga," Fredi giggled, then subsided with a yawn.

"Why," Edward demanded, "does she always sleep for you?"

"Because I am smart enough to let you wear her out."

Edward returned her grin with a smile so warm it could still bring tears to her eyes. Their life had been rich in warmth since their marriage, an event that caused less comment than she'd feared, due to the timely exposure of Charles Hargreave's affair with Millicent Parminster and his subsequent abandonment of his wife to a castle in Scotland. Poetic justice, according to Hypatia. Florence was simply glad her husband's old mistress chose to take her aunt along for company.

With scandals like this to entertain the peerage, the surprise evoked by Florence Fairleigh marrying the older rather than the younger Burbrooke was mild—especially when the newlyweds proceeded to live so quietly. A pair of stay-at-homes, society clucked, little imagining what the earl and his countess were getting up to.

Florence smiled at the memory of those days. Despite society's disapproval of their domesticity, Freddie's absence was mourned more deeply than theirs. Those few who guessed why he'd left kept quiet out of respect for—or, in some cases, fear of—the formidable earl and his equally formidable aunt. The consensus seemed to be that Freddie could do what he pleased, as long as they were not forced to know about it. Society being what it was, she expected this was the best reaction they could hope for.

Out of all of it, the loss of Merry Vance's friendship was her only regret. The two women saw each other, of course.

Edward was close to Merry's father; the duke and he shared a number of political interests. As a result, Monmouth's invitations were among the few the couple accepted. Merry always welcomed Florence warmly but Florence could tell her spirits were not what they'd been. She suspected Merry wasn't quite over her infatuation with the earl.

Her husband broke into her thoughts by stroking the curve of her cheek. "Something wrong?" he asked with the gentleness he reserved for those he loved.

She shook her head. "Just wondering if Merry Vance will be happy with that fellow her father seems to be grooming up to marry her."

"Why wouldn't she be? Solid man. They've known each other from the cradle. Plus, his positions on finance are impeccable."

She stifled a smile at this recipe for romance.

"Here's the turn," her husband said, pointing to the bell-towered church that marked it. He tugged at his collar, a sure sign that he was nervous. Florence patted his thigh, but knew there was little she could do to soothe him. Three years was a long time to go without seeing one's brother.

A short avenue of plane trees led to Freddie and Nigel's villa. The house was charming: soft gray stone with ash blue shutters and a roof of red clay tiles. White jasmine trailed from the windows, and the path to the door was paved with ocher brick. Everything was beautiful, but slightly unkempt, as if the people who lived here wanted the humblest visitor to feel at home.

The driver, a big, red-faced Frenchman, climbed down from the box and began untying their luggage. Since Fredi still slept, Florence handed her to Edward to carry out. Her long-awaited uncle bounded around the corner of the house just as Edward was lifting the knocker. Freddie was obviously dressed for gardening, in muddy boots and trousers and a simple peasant shirt. His skin was rosy brown, his hair bleached nearly blond. He'd gained weight since leaving England and it suited him immensely. He was solid now—no boyish rake but a man with his feet planted firmly on the ground. He grinned and covered his mouth when he saw his niece curled in sleep on her father's shoulder. Her ruffled pink dress, once quite fetching, was a hopeless mass of wrinkles from the ride.

"Oh, look at the little princess," he whispered.

"Wait till she wakes up," Edward warned.

Freddie merely laughed and gathered the sleeping bundle into his arms. "You made good time," he whispered over his shoulder. "We weren't expecting you until tonight."

"The princess wakes at dawn," Edward said. "Her subjects have no option but to follow."

Freddie grinned and swept his arm before him. "Welcome to Château Burbrooke."

His garden was a bower of daffodils and roses, with an ancient tinkling fountain and a table Nigel was frantically trying to cover with a cloth. Piles of clippings attested to Freddie's attempt to tidy up. More promising were two bottles of wine left cooling in a bucket of water. In the course of their journey, Florence was certain she'd swallowed half the dust of France.

"Oh, hell," said Nigel. "I mean, welcome to our home. How nice you could come straight back before you'd even seen your rooms."

The look he shot Freddie made it obvious this was not the sequence on which they'd agreed.

"Oops," said Freddie with a sheepishness so endearing Florence had to grin.

"Here," she said, reaching for the other edge of the cloth. "Let me help. I take it we're having a picnic lunch?"

"Yes," said Nigel. "That is, I'd planned a nice dinner but, well, at the moment we have bread and fruit and a wonderful foie gras they sell at a shop in town."

"Perfect," she said. "We very much like picnics and Fredi adores pâté."

"Like a pig in truffles," Edward muttered.

"Oh." Nigel looked looked slightly alarmed. "I hope I have enough."

"Don't worry," said Edward. "We won't wake the little beast till we've had ours."

This unparentlike declaration seemed to startle Nigel but also to calm him. Before he could assure Florence he could manage on his own, she followed him into the cool dark house, keeping up a friendly chatter that rather amazed her. She'd come a long way since her tongue-tied arrival in London. As they progressed through the hall, she gathered an impression of old polished wood and big simple furniture—a bachelor house, designed for comfort and ease. She knew just by walking through it that they'd all enjoy their stay.

By the time they emerged with the food, the brothers had their heads together over the table, where Freddie was sketching something on the back of a crumpled envelope. Like a trusting puppy, Frederica was curled in sleep on Edward's coat in a patch of sun.

"It's ten acres," Freddie was saying, "along the river. We had to replant where parts of the vineyard had grown bare, and some drainage needed relaying, but the soil is good and the rootstock is still productive. Right now, we're selling most of our harvest to Château Roudelle but we're thinking that, with the help of a local widow, we could develop a little label of our own."

"We're reeling her in," Nigel said with a laugh as boyish as Freddie's. "We've convinced her to take us under her wing. Teach the bumbling *Anglais* how to save their poor, neglected vines."

The ensuing merriment woke Frederica. Rubbing her eyes, she tottered over to the table and announced that she was hungry.

"Lord," said Edward. "Here comes the bottomless pit."

Despite his words, the facility with which he fixed his daughter a plate of precisely what she liked was a wonder to behold.

"Mm," she said, mouth full of bread and goose liver. "Fwance is good."

"I'll drink to that," said Freddie, and pulled one of the cooling bottles from the bucket by his feet. The dark green glass bore a handwritten label that said "Burbrooke-West, 1875 Bordeaux."

Florence clapped her hands. "It's yours? Oh, Freddie, how marvelous!"

"Merely a *vin ordinaire*," he said with a deprecating grin. "Most of our plants are young. The widow insists, however, that you can taste the shadow of future greatness."

He poured with great skill for a bumbling *Anglais,* tilting the bottle gently so that its contents would not be disturbed on the journey to the small tapered glasses.

"The interesting thing about grapes," he said, continuing this pretty ritual, "is that they thrive on struggle. The soil here is almost entirely gravel for several meters down. Water runs straight through it, along with the minerals the plants need to grow. So the roots"—he finished the last glass with a flourishing twist—"must dig deep if they want to drink. This makes the vine strong and the grapes sweet. Only through hardship can you get a true *grand vin.*"

With a teasing smile, he handed the glasses around, none more than half full, and Fredi's a good deal less. The two-year-old clutched it in chubby hands, as intently as if she held the holy grail. Edward made a sound of concern at this, but Florence shook her head. "Don't worry," she said. "Knowing our little sprout, most of it will end up on her dress."

"We should have a toast," Nigel said, his eyes shy but aglow. "To . . . to family, because the richest grapes grow closest to the root."

"To family," Edward agreed, clinking rims with his brother. Then he turned to Nigel. "And to love, because that is the best vintage of all."

To a one, the men turned red, though Edward did his best to cover it with a frown.

"To love," Florence seconded, loudly, before they could start shuffling their feet.

With a clearing of throats, the toast rang out. The cool new wine was tart and fruity, a burst of sunshine on the tongue. They smiled at each other as they swallowed and everyone there, even Frederica, knew that life was very sweet.